TAKING LEAVE

TAKING LEAVE

Jeremy Thomas

TIMEWELL
PRESS

First published in the UK in 2006 by
Timewell Press Limited
10 Porchester Terrace, London W2 3TL

Copyright © Jeremy Thomas 2006

A catalogue record for this title is available from the
British Library.

ISBN 1 85725 208 X

Typeset by TW Typesetting, Plymouth, Devon
Printed and bound in the UK by Biddles Ltd, King's Lynn

For Jane

Contents

April to July 1979

1

I've never liked hospitals. The sight and smell of them make me feel quite peculiar.

The outside of the Middlesex looks just as you might imagine an old London hospital to look – frightening. Once inside, it looks and smells even worse. I share the lift with an empty patient trolley until the fourth floor, step out, take a deep breath and walk into the Tennyson ward.

'Jesus, Mary and Joseph, would you look at what the cat just dragged in?' the cheeky Irish nurse says as I hover in the ward corridor holding a bunch of flowers aloft in one hand and balancing a silver dish on a tray with the other.

'Hello, Nurse, still wearing your watch upside down, then? You couldn't get me a vase for these, and a plate and two forks?'

'You've got more front than Selfridges,' says the nurse, smiling and walking away with the flowers.

'Hello, Mum, are you causing trouble again?' I call out as I walk towards my mother's bed. She waves her hand. She tries to fix her thinning hair and dab some powder on her cheeks. Balancing the tray on my arm, I bow flamboyantly.

The doctors say the disease is in remission but she still looks as if she has been run over by a Green Line bus.

'You look absolutely gorgeous! I've brought you some food, courtesy of the Venezia,' I say and sit down on the bed. She smiles a big smile with her watering eyes and points to her cheek for a kiss.

There is a broad red scar hiding in the fold of her neck, and an unfamiliar smell of something medical. I quickly sit back up.

I dab my finger at the bits of scampi lying in a bed of parsley on the restaurant dish. Then the nurse comes back and with a flourish puts a plate and two forks on the bed, performs a curtsy and leaves. I like her. She makes me laugh, which is handy in the circumstances.

'Mum, you said that the food was completely disgusting here, so try one of these.'

'I'll try one in a minute. I don't know what I'd do without you.'

I spear some scampi and look for the tartar sauce. I dip the scampi in it and swallow. Immediately, and with ridiculous exaggeration, I start fanning my face, miming that I've burnt my tongue. I then remember my mother has just had twelve radium needles removed from her tongue, but is still smiling a knowing smile. I turn to examine some flowers on the bedside table, cursing myself, but keeping the grin on my face and watching her from the corner of my eye.

'Look, Mum, it's all a matter of positive thinking; we've discussed it a hundred times before.'

'Marvellous, darling,' she mouths, sticking her thumb in the air.

I turn back and spear another bit of scampi, feeling as soft and useless inside as the creature I'm eating. I carry on smiling, stand up, and look around the ward. Her bedside table holds an ominous assortment of medicines and her family-collage photo frame.

'Ha,' I exclaim, clapping my hands with relief and sitting back down. 'I spoke with Diana and Charles last night and they told me about the plan for all of us to go to a Greek island. You know, with everyone together and a real recuperation for you. I hope it's not supposed to be a surprise. They have told you, haven't they? Dad, of course, is the one being difficult – can't leave the garden – we'll be burgled – the cats will eat all my lettuces – the house might explode – you know, the usual story.'

We both laugh and wave forks at each other.

I relax. Her pain seems to be lifting.

'I'm sure Daddy will find a way to sort out the garden. It's his life, you see.'

I shrug and offer her a scampi. She waves it aside and continues. 'We'll see what happens. I've got to get out of here first. Now, tell me, how is the flat, how is the love life?'

'Fantastic and even more fantastic!'

'What do you call the new love interest, then?'

'Loveday.'

'Is she keen on you?'

'It's possible.'

'Are you keen on her?'

'Yes, quite possibly.'

'Is she pretty? Is she kind to you?'

'Mum, for someone who's ill, you ask a lot of questions.'

'That's what mothers are supposed to do.'

My mother stares at the pieces of scampi remaining in the silver bowl as if they were pills covered in little spikes.

I laugh and wink at her. 'Are you going to eat the scampi or shall I take it away?'

She cuts a piece in half and slowly places it in her mouth. She starts to chew. Her head drops forward. She is having difficulty swallowing. She looks up at me and the fun that was there has gone and the pain is back. She starts making a pleading noise. Can I help? What is it? Oh, my God, she's going to be sick. Oh, no, where's the dignity? Never mind the fucking dignity, Tim, you cunt, find something for her to be sick into! Nurse Irish comes rushing over with a cardboard potty, pulls the curtains, and tells me that it's probably best, you know what I mean. I pick up my silver scampi dish and tray and leave. As I am going I try and catch sight of my mother but the curtains are all around now and all I can hear is the sound of awful retching.

I walk away from the hospital, kicking an empty cigarette packet along the street. I want to kick it to Kingdom Come but it escapes by falling sideways down a drain.

I join the lunch-hour on Oxford Street, a blur of Blondie T-shirts, big hair, safety pins, Hare Krishna, and brightly coloured Kickers. Everyone is pushing past the man wearing the leather cap and holding up a protest board as if it is a giant crucifix, saying: 'LESS PASSION FROM LESS PROTEIN: LESS FISH, MEAT, BIRD, CHEESE, MORE PEAS, BEANS, NUTS AND SITTING.' I cut across towards him, wondering, out of superstition, if I should buy his leaflet and give it to my mother. I stop, turn and start walking towards the office, telling myself: chop-chop and carry on.

The first thing to notice about my office is that it consists largely of glass. This makes it unbelievably cold in the winter and intolerably hot in the summer. It has a large desk. On the long suede shelf by the long street window sits my incredibly expensive hi-fi with its even more expensive speakers. Other than a discreet drinks cabinet, there are shelves everywhere, each one is covered in boxes of tapes and racks of cassettes. Every box is labelled 'Barracuda Records, a division of SCG'. I have one huge picture on my wall, a framed cartoon of New York depicting the city as the epicentre of the world. I also have a three-tier 'in' and 'out', not to mention 'pending', tray on my desk. These trays are always full.

I have three telephones. The grey one is chunky and connects me with my secretary. The second, my private line, is white, reserved for calls from girlfriends and from Rick. The third telephone is black and known as my 'internal'. In my three drawers I keep unpleasant things like bills that I have no intention of paying, or certainly not until we get records in the top five of the charts. In front of my desk is a rather nasty smoked-glass coffee table and two armchairs where nervous prospective singers, producers and songwriters sit.

There are always people dawdling, gawping, rushing past my Soho office window: some carry huge, flat tins of film; others, sweaty briefcases stuffed full of tapes from would-be disco stars or punk rock bands. Then there is the blind man who stands quietly and sells matches from a tray held around his neck by a single cloth strap. He wears a grey gabardine raincoat with an open and dignified express-ion and always looks straight ahead, the wind occasionally dislodging his brushed silver hair. For the four years during which I have run this record label, the man has always worn the same polished, brown leather shoes. He carries about thirty yellow packets of matches on a cinema usherette's tray which he grips gently with both hands as if standing to attention. A hand-written sign is sellotaped to the tray, advertising the fact that matches can be purchased for five pence. He has no sign to say that he is blind, just a thick white stick and eyes that stare upwards at nothing.

For a moment, I look at him and think that he must be hot underneath that coat on this surprisingly warm late April day. Maybe if you're blind, you don't feel these things so much.

2

The last annual conference and awards ceremony for the forty record labels licensed or distributed by OTE had taken place in the unheated banqueting hall of a hotel in Bromley. It had been a cheap and shoddy affair, resulting in half the participants contracting salmonella poisoning from the chicken Kiev. This year, Occidental Terrestrial Entertainment, to give them their due and full title, had hired the entire second floor of the magnificent London Sporting Club. It was a space that seemed the size of a football pitch and was partitioned in the middle by an enormous Japanese screen. One side contained a professional boxing ring and the other housed a stage upon which Barry White and Love Unlimited were playing.

Barracuda had won the award for the most promising label of 1979.

Jesus! I needed to breathe, to allow my smile to jump off the merry-go-round of congratulatory banter I had been subjected to all evening. While the bass and strings oozed through the intro of 'Let the Music Play', I leaned back against the far side of the canvas boxing ring where I hoped no one could see me and took a huge drag on my cigar.

That so many people had crashed the party was a good sign. The room was overflowing with a mixture of tight jeans, bulging chins and plunging cleavages. There were countless salesmen called Ron or Mike, A&R men called Al or Tarquin wearing identical leather jackets, not forgetting the air-kissing press officers called Magenta and Christof. The room was percolating with envy and disgust. A huddle of permed-hair disco label people were shifting their shoulders about, showing off their pink satin bomber-jackets with the word BOOGIE hand-stitched on the back. Staring at them disapprovingly were the two hairy beer-gutted bosses of heavy metal label Music for Vikings. Glaring suspiciously at the beer guts were the deathly pale chain-smoking owners of the new punk label Toxic Head.

I stood up and wiped the palms of my hands down the sides of my trousers. The room was clammy and too warm. I walked past several groups of people who yelled, 'Well done, mate', 'Well done, Tim', and to whom I said 'Thanks a lot, thanks a lot'. People I had noticed previously on similar occasions now leaned out of groups as I walked by to pat me on the arm, the back, the head, and some to kiss me on the cheek. I liked the kissing, especially when it came with the smell of perfume attached.

Fortunately, once the awards had been given out, the drink began to flow. Ties were loosened; people began to shout, running over to greet each other. While marketing graduates with dark bags beneath their eyes pulled at their chins and chattered anxiously to one another, bright young things with spiky hair shrieked and laughed out loud, all of them surreptitiously glancing round to see if someone famous or important had just walked in.

I sidled up to a small group that included my secretary Zannie Price and Abe Aberman, our whiz-kid company lawyer. Without saying anything, I knelt down on the club's chessboard floor and assumed a fish-eye view among the sea of legs. Most were clad in jeans or suits; a few wore crushed velvet or stood in stockings and high heels. Balancing the cigar between my lips, I caught hold of the glass tombstone award I had just received. The worm inside my head began to chant in a whisper that I was not as good, not as talented, not as clever, not a million times as cool and wonderful as these other people, that I was a charlatan and a fake. I told the worm to go fuck itself and noticed that both my hands were still shaking. I needed another shot.

'Are you all right, Tim? Not having a heart attack down there!' Zannie shouted, her face flushed. I looked up and saw her laughing and pulling wildly on her cigarette. I eased myself back up and draped my arms around Zannie and Abe's shoulders. I needed to pave the way for my exit.

'Is everyone having a good time? Got enough to drink? Anyone else I should be talking to?'

'We're having a great time, aren't we, Abe?' Zannie yelled, holding her cigarette aloft and wiggling her arse in time to the music.

Abe didn't say a word but let his eyelids close, jiggled his eyebrows up and down, and smiled a toothy grin. I clapped my hands and half-whispered in Zannie's ear: 'I've got a dinner in the country. You're going to have to look after things, OK?' Zannie threw me a knowing look, raised her glass in affirmation, and carried on swaying her hips to the music. I gesticulated to the men's room, said goodbye to Abe and walked off. Luckily, most of the people I passed didn't try to catch my attention because they were too engrossed in watching Barry White. Have a quick pee, smile, wave at Shamus Murphy the host and deputy boss of OTE, and piss off – that was my plan.

Just as I was approaching the men's room door I heard a loud, familiar voice.

'All right, sir, no need to struggle, we know who you are and we know where you've been!'

I swung round holding my free hand like a cocked revolver. It was Rick Fraser, my pal, dressed in his usual collarless shirt, blue cotton suit, trainers, square glasses and dark moustache. Right behind him was the tall Fozzie Bear figure of Gabe Morass, the drummer in our main band, Quantum Frog.

'Hey, Kojak how you doin'?' I said in my Lieutenant Columbo voice. 'I didn't know you two knew each other?'

Rick held up his palms in innocence, 'We don't really, not that well, but we're getting there, aren't we Gabe?'

'Yeah, man,' Gabe said in his loud Liverpudlian voice. Then he quickly excused himself and padded off to the balcony where, Zannie had reliably informed me, all the celebrities were to be found. Rick deftly picked up a glass of champagne from a passing waitress and asked: 'So, how did the presentation go? Did you knock 'em dead? Or was it a complete waste of time?'

I liked Rick for his realism, for his tough way with the truth. I liked him for his no nonsense 'I'm not going to be nice to people I don't fucking well like' attitude. It wasn't easy being the manager of an up-and-coming band like the Ox and I knew that although Rick always put on a brave face, he was always in some cash crisis or other.

Rick was full of contradictions. On the one hand he professed to live the rock-and-roll lifestyle, hanging out with bands, partying, playing it cool; but really, he was a traditionalist at heart. He claimed to despise the privileged world he had grown up in and downgraded his accent accordingly, yet Rick was and always would be a snob. He was also a creature of habit, religiously attending to his windowbox of plants each night, pouring himself and his girlfriend Victoria a gin and tonic, then doing *The Times* crossword. Rick was shorter than he appeared. A good friend, loyal and dependable, but someone who, if you got on the wrong side of him, could easily bite.

I flashed the award at him. 'The presentation went far better than even I expected,' I said.

'So did you really re-create the set of *General Hospital*?'

'A bit of it, yeah, that's right.'

'What, just to get them excited about the new Quantum Frog album?'

'Rick, have you ever sat through a sales conference? I mean, without wanting to hang yourself from boredom?'

'Fair enough; so what did you do?'

'I just spoofed the show complete with operating table, gas masks, screens and a sexy patient underneath the sheet.'

Rick bent his head forward and sniggered, in a Reggie Perrin drawl. 'Did she have *any* clothes on?'

'A well-secured set of bra and pants.'

Rick took a step back and laughed out loud, then, glancing around nervously, he lowered his voice and leaned in close. 'We can't say anything yet.'

We had a tacit understanding that our plans would not be discussed with anyone else. They were so secret that I had barely even discussed them with myself.

'Oh, yeah! I understand, Rick, no need to say any more.'

Rick took a long sip of his champagne and put down the glass.

'Now that you've won the award, you should get over to New York and put yourself about.' Rick was always encouraging me to go and chew on the Big Apple. 'A bit of self-promotion to the right people never hurt anyone, Tim.'

'You're right, Lieutenant Kojak,' I mimicked. 'Good idea.'

Rick clapped his hands and smiled. Then, changing the subject abruptly, he asked: 'How's everything with your mum, by the way?'

I wasn't expecting the question. 'Oh, you know, she's OK, yeah, I think she's going to be OK.'

'That's good. I'd thought it was more serious.'

'Listen, I've got to go. If you want Zannie, Abe or Gabe, they're out there.' I pointed towards the french windows. 'I'll call you soon.'

Rick stuck his thumb in the air, and walked away.

I drove back to Prince of Wales Drive with the roof open. The cold air made me realise that I was really quite pissed. It was always the same these days, just a matter of topping up from the night before. I needed to cut back. Noticing the sex gauge on my dashboard was flashing on empty, I also needed to have sex. My mind twitched between Loveday's breasts and my conversation with Rick. I needed to keep moving. I did not want to be on my own.

Back at the flat, I spooned cat food into Ned's bowl and telephoned my parents' house. To my surprise, my sister Diana answered the call, sounding rather crabby.

'Yes, Tim, cut the crap and hurry up. I'm busy helping Mum.'

'You wouldn't know busy if it came up and bit you on the bum.'

She wasn't in the mood for my banter and I wasn't in the mood for her. Still, I changed my clothes in record time, for some reason choosing my old cricket gear. As I was leaving, I had a quick game of football with Ned in the kitchen that ended when his bowl of milk was knocked over.

Just as I reached the car a superstitious feeling buzzed in my head, which I knew I had to fix. I went back inside, fished out a cloth, and cleared up the spilt milk.

3

I drove a 1967, four-speed, semi-automatic, sexy, black Citroën DS. There were few cars I wanted to touch, let alone go out with, but this was the one car I had always wanted. After all, if it had been good enough for Peter Sellers, it was good enough for me. *The Day of the Jackal* had inspired me to christen it the 'Gaulle'.

My strategy for driving on motorways was simple: keep the car safely in the middle of the fast lane, keep both hands on the steering wheel and one foot down hard on the accelerator. Somehow my mind was then able to go to a hundred different places and think about a thousand different things without ever having an accident.

Had I remembered to collect the laundry from the launderette? Had I remembered to take the laundry *to* the launderette? Had I left any food for the goldfish? Had I left enough food for the cat? Would the cat eat the goldfish? Had I had enough sexual partners for my age? Had I telephoned everyone I could about the band from Texas? Did Abe in the office really mean it when he said he did it *seven* times most nights? Did I really agree with Rick about only wanting to be rich and not at all famous? Should I go ahead and book the ticket for New York and wing it? If so, which hotel should I stay in? Would I ever settle down? Would I ever amount to anything at all? If a psychiatrist opened up my head and laid the contents on the couch, what the hell would he say: would he bolt, run a mile, or shrug in disappointment at something so *ordinary*? Maybe everyone hitting twenty-six worries like this.

As the two-mile sign for Hedgerly Cross appeared, I stuck another Marlboro between my lips, lit it with my Ronson, and pushed the new Talking Heads tape into the machine.

Minutes later, pulling into my parents' drive, I spotted a sensible estate car and a Renault 5 I didn't recognise parked neatly together by the front door. I deliberately slammed my car door shut and looked up for my father's enraged but friendly face at the window. It had become a sort of standing joke between my brother and me to try to irritate the old man by slamming our car doors whenever we arrived. I felt cheated when he didn't come to the window. As I walked towards the front door I remained determined to enjoy the familiar broken porch light and the mountainous heather garden in the centre of the drive. I gave the bell a long, hard ring. To my surprise the door was opened by a young woman, with a pretty and rather familiar face. She was petite, with brown eyes, white teeth and freckles.

'It's been a long time.' She smiled within her pageboy haircut.

'Hasn't it!' I said, desperately trying to remember who she was.

'I'm Jenny. Jenny Macmillan, you know, Moira's daughter. I'm over from Canada for a while and thought I'd come and lend a hand.

11

My ma is looking after your ma, and 'though I'm not a matron, I *am* a nurse.'

I stood in the hall smiling back at her like the village idiot and kissed her on the cheek, trying to remember what she had looked like the last time I saw her.

'God, I'm sorry. I didn't recognise you, Jenny. It's been ages.'

'Five years since I went,' she said crisply.

I glanced down at her left hand to see if there was a wedding ring, but just then her formidable mother swept out of the sitting room and headed straight towards me. A fiercely loyal friend of my mother, Moira was tall, athletic, red-haired and very, very Scottish. In fact, Moira was so Scottish I had difficulty understanding her. She was secretary of Hedgerly Cross Ladies' Golf Club where, behind her back-swings, she was known as Bodicea. More to the point, she didn't like me. She thought I was a waster, someone who did nothing worthwhile, contributed nothing to society, and only had a lot of high-falutin' fancy talk. Well, she was a stuck-up old bag who walked about the place as if she had a wire brush firmly up her backside. Worse still, the only man she thought was remotely worth bothering with was my own thoroughly irritating brother, Charles.

'Oh, I see, the big man has deigned to come down from his palace in London and visit us, then?' she half shouted. I took three quick steps towards her and, with as much charm as I could muster, put my arm around her shoulders.

'Had I known, Moira, that your beautiful daughter Jenny was here, I would obviously have come down earlier.'

'Aye, well you can forget any ideas like that, young man, because she's got a fella ten times better than you in Canada. Now get into the sitting room and say hello to your father. Go on with you, and I'll see if your ma is well enough to come downstairs.'

My father was sitting on his own, engrossed in the evening news. My sister Diana was framed in the French windows, looking out into the back garden.

'Hello, everyone! It's me.'

'Ssssh! Mum's asleep upstairs, stop shouting,' hissed Diana.

I felt as if I'd walked into the local library. 'Oh, hello, Timmy,' my father said, not taking his eyes off the television. 'Traffic all right?'

He always said that.

'No actually, Dad. There was a massive diversion to Saturn just after the flyover.'

My father turned his head slightly. 'Where? Where did you say?'

'Saturn, you know, turn left at Venus? Only joking, Dad, how are you?'

'Well, had a hard day in the garden. Had to mow all that lawn using only the hand mower, I think the petrol one's given up the ghost. Got it all done, though.'

I felt tempted to ask about my mother, but I knew from his face not to. My father was from the old school, unable to articulate many things without making them sound bald or trite. I went over and kissed Diana hello. She had a mass of jet-black hair, on top of which was balanced a pair of sunglasses, which she adjusted as I approached.

'Hello, sweetie, sorry I was sharp with you,' she said. 'It's been a bit tense round here. You've missed dinner, I'm afraid.'

'I noticed. Fancy a drink?'

There was no reply. Good God, this was like walking in at the end of a very bad party. What had happened? All the spark seemed to have been taken out of the place.

Come on everyone, liven up!

I helped myself to a whisky and switched off the television; a trifle disrespectful, but I had to get things going.

'Have you all been buying my records? Dad? Did you go into the village and get them?'

Diana came back to life and chipped in, 'I went and bought them for Mum and Dad, and bloody expensive they were too!'

'You're all heart Di, I bet you got Dad to pay you back, though.'

'You must be joking.'

'Have you listened to them, Dad?'

I knew this was too much to expect. For one thing, my father's taste didn't extend beyond *The Onedin Line* or *My Fair Lady*, and for another he couldn't understand the difference between 33 rpm and 45 rpm.

'Well, I can't honestly say that I have listened properly Timmy, but I know your mother put them on.'

Hooray! I thought, she's listened. And I know that even though she doesn't understand this kind of music, she'll say to me, 'It's got a jolly good beat'.

'But, Timmy,' my father went on. 'How does this success affect you personally? Will you be getting a rise in salary?'

My father thought in simple terms when it came to money.

'Yes, Dad, it will almost definitely mean that, but quite a lot more things besides. I've got something else cooking, you see, which . . .'

She had arrived. She was smiling away and taking tiny steps, and being supported under both arms by the Scottish and Canadian nursing corps. She seemed to be swaddled, no, shrouded, in layers of white nightgown and took an age to cross the floor. I walked quickly towards her, only to be waved away by Moira.

'Just let her sit down on this sofa, pet. Then you can say hello.'

Pet? Who the fuck does she think she's talking to?

Seeing my mother going along with all this was like seeing your favourite hard man happily helping the police with their enquiries.

Once my mother was seated on the now fading velvet sofa, I walked over and we carefully embraced. How thin she felt.

I stood up and threw my hands up in the air, exclaiming theatrically: 'So! We're both wearing white!'

'I know, darling, but you've got a dreadful grass stain on the bottom of those trousers.'

'I was trying to look athletic.'

'You are athletic, darling, and you look smashing.'

'How are you, Mum?'

'Super!' she whispered.

'Super, not *smashing*?'

She smiled and wobbled her head from side to side. 'No. Not smashing. Just super.'

Christ, she was beginning to accept defeat.

I sat down beside her and gently pinched the back of her hand. 'You can say that you're pissed off. It doesn't mean you're giving in.'

She looked at me and smiled again. 'I am . . . pissed off. Yes, I am pissed off!' she repeated.

Scratching my head and laughing, I stood up and wagged my finger at her like a bad actor. 'You've got to eat, you know. A little bird tells me that you've not been eating.'

She pushed herself back on the cushion, wincing and looking sideways as she did so. Her mouth opened to say something, and for a moment I thought she was actually going to tell me how painful it all *really* was, but no.

'It's you who must eat. I've had enough, thanks.'

There was a lull in the conversation, something neither of us would normally allow to happen, but it seemed necessary somehow. I leant back in my chair and played with a plate of food that my sister had just put on my lap. Providing I concentrated on the eyes and the middle of her face, she was still the same person, the same old Mum. And then, for no particular reason, I noticed her big toe. It looked horrible. It looked like the worst bits of my mother's illness had ended up in her big toe and were festering there. I tried to take my eyes away so she wouldn't notice me staring, but I couldn't. I looked around the room but my eyes kept being drawn back. I furtively compared this big toe with her other one to see whether it was all in my mind. It wasn't. This toe was swollen, the skin rising up around it looked purple and inflamed, and the nail thick and sharp, like an old-fashioned can opener. I sat there, self-consciously aware of how perverse I was being.

Then the smell. Somewhere deep down, I knew what that smell was, but I did not want to put a name to it.

I got up and poured myself another drink.

Diana suddenly spun her sunglasses round in her hand like a football rattle. Heeeeeeeeey! Mum, look, they're showing a Morecambe and Wise repeat on the telly. Come on, you love them.'

My mother was so keen to oblige her entourage that she immediately began to exclaim and laugh, but in all the wrong places. Then she started to smile in all the right places. Soon everybody was laughing along, even my father.

'Mary, pet, do you not think it's time to go back to bed?' said the matronly voice. I looked at my mother, thinking there was no way she would miss the end of 'Morecambe and Wise'.

'Yes, I do feel tired. I think maybe I'll go up and have a little rest and then come down again.'

I thrust my arm out as if dancing a tango around an imaginary partner. 'This is all a bit early, Mum. I thought you wanted to go out dancing.'

I was misfiring and knew that my stupid jokes were coming out all wrong.

'But I *do* want to go dancing!' she said smiling. She then started to turn slowly outwards from where she was sitting, like a climber manoeuvring up and around a jutting rock on a mountain.

'Well, you're not going to get very far dancing like that.' I goaded her.

Just then, the Highland Patrol moved into action.

'Tim Lomax, if you are not the most selfish young man I've ever met. Give your mother some room, please!'

At this point my father came to life from deep within his armchair behind me. 'Yes, Tim, quite right, come on, get out of the bloody way.'

This time my mother put up her hand to silence everyone, leaning heavily on my shoulder as she did so. I saw her grinning, as she whispered, with a glint in her eye, 'Why don't you just piss off?'

We looked at each other and burst out laughing. This was the sign I had been waiting for.

4

It was a couple of months now since I had first met Loveday. The whole thing had been such a cliché: it was across a crowded room, at an early evening party to celebrate Harry and Jessica's first flat in London; my eyes had locked on to her within a minute of walking through the door.

Harry and Jessica were just about my oldest friends. I had first met Harry when he moved to Hedgerly Cross when we were ten years old. Tall and gangly by fifteen, he grew his sand-coloured hair down to his shoulders, refused to wear any shoes but army boots, and vowed he would never be a part of the Establishment. Even then, Harry, being half Australian, loved to take the piss out of what he conceived to be the quintessential British type. He came to do this best when he was stoned or drunk. He was obstinate but, being rather amusing and good-looking too, was a great success with the girls. I can clearly remember the pangs of envy I felt visiting him in his first year at Oxford. He had told me about at least six girls and quite how he managed to walk down the high street without being accosted by some heart-broken female was still a mystery to me. It had been a matter of onwards and upwards for Harry. That is, until he met Jessica.

Jessica was not at all what I had been expecting before I met her. For a start she seemed much older than Harry and me. It wasn't that she didn't join in with the jokes and all the fooling, more that she always seemed to stand slightly to one side and rise above us. That she was shy and a hundred times more serious than either Harry or myself, there was no doubt. Yet her shyness was confusing. Although I never said it, during the first few times I met her, I got the feeling that the likes of me and some of Harry's other friends were being tolerated until we could be disposed of in some humane way. She was also different from any girl I had met before; she was the kind of girl I had only seen in French films. The fashion at the time was to wear everything very tight, and in as lurid a colour as possible. Jessica did neither. Everything was loose, everything was black, save a turban, patterned in gold and cream.

In those days, to Harry and Jessica and their bizarre entourage of friends, I was like someone from another galaxy. I had a company spaceship, and was able to bring them free samples of planet chips.

That was then and now was now. Still together, still the same save for a business suit or two, they were even still living with the yellow chair from Oxford they called the flat banana.

By Harry and Jessica's standards, this was not a big party, thirty people, perhaps. It had, however, taken me at least an hour to circumnavigate the room, being introduced to people I had no wish to talk to, moving slightly closer to my goal, until I summoned up the courage to introduce myself. I was nervous. I was mesmerised. After a few seconds of polite opening exchanges, I was hooked.

Close up, Loveday was far prettier than I had thought. Her skin was country-fresh, ivory and peach, not jaundiced-looking like that of so many other London girls. Her hair was the colour of lemon-honey and her eyes were wide and green. Those eyes were the killer, not to mention that she had the biggest pair of breasts I had seen in years. And in those guarded clever-clever moments of social introduction, where two people knowingly or unknowingly are trying to impress, pretending to be cool but measuring each other up, I could tell that Loveday was different from the rest. Despite a certain shyness, she looked you in the eye and did not allow her attention to be distracted. I asked if her name was French or made-up. She laughed, saying it was as French as clotted cream and that it had been passed down from her Cornish grandmother. Though she clearly had no need to be, Loveday also seemed to be genuinely self-effacing. For instance, she told me somewhat baldly that she worked for *Vogue* and asked whether I had ever heard of it. At this point I thought the game was nearly over. How could someone as gorgeous as this and working for a sexed-up thing like *Vogue* possibly be interested in the likes of me?

'Oh, I only asked if you've heard of it because not everyone has.' She spoke in a confident, old-fashioned British tone that was devoid of any arrogance. 'It's not that big a deal really,' she went on, 'not to me. Anyway, I'm sure you're not the type to read women's magazines.'

'I'm not big on reading them, no, except of course when I'm waiting to be tortured at the dentist. But it does sound very grand working for a magazine like that.'

'It probably is, if you're a model or in fashion editorial but I work in the advertising department, selling space.'

'Well, I think you're just as gorgeous as any of those models,' I said, keeping my foot hard down on the charm pedal.

Loveday laughed. 'You're a fast worker, aren't you! So, what do you do?'

Loveday admitted to me much later – after the third date in fact – that when I had told her that I ran a record label, Barracuda, she had nearly decided to leave, thinking that I would find *her* too boring.

We talked for a good hour at that party and I recall the flush on my face as she kissed me goodbye. Likewise, I remember thinking afterwards what an idiot I was for not asking for her phone number. Again, much later, she told me that she too thought I was an idiot for not having asked.

After I had manufactured a plausible reason, I rang her at the offices of *Vogue*. It was faintly embarrassing, as I didn't know her surname; but, then, how many girls are called Loveday? An invitation to the cinema and dinner was, after much riffling through a diary, duly accepted.

During that dinner certain facts came to light, some of them trivial, some of them not. She told me she had been a nurse and had felt no remorse at quitting. She told me she was the third youngest of four children and that her little brother had been killed in a motorboat accident in which she had lost half her little finger. She told me she was twenty-four years old. In testing her musical and literary taste it became clear that she was a serious romantic: Billy Joel's *The Stranger* and Daphne du Maurier's *Rebecca* were her favourite album and book. She said that she really didn't drink a lot, or couldn't take too much, and it must have been after the third glass of wine that it all came pouring out: she had caught her last boyfriend red-handed, *in flagrante delicto* with his secretary in his flat.

'Fucking bastard!' she hissed.

She didn't dress it up and she didn't dress it down.

'I had my own key, you see.' There was a pause while she dragged hard on her cigarette. 'They didn't even hear me come in. There they were, going at it like rabbits! He hadn't even bothered to take his socks off. Screwing her just like that.'

Loveday leant back in her seat, and dragged on her cigarette again. I smiled ironically in a *c'est la vie, c'est la guerre* kind of way. Although I found the idea of wearing socks quite amusing, I didn't quite know what to say. 'Had it been a long, you know, a long . . .?' I managed to stutter.

'Seven months,' she interrupted briskly.

I stared at my empty wine glass and tried to stop my thoughts racing. How could anyone do something like that when they had a girl like this? What would possess any man to be such a wanker? But then you never know . . .

Before I was able to voice any of this, Loveday pitched in, almost shouting, 'Oh, I suppose you're just like the rest of them, aren't you? Go on; say it, you probably think it's funny and that I am some embittered cow.'

It was as if I'd just leant out the window of a speeding train. I was shocked by the force of her anger and sat back with a jolt, dropping my cigarette on the floor as I did so. I bent down to retrieve it, took a drag and straightened my knife and fork. There was a brief silence, after which both of us let out muted whistles. I was beginning to feel as if I was the one who had fucked the secretary.

'Look, I'm really sorry.' Loveday picked up the conversation with a deep sigh. 'That all just came out in a rush. I didn't mean it, *really*. I hope I haven't ruined things, I mean the evening.'

I was about to mention the relatively painful break-up with my previous girlfriend, Vanessa, but changed my mind. After all, we'd come through it and were now, as they say, just good friends.

'Of course you haven't!' I said, taking hold of her hand without thinking. 'It's been a great evening but a bad story.' Trying to lighten the tone, I added with a hopeful smile, 'Maybe the secretary was blackmailing him?'

'Eighteen and hot in the cot more likely. The toad!'

I laughed and not just to relieve the tension. Loveday grinned, took a deep breath, and released her grip on the tablecloth. 'Anyway, let's not talk about him any more. Tell me about you and the music business.'

I gripped my throat as if I had just swallowed some revolting medicine. 'Are you *serious*?'

Loveday laughed, and raised her eyebrows for me to continue.

'OK, do you know much about the sea?' I asked, looking around the restaurant for inspiration.

Loveday smiled and whispered in a West Country burr: 'My parents' house be one mile from the sea at Padstow.'

Ignoring this information, I spotted a murky-looking lobster tank and launched into my familiar sermon about the music business: 'It's not nearly as glamorous as it sounds, really. Everyone thinks it's about listening to music all day, free T-shirts, sex, backstage passes, more sex and hanging out with bands. It isn't. What the music business is really all about is getting a hit.'

I dragged hard on my cigarette and slowly exhaled. 'Most people who work in it are addicted to having a hit and they'll do anything to have one. Whether you are a whale of a major record company, a licensed label shark, or a miserable indie mackerel, everyone in the musical ocean wants a hit. Even lobsters do. A company without any hits dies and decays into that slimy stuff at the bottom that nobody wants to touch.'

'Sounds disgusting,' said Loveday, wiping her mouth with her napkin. 'What about my brother's favourite weird bands, Pink Floyd or Tangerine Dream or whatever they're called? Do they want hits?'

'Probably not. But let me assure you their manager, their press officer, their A&R man and their plugger do.'

'Plugger? A&R man? What on earth are they?'

'Pluggers take new releases to radio stations and try to persuade people to play them. A&R men are the ones who actually go out and see bands in seedy clubs and so on. Personally, I think they're all neurotic. Most of them are incapable of making a decision about what sandwich to eat for lunch, let alone what band to sign.'

Loveday laughed, but shifted about in her chair, her green eyes starting to glaze over.

'But they're not the worst. The all-time worst are the managers. Their job is supposed to make it easier for everyone . . .'

I trailed off, sensing that she had heard enough.

'Would you like a coffee and a grappa?'

'How marvellous,' said Loveday seductively. 'Tim, would you mind if I asked you something?'

'Ask me anything you like,' I said, smiling into the candlelight.

'OK, then, tell me about your last girlfriend.'

Having shaken hands twice with the waiter and the *maître d'*, we left the restaurant just after midnight and stood outside underneath its salmon-coloured awning.

'It's been great,' Loveday said, giving a slow and smiling nod.

'Absolutely,' I said scratching my head.

'Thank you for a lovely dinner,' Loveday said.

'No, thank *you* for a lovely dinner,' I replied, looking her straight in the eye.

'Well, eh, I'd better find my car.'

'It's right behind you, where you parked it,' I laughed, pointing at her Hillman Imp.

Loveday playfully swung round and back. 'I completely forgot!'

'I do that all the time,' I said, taking three steps forward, so our bodies nearly touched. Noticing that she didn't step back or flinch I put my cigarette in my left hand and moved my right index finger towards her like a hypnotist. 'I hope you don't mind, but you've got this little speck of something on your cheek.' She moved her eyes coyly from side to side as I brushed my finger slowly down the side of her face. There was a pause as a current tingled down my arm. She chuckled and rubbed the end of her nose as if she was about to sneeze.

Despite the electric shocks each time we accidentally touched, I still had no real idea what she thought or felt. I already knew I was not interested in a quick game of poker but something with much higher stakes. I kissed her on each cheek and stepped back, blinking in the light. Loveday stepped forward and kissed me softly on the lips.

'That was for luck,' she whispered, blowing me another as she got into her car.

5

Another night, another family dinner. I sat for a few moments in the warm leather seat of the Gaulle, carefully listening to the lyrics of 'The Stranger', while freaking out about Loveday's holiday in Portugal, booked and paid for since Christmas, with old friends, and my trip to New York at the beginning of July. *We'd be apart for over three weeks!*

Reluctantly, I stepped out on to my parents' drive. The door was again opened by the lovely Jenny, only to reveal Bodicea breathing fire down the hall.

'Come and make yourself useful Tim,' she barked.

What is wrong with that woman? I muttered to myself, stepping across the doorway, kissing Jenny and heading swiftly for the drinks cupboard in the dining room.

To my surprise, Diana was sitting at the dining-room table, watching my father carve a leg of lamb.

'Hi, Dad. Hi Di! Everyone OK?' I called out enthusiastically.

'Ssshhh!' Diana, Moira and Jenny hissed, while my father jabbed the carving knife upwards towards my mother's bedroom. 'She's having a sleep, Timmy, so she can come down again.'

I smiled broadly at my father and whispered, 'OK, I'll speak very quietly.'

My father didn't look up but carried on carving the meat.

Once again I realised it was up to me to resurrect the party. I filled everyone's glasses while Diana dished out the food.

'Now, what's happening in the girlfriend department? Got somebody new, someone blonde, perhaps?'

How did Diana always know these things? I rubbed my fingers across the bristles on my chin, put my arms behind my head, and yawned. Then, mindful of the need for good karma in the house, I decided to disclose some details about Loveday.

'Oh, *her*. She's gorgeous, bright, likes my taste in films and music and seems to get on well with the cat. Her family comes from Cornwall and she used to be a nurse.'

Placing a plate of roast lamb in front of me, Diana announced, 'I'm going to call her the Cornish pasty. After all, there must be something wrong with her to want to go out with you!'

I laughed, my father laughed, even Moira laughed.

Then, after brief contemplation, Moira asked: 'And why did she stop nursing?'

My response was swift. 'She had a terrible accident with a sluice hatch and nearly got sucked down it. Lost half her little finger and has never been the same since. Terrible.'

Moira pushed her hands upwards and downwards, presumably attempting to demonstrate sluice hatch angles to herself, until my sister leant towards me. 'You just made that up.'

'I know. More wine?'

After dinner, while Moira and Jenny went upstairs to help my mother, my sister motioned me into the kitchen. Quickly flattening the pages of a travel brochure on the metal draining board, she whispered conspiratorially: 'Charles and I have decided we should go ahead and rent that villa in Greece at the end of next month, come hell or high water. That way we can all have one last big holiday together. Your job is to persuade Dad.'

I nodded and picked up the brochure, glimpsed the photos of white houses and light blue sailing boats, and put it in my back pocket.

Then, opening the kitchen door, I said, 'I'll leave it till later this evening, after he's had a few drinks. Come on, quick, he's waiting for us.'

It was back to the old days, with the three of us squabbling around a Scrabble board while waiting for my mother to come downstairs. My father's long legs formed a suspension bridge across the carpet to where my sister was slouching with her back to the velvet sofa. I knelt beside the board moving tiles, keeping score. The familiar family accusations started immediately. 'That's not a word! What does that mean? Get the dictionary!'

We were back on track again, the three of us laughing. I went into the kitchen and lit the gas to boil the antiquated old kettle. I pulled out the Greek islands travel brochure and began looking for anything horticultural that might appeal to my father. Soon my mind was focusing on one particular island and fast forwarding to making love to Loveday on a sandy beach. Just then, the kettle started whistling and I heard Moira shouting.

'Owen! Owen! Get up here quickly!'

At first I couldn't understand what was going on.

My flesh went cold.

'Quick! She's going! Quick, get upstairs.'

Through the half-open kitchen door I saw my father and sister running around the banister and up the stairs.

I did not want to go up those stairs.

I did not want to join in.

I *knew* what that smell had been.

I knew.

Going up the stairs was like mounting the scaffold to be guillotined. As I arrived outside the bedroom door I could hear my father sobbing, something I'd never heard before in my life. Perhaps there might be some mistake; perhaps she was just having a very bad turn . . .

At first it all looked so normal. My mother was sitting half-upright in the bed in one of her white gowns. But my father was lying diagonally across it, his arms, and hands reaching out towards her, crying and saying her name over and over again. Moira and Jenny stood at the end of the bed, looking very concerned, but professional. My sister was sitting on the edge of the bed, holding my mother's hand and whispering, 'It's all right, Mum. It's all right. Don't worry. You'll be all right in a minute, don't worry. It's all right, Mum.'

My mother's mouth was wide open, as if she'd had a terrible shock. She looked petrified. Her face was still, but there was movement in the eyes. It was as if a car had knocked her down and everyone around her was trying to help. Had she just had some terrible dream? Then I looked down and saw that the white sheets were covered in dark red spots of blood.

'It's all right, Mum, don't be scared, it'll be all right,' I heard myself say.

We were frozen in a tableau.

I kept staring at her face. I wanted to cry like everybody else but I knew it would be false, forced or untrue. I felt nothing; I was simply watching the spectacle, as if disembodied. I listened intently for the sound of her breathing in between the sobs. It was agonisingly spaced apart. Then, all I could hear was my own. I held it for all I was worth.

I could tell she had died even though her eyes were still open.

Someone needed to say it. God, give me some courage, I prayed.

'I think she's gone. Di? Dad? I think she's gone.'

I took a step towards Moira. 'I think I'd better go and phone Charles,' I said, switching to autopilot.

'Well done, darling,' she said sweetly. 'You go and do that and get yourself a stiff drink. Jenny, would you put the kettle on and I'll look after Mary here. Owen and Diana, in a moment, darlings, it's probably best if you go downstairs.'

The weeping grew louder. I turned to have one last look at my mother and saw Moira gently closing her eyes and, even more gently, closing that open and terrified mouth.

She was definitely dead then.

I walked down the stairs, feeling dizzy.

What on earth was I going to say to Charles?

My fingers were shaking so much I misdialled and nearly had an argument with the person at the other end. As I was redialling, Jenny put her arm round me, placed a lit cigarette in my mouth and pointed to a glass of whisky. I blinked at her and waited for the telephone to connect. It wasn't Charles who answered but Maya. I liked Maya a lot but felt a compelling sense of protocol about telling my brother first. He came straight to the point.

'What's happened? Where are you?' he said, slightly out of breath.

'Bad news, I'm afraid. Mum has just died.' I felt my voice trembling.

'You're joking. What do you mean?'

'No, Charles, I'm sorry, I'm not joking. I'm down at home now and she's just died ... five minutes ago. I think she had a haemorrhage and then, she just ... died. She's dead.'

'Christ!'

There was a pause and I heard him exhaling. I didn't know what else to say except to say what he would have said.

'Look, sorry to be blunt, but I'd better go and see how the others are.'

'What others? Who *else* is there?' he asked, suddenly angry.

'Just Dad and Diana. Oh, and Moira and Jenny Macmillan.'

'I'm getting in the car now and I should be with you in forty minutes at the outside.'

The line went dead.

The scene had no sense of time but a curious feeling of weightlessness. We were in the sitting room drinking cups of tea and whisky. Jenny had to keep taking Diana's cup and saucer every time she burst into loud fits of sobbing. Eventually a kind of pattern was reached; a burst of laughter quickly disintegrating into a mixture of wailing and stunned silence. My father sat slumped, beyond help, deep in his armchair, staring at the blank television screen. Occasionally, he would raise his head, and slowly scan the room as if looking to see if my mother, his wife, was still sitting in the room. His eyes and face were cold and empty.

What was Moira actually *doing* upstairs? There was no way I was going to go and find out.

'Don't worry, pet,' she'd said. 'I've just got to give your ma a bath and make her look nice.'

Give her a bath and make her look nice? Leave her alone! Christ, she's suffered enough; she doesn't need to have her fucking toenails painted.

After phoning Charles, I'd drunk the glass of whisky straight down before dialling the undertakers, and succeeded in having two cigarettes burning in the ashtray and one between my lips at the same time. For goodness sake, my mother had been sitting up in bed talking and even laughing only twenty-five minutes ago and now I was calling someone to take her away.

When the undertaker's voice finally came on at the other end of the line, he sounded calm and serene, precise and monotone, the way I expected the Dali Lama to sound. After taking the details he needed, he asked whether there were dogs (did dogs like biting undertakers?) and if our drive was large enough for their vehicle.

Vehicle? God.

'We'll do what we have to do,' I said.

As the clock chimed eleven, the doorbell gave a polite ring. We all looked at each other over the Scrabble board we'd returned to and before any exchange of information could take place, Charles was on his feet and out of the sitting-room door. I carried on playing my turn but listened intently to the muffled conversation taking place at the front door. Shit! It was the undertakers come to take the body away. There wasn't enough room in the drive, so would Charles mind moving his car so that they could get their vehicle nearer the door? Shit. Shit. Shit.

Charles opened the sitting-room door and presented the undertaker, who was younger than I had expected. Dark suit, black waistcoat, white shirt, black tie. He must have been in his late thirties, but was virtually bald. He wore a diamond ring on his middle finger. Professionally sensitive, he advanced towards my father and offered his condolences. I winced as my father started to talk about finances, but the undertaker quickly withdrew with Moira in unsteady attendance. He mimed at us, pointed upstairs and purposefully headed up to the bedroom.

We all tried to immerse ourselves in the Scrabble. We even speeded up the game so that there was never too long to wait between each turn. We tried to resurrect some kind of banter but there was too much movement upstairs to be able to concentrate.

'Zephyr is not a proper noun, you bastard,' Diana said.

'Look it up. Look it up if you don't believe me,' Charles said.

I dived to a nearby bookcase and started quickly flicking across the spines of the books with my thumb. As I was about to pull out the slab of a dictionary, the undertaker glided back into the room. He walked straight over to Charles.

Half-kneeling and half-whispering, he said, 'I'm sorry to have to ask you this, sir, but I wonder if perhaps you and your brother could lend a hand?'

I kneeled forward slightly, as if I had just realised I was on an aeroplane full of terrorists who were looking for a hostage to shoot. I heard Charles clear his throat and get out of his chair and straighten himself to attention.

'Of course, of course, absolutely . . . Tim?'

I carried on searching the shelves, feeling the heat of their gaze on the back of my neck.

No, please don't choose me, choose someone else.

Out of the corner of my eye, I could see Charles leaning round to see whether or not I had heard him.

The waiting seemed interminable but cowardice rooted me to the spot. I heard them move to the door, half-expecting Charles to call out again. I turned just as the door was closing and part of me wanted to run after them, to muck in, do my bit, but a bigger part refused to budge. I listened intently to every sound from above.

Footsteps and voices like removal men came down the stairwell.

'Down a bit . . .'

'Got it . . .'

'Over to your side . . .'

Diana appeared to be concentrating as hard as she could on the latest edition of *Cosmopolitan*. I looked around the room for my father and found him standing, staring through the white french windows. *What was he doing?* I felt a fountain of words surging up into my mouth. I wanted at least to have a dignified conversation. *For God's sake, is this it? Is this all the dignity there is?*

'Pity. It's beginning to rain. I rather hoped it would be nice tomorrow,' said my father, sinking back into his armchair and biting into a chocolate biscuit.

I watched Diana formulate her reply, still unable to take her eyes from the magazine.

'That's God crying, Daddy,' she said, turning the page.

There was a pause.

'Is it?' My father said, as if someone had told him that his answer to twelve across in his crossword was wrong.

I paced over to the door and opened it just wide enough to hear what was occurring beyond, but not wide enough to see.

What on earth are they doing now? All I could hear was the sound of plastic carrier bags being moved slowly down the stairs. *Surely, they aren't moving all her clothes? For God's sake, she's only been dead two hours! Show some fucking respect!* I leaned into the gap and listened harder. Yes, they were definitely bringing something down the stairs and it was definitely something plastic. I heard the removal men give directions again, but this time they were only coming from one person, the undertaker. My brother was silent at one end while the undertaker directed and encouraged from the other. I knew now what the package contained. I wanted to fling back the door, run up those stairs, take over from the undertaker and hold my end up with Charles. Instead, I stood there and did nothing.

Nothing. I did nothing except to think about that plastic and what that plastic was now surrounding.

August to December 1979

6

Travelling to Devon in Loveday's Hillman Imp that August afternoon made me think of a turkey slowly roasting in an oven. It wasn't
that the Imp was cramped, and only slightly more comfortable than
being driven in the grass-catcher of my father's lawnmower, or that
the temperature outside was 78 degrees. No, it was because I had
inadvertently snapped off both hot and cold levers on the heating
system, so it was now blowing out only hot air. Loveday laughed and
took it all with good grace, saying out of the corner of her mouth
that she would be sending me the bill. However, even with every
window wound down, it soon became clear that we were travelling
in a mobile sauna.

Determined that nothing should alter her happy mood, Loveday
asked me to hold the steering wheel while she tied her hair back,
leaned into the back, took a towel from a basket and spread it on the
seat beneath her legs.

'That's better!' she yelled, retrieving the steering wheel and singing
along to 'Ring My Bell' on the radio.

Despite my sweat-drenched shirt and trousers sticking to the
plastic seat every time I moved, I tried to remain cheerful. I tried
hard not to think of the Gaulle with its sexy sunroof, cool leather
seats, sweet smelling walnut dashboard, erotic up and down suspension, not to mention its eight track and cassette machine.

Loveday had flown to Portugal for her long-planned holiday the
morning after my mother's death, without knowing about it. By the

time she returned, the funeral had taken place, I was in New York, Quantum Frog were top of the charts and I had been banned from driving for six months, despite the best efforts of my lawyer, Johnny Darrell.

I hadn't told her the exact truth about why we had to drive to Devon in her Hillman Imp and not the Gaulle; I fully intended to explain about the drink-driving conviction but only when the time was right. About my trip to New York, I said it had been a riot from start to finish, with so many parties and gigs to go to. I didn't tell her about finding New York frightening and how I had spent most of the time in my hotel. I also hadn't told her how I felt about my mother dying. Well, I don't think I really knew. Loveday had been so wise and sympathetic, I had wanted to confide in her more than anything, but said we would talk at another time. I did tell her the whole truth about the house we were going to stay in, though, which belonged to my boss, Simon Caplow, and had a beautiful view overlooking the river Dart.

Loveday was driving in bare feet, wearing a white T-shirt and white jeans she had rolled up to above the knee. Her face was tanned and freckled and her body was brown with tiny golden hairs standing out on her arms and legs. She was wearing gold hooped earings and the silver turquoise bracelet I had bought for her in New York.

I listened to her talking about her flat and how she liked and sometimes didn't like Monica, her flatmate; how she liked the other girls at work, despite what they had said to her about Dartmouth being dreary. But we didn't just speak; we sang and yelled at the tops of our voices. At first I had pretended to be appalled when Loveday outlined her fascination with amending famous songs by inserting her own words.

'The key word until we get to Devon is *shag*, OK? Now this can be used as a noun, a verb, or an adjective. Ready?' Loveday chirped like an enthusiastic schoolmistress.

'Loveday! For God's sake how old are you? That's the sort of game people play when they are twelve not twenty-four,' I said as piously as I could, while straightening a row of Marlboro packets on the dashboard to stop myself from laughing. Loveday's smile faded.

I clenched my fist into an imaginary microphone and held it to my mouth, saying, 'However, have you ever thought of trying it with Abba?'

Loveday's smile returned.

'Do you know the song "Shagging me, shagging you"?' I enquired.

'I do now!' Loveday exclaimed, taking both hands off the steering wheel and grabbing the imaginary mike.

By the time the five-mile signpost for Dartmouth appeared we had successfully rearranged every single Abba song and were about to murder most things ever written by Hal David and Burt Bacharach. But a sudden heavy rain shower, lasting no more than fifty seconds, stopped us and slowed the Imp right down to a crawl.

'Tim? You know you completely ruined my holiday in Portugal?'

'How could I do that when I was six thousand miles away?'

'I couldn't stop thinking about you.'

'I missed you too.'

'You did? Even when you were in New York?'

'Yeah, I did, even more when I was in New York.'

'Well, I made a fool of myself every morning by insisting on walking to the nearest post box two miles away to send you a postcard.'

'Did your friends really laugh at you?'

'They changed my name to Moonface and said I only had one expression – miserable. I told them I had a migraine and to fuck off.'

'And did they?'

'Have you ever spent a holiday with five doctors and nurses?'

'Not lately.'

'You don't know what it is, to miss someone.'

'I slept with your photograph under my pillow each night.'

'You what?'

'You heard.'

'Did you really?'

'Maybe.'

She drove, smiling, not saying anything. For a few minutes there was a contented silence between us but one in which I was beginning to wish I hadn't made the admission about the photograph.

The house in which we were staying was right next door to the Regal, a decaying 1950s cinema, with a barely readable film poster of *Jaws* peeling from its walls. It was a three-storey holiday home that looked, from the outside, as if it had seen better days. The front door was on top of a steep slant of cobbles that ran on for fifty feet down a ramp to a weakly ebbing river Dart. We both gazed up at the peeling balcony overlooking the river and then back down again at the cinema and laughed out loud.

'This will do nicely, won't it?' I enquired as I turned the key in the front door. Once inside and halfway up the stairs, we stopped, looked up and saw lightbeams pouring from a spectacular domed light-well. 'God, you'd never expect it to be like this from the outside, would you?'

Five minutes later we were standing on the balcony. A dusty, warm wind blew into our eyes as we squinted into what remained of that day's sun. There was an unspoken sense of breakthrough, of arriving at an unselfconscious station in our journey. There were no other people, or it seemed that there was none, no outside frames of reference determining how we should be; just the two of us.

For some unknown reason, we didn't leave the balcony and make love straight away. In a peculiar outburst of responsibility, I insisted we walk through the house, to check for break-ins, burst pipes and bad air. After respectfully opening and shutting several doors, and carefully brushing dead flies from windowsills into a dustpan, Loveday suddenly chortled, rather maturely: 'Why don't I put some food together? Spaghetti carbonara?'

'That sounds delicious.'

'I'll go and peel the onions.'

As I heard Loveday clattering about in the kitchen, I sat back and tried to read the newspaper. I had a niggling feeling in my stomach that Loveday, just possibly, might not be the cordon bleu type. I stood up and clapped my hands together and walked into the unused musty kitchen. Loveday was straddled over a plastic dustbin, like a giraffe over a water hole, peeling an onion layer by layer into it.

'Ah, Loveday!' I exclaimed with as much *joie de vivre* as I could muster.

'Ah, what?'

'Are you sure that's the right way to chop onions?'

'Do you know a better way?'

'Well . . .'

I kicked the plastic dustbin to one side and stood very close to her, taking the knife, and casually lobbing it into the sink. I put my hands underneath the back straps of her dungarees and pulled her against me.

'You don't do it like that; you do it like this . . .'

With her feet balanced on top of mine, we shuffled out of the kitchen, our lips locked in a succulent kiss. I kicked open the bedroom door with a bang crash, the noise of which made us both laugh. 'Nothing but a wild thing,' I said in my best Elvis drawl.

Ravel's 'Bolero' was playing in my head as I put my arms around her legs and lifted her over my shoulder. 'E-a-s-y, tiger!' she yelled excitedly. I made it to the old-fashioned bed and laid her carefully on the mattress. Just before her head reached the pillow she pulled me down on top of her, putting her leg between mine and pressing it against my crotch. All I could hear was our breathing. I wished I could stop smiling. I lowered my mouth down to her neck and gently kissed every inch of it up to her chin. I moved my hand between her legs and squeezed through the dungarees. I wanted to find it sopping wet. I held back because of her innocence, or some old-fashioned shyness, wanting to wait until the time was right. Her leg started slowly rubbing against my cock.

I moved my mouth across to her ear and nibbled on its fleshy lobe. She moaned as if tasting something delicious. I licked my tongue in and out of the folds of her ear and she sighed, thrusting her hands inside the back of my trousers and tightening her nails into my flesh. As my mouth reached her other ear, my right hand unclipped the two straps holding up the dungarees. I pulled down the denim flap and fed my hand beneath her cotton T-shirt. I nearly came as my palm slid down her warm belly and reached a black line of thick wiry hair. She was breathing hard now and using both hands to grab handfuls of my arse as if she was planning on taking them with her. She was no longer rubbing her leg against my cock because I was rubbing it constantly against her. A flash thought told me I was no better than a rampant humping dog, but I couldn't help it.

I slid my face down to her belly and with both hands pushed up the T-shirt to reveal her suntanned breasts in a white embroidered bra. I bowed my head to smell and kiss each one. Just then Loveday made a barking sound. I looked up and saw that she was baring her teeth at me, snarling like a dog.

What the hell had I done?

But then she winked and carried on snarling. I stuck my lip out and made a silly face at her. She tilted her head towards me, blinking and opening her lips. On instinct I angled my mouth towards her in readiness for a kiss – yet suddenly with a passionate growl she lunged and bit me on the neck again and again and then on my cheek so hard I thought it was going to bleed. Partly in shock, partly in excitement, I seized hold of her wrists. She bucked her legs, thrashed her head and shoulders from side to side and cried out, 'You f-u-c-k-e-r!' She was strong but I was stronger and within two seconds I had her arms pinned either side of the pillow.

We were both panting, slightly out of breath. I smiled, she smiled. Then, when she looked away, I swooped down and took two bites on the side of her neck, not hard, but bites all the same. She turned round and yelped unconvincingly. I released my grip triumphantly, gently pushed her legs in the air and slid her white jeans and pants off, as she unclasped her bra. Pushing off my trousers, I eased myself next to her naked body and pulled her close to me so that our noses were touching. Loveday took hold of my chin and kissed me hard on the lips. As she started tearing at the buttons on my shirt, I grabbed hold of her with both hands and swung myself on top of her.

'Easy you t-i-g-e-r,' I said.

She laughed.

I guided my cock between her legs. Loveday sank her nails into my back and yelled out my name as I eased myself inside her.

We were looking into each other's eyes now. Something big was stirring in my heart telling me not to let those eyes out of my sight, to keep looking into them whatever happened.

The next day we talked our way around the town and then beside the river Dart, with Loveday asking questions about my friends and work.

'Tell me about Harry,' she said, 'and the truth about sadism and homosexuality at boarding school.'

'Nothing to tell. We were, and are, both very gay, but just don't show it.'

She sighed wearily and carried on walking in contented silence. Just before the place where the river narrows, Loveday stopped and announced she wanted to tell me something; something really important. Spotting a bench beneath a weeping-willow, I gestured for us to sit down, brushing bits of twig and leaves off the seat to make it more comfortable. I lit two cigarettes and handed one to

Loveday. She sat down and kept lifting her head as if to begin but would then look away at the river and the trees, forcing a nervous smile and letting out a secret breath.

The suspense was beginning to affect my smile. I repeatedly cleared my throat in the most cheerful tone possible, but remained mute, paralysed by some instinct not to say anything before she had spoken. My mind was bouncing back and forth like a rubber ball between the fundamentally awful and the ridiculously mundane.

She's going to tell me she had a child when she was fifteen. She's going to say she's already had three abortions and cannot have a child. She's going to say she's still seeing that awful boyfriend with the big socks. She going to say she's got a job in America. No, you twit! All she's going to say is that she's told you a little fib somewhere along the line. Maybe it's just something physical that you haven't noticed. Six toes instead of five, one bosom bigger than the other. Ah that's why she walks like a duck! No, don't be silly. God! Maybe this is something about me?

Loveday then coughed loudly. 'Before I tell you this, you have to promise on the Bible that you will never ever tell anyone what I am about to tell you.'

Slightly irked by the request for confidentiality that I had assumed to be implicit, I nevertheless made the promise. Immediately, I became irritated at the childishness of the situation. I sat back, breathed deeply and tried to make myself remember that nobody was perfect, not even Loveday.

The confession concerned the occasion when Loveday had shoplifted a bottle of hair dye from a local shop when she was twelve years old.

'And?' I said, when the story appeared to have come to an end.

'Well, that's it.'

I scratched my head for a deliberately long time and then delivered my considered judgment. 'Is that really it? I mean, is that all? One poxy bottle of shampoo from a poxy shop? Loveday, please – tell me something terrible.'

'Well, it's terrible to me,' Loveday shouted.

'OK. *OK*'

'No, not OK. You may have fantastic terrible stories you've been involved in, to do with the bloody music business or whatever it's called. I don't. I'm boring, you see! And this is something I have never ever told anyone. No one, in fact, except the man who ran the shop.'

'Why does he know?'

'Because he bloody well caught me the next time I did it, that's why.'

'Oh, so you went back and did it again?'

'I did it for a joke, you know, for a dare, to see if I *could* do it again.'

'And what did the man in the shop say?'

'He was very difficult at first. He said he'd seen me do it the first time and that he was going to call my parents.'

'And what happened? He let you off with a lecture?'

She hesitated. 'Sort of.'

'What do you mean "sort of"?' I said dragging hard on my cigarette and holding the smoke in my chest.

'He said he would keep quiet if I came to the back of his shop.'

I exhaled loudly, watching the smoke coming out of my mouth as I spoke. 'Was anyone else there?'

'What do you think?'

'What happened?'

'He asked me to sit on his knee.'

'You mean you went?' I said, trying to imagine the scene.

'I had no bloody choice, and also I didn't really know what I was doing.'

'So, you went into the back room and sat on this bloke's knee? *Then what happened?*'

'It only happened a few times.'

'*What did?*'

'Oh, Tim, I don't want to go on with this.'

'Tell me. I want to know. You can't start something like this and not finish it.'

Loveday's flushed face became pale. By now she was on her third cigarette. 'All that used to happen was that he put his hand down, you know, down there. I think he used to play with himself at the same time. Well, I'm being stupid, I know he did because I could see it.'

'How old were you?'

39

'Eleven, twelve.'

'Jesus Christ!'

'Yes, I know.'

'And you never told anyone at all?'

'No, you're the first. I started telling my girlfriend Sally once, but changed my mind. So now you know.'

On instinct, I knew I should put my arm around her and draw her close to me. On instinct, though, I didn't want to. I sat there, still holding her hand, and allowed my foot to dismember the cigarette I had dropped to the ground. I needed to buy myself some time to balance the volatility between my heart and head. Then I felt my hand being tightly squeezed and heard Loveday whispering, 'I'm going to have a wander up the bank.'

I managed to smile at her. 'I'm just shocked for you! I guess it was the last thing I was expecting. Funny, really. You probably feel better for getting it off your chest.'

Loveday walked slowly towards the steep riverbank, then turned and, smiling broadly, called back: 'Don't worry; I'm not all screwed up by it. I've worked it all out, you know. I just haven't gone round telling lots of people. Don't go off me, will you?'

'I went off you weeks ago,' I shouted back.

'Thank God for that.'

I held up two thumbs high in the air for encouragement and sat back feeling sluggish. Loveday had raised her arms by the side of her head in what seemed to be a comical attempt at a handstand. Then shouting something that sounded Japanese, she twisted her feet towards me and rolled into a summersault. I jumped up and acted as a buffer to break her fall.

'Jesus Christ, Loveday, that was fantastic.'

'Phew! Haven't done that in a long time.'

'I didn't know you could do that sort of thing!'

'Well', Loveday turned her head away as she patted her flushed cheeks and wiped her brow. 'It's a bit different doing that when you smoke, plus I'd forgotten how easy it is to get hit in the face.'

Puzzled, I mouthed the last part of her remark.

Loveday grabbed my finger, jabbing at her breasts.

'These, Tim, these are the things that can hit you in the face when you're in mid-somersault. Didn't you know?'

'Most obliged, Loveday, for the anatomy lesson. I had no idea. However, I'm much more impressed with the gymnastics. Anything else you haven't told me about? Sharpshooter? International financier by any chance?'

'I think I've told you everything, Tim.'

'It's not confession time, you don't have to tell me everything, you know.'

'I've never been a Catholic so I wouldn't know.'

A few moments later we were retracing our steps to the Regal. I felt like an actor with stage fright at the dress rehearsal. It was bloody stupid, but not too late to put right. Loveday walked with a permanent smile and, almost as an affirmation of her cheerfulness, kept wiping her nose as if she had just returned victorious from a cross-country run.

7

Rick and I had been sitting at a corner table with our backs to the rest of the diners for over fifteen minutes before we realised we had not ordered any food, but this was nothing new to the waiters of the Venezia. That day, it was the ever-watchful Frank, the owner, who kept replenishing our Bloody Marys, while we devoured every breadstick on the table.

Both floors of the restaurant were packed full of customers fanning themselves and devouring carpaccio, gazpacho, and plates of cold salmon and mayonnaise. Men sat with shirts unbuttoned and jackets hung over the backs of chairs while women in white dresses showed off their suntans. Hot, hot, hot. So hot that Frank had brought out two ancient electric fans. The noise of twenty conversations was growing, as yet more bottles of Pinot Grigio were hastily clinked across the room and despatched to the tables. Frank managed to maintain his calm exterior, only occasionally raising his voice, slightly, to hurry up the chef. For late September business to be this good, Frank must have been doing something right.

Grabbing a paper napkin from a wine glass, Rick dabbed his sweating forehead and said, 'So?'

'Sorry, Rick, I was miles away. What did you say?'

Rick took off his glasses and placed them emphatically in the middle of the table.

'So, what happened?'

'You are not going to believe this!'

'Tim? Just tell me!' said Rick snapping a bread stick with both hands.

'OK, OK. Are you ready?'

'Yes!'

'Here we go, then. So, usual form: I get up there, you know, Caplow's inner sanctum, one minute before our usual meeting. The two secretaries are being far nicer to me than usual, but I'm nervous, right? Then, Brian Boore, you know, Finance Director, comes out of Caplow's office looking smug as usual but this time he gives me a pat on the back and says, "Well done, my lad".'

'My lad indeed, cheeky fucker!' Rick chuckled.

'Anyway, one of the secretaries tells me to go in. I have to say I wasn't looking forward to it, not one bit. The room's in its usual darkness – you know, blinds half-drawn, one lamp glowing and there he is, behind that intergalactic desk, puffing out smoke from his pipe as if his head's on fire. "Come in, come in," he says, far too bloody cheerfully. Immediately, he zooms off on a tangent, talking about how great the weather is and how Brian Boore reminds him of Bowie's manager on a bad day but without the personality.'

Rick laughed loudly.

'He then spins back to how pleased he is with the daily sales figures. I ask him how on earth he got them and he says he's trained Zannie to give him a copy without me knowing. We have a laugh about that. I swear he knows what's coming. Then he hands me a bunch of cassettes sent from Aaron Stein in America and says he would be grateful for my opinion, when I have the time. He wasn't going to stop, so I had to bite the bullet and jump in.'

'What did you say?'

'Well, after a lot of umming and erring, I told it to him straight. God! It was awful. I said I wanted to be up front about it and that I had decided to leave to pursue something else. He didn't let me finish and calmly put his hands up in the air and asked which company had offered me a job. I told him that it wasn't another company, but I was going to start a new one with you.'

Rick leaned forward. 'Did he go completely mad?'

'No. He just sat there, puffing slowly on his pipe. I told him I was grateful for all that he had done for me and how I'd never forget the experience etcetera, but I felt the time had come to try to do something for myself. Then he interrupted me and asked if I couldn't be persuaded to stay on. I rambled on about my age and opportunities and having thought it through and so on. He said he respected my decision, and was grateful that I had the decency to tell him in good time. He then asks, am I prepared to work till the end of my contract? Of course, I tell him.'

Rick raised his eyebrows and said, 'You don't have to, you know. These days a lot of people don't.'

'Yes, well, I think that's wrong. Why have a contract in the first place? Anyway, stop interrupting; I'm just getting to the good bit. So then he says, and this came out of absolutely nowhere, he says, *do we have a backer?* I nearly fell off my chair! I quickly made something up and said we were just starting to talk to people about that side of things.'

Rick was on the edge of his seat by now.

'What did he say?'

'He said to give him a few seconds while he thinks something through. I can tell you, for the next sixty seconds all sorts of things were going through my mind.'

'And?'

'And then he leans back in his chair and quite casually asks exactly how much money are we looking for? I didn't know what to say, so I just pulled a number out of my head and said one hundred thousand pounds. He didn't blink, but said he thought that was a sensible amount. My mouth was completely dry. He then said that, on reflection, and knowing his American partner's belief in me, and the fact that he rated *you* very highly, that he would like to provide the backing rather than anyone else. And would we please come and see him as soon as he's back from his holiday and when, of course, we're ready.'

'Christ! Did he really say that?'

'Yes, Rick. He really did say that.'

'Clever old bastard. He wants to make sure his investment in you carries on paying off.'

'A hundred thousand pounds!'

'It goes very quickly, Tim, believe me.'

'Well, I know, but it's quite a start, isn't it?'

'It's more than a start. When does he get back from his holidays?'

'Early October, I think.'

'I think we'd better eat, don't you?'

'Come on, Rick. We should be drinking champagne.'

'Look, don't misunderstand me. It's great news, but always remember: "Truth is a cleared cheque in the bank".'

Frank put a large plate of asparagus on the table, then leaned down by my side, waiting for a lull in the conversation, and almost whispered, 'Tim, I just thought I would enquire how your mother is.'

I felt my mouth stretching and ran my hands over my face.

'Oh, that's very kind, Frank. She died just nearly three months ago. I thought I told you.' Frank looked genuinely upset. 'It's all right, Frank; it's all over now and she died peacefully.'

Frank was still looking at me. 'Good,' he finally said. 'That's good. I am glad she did.'

I said goodbye to Rick by the aluminium revolving door to the five-floor building of SCG, the Simon Caplow Group. We cracked a joke, shook hands in the creepy Masonic way that always made us laugh, and went our separate ways.

The record company section was on the ground floor and I peeked through the glass window of the general office which was big enough to accommodate seven desks, or workstations as Zannie called them. In the middle of the room was a long white table where we held daily prayer meetings to discuss tactics. I knocked on the glass and Hugo, Jolian, Rufus, Jasper, and Emma all looked up and waved as they continued gabbling on the phone. All this activity was good and made me feel better. The place could survive without me.

When I'd told Loveday about my plans she was cautious. 'Are you totally sure about Rick? I mean, can you trust him?'

'He's my best mate in the business,' I'd said defensively.

'Look, I know I'm a bit thick,' she said slowly, 'but why all the hurry? Isn't it best to stay and build on the success you've got?'

'Yes, but if you've done it once, you can do it again. Get it?'

Loveday shrugged and feigned acceptance. 'I guess if you don't do it now, you'll always regret it.'

Now I pushed open my office door and smelt a strange mix of menthol cigarettes and perfume. I walked in half-titillated, half-annoyed that someone was in my office.

'Only me!' came Zannie's voice from somewhere behind my desk, her cigarette burning in my ashtray.

'What are you doing in here? What have you lost now?' I liked teasing her.

'What?' she laughed, walking round to sit on the front of the desk. 'What have *I* lost? That'll be the day! When have you ever remembered to walk out of here with the right tapes or files? And you're usually wearing someone else's jacket by mistake.'

Zannie laughed in a theatrical way that made me suspect she was drunk. She eased herself off the desk, pausing mid-laugh to bend down and lift up the bottoms of my trouser legs. She threw her head back and whooped.

'Yeah, yeah, Zannie, what's so funny?'

'Oh, I'm just remembering the time with the astrology book. You know the one with the yellow cover that said to look under your boss's desk and see if he was wearing different coloured socks. You were then, and you are again today.'

I knew she was right but I also knew I wasn't in the mood for much more of this. I sensed that there was a lot more to what she was saying than just banter about my absent-mindedness. She began picking things off my desk, and examining them in the light. She held up a plastic weasel with an engraved plaque on its chest that said, 'Weasels ripped my flesh UK tour 74 thank you from Frank Zappa.'

'Do you remember those days at Zenith? You were driving all over the country for those radio tours. I was doing all the work, as usual, typing out those dreadful itineraries. Takes you back, Tim, doesn't it? We've been together a long time, eh?'

'Price! Have you been drinking?'

'Don't call me that! You know I hate that!' she shouted, gripping the glass ashtray so tightly it slipped out of her hands and spilt its contents on the floor. 'Shit!'

'Zannie! Calm down, what's wrong?'

'Nothing's wrong!' she yelled, looking away and reaching down to pick up the scattered cigarette butts and paperclips.

I took a deep breath, crouched down in front of her, and scooped up the remaining paperclips.

'Look, why don't you just sit down and have a break? In fact, why don't you have a Kit-Kat?'

Zannie shook her head slowly and raised her eyes to heaven.

I got up and sat behind my desk.

'Bloody hell, ZZ Top, Caravan and Frank Zappa – they do seem a long time ago now!' I said, hoping she would go back to work, but Zannie opened up a new line of attack.

'Funny how you haven't asked for the sales figures, isn't it?'

'Funny how someone hasn't given them to me, as requested, Zannie.'

'The morning sales figure was fifty-eight thousand.'

'Just this morning! Shit, that's fantastic!'

'It is, isn't it? All that hard work we've done is finally paying off.'

'Yeah, it's brilliant,' I said, aware of how flat our voices sounded. I wanted to clap my hands and say let's get on with things, but Zannie's dark eyes were staring at me, her mouth biting at a cuticle, ready with another question. She delivered it slowly with more than a hint of sarcasm.

'So, how was Rick and how was lunch?'

'How did you know I was seeing Rick?'

'I know everything there is to know about you.'

'Oh Christ, not another one.'

'Well?'

'Zannie, I love you dearly but I'm not obliged to tell you every single little thing that happens in my life, am I?'

'Something to hide then?'

'Jesus! What is this?'

'Well, is there?'

'No! Of course not.'

'That's not what I've heard.'

She was behaving like a scorned wife and I was acting the part of the cheating husband. In some ways I felt she was entitled to, but I was also aware of my pledge to keep things as quiet as possible for the moment. I got up from the desk.

'Zannie, I've got a very important meeting next week. I can't say what it's about, but once I've had it, I promise I'll tell you what's going on. OK? In the meantime . . .'

'You know I won't say anything.'

'No funny comments to anyone, not to anyone in the whole building, anyone in the business in fact, including Rick, OK?'

Zannie sniffed. 'I'm sorry. I was really worried. You know I'd do anything for you.'

'Thanks, Zannie,' I said, giving her a hug and gently squeezing her backside.

Zannie stepped back from the embrace, rubbing her hands together as if she were cold, looked up and said: 'You and your words. Ha! Success at *Zannie Price*! You're mad, you really are'

8

I stuffed a five-pound note into the taxi driver's hand and without waiting for the change ran into the OTE building. I looked up at the clock. Not only was I more than five minutes late, but the date was 12th October. Time was moving fast.

'You've got to come and sign the book first!' warbled the grey-haired receptionist. I scribbled furiously into the OTE Records visitors' book and looked up at a younger receptionist who was staring at me with such disdain I wondered if my flies were undone. She was a peroxide blonde, and wore a pair of pink dungarees that looked at least two sizes too small.

'Are you new here?' I said, managing a smile.

'Yeah, that's right,' she mumbled.

'Tim Lomax from Barracuda.'

'Barracuda? Is that a band?'

I hesitated for a second, wanting to let her know *exactly how important* I was, but thought better of it and rushed over to the lift.

On the fifth floor, I tried to speed-walk up the corridor to the hushed and revered world known as the Directors' Suite.

Clare Doherty, the senior secretary, reassured me that '*this time*' I was not too late and that Shamus Murphy would be along shortly. She showed me into his office and to brown vinyl chair. The air seemed sweetly acrid. When Clare left the room I sniffed repeatedly, trying to identify the offending odour. It was familiar but something I had not smelt in years. Then I realised it was the aftershave, Old Brute. Loveday's home-made bacon sandwich swivelled in my stomach.

There were the usual self-congratulatory photos of Shamus shaking hands with various celebrities, and gold discs mounted expensively around the walls. I began comparing his office to that of Simon Caplow. His piles of records, music scores, the tobacco smoke. I began to imagine what Rick's office looked like and pictured high ceilings, white walls, high-backed wicker chairs and cool Moroccan carpets; people walking barefoot. Leaning forwards, I pulled a large silver photo frame across the desk towards me. It showed a summer scene in the country, with a radiant Mrs Murphy sitting on the lawn surrounded by three toothy children. This rather elegant middle-aged woman somehow didn't match up with the Shamus Murphy I knew. I began to examine the theory of 'It takes all types', but just as I was reaching a conclusion, a hand slid slowly down my shoulder, and an Essex voice sang out: 'H-a-l-l-o, m-a-t-e! How are ya?'

Shamus Murphy was the closest thing to a human slug I had ever met in my life. Big collar, wide tie, you only needed to shake hands with him briefly to know. In fact, it was altogether easier to think of him as Shamus Slime, or indeed just the Slime.

The Slime was a very big bigwig at OTE. To be exact, he was the deputy managing director. Had I met him in a different location and when he was not wearing his three-piece suit, I would have been forgiven for thinking that his main occupation was selling fake perfume on Oxford Street.

He wore a shamrock pinkie ring, even though the only Irish thing about him was his late grandmother's linen underwear. Apart from the sixty-a-day he smoked, it was said that he only lived for two things, work and sex – or, as he would say, 'wedge and pussy'. To be more precise, he considered fucking anything that moved, provided it was wearing a skirt. How any female could remotely consider sharing even a biro with this man was beyond my comprehension.

But then it was still beyond me, even at the advanced age of twenty-six, to understand that some people will do anything to get ahead.

After Shamus had asked me whether I wanted coffee and had told me how many trillion records OTE had sold the day before, I was able to get down to the serious business of taking the piss out of him. It had taken me a long time to get to a position where I was able to do this and now I couldn't stop myself.

'I see you have a new receptionist downstairs, Shamus. Very attractive! Is she new?'

'Oh, have we?' Shamus asked, leaning back in his chair a little too quickly.

'Yes, you have. I'd say she's very bright.'

'Really?' said Shamus, playing with his cigarette box and looking almost coy.

'I bet there'll be a few people wanting to show her their etchings!'

I knew that this last remark would force Shamus out into the open. The one thing you could be sure of with Shamus was his uncontrollable need to tell you about it. He jumped out of his chair and strode to the door, shutting it carefully enough to make it look as if we were having a really confidential business discussion.

'Strictly between you and me, right?' He said this every time he was going to impart details of his latest staff conquest. I smiled and nodded – I always did.

'Fuckin' hell!' he stuck his tongue out and put his hand around his throat. 'Like a fucking train! I tell you, I'm getting too old for all this, know what I mean? She's only bloody seventeen,' he added, wheezing and building up steam. 'But I tell you what, these days they know more about it than we do! Fuckin' 'ell, know what I mean? Right saucy little thing she is. I tell you, when we got to that golf club I thought I'd be home by eleven. Stone me if I didn't stagger in at one in the morning! Lovely little arse on her . . .'

With that he made a curious slurping sound, slowly wiping the back of his hand across his nose and mouth before saying, 'So, what d'you need, then? I know you only come 'ere when you want something.'

'Well . . .'

'Look, let's not beat about the bush, young Tim, we know the deal's up at the end of the year, and you've had your first real run of hits, so you probably want to renegotiate the contract. Smart move of mine licensing Barracuda all that time ago, wasn't it? Yes, well done, Shamus. And *you've* done well, lad, no one can take that away from you. You want to redo the deal and get better terms, don't you, Tim? Am I right or am I wrong?'

He gave a long, music-hall laugh. I laughed back for as long as possible, first to give myself some time to think, and second to see if he wanted to disclose his position further. Keeping shtoom was not one of Shamus's principal skills; I had known that ever since he first started sharing every sordid detail of his sex life. However, I also knew that because he was so utterly unscrupulous, Shamus was in fact quite skilled at making deals for himself. He was gifted or tainted – depending what side of the street you were walking on – with the ability to use expressions such as, *'Let me be absolutely straight with you'* or *'I shouldn't be telling you this at all'*, with such sincerity that you believed every word he said. If he had to, he was ready to let you think you were his best friend or that he was yours, or that, frankly, today was the very last day that he was going to be working for this company. I truly came to believe that if the deal was big enough, or important enough to his boss Pierre King, Shamus would have donned a skirt and fucked himself up the arse, if necessary.

'Well, in a way it is about the contract, Shamus, yes,' I said, feeling my way into the conversation. Shamus jumped in immediately.

'And?'

'Well, this is difficult because it's really about me in a way . . .'

'I take it you've been well rewarded for the recent hits?'

'Obviously,' I lied.

'So this must be about the key-man clause we asked for. I can tell you now, and you can tell Mr Simon Caplow, your guv'nor, that we're not doing it without a guarantee that you are in the frame. Well, not at that sort of money anyway,' Shamus sped on, not pausing for a reply. 'Look, it's far better for you to be on a key-man clause; that way they have to pay you a whole load of money to get rid of you. Or don't you want to be in the frame?'

'Well, obviously I do, but it's just that another opportunity has come up, that's all.'

Shamus looked genuinely stunned. He leaned forward open-mouthed, his three chins quivering as he frantically stubbed out his cigarette.

'You're leaving? What! After all we've done? After all the money we've spent? After all the hard work? After that award and fantastic party at the Sporting Club? Fuck me!'

I sat there, swamped by a guilt I had not anticipated.

'I'm not going to leave anyone in the lurch, if that's what you think, Shamus,' I said feebly, wishing I had rehearsed the whole scene first.

Shamus sat hunched over his desk pushing his cigarette box back and forth with his finger. He did not look up but said in a new and serious tone, 'I can tell you, Pierre is not going to be happy about this. I think I'd better go and tell him right away.'

Shamus stood up and looked at me as if enquiring whether I had anything to say before being sentenced. God! Barracuda was only licensed to them. I didn't work for them. Why was he taking it so personally? Or was he? I decided to take the slug by the horns.

'Shamus, I'm leaving to start a new record label with Rick Fraser.'

'Who?'

'You must know Rick Fraser,' I exclaimed indignantly, inwardly concerned that he didn't.

'Never 'eard of him. Back in a minute,' he said, leaving the room almost theatrically.

I sat there feeling vaguely confused. Was he playing a game with me or not? Simon Caplow's reaction had been very different, and he was my boss, for fuck's sake! It was true I had persuaded OTE to spend an awful lot of money on marketing the label, cajoling them and playing every form of politics I could to keep them moving. But, surely, they had made a lot of money too? Maybe they hadn't. Maybe they wanted some form of payback. I stood up quickly and started to breathe deeply. I was hearing a familiar voice inside my head. It was that chanting worm eating away at my thoughts again. I hummed loudly but it wouldn't go away. *They're going to find you out. You've gone too far this time, bitten off too much, you're fucked.*

Suddenly the Slime bounced back into the office as if he had just won the football pools. 'Shift yourself, Tim. Pierre wants to see both of us in his office.'

Pierre King's low-lit office resembled a posh Bond Street florist's with vases of flowers everywhere, a big desk and lots of telephones.

51

The only concession to the music business that I could see was a neat pile of records on the corner of his desk.

I sat on the Chesterfield listening to Shamus in amazement as he sped through the history of the association of our two companies. As he droned his way through the details of what he and his team had done to bring about our success, I was pleased to see that even King was becoming irritated. Undeterred, Shamus then listed *my* talents: . . . determination, that's what he's got, like a bull! God's gift to having good ideas, you know, like the nurse on the operating table at the conference, very good that, don't worry, Pierre, I'll fill you in later. Everything he's working on is turning to gold, Pierre; he's got the Midas touch, I'm telling you! And on top of all that, the poor chap's had to cope with losing his mum. Nasty that, wasn't it, Tim?'

I nodded, embarrassed that this information was being used as conversational currency. Before I had time to calculate exactly where this volte face of Shamus's was leading, I heard Pierre King calmly enquire, 'So how much money do you imagine you and Mr Fraser will be requiring in the new venture, Tim?'

He had gone straight to the point. I was stunned. Here was a man to take seriously: no crappy chit-chat, no talk about the fourteenth hole.

'In the region of one hundred thousand pounds,' I heard myself say.

There was a brief pause as King wrote this down and then I heard him say, 'Presumably that figure covers your first year. The deal would be a licensing deal for the world, yes?'

Christ! This was all going too quickly. What the fuck should I say?

'Well, yes and no. The deal is for the first year, but we intend to retain as many overseas territories as possible.'

King made another note, put down his pen, and stood up, smiling.

'Good. That's very good. We'll have to discuss the overseas position, of course, but let me say that we're more than interested and we would like you and Mr Fraser to come and see us before you see anyone else. I imagine you're busy finding your successor. When do you actually leave?'

'We start the new label on the second of January.'

'The first working day of 1980! Sounds to me like it's going to be your decade. Come and see us as soon as you're ready. Goodbye.'

The whole meeting had taken less than ten minutes. Ice cool.

I managed to disentangle myself from the Slime's endless pumping handshake and escaped into the lift. As I watched the floor numbers flash past, I kept repeating *a hundred thousand pounds* to myself like a mantra. First Simon Caplow's offer, now this. I couldn't believe it.

When the lift doors opened, I walked straight over to reception. 'May I borrow this phone? Don't worry, it's a local call.'

Miss Goes-Like-A-Train looked dumbstruck and turned quizzically to the grey-haired receptionist. As I heard Rick's direct line ringing, I asked the former: 'Do you like golf?'

She stared at me. 'Are they a band?'

9

The Crooked Billet was just across Albert Bridge from Battersea. It was three hundred years old, with open fires, worn stone floors, long benches and wood panelling that smelt of beeswax and old beer.

Rick arrived shortly after opening time, wearing an orange baseball cap and nearly tripping up over an uneven flagstone. He happily accepted my offer of a gin and tonic, and then went and lay down on the long wooden bench by the fire. Balancing the drink on his chest with one hand, he casually placed his other hand behind his head and promptly fell asleep. Fred, the pint-sized barman who seemed older than the pub, gave me a questioning look as if to say *is he with you?*

'It's OK, Fred, let him sleep for a few minutes, he's not used to being in such a nice place. He's a West London type, wrong side of town, know what I mean?'

Fred screwed up his face in mock horror and straightened a beer towel over the bar.

After downing my first whisky, I ordered another, then walked over to Rick's bench. 'Good evening, sir!' I boomed in his ear.

Rick awoke with a start but managed to keep hold of the gin and tonic. Like a bedridden patient he lifted his head and sipped from the glass.

'Christ, that's better! I thought I was going to fall asleep in the car coming over.'

'Out late last night?' I enquired.

'No, another boring night in front of the TV, waiting for Victoria to give the word.'

'What word? Oh, yeah, all this pregnancy malarkey.'

Rick heaved himself up on one elbow. 'It may be malarkey to you, but it certainly isn't to her. You wait till it happens to you.'

'It won't happen to me. Not for a very long time,' I declared emphatically.

'I tell you, they're all the same, Tim. This biological clock thing is no joke. I've had to take hot and cold baths, stand on my head, run up and down the stairs and wake up at all times of the night. Last night I even had to use half a dozen ice cubes.'

'Jesus! Where did you put those?'

'Where do you think? Behind my ears?'

We both laughed.

'Anyway,' he announced, swinging himself off the bench and pointing to a nearby table, 'let's get on with the business.'

As he sat down, clicking open his briefcase, I was amazed, as ever, by his ability to switch so quickly from larking around to being deadly serious.

'OK, Tim,' he said, peering over his glasses. 'Am I right in assuming we want to make, or rather you want to make, three albums and six singles in the first year?'

I opened my Book of Lists and, leaning heavily on the appropriate double page so that it lay flat on the table, said, 'Yeah, that's right, but why put it like that?'

'Like what?'

'Like this is only to do with what I want.'

'You're the one with the interest in making records. I don't care, remember. It's only a means to an end for me.'

'Oh, come on, Rick, don't make out this is just something to indulge me and my weird taste in music.'

'Of course I'm not saying that. It's just that you're the one who knows what's good and what's bad. I don't, not really. All I'm good at is adding up the sums and telling people what to do.'

Rick let out a stuttering laugh. I joined in, then went to the bar for a refill.

'OK, sorry,' I said, when I returned. 'Look, Rick, I do know about these things and I'm telling you this label is going to be tremendous.'

Rick took a sip. 'Let's hope you're right.'

'Work it out for yourself. We've got Simon Caplow *and* the guys from OTE gagging for a deal and they're the only ones we've seen so far. So add up your fantastic talent and mine and the fact that there's no one as brilliant as us two, and you'll see what I'm talking about. This has got the potential to be really huge. Do you understand? You do want to do this, don't you?'

Rick took off his glasses, rubbed his eyes, sniffed loudly, and smiled.

'Of course I do, otherwise I'd be at home watching "Match of the Day". I know it's going to be great. I don't need convincing, Tim!' Taking two pieces of paper from his briefcase, he continued, in a more enthusiastic tone: 'This is a summary of how and where I think we would spend the money in the first year.'

'I see,' I said looking at the handwritten columns and not really understanding anything.

'And this other page contains a detailed chart demonstrating income stream.'

'Oh, yes,' I said taking hold of the paper as if it were part of some school exam.

'Now, as much as Simon Caplow and the blokes from OTE are going to want to hear about music, they're also going to want to know about costs.'

'Anyone can produce costs, Rick. Costs don't make money, hit acts do.'

Rick cleared his throat loudly. 'Obviously it's about having hit records from hit acts! But in my experience, people don't give you money unless you show you know what you're going to do with it.'

Thirty minutes later, we had agreed the details of the expenditure as well as a schedule of recording plans. By now the pub had filled up with a dozen noisy people who all chose to come and stand by our table in front of the blazing fire.

'Fuck this for a game of soldiers! Another drink, same again?'

Rick nodded as I strode to the bar.

As Fred filled the glasses, I gazed up into the horizontal mirror high above his head, trying to find my own reflection. I liked being by the bar, striking matches on the side of bricks, flicking back whisky to make the back of my throat glow. Glancing up at the mirror again, I saw three familiar figures entering the bar. Loveday, in her red woollen hat, was closely followed by Harry and Jessica.

'Bloody hell, on time for a change!' I said, kissing Loveday and Jessica and giving Harry a friendly punch. Harry stiffened. Now that he had joined a merchant bank, he thought he had to be seen to be behaving in a certain way. He knew I disapproved, but before I could say anything, he mumbled, 'Get the drinks in, Tim!'

'Your round, I think, Harry,' I said smiling. As usual Jessica reached for her bag.

Rick laughed and stepped towards Loveday.

'So, Loveday, how's life in the fast lane?'

'Have you two met before?' Harry asked.

'Oh, yes, I've met Rick at least three times – if not four. We're getting married soon,' Loveday said, grinning.

'Don't you think we ought to live together first, Loveday?' Rick replied as quick as a flash.

'Yes, but I want to get married, Rick, and have kids. You know, do the whole thing.'

Rick paused and cocked his head towards me. 'You want to have kids, do you?'

I decided to interrupt as quickly as possible. Luckily, Harry spoke up first.

'Excuse me interrupting your breeding plans, Loveday, but what time do we have to get to the Excuse, Tim?'

I had asked them to come with me to a club in the King's Road for dinner and to hear a new band.

'Fancy coming along, Rick?' I asked.

'No. I've got to go. Victoria's waiting for me with some awful task at home. Enjoy the band and see you all soon.' He picked up his briefcase and walked towards the door.

'Come on then, who wants a drink?' I said, keen to pump myself up before getting to the Excuse.

* * *

The disagreement between myself and Loveday had started simmering after leaving the Crooked Billet and was nearing boiling point before we arrived at The Excuse. It was a friendly enough argument at first: Loveday slammed the door of the Gaulle just a little too hard. Now, I could never be exactly described as car-proud, certainly not in terms of the state of the interior, but I was proud of *this* car. Likewise, it was my first month back on the road after the ban, and without any doubt at all, it felt absolutely, fucking, fantastic.

We parked outside the Duke of York's barracks. By this time, it was clear what was really bothering her.

'You didn't tell me you were seeing Vanessa next week.'

'What?'

'You heard.'

'How did you know that?'

'You left your pocket diary on the dining-room table.'

'And you read it, Loveday?'

'I was only going to write my birthday in there, so you didn't forget. So, what about Vanessa, Tim?'

'What about Vanessa?'

We nipped and pecked at one another in the lift that took us down to the chrome-door entrance of the Excuse and then stood silently waiting for Harry and Jessica to arrive. Fortunately, Loveday was temporarily anaesthetised by the cool atmosphere and soft golden light that glowed from every corner of the room. Fleetwood Mac's *Rumours* oozed from the ceiling speakers while the young and beautiful sat murmuring in white cane chairs around white cane tables. It was like a Cinzano Bianco commercial, but sadly without Joan Collins and Leonard Rossiter.

The manager showed us to our table. Sitting there, proprietorially, was Abe Aberman.

Now, if Woody Allen had an alter ego, Abe was it. Abe Aberman had been working for two years on secondment as a lawyer within the SCG Group. In his words, we had 'kinda clicked' but, in mine, not exactly tied the knot. I had recently decided that he was the sort of guy who was great in a one-to-one situation but unreliable in a group. Pale and so thin he looked like an X-ray, Abe was also the walking embodiment of self-deprecating charm. He'd spend an hour complaining about how generally run down he was feeling, and then limp sadly on to the tennis court and thrash the living daylights out of you, especially if there were any females about.

Abe stood up smartly and greeted Loveday with a little too much ebullience. Then we all sat down and studied the menu.

The first half of dinner went pretty well. Harry and Jessica enjoyed the band and we chatted happily, like expert conspirators, about the future of the music business. During the day, I had privately announced my plans about joining forces with Rick, but had asked everyone concerned to treat the matter as confidential. The reaction had not been as enthusiastic as I had expected. I told myself that it was a difficult thing for people to understand, and everyone would simply need a bit more time. Abe had definitely been a little off about the idea, but I had decided to give him the benefit of the doubt.

It was during the second half of dinner that things really began to go askew.

'Tim, you weren't seriously thinking about signing *that* band?'

'Do we really *want* another bottle of wine?'

'Mind if I change places with Harry, so you can tell me all about yourself, Loveday?'

It was not just Abe's digs about the band or the way he had queried the wisdom of my ordering more wine that had got up my nose, but the way he was monopolising Loveday. Initially, I had been pleased not to have to worry about her and, what with the business about the stupid diary, it was almost a relief to have someone else take up the strain. That is, for about ten minutes.

After another fifteen, I began to cock my head towards them to overhear whatever it was that was so absorbing.

'You don't like Hemingway? Loveday, I'm shocked!' said Abe.

'I'm afraid so,' Loveday said, sipping her wine, 'but I'm mad about F. Scott Fitzgerald if that helps.'

'You know, you remind me of that actress in *Rosemary's Baby*. Do you know who I mean?'

'Do you mean the one who was opposite Robert Redford in *The Great Gatsby*, what's her name?'

'Yes, that's the one, very pretty, very sensual and intelligent-looking.'

'I don't look anything like her, well maybe a tiny bit . . .'

Surely Loveday wasn't going to fall for that crap? Telling myself not to be so uncharitable towards a displaced and well-meaning American, I sank back into Harry's pontificating about the benefits of diplomatic negotiation in Iran compared to the use of military force.

Ten minutes later they were still at it. By now I was convinced that Loveday had foolishly allowed herself to be spun right into the centre of Abe's sexual web. Worse, maybe it was the other way round. Abe looked up in my direction.

'So,' he said, 'who is going to have the final say in whether you sign a band or not? You or Rick?'

Abe was good at this sort of thing; he made it all look so effortless. He was like a footballer dribbling the words right up to you and then ducking and weaving them behind your back. I told myself it was just a case of plain and simple envy: it was happening for me and it wasn't for him. He was returning to America at the end of the year.

Loveday was resting her chin in the palm of her hand, tilting her head on one elbow, and smiling across at Abe. She was wearing a tight thin cashmere sweater and looked like the perfect mixture of innocence and sex. I knew she knew I was watching her. All of a sudden she interrupted Abe's monologue with an emphatic 'Excuse me' and leaned towards me. The table fell silent, perfectly on cue, as she said: 'Abe doesn't think you should join up with Rick. He thinks you should stay put.'

The silence remained underneath her full stop. Loveday sat back, more than a little drunk, lowering her eyes and running her tongue along her bottom lip. Abe shifted in his chair and slowly took off his glasses. Harry and Jessica looked confused and then smiled politely into space.

Abe raised his head. 'I just said that maybe you should stop and think about life out there in the cold, without any real money. Hate me, by all means, but I don't think you've thought this through.'

I managed to sit there, grit my teeth and smile while Abe nodded at his empty ice-cream bowl. I was about to make a crack about certain people not having enough lead in their pencil when a cheerful Liverpudlian voice came out of nowhere.

'Hey, Tim! What's *happening*?'

It was Gabe Morass, swaying, slightly stoned and dressed in a white polo neck sweater, jeans, and tan suede jacket.

'Gabe, my old pal! Come and join us?'

Gabe beamed his usual broad smile, scratched the back of his wild hair, shook hands with everyone on the table and said: 'Love to join you guys, but I'm meeting someone at the Speak. You coming down? Good band, apparently.'

People liked meeting Gabe, not only because he was a famous musician but also because he was genuinely down to earth.

'Save us a table, Gabe!' I called out, as he sloped off towards the door.

'Was that *the* Gabe Morass?' Harry asked in a schoolboy whisper. 'I would really like to meet him.'

'Of course, Harry, once we get to the club,' I said, rubbing my hands together and turning my attention back to Abe. 'Are you going to join us, Abe? Or is it past your bedtime?'

10

The Speak possessed only six normal lightbulbs. Two were situated in the kitchen, two were in the toilets, and two were hung over the cash tills. All the other bulbs were red. Curiously, the Speak was the place to be seen.

Once down the wrought-iron staircase, past the doormen, the club consisted principally of three rooms. First, there was the green room, which on a good night resembled a cocktail bar out of *Cabaret* and, on a bad night, a dimly lit launderette without the washing machines. Second, there was the restaurant, an oblong room lit by a multitude of candles in empty wine bottles, with expensive-smelling food that, despite an endless queue of customers, was curiously inedible. Third, there was the big room where people sat and drank as much as possible, studiously ignoring whatever band was playing on the tiny stage.

The big room was half-full, but we decided to stay and ordered a round of drinks. Just as the waitress served us, a three-piece band shuffled on to the stage and began playing at full blast. Abe and I pretended not to notice. Harry and Jessica walked off towards the band who were playing a choppy white reggae, similar to the Police but more intense. Suddenly, as the drummer started bashing out the intro to their second number, I felt someone jabbing my arm. It was Loveday. She leaned sideways and yelled in my ear.

'I don't feel very well. I think I'm going to be sick.'

Now the one thing you don't want in a club like the Speak is a girlfriend who is going to be sick.

'Are you sure? Put your head between your legs,' I yelled back, pointing downwards and trying to make myself heard above the noise of the band.

Loveday let herself flop on to my lap and passed out. The need for cold flannels, smelling salts and a stretcher raced through my mind until I lowered my ear to her face and heard her happily snoring. I eased off my jacket and carefully draped it over her, exceedingly grateful to her for not throwing up.

When I turned my attention back to the band, I was transfixed by the sight of Harry slumped in a nearby chair while Jessica pinched the bridge of his nose. She pointed to the stage and shouted something unintelligible. Seeing that I was none the wiser, she screwed up her hand, looked at the stage, and swung her fist in an arc towards Harry's face. I turned towards the stage to discover what she was pointing at. More people were crowding into the room now, but they weren't looking at the band. They all seemed to be cheering the drunken fool pawing the guitarist's strings. The spiky brown-haired man swayed, and staggered and then, putting his knee on the stage, heaved himself up, turning his head to acknowledge the crowd.

An arm and a hand appeared, and the man was wrenched off the stage. In a flash he recovered his balance, and swung his fist into his captor's face. I winced as the punch connected, and my adrenalin kick-started as I realised the face belonged to Gabe Morass.

He did nothing in response, but smiled.

The crowd started chanting and laughing.

'Sid, Sid, Sid!'

No one seemed to recognise Gabe, despite recent Quantum Frog appearances on the 'Whistle Test' and 'Top of the Pops'.

'Go on, Gabe, hit the fucker!' I heard myself shout.

Gabe kept smiling and gesturing to the man to leave. Then the man leaned into Gabe, jerked back his head, and spat in Gabe's face.

The band stopped playing. Gabe slowly wiped his face and gently pushed the man towards the door. The man snarled and screamed and drove his fist into Gabe's arm. The deep slap echoed round the room. Nothing.

'Come on, Gabe, please! Hit the bastard!'

Gabe stepped closer to the man and smiled. The man took a step back and lunged at him again, but this time Gabe blocked the punch with his forearm, grabbed the man's shoulders, and nutted him smack on the forehead.

There was a moment's pause, and then the man doubled up.

The crowd were completely silent, all except for me. I could not understand all this reverence. Then Gabe lifted the crumpled heap high above his shoulders and started walking slowly through the crowd. He looked magnificent.

I knew better than to go after him with congratulations, although I wanted to. He was odd, Gabe. Unless he was on stage, he didn't like being the centre of attention. I turned round to see how Harry was faring, but instead found the smiling face of Abe.

'Do you know who that was?' he said, appearing to choke back an orgasm.

'That was Gabe Morass, the drummer from Quantum Frog. You've already met him.'

'Not him! The other guy, Sid Vicious!'

As I stood there registering the fact, the crowd and the band started up again drowning out my reply: 'Bye, Sid! Thanks for coming! Come on you, Sid! Regrets I've had a few! Regrets I've had a few . . .'

Having given Harry a handkerchief full of ice cubes for his nose and made sure he was getting the best of attention from a recovered Loveday and Jessica, I went outside to find Gabe. He was crouched on the pavement with his back against the club's railings, whistling to himself. His polo neck was spotted with blood and he seemed a little shaken. I offered him my brandy. He took hold of the glass, and downed it in one.

'I think I'll be calling it a night, Tim. See you soon, yeah?'

* * *

The drive home that night to Battersea was beautiful. At first.

The Gaulle cruised majestically through the deserted London streets, with only the occasional black cab passing us. A little accordion music and we could have been in Paris. As we swept into the empty circle of Hyde Park Corner, Loveday leaned her head on my shoulder. Apart from a series of meaningless profanities about the lateness of the hour we had said little since getting in the car. I pushed a cassette of Burt Bacharach songs into the machine, pressed play and listened to Dusty Springfield singing 'The Look of Love'. For a brief while, the world was a wonderful place.

Even when she was fast asleep, Loveday always seemed to know when there was trouble around. Instinctively, she moved away from my shoulder and wound the window down. The police car in front of us was definitely driving too slowly. I slowed down slightly, the police car seemed to do the same, and my heart began to beat a little faster.

'Let me do the talking if they stop us, Tim. Don't open your mouth unless you have to.'

Although pleased to have someone in the car adept at dealing with these situations, a part of me preferred Loveday fast asleep or slightly pissed. Then, to my horror, I spotted several police cars with their blue lights flashing, parked two hundred yards ahead just before Chelsea Bridge. Confirming that the police car in front of us was still there, I looked quickly in the mirror to see if I could casually stop and turn around, only to see another police car right behind us.

'I'll do the talking, Loveday, if you don't mind.'

'Don't be so ridiculous. You're completely drunk.'

'I'm completely drunk? Well, what the hell are you?'

'I'm not driving the bloody car, am I?'

I couldn't muster the necessary logic to continue the argument, notwithstanding the fact that by now policemen bearing torches were waving us to the side of the road.

'Would you please step outside the car, sir?'

As I stepped unsteadily on to the kerb, I felt all my bravado disappearing down the drain along with my driving licence, for the third time.

'Driving licence, please, sir. Is this your car, sir?'

A minute later and just as I had nearly bitten through my bottom lip, a burst of frantic talk came crackling through the policeman's radio. He took a step back and cocked his head to listen. Once I heard the anonymous voice confirm my address and the registration of the car, I realised I was done for. The next step was the breathalyser, court, then prison. I looked across at Loveday and shrugged. She smiled back. Then, with the smile never leaving her face, she opened her car door.

She used her sweetest, silkiest voice on the police officer.

'Is there was anything I can help you with? You see, my friend didn't want me to walk home at this time of night and kindly offered to drive me home – it's only just over that bridge there . . .'

'For the fiftieth time, I am *not* starting a row about it. I was just saying you're very lucky not to have been arrested, that's all.'

I stood in the kitchen watching Loveday spoon a ridiculously large amount of cat food out for Ned. I was still shaking like a jelly, so grateful that I had escaped from the clutches of the police that I was convinced an Act of God had just taken place. Loveday had refused to join me in a celebratory whisky.

'I thought you were tired?' I asked, penitently drying as she washed up some dirty plates.

'I am tired. I am so tired I can't go to fucking sleep.'

Long silence.

I was just going to put on a record when she began again, 'Well, I never thought I'd say it, but thank God for the IRA. If it hadn't been for that bomb you'd have been for it.'

I looked down at the cat for support. 'But I had the whole situation completely under control, didn't I, Ned?'

Silence again, save for the sound of Ned chomping his food. The cat had heard it all before and didn't even raise his head from the bowl.

Eventually, we went upstairs to the bedroom.

I switched off the light and instantly a disembodied voice said, 'Before you get excited, I've got my period.'

'Oh, thanks very much,' I said, knowing that she was lying.

Three minutes of silence ensued, punctuated by Loveday thrashing about like a stranded fish. I kept thinking it would all suddenly become a joke, that she would turn round and scream or laugh. Instead, she kept sighing and tutting. I thought briefly about trudging downstairs to polish off the whisky and play football with the cat, but a final loud sigh changed my mind. As determinedly and dramatically as possible, I swung out of bed, switched on the light, and stood in my boxer shorts, arms folded, looking every inch like Charlton Heston in *El Cid*.

'Right! What's this all about? Come on, let's sort it out right now.'

'Oh, shut up! Put the light out and get back into bed, you look ridiculous.'

Sensing a possible thaw I persisted, but added a touch of affection to my tone.

'Loveday, darling? I don't want to go to sleep on a fight. Let's sort this out.'

Bad idea. Loveday resolutely sat up, folded her arms over her T-shirt, and began. Never had I heard a woman, or anyone for that matter, talk for so long without seeming to take a breath.

'You really want to know what's bothering me? Well, I'll tell you. One. Why didn't you tell me you were seeing that cow Vanessa? Why do I have to read your fucking, squirmy little diary to find out you've been seeing her? Two. Why did you leave me on my own tonight with that groping American while you wandered off for three hours showing off to your friends about how brilliant you are? Three . . .'

And so it continued.

11

The following morning, it took ten stupid minutes to locate where I had parked the Gaulle the night before. Driving to work, the radio appeared to play only two songs 'Ghost Town' and 'Watching the Detectives'; neither of which made me feel any better.

It was a quarter past ten when I managed to sneak past Zannie and get into my own office, shutting the door before actually being sick.

Usually I managed to slop out the waste-paper basket discreetly into the men's toilet in the basement but on this, the last morning of my last day at Barracuda, I still felt drunk and superstitious. So instead of legging it down to the bog, I threw a load of newspapers into the offending bin and sprayed the room with air freshener.

I'd already said most of my goodbyes and a leaving party was planned for that evening in the pub across the road. The meeting with Zannie had easily been the worst. Not that she'd said much, but I could tell from the way she avoided looking me in the eye, by the way she kept turning her head away, that it was bad. I had been putting off telling her because I knew it was going to be difficult, and because I knew I wasn't going to take her with me. I thought I should be starting afresh, with no old attachments to give me an advantage. However, I had said to her, by way of compensation, that she was going to be promoted, that it was time for her to move up and be doing something more important than making me cups of tea. She had said thanks, but she'd been thinking of leaving for a long time anyway.

The rest of them, the two pluggers Jasper and Hugo, Jolian the international man, and Rufus in production, hadn't been shocked at all, seemed almost to have expected it and wished me well. I could tell they really didn't give a shit and were far more interested in knowing how my move would affect them. Only squeaky Pete the runner and Emma the press officer had expressed any genuine good-will. But there you go, I thought. What can you expect in this business?

Ten minutes later, and after some deep breathing exercises in between puffs of a cigarette, I began to feel much better. I got up and walked out of the building. There, right in front of me, was Super Blooms. I pushed open the door, noticing a large green credit card sticker that proclaimed: 'It says more about you than your money ever can.' I walked into the shop, inwardly berating the crassness of advertising, but also secretly pleased I had been given a card. A friendly-looking middle-aged lady smiled at me from behind the counter.

'What would you like, sir? Some nice roses perhaps?'

'I'd like six tiger lilies, six red-and-white carnations, assorted iris and freesias set against a big spray of winter berries, to be delivered to this lady within the hour.'

Putting my credit card on the counter, I added, somewhat cockily, 'Think you can handle that?'

The woman blinked for a moment or two, picked up my credit card, and said, 'Of course we can do that, sir. Are you sure there's nothing else you would like? No? Then just sign here, please.'

By lunchtime I was on my way to the future. I took a cab to Rick's office in Acton. It cost a fortune, but I didn't care – there was going to be plenty more where that came from.

When I stood outside the offices of the Delta Entertainment Group, my new home, on the Lower Hades Road, at first I thought there must be some mistake, or that it was an extremely good joke.

The immediate area was grey, dirty and dismal. I then recalled the only time I had been to Rick's office before was for a party held on the day of the Queen's Jubilee. It had been to celebrate the launch of the Ox's new album *Who Cares?* The band's singer and guitarist had felt upstaged by the people singing and waving Union flags behind tables on the pavements outside overflowing with food and drink. Despite Rick's patient and good-humoured counsel, they both behaved like prima donnas and walked out. Rick simply shrugged his shoulders and made sure that everyone enjoyed the remainder of the party; eventually getting so stoned that he led a conga line down the stairs to join in with the street party outside.

Delta was based on the third floor of an ugly 1960s building above Double Day, a discount shop that sold out-of-date shoes. Apparently, most local customers had deserted the shop after the new owners stopped disinfecting the pavement outside each morning to combat the smells deposited there by vagrants the previous night. They had also ceased their daily collection of lager cans and empty cider bottles, preferring to bag them up on a Saturday in the hope of some money back on the empties. The one thing they had not stinted on was new security grilles for the shop windows and the door.

A concert promoter called Johnny Bird occupied the first and second floors. He had an unfortunate reputation for losing his temper, but managed to maintain credibility by always picking up on a hot band before anyone else. He weighed nineteen stone, was six feet five inches tall, and owned a 1966 blue-finned Cadillac, which he kept parked across the road.

This is the real world, not the artificial world of Soho, I kept telling myself. Seeing that the front door was open, I walked inside and made myself take the stairs three at a time all the way up to the third floor. Coming out of the door was Starling, Rick's American secretary. I had met her before at gigs, and although she seemed to have a mouth on her, I thought she was all right. Starling was over thirty, slim, with a pretty but gaunt face, a lazy eye and, long brown hair. She was wearing lace-up boots and a fur-lined quilted anorak.

She greeted me with a bad-tempered wave of her hand.

'Hi, there, everyone's gone out for lunch except for Rick and me. I'm not waiting any longer for someone to come back. So it's going to be just you and Rick. Hang on.'

She pushed her head back inside the door and shouted, 'Rick! Tim is here. Shall I send him in? Yeah? OK.'

She sighed, slung her bag over her shoulder, and said to go in.

'Thanks, Starling, that's great,' I said, telling myself that my impression of being unwelcome was ridiculous.

'Call me Star, everyone else does,' she yelled from the stairs.

Inside I was immediately surprised by how dark everything was. An odd smell, like damp clothes, seemed to be coming from the carpet. There was one large room and six much smaller offices, three of which were not being used. And it was cold. Fucking cold.

Rick's office was the first on the left. I knocked rather formally on the door and he opened it, already putting on his jacket, as if in a hurry to leave.

'Hi, Tim. So you found us all right? That's good,' he said. 'Listen, I've had a day of it already. Let's go out for a sandwich. OK?'

Despite the smile I could see he was in a foul mood.

'Let's go straight to lunch and look at the office later,' I suggested.

'Great idea, I'll have a pee and then we'll go.'

As I waited for him, I stood there, remembering the crush of people from the Ox's party two years ago. Today, apart from the buzz of an overhead light and the traffic outside, the office seemed eerily quiet. I decided on a high-speed peek behind Rick's door. I think I must have been expecting to see a couple of belly dancers or something because I was very disappointed with what I saw. Rick's office felt like a double riding stable with only one horse in occupation. Its furnishings were plain, with a desk and two chairs and one framed photograph of the Lake District on the wall. On his desk were two telephones, four neat piles of paper, and a large white calculator. A brown-painted hatch in a connecting wall would, I imagined, be the main means of communication between us if I occupied the stable next door. I quickly pulled the door to when I heard the toilet flush.

Rick reappeared holding a bunch of keys in his hand.

'Funky offices,' I said, cheerfully.

'Yeah, very funky,' Rick grunted and carried on walking.

As we descended the stairs in silence, I told myself that I had simply become too used to the polished bonhomie of Barracuda, and that everywhere new seemed strange at first.

'Bad dentist appointment this morning?' I ventured.

'Meeting to do with the band,' Rick said.

'Oh.' I wanted to ask more but didn't.

In the end we drove to Shepherd's Bush in Rick's gold-brown Granada to have a pizza, the local sandwich bars being uninviting to say the least. By the end of lunch I had managed to cheer Rick up considerably and we parted having renewed our resolution to conquer the music business and buy each other Caribbean islands.

Back to Soho's street of dreams for some last-minute desk clearing.

The second I walked into my office, the internal phone rang. It was Stella, Simon Caplow's senior secretary, neurotic and up her own arse as usual. As I held the phone away from my ear I heard her non-stop sentences running into each other like a telex machine, informing me that Rick Fraser and myself were urgently required to meet with Mr Caplow at five-thirty that afternoon.

First a call to Rick.

'Tim it must be all of twenty-seven minutes since I last saw you. Can't stay away, I know . . .'

Then a call from Loveday.

'Thank you for the flowers, sweetheart. You know, maybe we started fighting last night because it was so late. I know you and Vanessa are just friends really . . .'

The world was starting to feel right again.

* * *

I had always felt that waiting outside Simon Caplow's suite of offices was akin to waiting outside the Headmaster's. It didn't matter how long I'd been around or how well or badly I had been doing, I was always a little nervous. I was reassured when Rick arrived, out of breath, to see that he was nervous too.

'Come in, gentlemen, come in and make yourselves comfortable.'

Simon Caplow had a knack of making sure you never knew exactly what mood he was in until the conversation had begun. His style was always dry and economical and he was the only person I had ever met who could use the lighting of his pipe to control a conversation. I felt comfortable, though, and reminded myself that the air of formality hanging over the room was most likely a necessity given the large amount of money he was going to invest in us. I stared out of the window, happy that my new partner in crime could successfully handle any difficult financial questions. Rick was good with people and had pre-empted the conversation with an enquiry as to Caplow's latest theatrical project in the West End. I continued staring at some pigeons on the window ledge and heard the familiar sound of a match being struck and the faint crackle of tobacco being lit. I turned back to join in the conversation. I had been through this sort of procedure a hundred times before.

Caplow cleared his throat loudly and said, 'Well, I'll come straight to the point and would ask you to respect that what I am about to tell you is absolutely confidential.'

Both Rick and I solemnly nodded our heads, only just concealing our excitement.

'Well, I'll get straight to the point. My partner and I have decided to call it a day and separate. And therefore . . .'

In the seconds that he took to relight his pipe, I guessed he was going to say something about joining forces with us in a more substantial way.

'And, therefore, it is regrettably not going to be possible for us to make the investment that we said we would make. Without wishing to rub salt further into the wound, I am unfortunately quite certain that it will not be possible for me to invest as an individual for quite some period of time, much as I would like to.'

I sat there, probably with my mouth open, feeling as if a brick had just been dropped on my head.

'Presumably,' said Rick as if he was commenting on a game of cricket, 'presumably there is a mass of red tape regarding each other's exclusivity in respect of service contracts before either of you can do anything?' I was amazed at how calmly he was reacting.

Caplow nodded and puffed on his pipe, ensuring he did not make eye contact with me. I certainly wasn't swallowing all that bullshit. The fuckers had simply broken their promise. Nevertheless, without further ado, we were all shaking hands, *no hard feelings*, and Rick and I were being walked to the door. Thirty seconds later we were downstairs, standing opposite the revolving door at the entrance hall of the building. The whole meeting had lasted no more than three minutes. I was furious with myself for not having spoken up at the meeting, not fighting for the money, *our* money.

'Well, I'm sorry, Tim, but I think that puts the kibosh on our plans.' Rick shrugged.

'What?' I asked, as if someone had just punched me in the throat.

Rick shrugged again and pushed the revolving door. 'Look, it's very simple. We don't have the money any more. We can't go ahead.'

WHAT? Can't go ahead? I can't believe I'm hearing this. I can't believe I'm hearing myself like some fucking hopeless wet rag beginning to agree.

'Look, Rick,' I said, pressing down hard against my instincts, 'we agreed to this. The fact that they've chosen to bail out doesn't mean we shouldn't do it. We've just got to get the money from somewhere else, and I am sure we will. We've still got OTE for Christ's sake!'

Rick gave the revolving door another push and shook his head wistfully. 'Well, I don't trust them and I'm not sure that anyone else will definitely come through either.'

'But I'm sure, Rick. We agreed to be partners!'

Rick halted the revolving door, stepped halfway in, thought for a while, and slowly began to nod his head. I played my last card.

'Rick,' I said. 'You did agree, didn't you?'

He stepped back out of the door, took a deep breath, and wiped his hand against his mouth. 'OK. I did agree. You're right. We'd better talk about this in the morning and work out a plan of action. I'll see you later, then.'

With that he revolved out of the building and was gone. I walked back to my office stunned, but pleased that not quite everything had slipped through the net. What I needed was a drink. But just as I sat down, the internal telephone rang. It was Stella again, saying would I go up immediately.

It felt strange walking up those stairs. When I got to the top, there he was waiting for me. Simon Caplow. I could hardly look at him I was so angry. He put his hand on my shoulder and said apologetically, 'Listen, Tim, I'm sorry about all that. I can tell you, *confidentially* though, that things are going to get a lot worse round here. I think the whole business is about to go into recession. Quite seriously, I'd like you to stay. I think you should definitely stay. Don't be too proud, Tim, please? There'll always be another time to do this. It's not too late. Stay. What do you think?'

I thought nothing and looked him in the eye as directly as I could. Then, as I turned to walk away, I smiled and shrugged.

'I think not. But thanks for offering.'

12

My father decreed that Christmas didn't count this year. We spent the day and Boxing Day at a hotel in Hedgerly Cross. Loveday telephoned on Christmas morning to say how much she liked all of my badly wrapped presents. I thanked her for her perfectly wrapped six, telling her that my favourites were the Rubik's Cube and silver cigarette box.

By the time everyone was sitting by the inglenook fireplace, half asleep in the post-Christmas lunch cliché, my brother and I had itchy feet. I needed to beat him at something and he needed to beat me. Squash and Scrabble were our usual games of choice, but in their absence we settled on table tennis.

The hotel sports room was white-walled, over-heated, and smelt of salt-and-vinegar crisps. It didn't matter. After we had been playing for a few boisterous minutes, Charles paused and scowled at the cloud of cigarette smoke travelling towards him.

'Do you have to?'

'Do I have to *what*?'

'You know perfectly well. Why don't you give up?'

'Why should I? I happen to like it.'

'Well, it's bloody anti-social.'

'Just because you've never smoked.'

Charles had always been the opposite of me: well-groomed, slightly overweight, financially articulate, never a penny out of place. Having said that, he was not boring, not boring at all. He was simply a country squire imprisoned in a pinstripe suit, a man who drew his breath from a bygone era when hunting, shooting and fishing were daily rituals – where men were men, chaps were chaps, black was black, and white was white. Charles liked a sense of order to things, a sequence, a protocol for behaviour. Quite why he sounded so much like a newsreader was a mystery I could never fathom.

'Nineteen-eleven and it's your serve,' I said smugly, chucking the ball over the net.

Charles picked up the ball and drew his bat towards him in readiness for another killer backhand serve. But he served the ball too hard and lost the point, then did exactly the same again.

'Two games to love. Another one?' I said cheerfully.

'I'll thrash you in a minute, you've just been lucky so far, that's all,' Charles yelled as he walked around the empty room making driving movements with his ping-pong bat.

'So how's everything going? How's the dog? How's work?'

Charles sniffed haughtily and then laughed. I knew that he carried a photograph of his golden retriever around in his wallet alongside one of Maya.

'Work is pretty good, thanks. Yes, I have to say it's p-r-e-t-t-y good.'

For Charles to use or imply any term better than 'not bad' meant something important was occurring in his life. He told me that the company he had helped to found was set to go public by the end of the year.

'Obviously, we won't be having a full stock market listing yet,' he announced, 'but we'll be on the secondary one.'

'Great,' I said, noticing Charles's bitten-down fingernails.

'So, what's the position on your new venture?' he asked.

'I've told you, it's going to be fantastic. Not bad at twenty-six, eh?'

Charles forced a smile. 'No, not bad, you're right, not bad at all. Got a balance sheet I could look at?'

'A balance sheet? What on earth do *you* want one of those for?'

'OK. Put it another way – what capital does the company have?'

'Capital? Do you mean money?'

'Christ almighty, Tim! What do you think I mean, chocolate biscuits?' Charles sighed loudly and began rolling the ping-pong ball round the table with his bat.

'For Christ's sake, Charles, stop being so bloody pompous. You know very well we've been trying to raise the money. Anyway, I think we've got it.'

'Tim, we all know you'll never win any major prizes in mathematics, but I did think you had some idea of basic economics.'

Charles turned to face me. I was becoming increasingly irritated by his lecturing tone but I was also confused as to whether he really had a point or whether his nose was out of joint, due to my success. Whatever, I was not going to take it lying down.

'Look, Charles, in your city-slicker world maybe everyone knows about capital and balance sheets. Well, in my mind, in my world, it's a matter of horses for courses. I'm good at making records and my pal Rick is good at looking after money.'

'Well if your *pal* Rick is so good, where's the money?'

'God, Charles, you'll be asking what school Rick went to next, won't you?'

Charles took a step towards me, shaking his head.

'Tim, maybe Rick is a great chum of yours but how do you know he has any money?'

'I never said he *did* have any money. Anyway we're about to be given . . .'

Charles slammed his bat against the end of the table. 'Great! So how do you know his company isn't in massive debt? You don't, do you? Tim, you can't run a business without having capital. You can't build up a company that's in debt and has no capital. Does your friend Rick understand that?'

I walked smartly round to Charles's side of the table, took the bat and ball from his hands and carried on towards the door. I was not prepared to hear any more derogatory remarks.

'You're out of order, Charles, and you know it. I'll get the money, just you wait.'

'I'm only trying to help, *you* know that.'

I shut the door behind me.

January to June 1980

13

The Christmas holiday break had been a long one. On New Year's Day the temperature had dropped to −5° Centigrade. In London, the Serpentine Swimming Club's traditional icy plunge had lasted one minute instead of its usual ten. People returned to their offices on 2nd January, a Tuesday, to discover burst pipes and frozen cisterns; within forty-eight hours plumbers all over England were reporting record business. Fans of John Lennon were happily intrigued to read that he was working on a new album, entitled *Starting Over.*

Spunk, once thought of as a label only for infantile students, was now setting records of its own. When the first top fifty of the New Year was published, it had an unprecedented five records in it, proving that anarchic imagination and flair were more vital ingredients to success than the financial muscle of the major companies. The news of Spunk's amazing success only helped to fuel our plans at Delta. I had already made what I thought was a brilliant presentation of our plans to OTE's four-man, one-woman evaluating team and they had even applauded at the end of it. Additionally, as a parting gesture, Shamus Slime had given me the thumbs-up and whispered that it was only a matter of a 'bit of red tape and then you'll be safely on board'.

So, when Rick and I went to the OTE building we were ready for more applause, ready for the red-carpet treatment, ready to collect gold.

Shamus leaned back in his chair.

'Sorry to piss on your strawberries like this, but I hope you understand it's nothing personal? It's the recession, Tim. We've all got to tighten our belts.'

I stared at him, unable to formulate a response.

Rick sniffed, closed the lid of his briefcase and said calmly: 'Just so as I completely understand the position, Shamus, do you mean that you can't do the deal you *were* proposing, but you could do something else?'

Shamus took a big suck of air and then accidentally coughed all over his silver cigarette box.

'Shit!' he said, wiping the top of the box with his jacket. 'Look, let me speak plainly. We're not in the market for handing out any more licensing deals with money attached. I'm sorry Pierre isn't here to explain in person.'

'We understand, don't we, Tim?' Rick said.

Shamus slobbered on: 'I tell you what, maybe we could give you a distribution deal and maybe when things get better, well, who knows? No money now, and maybe not for a year, but then we'll see. What do you say, Tim?'

I wanted to stick a set of golf clubs up his arse but instead I smiled.

'You sound like one of your little girlfriends, Shamus, saying it's over, no more hanky-panky, but couldn't we just be friends?'

Shamus convulsed with laughter, sounding like an overweight walrus having an asthma attack. 'Oh, very good! Very good! But, sssshh, don't say things like that.'

I looked at Rick, stood up, and managed to shake hands. I said that we would let Shamus know if we had any interest in pursuing his offer.

I walked out of the OTE building feeling that I had been betrayed. Moreover, Rick's whistling cheerfulness only made matters worse. Maybe he thought I had made the whole thing up in the first place . . . After all, this was the second time it had happened.

He did have a certain swagger as he walked back to the car.

'Don't take it so personally, man. Fuck 'em. Things will work out. They always do,' he said.

For the first three days at Delta I had worn a pin-striped suit. It had been Loveday who insisted I wear it, saying that's what people did in an important new position. On my fourth day at Delta I burnt the suit by standing too close to the calor-gas heater. By my second week, I was wearing jeans and a big sweater, just like everyone else.

And still Delta was cold.

Compared to Barracuda, everything was different. Even the sound was different. The only record player that was working was stashed in a corner and not used. There was no traffic noise, no hustle, and no bustle. No noise at all.

Cold, fucking cold.

I wasn't going to let it get to me, though. No, I was a positive person, and thinking big, thinking positive was the way to get ahead. I knew that I had reacted badly to the meeting with OTE. I could sense it in Rick's voice. Of course, he had probably seen it all along, had seen exactly what was going to happen. But I hadn't. Now it was time to get back up to speed.

'Hey, Rick,' I said. 'What about an office meeting? You know, to set down objectives and make some plans.'

Rick swivelled round in his chair. 'How about a meeting between ourselves first?'

'Absolutely,' I said, making myself comfortable.

'The way I see it is this,' Rick began, and continued at speed. 'We now know we're not going to get the money from OTE. In my view, although there are other people out there who *could* be interested, they probably won't be until we have an act they think could be big. In any case, I've made calls to the two other people who rate us, Rob Richards at Polygone, and Bill West at EXM, and they'll be calling back. I think it'll be possible to get outside investment, eventually.' Rick paused for breath. 'But, we have to get ourselves more organised first. They won't invest purely on the strength of our names. That's one thing we've learned. Agreed?'

Rick picked up his mug of coffee, leaned back in his chair, and took a sip. I clicked on the Ronson and lit a cigarette. I was delighted to be reminded that there were two other players in the game who were still interested.

'Yeah, I agree, Rick, that's great,' I said waving the cigarette smoke back into my own office. 'I'm just a little worried about what happens if neither of these options materialises. Know what I mean?'

'I know what you mean, but worrying about it won't solve anything, will it?'

'No, absolutely right! Of course.'

'Basically, what *you* need to do is come up with some acts and get the label into shape so that we can do some international licensing deals. It's as simple as that, really.'

As simple as that?

'Right. OK. Well, we'd better have the office meeting, then, and see exactly where we are.'

'Whatever you say. You're in charge. Just tell everyone when you want to start.'

Back at my desk I began writing out an agenda and thought back to the office meetings I used to hold at Barracuda. Zannie, Hugo, Jasper, Rufus, Jolian, Emma and I, would sit round the big table, all wearing promotional T-shirts, chewing on cheese rolls and drinking mugs of tea. The phone would ring on the dot of nine-thirty. It would be OTE. Zannie would answer it and then announce the new top fifty chart positions, after which the meeting would begin. As usual, squeaky Pete would move next door to man the telephones until the meeting had ended. In order to keep people motivated each week, I ensured that a different person would chair the meeting. Each record and band were discussed and noted in separate categories with an action column containing the initials of the person responsible for carrying out each task. Within half an hour of the meeting, the minutes would be typed and copied to Simon Caplow and all attending, with individual actions highlighted in coloured pen.

The office meeting at Delta was due to commence at midday.

'It won't take longer than an hour, will it?' Rick called out to me as he was waiting for a telephone call to connect.

'Well, it'll take as long as . . .'

But he was already speaking before I could finish.

The meeting started at twelve-fifteen. I wanted it to start it at twelve, but Star had decided to go out for a sandwich in case she missed her lunch. Then another important call about the Ox came through for Rick. Meanwhile Susie, who appeared to have a mental age of twelve, had begun teasing Chalky about his moustache. In turn, Chalky began teasing Susie about the hippie-whining way in which she spoke. Susie was half-Moroccan, half-Rodean, petite with shiny black hair, dark eyes, silly and definitely sexy. Star came back, sat down, and angrily began to munch her sandwich. A call then came through for me, and to my embarrassment it was from Loveday. I stoically refused to take it and carried on.

'While we're waiting for Rick, would somebody volunteer to take the minutes, please?'

Silence.

'What I mean is, could someone please make a written note of what we discuss?' I looked across at Star with as straight a face as I could muster. I knew that, underneath all that nonsense, Star would try to be professional, or at the very least polite.

'Yes, of course, Tim,' she said, looking at Susie and pointing at her sandwich. 'Susie, you do it, my hands are filthy.'

'Oh, fuck off,' Susie whined. 'You do it. I'm not going to.'

Just as I was getting to the end of my tether, Rick walked into the room.

'Who is not going to do what? *Susie?*'

'Oh, all right then.'

Star, Susie and Chalky reminded me of uncared-for pets who needed an equal amount of attention and a firm hand. Once our discussion had built up some momentum, however, I was surprised at the level of the contributions being made. Tasks were handed out and greeted with a mixture of incredulity and shock. I had made sure that I had given myself the largest pile of actions, and left the room feeling that at last I had something positive to get my teeth into.

I waited for the best part of the afternoon for the minutes to be typed. Rick had decided to leave early but had suggested going to lunch the following day and said he would call me that night. It was then discovered that the photocopier didn't work and that someone would have to go down to Johnny Bird's office. Immediately an argument erupted about who had gone down the last time. I soon realised no one would go.

'You must be bloody joking!' Susie yelled at Chalky, climbing on to her chair as if she was a cartoon mouse running from a cat.

Chalky was a cheerfully camp Glaswegian, older than the other three, who wore flared trousers, chunky shoes and a multi-coloured tank-top.

'Look, I've got an urgent report to do for Rick's meeting with the bank.'

'Don't threaten me with Rick; I'm not going down there and having my head bitten off. Star, it's your turn,' Susie said, giggling.

'Yeah, go on, Star, he fancies you. He thinks you've got great tits,' Chalky said, sticking both his hands out from his chest.

'Enough already!' Star shouted. 'Come on, stop being so ridiculous. This is Tim's first week in the company. We don't want to give him a bad impression. Do we?'

Everyone seemed to hesitate before laughing reassuringly.

'I haven't formed a bad impression. We just seem to need a new photocopier,' I said, trying to be the chirpy cheerleader.

'Right now we don't have enough money to buy a new kettle, let alone a photocopier,' Chalky said.

I suddenly realised how stupid all of this was. It was time to get serious.

'Where are the office minutes?' I said loudly, in my snootiest tone.

'Why?' said Star, handing them to me.

'Because I'm going to go downstairs myself and get this bloody well sorted out.'

'No, don't do that,' Star said, taking the minutes off me. 'You shouldn't be doing that. Susie, go to Patel's newsagents and ask them if they can do it. Say we'll pay them back next week. You can go home early if you do it.'

'Oh, all right, then.'

When Susie returned an hour later to announce that the photocopier in the newsagent's had broken too, everyone laughed, and in the end so did I. Why it had taken her an hour to establish this fact I didn't know, but I was beginning to understand that everything at Delta seemed to work this way.

Late in the day, the telephone on my desk buzzed three times. I knew before I picked it up that it was Star, because I could hear her shouting from the other room. She had a habit of abbreviating everything to the minimum.

'It's some guy from Ireland. Says you know him from Barracuda. Band called B Square. Line three. Kay?'

She put the call through. A soft Irish voice spoke without waiting for any reply.

'Hi, Tim? Yeah, it's Donal Stout, you remember, from B Square! God, I've been looking for you everywhere. No one was at your old office, you see. Difficult to get your new number and all that. Sorry, what? What did you say? When was the last time we met?'

He then explained how he had come to see me twice before at Barracuda, and how grateful he had always been for my advice, giving him the time of day when no one else would, etcetera. At first, I was suspicious that this was yet another wanker giving me some 'grateful' line, but then I remembered the band. He carried on talking, telling me about how much the band had improved, and how this person and that person were now taking it seriously. They were doing a gig the following night in Notting Hill Gate . . .

I was only half-listening, preferring instead to use my gut to tell me whether what he was saying held any weight. It did. He spoke with a mixture of confidence, charm and respect that made me want to take him seriously. I wanted to whistle my excitement. I started to plan the party.

'You were right the last time, and the time before. I didn't want to admit it, but what you said was true. You were the only person to take the trouble to say exactly what you felt. That's why I'm calling you. We're ready to roll now. Ready to do a deal. We've paid our dues, got the songs sorted out, got rid of the rough edges, and we're chomping at the bit, ready for the craic. Are you ready, though?'

I smiled and nodded to myself, certain that I was not going to answer that particular question, just yet. Then he dropped a little bombshell.

'But to tell you the truth, Tim,' he continued, 'there is one other company very seriously interested. Well, should I say one man, Charlie Crosse at Palm Tree, to be precise. Now, Tim, as a band we always held you in great respect and so we wanted to see you first. We know exactly what we want, so we won't waste your time . . .'

Charlie Crosse's judgement was worth a lot in anyone's currency. He was one of the few people, aside from Rick and Simon Caplow, for whom I had any respect at all.

'What are you looking for, just out of interest, Donal?'

'I'll tell you exactly. You can have the band under contract and a whole album, including recording costs, for twenty-five thousand. No more, no less.'

'An album? I think that's a bit premature, don't you?' I said forcing a laugh.

'No, that's what we want. As I said on the phone, Charlie's interested and he said if we decide to go ahead they'll want to do an album. The money's not a problem for them, you see.'

'Nor is it for us, Donal! It's just a question of doing things step by step. I'll come to the gig tomorrow and in the meantime have a chat with my partner. Don't do anything impulsive, will you, now?'

I reached for my diary and made an appointment to see them. I then quickly started jotting down a new list in the Book of Lists of all the things I needed to find out about B-square before the gig. At last I was beginning to get a bit of the old blood back flowing through my veins.

14

The Hillgate Theatre was better known for putting on the latest in theatre workshops than rock bands, but judging by the amount of people inside, it didn't matter. I walked in with a minute to spare before B-Square came on stage. I handed over the one pound fifty entrance fee and didn't check to see if my name was on the guest list; I wanted to pay for my ticket – I knew it would count later on.

The seating was fifteen rows of metal chairs, the uncomfortable type you often see in films being held aloft and used in fights. The floor was made from hardwood and smelt of academia. Tall church candles burned in each corner of the room, and at the front of the stage was a line of bronzed oyster shells casting shadows across the curtains. I did a rough headcount and calculated the crowd to be between fifty and sixty. Most of them were male, loud, knocking back the ale and talking animatedly in small groups. Something about their cheerfulness told me they weren't from London. I made a quick 360-degree check of the room. The good news was there wasn't a leather-jacketed A&R man in sight. The bad news was that I spotted Johnny Bird, the concert promoter from downstairs, leaning against a pillar, and stroking the stubble on his chin with the top of a bottle of Coca-Cola.

Suddenly, the curtains flew back and the band came on. No fucking about, it was straight into a song, a solitary spotlight on the singer. The band was tight, played well together, knew where they were going and, although it was obvious where they could improve, they made a real impression. There was an economy to their songs not present before. After the fifth number, the crowd shifted up a gear and began shouting and jumping up and down as if this were a punk rock show. The band responded by speeding up, and the guys in front of the stage pulled off their T-shirts and shook their heads and shoulders at one another as if they were having epileptic fits. The music wasn't the best I'd ever heard, but I knew instinctively that the band could do well, in a superior meat-and-two-veg sort of a way. Americans were going to like this band. They would like the singer and the guitarist, of that there was no doubt. This could be the way through the jungle to the clearing, where the little aircraft was waiting to take off and get us out of the shit. I knew I had to sign them.

It didn't take me long to figure out that most of the crowd came from Dublin. As the two guitarists retuned their guitars, I casually asked a podgy guy wearing a T-shirt saying 'never mind the bollocks' where he was from.

'Oh, we came over on the ferry last night. Stopped in Holyhead and then straight down on the good old coach to London. D'ya like the band, then? Are ye from a record company? Ye are, aren't you? Me mates and I clocked you coming in. Well, if you want my advice you'll be snapping up this lot bloody quick. They're going to be bigger than Jaysus Christ! My sister used to go with the bass player, stupid girl dumped him for a dentist – can you believe that!'

The band continued for only another twenty minutes and cleverly did not play an encore. Backstage, the atmosphere inside the dressing room was friendly and cheerful, though the room resembled the inside of a weighing room after a serious horserace. The four band members sat balanced on various bits of a sofa, steam rising from their sodden heads, wiping themselves down with the T-shirts they had worn on stage. Donal Stout stood fanning them with his jacket. I shook hands with him, shook hands with the band, and sat down on a barstool.

'Tim, grand to meet you,' said Skull, the singer. 'Donal told us about you a long time ago. Thanks for all your support.'

'Well, it's a long and winding road, isn't it?' I said shrugging my shoulders and pulling a big grin. 'Are you making much money from being on the road?'

'You must be joking!' shouted the pasty but muscular drummer.

'We make a little money in Ireland but that's only been in the last six months. We don't make a bloody penny when we come here.'

'Well, I bought my own ticket tonight,' I said shaking my pocket full of change.

'You didn't have to do that, Tim.'

'No, man, you were on the list.'

'Well, in my view, record companies like us who've got the money shouldn't be tight about spending it on tickets.'

'Good man, Tim. Excellent!'

'We like that, don't we, lads?'

'Oh, I'm just another smarmy wanker really,' I joked, and then asked: 'Do you want to have a meal, or would you like to go back to your hotel to talk?'

From behind my head a slightly nervous Donal piped up.

'Yes, eh, why not come back to the hotel? Do you know the Brazil?'

'Yeah, of course, that's a good idea. I'll meet you there in thirty minutes?'

The band put their thumbs in the air and shouted, 'See you later'. However, something in the way that Stout patted me on the back as I saluted him goodbye made me suspicious.

The novelty of sitting in the residents' bar at the Brazil Hotel and watching bands in various stages of inebriation was still a turn-on for me. It was where every band on the way up or on the road to nowhere always stayed. I was sure the 1939 brown flock wallpaper was going to end up in a museum one day. Five rounds of drinks and five annoyingly expensive sandwiches later, I was in the closing stages of trying to secure the deal by talking endlessly about the benefits of Delta.

'You see, I've worked in big record companies. I know what goes on. I know how bands get lost; get passed from one department to the next, ending up in some basket of internal post, forgotten about in the corridors of power.'

'Oh, no, stop, this is terrible!' Vince the bass player shouted.

'I'm not joking. You see, what you've got to remember is that these big companies have got so much money, the likes of you can easily become a numerical experiment that either does or doesn't work. In the end, it doesn't matter at all because as long as one of the ten or fifteen bands they sign each year shows some promise, they'll be OK. Don't think for a minute that you won't be one of those fifteen, and then one of those thirty, and then one of those forty-five. You'll become another blip on a radar screen, waiting behind twenty other bands to get into the studio. Oh, yeah, and all these companies will want at least a five-year contract. Now don't get me wrong – I have a lot of respect for these companies, I really have – but not when it comes to helping to break a band. You need a small team like Delta. Five people who will put you at the top of their list each morning, five people who will eat, drink, and breathe B Square. People who will stand up and be counted as serious supporters of your cause. To sum up, guys, it's really very simple: small is beautiful. Over to you.'

Trying hard to suppress an image of Star, Chalky and Susie arguing in the office, I waited for their reaction. Judging by the nodding heads and the way the band were shaking my hand, I knew I had hit home. It was only a matter of time now.

Eventually the band's conspiratorial conversation subsided and Donal Stout tapped the side of his glass with his pen.

'No need to make a speech, Donal,' I joked.

Looking down at the debris on the table, he smiled, let out a laugh and said, 'We're really keen, really interested, Tim. Aren't we lads?'

'You bet we are! Too fucking right!' came the chorus of Irish voices.

'That's what I like to hear! So, what's the next step?' I said cheering up.

Donal Stout hesitated so much with his next sentence, I knew it was going to contain the word 'but'.

'The thing is, Tim, we're a bit torn. I'll be frank and tell you exactly what the position is. We really want to be with you but Palm Tree offered us seventy-five thousand pounds this afternoon . . .'

'Seventy-five thousand! Christ.'

I could tell from Donal's face that he wasn't bluffing.

'It's a lot of money, Tim, you know that yourself,' Skull the singer said philosophically, as he rolled a cigarette between his nicotine-stained fingers.

'Money isn't everything, is it?' I said, wanting to go home.

'No, of course it isn't. We wouldn't be here having this conversation if we didn't think so, would we?'

'Why don't we all meet up tomorrow and I'll make you an offer that will put hairs on your chest?'

'Better make it a good one, Tim.'

We met again at the Brazil.

I pleaded with them not to rush.

I promised that after two singles we would give them sixty thousand pounds.

I promised them commitment, dedication and devotion.

But they were already walking down the aisle with Charlie Crosse from Palm Tree, and there wasn't a thing I could do to stop them.

15

Apparently the fire had started in the early hours of the morning. There were no witnesses, and by the time the firemen had arrived it was too late. According to Rick, you didn't need to be Bamber Gascoigne to figure out that it had been deliberate. I thought that Double Day Shoes never seemed to be doing any business, but tried to look as casual about it as I could. It was another nail in the coffin of the Lower Hades Road as far as I was concerned. It was just a disgusting road, long and ugly, teeming with discount carpet shops and broken washing machines – a road where God had turned the brightness down, adjusted the contrast to make it bearable. Empty cans of Special Brew were spewed along the pavement, alongside empty cartons of fried chicken stained with ketchup. Everywhere I looked there was rubbish. Heaped in doorways; clustering against cars. Not pretty, black bin-bagged rubbish, just rubbish nobody cared about. If you don't care about the rubbish, then what will you care about?

It was not a cheerful morning. In the three weeks since the B Square débâcle, I'd felt my spirits plummet lower each day and I almost wished the fire had reached the third floor instead of just charring the hallway.

Rick had asked the carpenters repairing the stairs to be vigilant about keeping the front door shut, not only to stem the curiosity of the odd vagrant, but also to keep out any of the hundreds of stray dogs living in the area. But one of the carpenters had left the door open long enough for a mutt to come in and piss all over the first three steps. The carpenter had eventually cleaned it up, but not before the urine had soaked in sufficiently for the smell to register long term.

Irate phone calls demanding that bills be paid were increasing every day. Buoyed by several overseas companies interested in licensing the new label, Rick was able to whistle and hope that the fortunes of Spunk would soon be ours.

'You know as well as I do, we only need one hit act and then everyone will want to be our friend. They'll be covering us like flies, just look at the guys at Spunk. You'll find a far better band than that Irish lot, I'm telling you.'

'Yeah, but how are we going to do that without any money?'

'You find the band first and then we'll use the money from these deals.'

'But I thought you said we needed to use that money to pay the bills.'

'Tim, lighten up, would you? For fuck's sake, everyone in this business has creditors and everyone robs Peter to pay Paul. Just relax and find another band and let me worry about the money. OK?'

'Sure.'

I was confused by Rick's optimism. Until now, he had always been the voice of doom regarding money. I began to wonder if his cheery mood had more to do with the stellar climb of the Ox than with any confidence in my abilities.

I walked into his office, pointing to a picture of the Ox in a copy of the trade magazine *The Business*.

'Jesus! I didn't know they were that popular. Look at how many dates they're doing. What a bloody shame we couldn't have offered the support spot to B Square – that might have done the trick,' I said, pointedly.

Rick didn't look up from the calculations he was making on a piece of paper.

'I'm pretty sure the band wouldn't have wanted a group like B Square on the bill.'

I curled the magazine into a tight roll and flicked it hard against the side of my leg.

'Well, we're all paddling in the same canoe, aren't we? Couldn't you have persuaded them?'

Rick took off his glasses. Clutching the pencil between his teeth, he forced a grin and pointed at the corduroy chair next to his desk. I sat down.

'Look, you'd better understand a few things about me and the Ox; otherwise we're going to fall out.'

'I see.'

Rick then gave me a short lecture about how long it had taken him to make the Ox successful and how hard it had been to win their trust to handle all of their money. He carried on speaking, occasionally hitting the desk with his pencil.

'Not to put too fine a point on the whole matter, the only person making any decisions about the Ox will be me. So, just for the record, and so that we're both clear about it, the reason the band is important is that they are the only thing round here that makes any money. Right now we don't have a lot of money. It's really very simple: you, Tim, concentrate on getting in the acts for the record company, and I'll help, but in the main I'm going to concentrate on running the band so that we at least all get something to eat. OK?'

I nodded my head, stood up and returned to my office.

And so the weeks dragged on. Sitting in my office was like being in a cheap motel room with a clock ticking loudly; nothing seems to have any value and you don't want even to open your suitcase, let alone unpack it. I was slowly slipping into quicksand. It was very fine, black quicksand that only I could see.

Nothing is working. Nothing will work, the worm in my head said again and again.

Yet more bands were ringing up, wanting to make appointments, to play me their tapes. Their endless chirpy patter of how big they were going to be was becoming so excruciating I asked Susie to take messages instead.

It was also becoming difficult to have a phone call of any length with Loveday.

'Tim? It's me.'

'I know who it is. What do you want?'

'There's no need to be like that. What's wrong? Is there someone else in your office? Shall I call back another time?'

'Yes, no, wait, don't do that.'

'I just phoned to see if you were all right.'

'Why shouldn't I be! I'm absolutely fine. Now go away and leave me alone.'

'Tim I'm only trying to help. Don't be so horrible.'

'I've got to go, Loveday. I've got meetings all day. I'll see you later.'

'OK, sweetheart, I understand. Bye.'

I sighed, and dropped the telephone on to its cradle. I was aware of a filthy lightbulb blinking in my head: Loveday was the quicksand. Loveday was the problem.

Rick had noticed it first. As I put down the phone after another long call he said, 'Christ Almighty, Tim! Was that Loveday bending your ear again? She must drive you crazy, calling all the time like that.'

'You're not kidding!' I said, with an unconvincing laugh.

Rick was like a rat up a drainpipe, straight to the point: 'Are you not in love with her any more? Is that it?'

'What?'

'I'm not saying that's it, I'm just asking, is it?'

I hesitated, uneasily aware that whatever I said might be set in stone and used against me.

'Yes, you're right, that is it. I feel really bad, though. It's stupid, I know it's stupid but I do.'

'It's not stupid; it's just how it is. I sympathise.'

I sat back and rolled the words 'I sympathise' between the fingers of my mind.

'Do you understand? I feel really bad, but I think I have to do something, the right thing.'

Rick took his time in answering. I exhaled a long belt of cigarette smoke and swallowed, wishing I could erase this last sentence and substitute it with something tough from Raymond Chandler.

'Tim, I do sympathise and, yes, I do understand,' he replied, sounding even more sombre and sincere. 'Although it's different for me because I've been with Victoria for so long now. But, yes, I know how difficult this must be. It's tough. I know people who have stayed together despite – well, you know, not being in love. Safer to be with someone, than not. Few people seem to travel solo these days. It takes guts. But you'll feel better when you've made the decision, I promise. And trust me, Tim, there are a lot of other dolls out there . . .'

There was a pause and then we both laughed in unison. I shifted forward in my seat, wanting to steer the conversation into deeper waters, but was thwarted by a loud American voice.

'Rick?'

We both looked up. Star was standing in the doorway with one hand on her hip, the other holding a piece of paper in the air.

'Yeah, what is it?'

Star flicked back her head in a semi-petulant way and grinned sarcastically.

'There's a man out here from the bailiff's saying if we you don't give him some cash right now, he's going round to the rehearsal rooms to repossess all of the Ox's amplifiers. OK?'

Rick turned away to look through the window. 'Make him a cup of tea and tell him I'll be out in a minute.'

Star shrugged, threw the letter on Rick's desk and marched out of the office.

I didn't need to look at Rick's face to know that our discussion had come to an end.

16

Loveday phoned again that afternoon. When I snatched up the phone to tell her off for calling, she started singing my favourite Al Green song. She sang it breathlessly with a country twang but to her own words: 'I'm so t-i-r-e-d of being a moan, I'm so tired of being a moan . . .'

I didn't say anything.

'Tim, I'm sorry for what I said earlier, I was being a selfish old cow. I know that it's new and difficult for you there. Come and have a cosy supper tonight, just the two of us.'

'OK. What time should I come?' I heard myself replying as if we had just met.

'Whenever you want. Seven-thirty?'

'Seven-thirty it is.'

'Do you want Harry and Jessica to come as well?'

I dragged hard on my Marlboro.

'No. Just the two of us,' I said, feeling a bad twinge of Judas in my stomach.

'Great. Must go. I've got to catch the shops. See you real soon.'

Loveday was so cheerful as she said goodbye that I thought the telephone was going to hover off the cradle when I tried to put it down. I swung round in my chair to look through the window and saw that the streetlights were already on. What the hell was I doing even thinking about ending it? Loveday was being so cheerful I wondered for a second if I had forgotten my own birthday. I turned round to the desk and began mouthing an argument with myself. This was all wrong. Maybe we should be living together, like Rick and Victoria, like Jessica and Harry. Is this what lay at the heart of the problem?

I arrived early at Loveday's flat in Dayton Street. It was raining. A miserable song I had heard on John Peel entitled 'Love Will Tear Us Apart' kept repeating in my head. In an effort to kill time and the song, I sought sanctuary in the Footman, a small pub with large, bow windows. I pushed my way to the bar past a load of rain-coated people, bought a large whisky, and sat down feeling unpleasantly selfconscious. A discarded newspaper headline about Idi Amin, living in luxury in Saudi Arabia, made me feel even worse. Periodically I raised my head from my glass to look at the twenty or thirty people all chattering around the bar. They seemed shockingly happy. I wondered if there was a telephone number you could dial to report such people. If you see any suspiciously happy people, please don't attempt to move or touch them. Just call the Happiness Disposal Team on Bayswater 8552.

I studied the faces of the women to see if Rick was right about there being plenty of willing replacements out there. In the middle of my appraisal I felt a tap on my shoulder and a breathless female voice gasping, 'Hello there, Tim!'

I took in the warmth of the moment and thought that normally these things only happen in the back pages of men's magazines. I swung round and smiled up at the rasping sexy voice, and saw that it belonged to Loveday's flatmate Monica, dressed in her nursing cape and grinning like a maniac. She had a habit, did Monica, of smiling at you with her mouth wide open for a considerable length of time. I had concluded some months earlier that this was either on account of her spending too much time trying to persuade patients to put pills in their mouths, or that perhaps she was powered by some gigantic battery.

When she finally stopped smiling she went straight into auto-prattle: 'I know what you're having for dinner tonight!'

Welcome to Mensa, Monica. She leaned down towards me and said, 'Don't ever say that I told you, but the meal you're having tonight does not exactly come from Loveday's fair hands . . . I think . . . in fact, I know it's come from the local Chinese!'

If only I cared what you thought, Monica. I swallowed my whisky and smiled. Monica was one of those girls you had to ignore for a minute before she would smile and walk away, having come to some frightfully important conclusion about your relationship and odd state of mind. She was walking away now, stopping every few paces to give a childlike wave before eventually stumbling out of the door.

As I slowly walked up the stairs to Loveday's flat, I was grateful that it was on the third floor, giving me the opportunity to rehearse my lines one final time. I stopped and turned on the thirty-third step and gripped the banister with both hands. I let out a long slow breath and thought of Rick. His comments about Loveday had made so much sense.

I was not at all prepared for how gorgeous Loveday looked when she opened the door. The perfume, the make-up, the shirt buttons undone. I wanted to call the referee over and have the match restarted or at least call a member of the Happiness Disposal Team.

Handing me a whisky she told me just to relax and make myself comfortable and joked that the doctor would be in to see me shortly. As much as I didn't want to, she was already making me laugh. I walked into the sitting room and spotted the recently purchased bottle of whisky next to two lit candelabra on her mahogany foldout table.

Loveday moved in and out of the kitchen, telling me a story about two girls at *Vogue* who wanted to be models.

'You'd think they would have had a bit more up top, wouldn't you? I mean, one of them is shorter than my grandmother and the other looks like she's got a coat-hanger for a nose. I'm not being a bitch but they're hardly, well, you know, now where was I? Oh, yes.'

Standing by the table she tore off two pieces of kitchen towel and put one on each side plate, not noticing the ones already there. Repeatedly pushing a bunch of hair behind her right ear, she bent down towards the candle and lit a cigarette.

'They've got no idea these girls, Tim. They've no idea of what it takes to model, no idea what's required. They just think it's a lot of hotels and foreign travel, which of course it is but . . .'

From the way she never stopped talking, I could tell she was nervous, like an anxious cat trying to protect her kittens. As she walked out of the room, I wondered if I should bring the conversation round to the subject of a temporary separation. Should I wait until the first course had been eaten before mentioning the idea of a break? Or should I hold it all until the coffee?

Just then, just as I was looking for the shred of courage that I needed, Loveday shouted through the door, 'Tim? Meant to tell you. I bought these yesterday at Harvey Nichols. A hundred and sixty-five quid! Thought I might take them on holiday with me to New York.'

'New York? You never said anything about that. What on earth is going on? You haven't got the money! What are you talking about?'

Loveday was now standing draped within the doorway, just this side of irresistible, and dressed in a pair of black skin-tight leather trousers that left little to even my imagination. A collision took place in my mind between the convenient idea of Loveday actually going away for a while, and the temptation of what lay within those trousers.

'Like them?' asked Loveday, smiling for all her eyes were worth. I was completely powerless.

'Yes, of course . . . I like them.'

I swallowed hard, cleared my throat, and shook my head like some belligerent horse. There was a heavy perfumed pause, during which I realised it was up to me to go on talking.

I stared at the trousers, trying to avoid those come-to-bed eyes. My head began to churn: don't be such a coward, don't be a wanker all your life. Tell her it's over. Tell her you're through. Tell her it's not her, it's you. Tell her she'll make someone a marvellous wife. Tell her, Tim! Do you want to be successful? You can't have your piece of cake and eat it, remember? Don't put off to tomorrow what you can do tonight, you gutless piece of lice.

My mouth opened but as I was about to speak I saw Loveday smiling. I pressed my pause and freeze-frame. This woman didn't, couldn't, and shouldn't know anything of the poisonous worm living inside my head.

'Loveday,' I said as seriously as I could, 'where did you get a hundred and sixty-five pounds to spend on a pair of trousers, and what's all this about going to New York?' I hesitated and suddenly had an unpleasant feeling: 'Have you met someone else?'

Loveday milked the sentence for all it was worth, waiting a very long time before replying.

'Oh, you stupid fucker! Of course I haven't met anyone else. I got the trousers free from work. One of the models said they were too big so she gave them to me. And I'm not going on holiday to New York. I'd like to go, but only with you.'

Like Bob Hoskins in the final scene of *The Long Good Friday*, I sat back smiling and blinking over Loveday's elaborate trick. It had obviously been a game to see if I cared.

But in the end, as we finished eating, it was Loveday's innocent mention of Rick, and her request to see the new offices, that brought things to a head.

'Are you afraid I'm going to embarrass you in front of your funky new friends?'

'Nothing of the sort, don't be so stupid. You've met Rick loads of times before, anyway.'

'So, what's the problem, then? Don't you want me to come and have a look?'

'Of course I want you to see it. It's very cold, that's all. Maybe you could come one weekend when it's warmer.'

'Why on the weekend? I want to meet everyone who works there.'

Loveday stacked the plates and carried them to the kitchen. I hunched my elbows forward on to the table and put my hands on my head, wishing I were one of those stupid monkeys that hears, speaks or sees no evil.

Loveday came back in and knelt beside my chair. Judging by the anxious look on her face I thought that she was about to tell me it was over rather than the other way round.

'Tim? I know you think I'm a nag and stupid and difficult, but tell me, honestly, is there something wrong?'

'Wrong?'

'I know that you're really down at the moment and I want you to be happy, that's all.'

'I'm fine. Really. Just a bit tired, that's all.'

It was my turn to get up from the table.

'Tim, come on! I know you. I know there's something wrong and I know what it is.'

'Really? And what, pray, is it, then?' I said, looking round for a comfortable space to sit down on the sofa.

Loveday got up, lit a cigarette, and pulled up a chair right next to me.

'It's Rick, isn't it? I'm sure it's not working out how you thought it would. Is it?'

I drew breath and hesitated before responding to such a direct hit. 'W-e-l-l, maybe . . .'

'Maybe what? Come on, it's me you're talking to. I'm not going to tell anyone, Tim. If you can't talk to me about this, who can you talk to? Harry?'

'No, I can't talk to him, you're right, not at the moment, anyway. Maybe when it's all clear and up and running. Maybe then.'

'Maybe? Come on, Tim, it's 1980 not 1940, spit it out. It's the money, isn't it?'

I let out a long, hollow laugh at yet another near direct hit. Loveday smiled in frustration.

'Have you got enough money to do all the things you need to do?'

'What do you mean exactly?'

'Come on, Tim, I'm not stupid! Stop being so bloody obtuse!'

I jerked my head towards her and shouted: '*I am not being fucking stupid!*'

Loveday sat holding her wine glass in mid-air, open-mouthed.

'Sorry. Sorry,' I repeated loudly.

Loveday put down her glass and took hold of my hand. 'I didn't say you were being stupid. OK? Calm down. I just want you to tell me what's happening. Listen, I do understand, you know. This sort of thing happens all the time. Maybe it's not the right thing for you after all. Maybe it's best to cut your losses before it's too late?'

'You mean, cut and run from a sinking ship?'

'Is it really sinking?'

'No, and I'm not a rat. Not really. I've just got to get more on the case. Grasp the nettle. Do the deed. Pull it out of the bag.'

'Tim, you've had too much to drink again! Come on, what on earth are you talking about?'

I took another deep breath, and pushed the palms of my hands up and down my face. I tried to speak but Loveday cut me off.

'I've never known you to be like this, so serious.'

'I don't know how to say this, but work is not the only problem.'

There was a pause and then Loveday launched in.

'Look, Tim, there is this adorable country post office in Devon. It's for sale and it's seven thousand pounds. It's about to be advertised in the *Western Morning News*. I've seen the photograph and it's beautiful. Built in 1880. It's an old redbrick house covered in laburnum with a postbox embedded in its wall. Apart from the post office downstairs, there's a sitting room, kitchen and dining room and three bedrooms above. And there's a garden with an old-fashioned swing and two cherry trees.'

'You sound like you've fallen in love with it already.'

'I'm trying to find a solution, Tim.'

'Sorry, go on. What's the idea?'

'The idea, Tim, is that we go and live there. We could pack up everything and just leave. It can't be that hard to run a sub-post office. We could do it between us. Then you could have your music and I could have my books and the rest of the world could just fuck off.'

Loveday paused. She was slightly out of breath, but smiling broadly.

'Just imagine how much Ned would like it. Think about how many mice there would be for him to catch. Think, Tim, there would be no one to worry us, nothing to bring us down, to stop us from being happy. I don't think it's running away, I think it's a choice we'd be making. What do you think?'

I stood up. Loveday cocked her head to look up at me. She looked exquisite.

'Loveday?' I wiped the back of my hand over the saliva that was bubbling in the corners of my mouth. Although I felt dead inside, my heart was beating fast. I swallowed hard. 'I don't know how to say this. But this has got to end.'

'You're not making sense, Tim. I don't think you know what you're doing.'

'I do know what I'm doing. It's got to stop. It just isn't right to carry on. I'm sorry.'

There was a long pause, at the end of which Loveday let out a loud and angry sigh.

'Isn't right, did you say?' she enunciated bitterly. 'Do you think I'm stupid or something? Do you think I haven't understood every time you've said something about us "not being right" and how you "need to focus" on your work? I've been hearing this for the last ten years or so it fucking well seems.'

'Look, Loveday, nothing is black and white . . .'

'Don't bother to make any more excuses, Tim. Don't bother to say all the crap about not wanting to hurt me or that it's just the wrong time. Christ, in a minute you'll be saying it's nothing personal.'

She stood up, covered her eyes with her hands and sobbed.

'Loveday . . .'

I only got as far as uttering her name before she swung round and grabbed my shoulders tightly with both hands. No longer caring if I saw her crying, she fixed me with her eyes and yelled, 'Shut up and listen! I'm not like one of your stupid bands that you can simply drop when you've had enough of them! I'm worth a million times more than them. You bloody fool, don't you see that! Why do you want to fucking ruin everything?'

17

For some reason the pub was empty. I never liked being in the Crooked Billet on my own. In fact, I never liked being on my own at all. Too much time to sit and dwell, too much time for the worm to piss its acrid bile.

I took hold of the drinks from Fred, walked over to the fruit machine, and idly put a 10-pence piece in the slot. Nothing happened. I nudged it. I pressed the square buttons on its front. Nothing happened . . . I slugged back some whisky, looked over my shoulder, and kneed the machine right where its balls should have been. It started flashing. Good. I finished the whisky, started glugging back the pint, and pushed in more 10-pence pieces. The machine fizzed and fruit symbols spun and juddered to a halt on its horizontal display. No win. I continued pushing the square buttons, superstitiously hoping that if a winning line appeared, the debating chamber in my head would fall silent.

– For God's sake Tim! Why didn't you tell us about you and Loveday?

– You're making a huge mistake.

– Tim why didn't you remember you had a meeting with the Japanese company? They were interested in doing a deal with us, for fuck's sake!

– What do you mean you need more time to listen? Can't you make a decision?

– No, Tim the appointment was for tomorrow, not today.

– How could you have left those tapes on the roof of a taxi?

– I thought everyone had been told about Barracuda closing.

– Between you and me I never thought you and Loveday were right together.

– Get your work sorted out, then everything will follow.

– Maybe this is a sign to change direction?

I sat back on the stool, staring at the fruit machine flashing TILT on and off. My head was spinning like a top with other people's advice; it was a debating chamber with no one keeping order. I tried hard to empty it of its furious shouting and start again, but without success. Instead, I sank further into the dark.

The previous week had been terrible, and not just because of the situation with Loveday. I was making big mistakes at work, mistakes concerning calculations, estimating costs, budgets, timetables, forgetting appointments, forgetting people's names, forgetting who I was.

I emptied my glass and walked back to the bar. I sat down, picked up an old cocktail stick, and started twiddling it round a crumpled cigarette butt in the ashtray. Should I have one more drink? Or should I leave? I held my pint glass up in the air to see what would happen. Fred walked over, took hold of the glass and, lowering his voice, leant towards me and said: 'Excuse me for saying this but are you OK? You planning to drink us dry?'

For a second, I couldn't think of a reply but then remembered a line from a movie.

'Didn't even touch the sides, Fred.'

'Really?' Fred stepped back from the bar and then leaned in again. 'You commiserating or celebrating?'

'Both,' I said, quickly opening my newspaper.

Twenty minutes later, Harry arrived. No Jessica in tow this time. At first it was a welcome distraction to hear his news. He had been promoted that week to the international section of his bank, and been given a whopping pay rise.

I could tell, although I didn't say it, that Harry was starting to shed skin from his past. There were no more comments about capitalist bastards, about being a cog in the wheel or joining the bourgeoisie. No, it was now full speed ahead along the rails to success and mega-wealth. I didn't mind at all. For me Harry was Harry, and whatever old bollocks went along his surface, be it Socrates, takeover bids or Aristotle Onassis, it was perfectly all right with me. It was just that he went on a bit too long about how brilliant it was all going to be.

'Same again, gents?' asked Fred, taking hold of my empty glass.

'Thanks,' I said, watching Harry drain his pint beside me.

'Give us that and I'll get you another,' I said, holding my hand out to him.

Harry held on to the glass and flicked back the cuff of his sleeve.

'Oh, shit, I can't. I promised I'd meet Jessica outside Sloane Square tube bang on eight o'clock.'

'Oh?'

'Sorry, Tim. I promised her a celebration dinner tonight.'

'You wanker! I thought we were all set for an evening out?'

'Yeah, I'm sorry, but, you know.'

All I knew was that I was really disappointed. I wanted us to go and get steaming drunk and perhaps talk about what was going on at work.

'Sure, no problem,' I said taking a big drag on my cigarette.

I hadn't even had the chance to talk to him about Loveday.

When I left the pub, my head was spinning and I found it hard to concentrate. I located the Gaulle and sped off down the Embankment. Just as I turned left from Albert Bridge into Prince of Wales Drive, distracted by some thought about the office, I drove over a concrete bollard in the middle of the road. The sound of the two tyres exploding was funny at first, but the noise of the concrete ripping into the chassis was not. The good old car managed to heave and hiccup into a side street opposite.

I knew the car was wrecked but suddenly I had my wits about me. I killed the lights, rammed the handbrake on, and quickly got out. I looked up towards Battersea Park Road and behind me to check if anyone was coming or might have seen the accident. The area was deserted. I slid my hand over the warm bonnet of the car, and felt a sentimental lump in my throat, almost as if the car was a dying horse.

I walked the rest of the way home and spent the remainder of the evening watching 'Telford's Change' on TV and talking to the cat.

18

Every day is becoming harder. Every day I feel the net drawing tighter. I am in the middle of a field with everybody watching as, one by one, my clothes are being removed. I stand there naked without even a fig leaf, squirming with shame as the crowd comes closer to inspect what lies beneath my skin. Until now I've avoided all the searchlights. I've always run between them, or outglared them; always had the front to stem any real enquiry. But now the ball of wool that makes up my life is unwinding as it rolls down the stairs, and like a child, I cannot catch it.

The office was ironic. Stuck in funky Lower Hades Road and dealing with bands from CBGB'S in New York and the Albuquerque in London, we could have, should have, been on the cutting edge of cool. Yet, inside, the tone was more that of two disgruntled occupants of some gentlemen's club. When the feeling of being naked grew to extremes, I had to go. I would stand there in his doorway, clutching my empty briefcase, frozen speechless, and Rick would look up from his desk, force a smile and ask, 'Going somewhere nice?'

I always mumbled something about going to the dentist again or a meeting with some prospective band, and he would always take it, always accept it as it was. In reality, I never knew where I was going, except that it was away from the world of Delta and the spectres that were battering inside my head. I would run and run up the Lower Hades Road, praying nobody would see me. I always felt the same old guilt, the same sense of letting Rick down, of leaving him to cope with all the shit.

The theatre was Jessica's idea; Loveday was Harry's. An evening at the National followed by dinner overlooking the Thames: what better way to put them both back together again and cheer up good old Tim?

The four of us exchanged familiar jokes and banter as if nothing had occurred in the intervening weeks. I was pleased I didn't have to do too much of the talking. While Harry and Jessica skilfully ensured that the conversation remained pleasantly neutral, with nothing too personal being discussed, while I managed to catch Loveday's eye a few times and exchange knowing looks.

I sat down next to Loveday at the beginning of the play, painfully aware that I would not be able to smoke for the next two hours. I glanced at her programme and saw that the play we were about to witness was *Death of a Salesman*. I don't know why I hadn't asked what we were going to see, but I had just assumed it was going to be a comedy.

Death of a Salesman? A massive wave of paranoia rolled in my stomach. I thought I was being set up by the others to endure some form of therapy. I wanted to say something discreetly to Loveday, make my excuses, and push past everyone in the row before the curtain came up, but Harry and Jessica were talking to her. I needed a cigarette there and then and looked over my shoulder to check where the exits were. Then the house lights dimmed and before I knew what was happening it was dark and Loveday had moved her hand so it was just touching mine.

I wanted to take hold of her hand, squeeze it, and keep it warm between my legs but I didn't. I sat there, immobilised, smelling her perfume, feeling her touch, but unable to look at anything but the stage.

After the first few scenes, Loveday turned to me and whispered: 'This is seriously depressing, isn't it? Come on, let's go outside and have a fag.'

I turned to her and shook my head. All my energy had gone, and I felt manacled to my seat. As Willy Loman's sense of failure became more obvious, I realised I was looking into a mirror. It was as if my past had caught up with me and smacked me on the jaw.

The meeting between Rick and myself was brief.

'Take a week off or however long you need,' he said. 'Go away somewhere nice and think things through.'

I did absolutely nothing that week, other than stare at the cat staring at me.

Ten days later I met him at the Crooked Billet.

He sat down at the table, his hands cradling a gin and tonic. 'I've ordered some cheese and tomato sandwiches. Seems strange being in here at lunchtime, doesn't it?

'Yes, I suppose,' I said guiding the end of my cigarette around the perimeter of the already full ashtray.

'So you didn't go away?'

'No, I started to build a wall on the roof-terrace instead,' I lied.

'I'm told that building walls can be very therapeutic.'

I shrugged, stubbed out my cigarette, and let out a long, pissed-off sigh.

'Look, Rick, I'm sorry, but it's bad day at Black Rock.'

'I'm not with you. What do you mean?' Rick asked, taking off his baseball hat and running his hand through his hair. There was a long pause in which the ticking of the large pub clock became apparent. Twice I opened my mouth to speak but could not settle on a clear line of explanation.

'I don't know if this is going to make any sense.'

Rick smiled sympathetically. 'Tim this is not a police interview. You don't have to say anything.' Then, pausing to gulp down his drink, he continued. 'Look why not have a few more days off? Go away this time, go somewhere hot and lie on a beach and sleep. You look terrible.'

'No. I can't do that now. Look, Rick, it's time for me to go. The last thing I want to do is let you down, but it really is bad day at Black Rock.'

Rick turned his head away as if he were going to sneeze.

Ultimately, in an attempt to say something non-personal, I settled on one constant: that I had unfortunately lost all enthusiasm for the business, and really didn't know what else to say. Yet there was an unconvincing ring to it, and we both knew it.

Eventually, Rick put his hands up for me to stop. 'OK, OK. I hear everything you say and, believe me, I am sympathetic.'

He then began mumbling a series of disconnected philosophical statements about work not being the most important thing in life, and how he was often tempted to quit and start something in the country with Victoria. Eventually, he got to what he really wanted to say.

'For my sake, however we choose to handle this between us, in terms of the outside world all I ask is that you handle things in an adult way. Come in on Monday and we'll sort it out.'

'Why, yes, of course,' I replied, as if someone had just asked me the time.

Rick continued to talk about the different possibilities remaining for him in the music world, and how perhaps we should never have gone down this road in the first place, but I was not really listening. I was thinking about Rick's request that I should try to handle things in an 'adult way'. Despite all the words of agreement I was muttering to Rick about turning up at the office on Monday and being careful not to tell anyone anything, all I wanted to do was write a cheque for whatever the experience had cost him and disappear into thin air.

Rick drained his glass, put his hand on my shoulder and wished me a good weekend.

* * *

Someone was watching.

I walked. I ran . . . I had three sanctuaries. The sweet shop, run by a gleeful Indian couple, would last only for a minute providing, that is, no other customer was in front of me. Even then I still could not simply ask for a large bar of chocolate. It was not as if I was buying porn or contraceptives, but I had to wrap the chocolate inside a newspaper and then buy forty cigarettes as well.

Leaving the sweet shop, I would walk swiftly across a rubbish-strewn side street full of abandoned cars to the entrance of St Joseph's church. There the pattern was always the same: I would walk up and down outside pretending to wait for some mysterious person to arrive, reading the newspaper to provide extra cover. It would always take at least three or four minutes before I felt able to go inside. Once inside, the worm would rise.

– Who invited you?

– Well, no one in particular, I just need to be here, that's all.

– Oh really? You thought you could drop in at random again, pop in at will. Behave like a gunslinger; do all the things you've done and still wear your gunbelt even in here?

In the appalling silence that followed I would always feel like saying that I'd be happy to unsling the gunbelt, happy to unsling anything at all in return for some answers, some directions, some peace. But it never worked out that way.

So I'd hurry off, desperate to reach the allotments. I would happily have traded my apartment for an allotment of my own. I would have erected a tent – cleverly camouflaged, of course – and moved Ned and myself in there for good. After a short period of time I would have gone off in search of the blind man selling matchboxes and given him his own patch, so he could still go on selling matches but would have somewhere comfortable to sit. Later, I would invite selected friends round for a very short stay and calmly explain my new way of life. I would wait until the allotment was almost at its best to invite my father to spend an afternoon discussing whether it was possible to improve on *my* vegetable garden.

And Rick?

Well, Rick would be invited for a gin and tonic at six o'clock, and to take some of the tomatoes I'd grown for him.

And Loveday?

I'd see Loveday every ten minutes. High above the allotments to one side in the hazy distance there is a straight road, balanced on top of a grass ridge. On this road she travels slowly back and forth. Sometimes she is staring straight ahead; sometimes she looks down in my direction. Although I can see her throwing back her head and laughing, I cannot see whether she is sad, bored or happy. I know deep down that she is looking for me. Clutching the last straw of my courage, I manage to turn so she does not see me and I let her pass on by. Then I hear a mechanical procession of rumbling motorcars travelling along the ridge in the opposite direction. A creamy-white line of open-topped cars, and the sun is dappling, bouncing off its suntanned occupants. I hear gentle laughter coming towards me.

As the first part of the procession reaches the point opposite me on the ridge, the laughter stops and everything changes to a funereal pace. The cars move slowly past like a line of gondolas and I can see a different girl standing in each one and turning to stare at me. As the faces slowly swivel by, I know them to be faces from my past coming to say farewell, adieu, until the next life then, thanks and cheerio.

19

It's the end of May. I am lying on my back, brushing my tongue from side to side along the ridges of my upper teeth. I focus all my attention on doing this and realise that I have a helicopter in my mouth. For a moment I laugh at the absurdity of my thoughts but then the sound reminds me of blades beating through the air across a jungle in *The Deer Hunter*. I think of soldiers being forced to play Russian roulette.

Would I have the guts to play and pull the trigger?

Cambodia is the place to be, or somewhere like that, where life doesn't really matter. Somewhere where no one is watching. Somewhere where people live and die within a twinkling of your eye, but where the game goes on regardless until there's no one left.

The telephone rings its feeble trill and I stretch across to answer it, noticing that the time is ten past midnight.

'Hi! I'm ringing from a nightclub,' Loveday yells.

'Yes, I can hear that.'

I pick up a tennis ball from underneath the bedside table and squeeze it for all I am worth.

'I'm having a fantastic time,' Loveday says, teasing.

'Is that why you're ringing me?'

The Bee Gees' 'Staying Alive' suddenly blasts down the phone as a door opens and closes behind wherever she is standing.

'I said, I am having a fantastic time.'

'All right, I expect you are. What's his name?'

'Hugh and John and Mon. There are four of us, you see?' she says in a loud whisper, slightly slurring her words.

'How fascinating.'

The throb of muffled disco music continues in the background.

'Fantastic meal, and now there's dancing.'

The Bee Gees or whoever it is gets louder again. I picture Loveday holding the phone behind her head to demonstrate where the music is coming from.

I yell at her. 'Did you really ring to tell me that?'

'Well, aren't you jealous?'

I hurl the tennis ball at the wall; it bounces straight back and hits me on the cheek. It stings like fuck but I carry on the conversation.

'Are you very, very drunk, or just drunk?'

'All three.'

'Loveday, don't kick a man when he's down.'

'What?'

'You heard,' I say, pushing the duvet away with my legs.

'Oh shut up, you miserable misery. I was just worried about you, that's all.'

I cradle the telephone between my neck and shoulder, light a cigarette and say: 'There's no need to worry. Just don't tell me if you fuck him, that's all.'

'You sound terrible.'

'Well, I feel terrible, so terrible that I think I'm going to live in Phnom Penh. But it's my problem and I'll sort it out.'

'Martyr.'

'Fuck off, will you? You spoilt nightclub bitch.'

'Do you miss me?'

'Oh God . . . you know that I . . .'

'Do.'

'Look, please don't . . .'

'I'm sorry. Shall I come round?'

'You're in a fucking nightclub with Mr Fucking Date, for Christ's sake!'

'Well, I can fucking well just leave if I want to, can't I?'

She sweeps through the open front door wearing a fur coat and red velvet skirt and jacket looking glamorous, very sexy and very, very drunk. It is one o'clock in the morning. Big deal, but I tell her I am not safe from anyone unless I am under the bedclothes. She thinks this is funny. Maybe she is right. As she climbs the stairs she is laughing more and more, stopping only when she reaches the bedroom door.

'A long time since I've been here,' she half-mumbles, half-hiccups as she sits down unsteadily on the edge of the bed.

The talk is like a lift stopping at random between three floors of conversation.

'Great meal at the restaurant, they had those potatoes you like.'

I want to ask her about Hugh or Stew but I resist.

'Really? Is that all you had? Just potatoes?'

She pretends not to have heard, then carries on as if we changed the subject some time ago.

'Did you know Arthur Miller was married to Marilyn Monroe? No wonder she topped herself!'

'Oh, is that why you're here tonight?'

'What?' she asks in a bewildered tone while slipping slowly off the bed.

'Careful,' I say hooking my arm round her waist and pulling her back.

Loveday rubs her eyes and yawns. She is like a child that has just woken up. She runs her hands over the duvet and finds the bulge of my feet. As per our unspoken ritual she yanks my big toes from side to side and nearly topples over again as she looks up at me. I shake my head, give her a smile, thinking the scene is unreal. I bring my feet back, so my legs make an arch and guide her to lean back against my knees.

'Oh, that's better! Tim, please . . . give my shoulders a rub?'

I begin gently and not so gently kneading the warm skin on the top of her neck. I slide my fingers underneath her hair and up to the back of her ears, and then let them fall and trace the round softness of her perfect shoulders. For a strange moment I imagine we are back in Dartmouth. She chatters away drunkenly, half about the excitement of her evening, and half about her desire to go and run the post office in 'Nether sodding Wallop'. I want to hold her and cup her breasts; I want to put my hand between her legs. I want to pull her clothes off. I want her smell. I want her naked body right beside me. I want, yes, but my body seems locked, submerged in a diving bell beneath the surface of the duvet.

To take my mind off this impossibility, I suggest perhaps considering a sub post office in Phnom Penh. She puts her hands on her head and bursts out laughing. I think she must have misheard me, but then, in a bizarre mixture of Billy Joel and the *Mikado*, she sings a line about having a 'wanting to go to a sub-post office in Phnom Penh'.

Without meaning to I yawn, and then think that one of us had better inject some sense into the conversation.

'All right, Loveday, let's get back to being sensible.'

'You what?' She turns around and points her finger at me in mock shock. 'Tim? Being sensible doesn't suit you.'

I laugh.

We both want her to stay. We both know that maybe she shouldn't. I wish I was drunk. I wish like fuck I was drunk! I know I have not had a bath in over a week. I also know that I am currently incapable of even screwing a plug into a wall. But I want her to stay. She starts stroking my hair as if I'm a child. It all now becomes an erotically tinged memory of my mother in fur coat and perfume, kissing me goodnight before going to the theatre. I want to write a cheque for this post office she wants. I want to take her there right now, but I know that I'm falling asleep. I want her to be beside me when I wake up in the morning but somehow I know that she won't be.

20

Sunday morning seemed to be the best time to do it. In my own way I had said a goodbye of sorts to Loveday, and it would spare Rick from any further embarrassment. I had bought the cheapest ticket possible and then travelled aimlessly on the Circle Line as far as Edgware Road, round to Tower Hill and back again. Ultimately, I knew I was going to change on to the District Line and then change everything.

Fulham Broadway station appealed to the dramatist barking in my head: 'An unidentified male in his twenties died today as a result of multiple injuries sustained from jumping in front of the eleven-thirty Wimbledon train as it pulled into Fulham Broadway station. The station was closed for over two and a half hours while firemen used winching equipment to raise the train. An eye-witness . . .'

When I actually did arrive at Fulham Broadway, both of its platforms were deserted. There was a smell of rotting litter and dog shit that reminded me of the Lower Hades Road. As the train I had been travelling on shunted away into the distance, I stood and surveyed the desolate scene, wondering why there were so few people. My answer came as I detected the chanting of a football crowd drifting in and out of the station. I shrugged it off and looked up at the indicator for approaching trains. Two minutes until the next one to Wimbledon.

Without thinking, I took out my camera and began to photograph every aspect of the platform; the rails, the ticket barrier, the gap dividing the glass roof-panels, the sky. I wanted to have a memento of where I had been, something to look at from wherever I was going. I was taking so many pictures I was actually beginning to enjoy myself. This was weird! Having nearly finished the film, I reflected that it was imperative to have at least one picture of the thing that was going to carry me off. 'A matter of respect,' I told myself.

I began debating whether I could photograph the train as it emerged from the tunnel and still have time to jump in front of it. I paced up and down with my hands behind my back trying to think what would be best and wishing my father was there to advise me on trajectory, projectory, angular incidences and generally the correct way to do this, bearing in mind the principles of advanced mathematics.

'Oh, bollocks, fuck off!' I yelled at the skylight. My father wasn't with me and I could work it out for myself. Within a matter of seconds, a movie began running in my head with me in the starring role. I was Kenneth More in *A Night to Remember*, on the *Titanic*, wearing a white Aran sweater, and oilskins, battling to get the passengers safely into the lifeboats. I made myself go forward to the very edge of the platform, pretending to be a nervous passenger wanting to be pushed. 'No, I'm sorry, sir; we haven't got time for photographs. Please put the camera away and wait for the signal to jump . . .'

Somehow, this lifeboat scenario made everything much simpler. I braced myself and stood back a little as I felt the rush of wind as the train sped through the tunnel.

Now was the moment, now was the time.

I stood there, rocking back and forth, the lights of the train now so bright I could nearly see the driver. I looked again at the spot I must jump to in-between the rails. My heart started beating a deep thump-thump-thump and my breathing was getting shorter and shorter. I thought about saying a prayer but there wasn't time. To stop myself being sick, I put my hand round my throat, took one more look at the rail, shut my eyes and leaned back ready to jump.

Suddenly the train screeched and shuddered to a halt. A moment later there was a crackling on the platform speakers, a tapping on the microphone, a clearing of the throat, and a bored nasal voice said: 'Sorry, ladies and gentlemen, the power has been cut on the District Line due to an electrical fault at Bayswater.'

Selfish bastards! This was supposed to be my turn. I'm phoning the duty manager.

I stood there silently mouthing this vitriolic nonsense until finally there came what I thought was the inevitable intervention of the platform manager. Tap-tap-tap on my shoulder.

No, go away! I'm off, I'm departing from platform 3 any minute now . . . please, can't you see I'm busy?

Then it came again, tap-tap-tap on my shoulder and a familiar voice. 'Haven't you forgotten something, Mr Lomax, sir?'

I turned round. It was Simon Caplow standing in unfamiliar weekend clothes. He was holding the carrier bag I had left sitting in the middle of the platform. It looked strangely irrelevant.

'I saw you from the other side,' he said.

I smiled a what-the-fuck-do-I-say-now smile.

'Aren't you a bit close to the edge?' he said with generous ambiguity.

'Oh, yes, perhaps I am. I was trying to take a photo of the tube as it came out of the tunnel,' I said, quickly remembering my camera.

He looked directly at me for a second and then returned to his usual pose of staring down his nose at the non-existent smoke coming from his pipe. He was not used to making running commentary, but bravely continued to explain the reasons for his presence in such a place.

'I decided to see how the other half live and not take the car out today.'

He was used to me picking up the thread but no words would come. He shuffled on the spot, still waiting for me to say something. A train arriving on the opposite platform broke the silence.

'Anyway, it's not as bad as I thought. Hang on, there's my train.'

He started running down the platform in what seemed an entirely inappropriate manner for someone of his position. He had only run ten yards or so when he stopped, turned and shouted back to me, 'Come and see me Monday or Tuesday. I've something rather interesting you might like to consider. Don't forget, will you?'

I waved after him all the way across the footbridge until he disappeared inside the train. I felt ridiculous now. All dressed up and nowhere to kill myself. Plus, I now had an appointment of sorts, which I knew I would have to keep.

Besides, whatever would have happened to Ned?

I ambled out of the tube station, on to the Fulham Road, and headed towards Parsons Green. It was as if I had just emerged from a terrible dream. I picked up a stick and joyfully whacked the sides of my legs. I spotted an old red telephone box on the other side of the road. It was on the corner leading to Wandsworth and Battersea and seemed to have been there for the last hundred years. I crossed and yanked open the door, and dialled Loveday's number.

'Hello, is that Phnom Penh 9889?'

There was a slight pause, then Loveday said, 'Yes. It most certainly is.'

'Thank Christ for that,' I said, happily sliding down the side of the call box.

July to December 1980

21

Despite the crowds, the rendezvous at Battersea Funfair had been effortless. Here we were: Harry and Jessica walking alongside Rick and Victoria with Loveday happily sauntering along between them. What a turn-up for the books! All of us, except for the pregnant waddling Victoria, had already drunk a considerable amount that evening. It still seemed incredible to me that things had turned around so quickly.

It was exactly six weeks since that fateful meeting with Simon Caplow at Fulham Broadway station. I did not want to think about it much now, afraid that the glue that was keeping me together might become unstuck.

Caplow had sat within the usual cloud of smoke when I went to see him. Then he uncharacteristically leaned forwards so that his chin was nearly touching the desk and said: 'Life is short enough already, Tim. We can't have you trying to make it any shorter, can we?'

I laughed an awkward laugh and started to say: 'But you don't . . .'

'But I do,' he interrupted, 'and, anyway, that's not the point. I want you to come back and run the studio here for a while. It needs someone like you to shake it up and get it moving. I thought we could pay you ten thousand and a bonus. It would keep the wolf from the door. Think about it and let me know.'

I had walked down the stairs from his office at least six inches off the ground. It was all I needed to hear. By the time I got through the revolving doors of the building, I had formulated an idea whereby Rick and I could combine running the studio together as well as Delta. It would mean much-needed income for the pair of us, and some possible new opportunities as well. To my surprise, though, when I explained the idea to Rick, he was less than enthusiastic about it, saying it would be impossible to be in two places at once. After a week back at work in the Lower Hades Road, I felt so reinvigorated that I decided not to pursue the studio idea but to recommit myself to making Delta a success. I told myself that if Bjorn Borg could win Wimbledon for a fifth time, anything was possible.

As we meandered into the fairground, cascades of high-pitched screams came tumbling through the air. We stopped and gazed up at the sky. Just above the tops of the trees, the open, badly lit cars of the big dipper could be seen, like some Mary Poppins nightmare, travelling quietly along a straight rail before making the ultimate screaming descent.

'Flaming Nora, I'm not going on that!' Loveday yelled out.

Everyone laughed.

Harry, Rick, and myself decided to race one another to the shooting gallery. We charged away like laughing schoolboys and were neck and neck all the way until I collided with two mohicaned punks who were carrying a small plastic bag bulging with water and a solitary goldfish.

'Bollocks!' I shouted, as I peered round one of the punk's blue quiffs and saw Rick and Harry trying to hold each other back as they came to the entrance of the shooting gallery, panting and completely out of breath.

After brushing the water off my own shirt and theirs, I looked down at the plastic bag and was relieved to see that the goldfish was still swimming. Uncharacteristically, I thought, one of the mohicans stuck out his hand like a boxer at the end of a fight to shake hands and confirm that he and his goldfish had no hard feelings.

By the time I reached the counter of the shooting gallery, Harry and Rick were already cocking back the barrels of two of the three available guns. As I grabbed the remaining rifle, a gruff fairground voice boomed straight over my head.

'Sorry, mate, that one's broken; you'll 'ave to wait till the next round.'

'Bloody typical!' I shouted as Rick and Harry took their first shots.

I turned around, and spotted Loveday staring up again at the Big Dipper. I walked over and took her hand. 'Are you all right?'

'Yeah, I'm fine. Just feeling a bit disconnected, that's all.'

I ran my finger softly down her cheek and hooked my arm around her waist.

'Where are the others? Has Victoria disappeared into a drum of candy floss?'

'They've gone off to find the old bag who dresses in a shawl, has enormous tits and calls herself Psychic Anastasia.'

'Why aren't you going?'

Loveday let out a short laugh and said: 'Because I happen to know her real name is Beryl and the only thing psychic about her is her ability to tell you what you want to hear.'

'Don't you want to know about your future, then?'

'I wouldn't mind, but not from Beryl.'

'So, do you fancy a ride on the big dipper? Think you've got the nerve?'

'WHAT!' Loveday yelled, grabbing hold of my lapels.

'Well, maybe you haven't!' I said, teasing her and breaking free of her grip.

Loveday swung round and stood like a cowgirl with her legs apart and her thumbs sticking through the loops of her belt. 'Have I got the nerve! Are you s-e-r-i-o-u-s?'

I smirked and shrugged in mock machismo.

'You cheeky sod! You're the one who normally never wants to go on these things!'

I didn't reply but turned around and offered her a piggyback. 'Whenever you're ready.'

I felt the warmth of her body against mine as her arms tightened around my neck and her thighs gripped the sides of my chest. I walked us both slowly across the damp and muddy fairground: past the schoolboys hurling balls at the coconut shy; past the old women throwing plastic hoops over poles to win a goldfish; past the three darts in a playing card stall, and on towards the drunken whirring sounds of the merry-go-round.

We stood a few foot away from the running boards, watching the mad staring horses gallop mechanically up and down. It looked like a gigantic spinning Christmas cake. I turned to look at Loveday and saw her face speckled in gold and orange light.

'Why the fuck is nobody riding on this?'

Loveday laughed knowingly and eased herself off my back. 'I think you'll have to ask Beryl about that.'

'Well, I don't think the big dipper looks safe; something tells me we shouldn't go on it.'

'Ha, ha, I thought as much. You're losing your nerve, aren't you?'

'I'll show you what nerve is, Nora.'

One minute later we were standing back to back, waiting in the queue for the dipper.

I decided to ask her there and then.

'Loveday?'

'Yes, Tim?' she replied suggestively, as if she knew what I was about to say.

'There's something I want to ask you.'

'Oh?' she said, squeezing my hand.

'Would you . . . like to go to Dartmouth for another weekend?'

There was a pause in which all I could hear was the whirr of the merry-go-round and sirens sounding the end of the dodgem.

'Are you sure that's all you wanted to ask?'

I turned Loveday around so we were facing one another and put my face next to hers whispering, 'You'll have to come to Devon to find out.'

I put my arms tight around her and kissed her softly on her eyes, her nose and, in a moment of unselfconscious passion, on her mouth.

Two minutes later, amidst terrified screams and whoops of excitement the big dipper commenced its deceptively slow roll into the first of its three-hundred-and-sixty degree turns.

22

At exactly midday on the 12th of September, I bounced into Rick's office waving a cassette. Rick looked up for a few seconds, then carried on reading a letter from the bank.

'Tim, if it hasn't got any money in it, I'm not interested, OK?'

'But, Rick, this is going to be the answer to all our problems.'

'We've got bugger-all income, Atlantis are reassessing the Ox's contract and Frankie from Spunk just called to say they've got a monster called "Stop the Cavalry". As if they need any more hits.'

'Ahem, Rick, hello?'

'We need something, that's for sure,' said Rick, watching me out of the corner of his eye.

'Well, here it is.'

I lifted the cassette above my head like a sacrament, and in my best Benedictine voice, sang out, 'in nomine padre, spiritus sancti – amen!' Rick put down his letter and scratched his chin in bemusement.

'What did you sprinkle on your cornflakes this morning?'

I laughed and handed him the cassette. 'You've got to hear this right now.'

'OK, OK!' Rick mumbled, taking the tape and putting it into the cassette player underneath his desk.

Two minutes and fifty-five seconds later, Rick was embracing me like a flapping seal. 'It's fantastic! I love it, Tim. What can I say? Put it on again.'

I knelt down and pressed rewind on the tape machine.

'I'm glad you like it.'

'Like it? I'm in love with it. Who is it?'

'It's a band called the Dogs. I saw them at the Excuse ages ago. Stand by now.' I turned up the volume and pressed play.

Within seconds of the chorus, and to my great amusement, Rick did a John Travolta shuffle to the window, pointed one arm up to the sky and clicked his fingers in time to the beat.

Halfway through the song I looked behind me and saw Star and Susie leaning around the half-open door like stooges, nodding their heads to the music and pointing in astonishment at Rick.

What we had all just listened to was, in anybody's terms, an unequivocal, unstoppable, unquestionable HIT. Could we, could I, secure the deal? That was the question.

For the next seven days I did little else but talk, eat, sleep and think about making the record a success. The track in question was called 'Rhiannon's Café' and had been written and performed by two eighteen-year-old Welsh boys called the Dogs. It had been made independently of any record company in a small studio in Anglesey. Dave and Neil, the singer and guitarist, and their manager Andy Grave, had spent two weeks in London trying to sell the tape to record companies but had been rejected by every single one. In a rare moment of fantastic fortune and coincidence, and on their last day in the big city, they had met Zannie Price. Even though the record company Zannie was now working for had rejected the tape, she had been impressed, certainly impressed enough to get in touch with me.

Well done, Zannie. It was also Zannie who then persuaded the downhearted trio to wait for me in a pub off the Tottenham Court Road. To hasten the journey, I borrowed Rick's Granada but became snarled up in traffic. When I eventually arrived, I gave Zannie a big kiss and was swiftly introduced to the Dogs and their manager. Ordering a round of drinks, I persuaded the landlord to play the band's cassette through his sound system. I only needed to hear the first minute of the song before I was convinced it was a hit. Confidently ordering another round of drinks, I sat down and went into performance mode. As I spoke, I ran another separate conversation inside my head.

'So, tell me about the band. Have you got any photos? A video perhaps?'

– The question is, why has no one else picked up on this track? Is it too bloody obvious even for them?

'Oh, yes, yes, I see. Now, what about other songs? How many have you written and exactly how many have you recorded, either as demos or masters?'

– That'll keep them talking for a bit. Now, where was I? Yes, why has everyone passed on this tape? Come on, you've got to be quick. Well, it's obvious, isn't it? It's the two lads and the manager. I mean, they're very nice and from Wales and all that. But Anglesey? Who's ever heard of a hit from Anglesey? No, the real problem is sitting over there with the brown suit and big mouth. Yorkshire git! Thinks he knows it all. Still, he's the one I've got to convince. Christ, I hope they don't want any money.

'Well, thanks for giving me all that information. Now, let me be completely frank, may I?'

'It would make a change from most of you bloody people. All hot air and no trousers,' said Andy Grave, smirking and emptying his glass.

The two earnest-looking band members grinned nervously, and leant towards me.

'I sense,' I said, pausing for effect, 'that you have been given the run-around something rotten. No one in these big companies has taken you seriously and probably those that said they would ring back never did. Am I right?'

'Absolutely! Got it in one!' exclaimed Dave and Neil.

'And you're here to tell us that Delta Records, is different. Pull the other one!' chimed Grave in a heavily sarcastic tone.

'I can see you weren't born yesterday, Andy,' I replied, keeping my cool.

– Christ Almighty, why ever did I agree to this? Because this is a hit record. Now tell them what they want to hear and invite donkey brain over there out to lunch.

'I don't know whether we're completely different or not, but what I do know is that if we release a record it's not one among ten that we release every week; it's one out of one. That is to say, you don't have to wait in a queue while big artists get released before you and you don't have to wait for your record to be made a priority because it already is. We could have this record out in four weeks flat, yes, just in time for the Christmas market. And when you deal with Delta you don't have to deal with a thousand trumped-up secretaries and their trumped-up bosses – you deal directly with either Rick or me. Now, what do you think?' I said, smiling at them triumphantly.

'Brilliant! Just what we want. Isn't it . . .' Dave began as Andy exhaled loudly and interrupted, flicking the end of his nose with his finger.

'What I want to know is, firstly, why are you in such a rush to release the record? And secondly, who is Rick?'

'Look, Andy, I came here at extremely short notice on the understanding that you were interested in doing a deal sooner rather than later. If I'm wrong, then let's put this on ice and get together later in the year. No hassle, no problem. On the other hand, you could come to the office tomorrow morning and meet my partner Rick, and perhaps afterwards we'll have lunch and see if we still have something to talk about. Yes?'

I gave Zannie a lift home and thanked her profusely for the tip, promising her a cut in the record's success. As she unbuckled her seat-belt, Zannie fixed me with a look that was difficult to misinterpret.

'I'm much more interested in getting a decent job, Tim. You know, like the one I used to have?'

Kissing her goodbye, I asked what length of notice she had to give to her current employers.

'A month, but I could persuade them to let me go in two weeks.'

There was a brief pause as we smiled knowingly at one another.

'Let me think about it. I might have an idea.'

I then headed across town to Fulham to join Harry, Jessica and Loveday for dinner. I played the tape several times at varying volumes during the journey and each time became more and more convinced I was right. I knew that the decisive test would be to play it to the others.

A candlelit dinner was noisily underway when I arrived at the flat. I couldn't restrain myself, and after a few gulps of wine handed the cassette to Harry and asked him to play it. Five minutes later everyone was singing 'Rhiannon's Café' as if they'd known it all their lives. At one point Harry even lifted himself drunkenly on one elbow and slurred out a toast: 'To Rhiannon's Café and Christmas in New York.'

After the clinking of glasses had stopped and the last murmur of the song had died away, I picked up on the cue and leaned across the table to Harry.

'Harry? Is this really true?'

'I'm afraid it is, old bean. The bank has offered me a one-year contract in New York, including a subsidised apartment. Sorry I couldn't ask you for permission first. From 15th November our new address is going to be Little Italy!'

'You jammy bastard!'

'Tim! Why don't we go over and visit? Come on, it would be great. You could sell that dreadful old car to pay for the tickets!' Loveday teased.

'Too right, mate,' yelled Harry in a Les Paterson Aussie voice. 'Sell that heap of a shit and get yourself down to Pan Am!'

'I didn't get where I am today by selling a national treasure like that!'

Loveday looked like an excited schoolgirl. I wanted to book the tickets there and then, hand over the surprise of an autographed copy of Billy Joel's *52nd St* album and make rampant love to her in the back seat of the car.

'No hotel costs and the best spaghetti ever, just around the corner!' enthused Jessica.

'We're really going to have to think about this v-e-r-y carefully,' I said, in my best Mrs Thatcher voice.

'Oh, Tim, stop being so boring, let's find a way?'

'Loveday, you're so *impetuous*!' I said, teasing, having decided to do exactly that.

The following morning at Delta, there was an atmosphere of real excitement.

'I think they're here! I think they're outside now,' Susie squealed, leaning on my desk, and panting like a cocker spaniel.

'Right, chaps, this is it!' I yelled in a squadron-leader voice.

Star gave her lips a last swipe in the broken toilet mirror, and kept those lips smiling the whole time she spoke to the musicians as they waited in the Delta reception. Both Dogs were dressed in Arran sweaters, blue jeans, black and yellow oilskin coats respectively, and brand-new Cuban heels. Neil, the shorter, mop-haired partner, had already taken off his coat and was now rolling a 'bit of a herbal' as he called it.

'Can we get you some tea or coffee?'

'Here, take these records, they're all the ones ever released on Delta.'

'Hey, Dave, would you like to go to a gig tonight?'

'Nice track, boys!' Rick said. From Rick, that was staggering praise.

Rick liked the music, maybe even the band, but the critical relationship was with Andy Grave, who was ten minutes late and sporting a hangover.

'Andy, I'd like to introduce you to my partner Rick.'

Rick stood up from his desk and shook hands. 'Good to meet you, Andy.'

Unfortunately, Andy wasn't looking at Rick when he shook hands, but at the view through Rick's window.

'Can't be much of a record label if you have offices in this dreadful shithole? Let's face it, you haven't even got central heating, I mean, the girls next door must be bloody freezing in winter. How d'you expect them to do any work?'

I began to see the record that was to be our passport out of debt, and my and Loveday's passport to New York, disappearing at high speed down the M40 back to Wales.

I heard Rick sniff. 'Been in the business long, Andy?'

The situation was growing worse by the second.

Then, without waiting for Andy Grave to stop shuffling his feet and reply, Rick continued: 'No, I didn't think you had or you wouldn't be making such crass remarks. As I understand it, you've been round and round the houses with this track and nobody wants it. We are in a position to release it and turn it into a hit for you. Frankly, I am amazed that you think our location or whether we have central heating have any bearing whatsoever on whether your record will be successful.'

I wasn't going to hang about to hear Grave's reply. I made some lame excuse and rushed into Chalky's old office. I missed him and was sorry that he had decided to leave a few weeks earlier. I grabbed the phone, and dialled Rick's private line. I had to stop this before it turned into a punch-up.

'Rick, it's me! I'm phoning from the other room. Call me Bjorn, or whatever you like.'

'Bjorn, make it quick, I'm in a meeting. What's the problem?'

'Listen, I know this guy is a total twat but . . .'

'You can say that again, Bjorn.'

'Look, Rick, just leave all the talking to me and bluff it out a little longer. I've got all the plans worked out on paper. They're brilliant, you'll see. But don't get into a fight with this guy, please! He's a knobhead who knows nothing. We've got to do this deal. I know this record is a hit. Talk to him about cricket or something.'

Rick by now understood the situation and had obviously decided to enjoy the game. He took a deep breath. 'Well, all right, Bjorn, I didn't realise that was the position. If you need time to pay, that's OK with me, providing you pay when you say you're going to. Oh, and thanks for the news about the cricket score. Just what we didn't need. Bye.'

As I returned to Rick's office I could hear Grave's Yorkshire origins coming to the fore. 'Cricket news?' His tone changed the minute the words were out of his mouth. 'That score wouldn't be about the Test Match would it?'

'Yes, Andy.'

Grave's arse was squirming in his chair, itching for information. 'How many wickets do we have left?'

'O-h . . .' Rick acknowledged distractedly. He was savouring every millisecond of the moment.

'So, you're a cricket fan, are you?'

'Apart from the Dogs, and selling life insurance, it's the only other thing I'm interested in,' Grave said somewhat contritely.

'Life insurance?' Rick queried as if he had just heard the word paedophilia.

'Yes, life insurance, endowments, you know. I help people get mortgages. It pays the rent,' Grave added.

Rick gave Grave's suit a long dismissive look and then decided it was time to get back to cricket.

'Are you a Yorkshire supporter by any chance?'

'Yes, I am. How did you know that?'

'Telepathy.'

He who confesses first is doomed . . .

The rest of that morning was taken up with Rick and myself nailing our man, and, in our own words, 'rising' to the occasion. Rick arranged for a contract to be drawn up at top speed and to have time reserved at the pressing plant.

'Bearing in mind the Christmas rush?' Rick said.

'Of course, I completely understand,' said Grave.

As he was about to descend the stairs, he asked, 'What *was* that cricket score?'

'Oh, didn't I tell you? England were one hundred and eighty for six at the close of play last night.'

As soon as Rick closed the door behind Grave, we both slumped to the floor, laughing our socks off.

'Well done, Tim. Brilliant team work.'

'Well done, Rick! I've never seen cricket used as a method of torture before.'

'Onwards and upwards, Tim, onwards and upwards!'

23

I was sitting, very patiently I think, in a traffic jam in the Gaulle. After much negotiation and several hefty bills, I'd managed to resurrect the dear old thing. It seemed to be shaken but not too stirred by its tête-à-tête with the bollard. I was on a slip road leading to the M40 down to Hedgerly Cross, heading to the homestead to see my father for lunch. I felt happy, trebly happy, because everything, well, most things, had been such an amazing blast.

The radio deejay gabbled out the date – 21st October – over the intro of the latest Blondie single, 'The Tide is High'. I could not believe the date nor that Blondie were having yet another hit. Time was rushing past. The good news was that we had already had three pre-release plays on the radio of 'Rhiannon's Café'.

Things were finally slotting into place. Harry had once said to me, 'This isn't a dress rehearsal, Tim,' and yet I felt that everything that had gone before was. I was praying that this was the real thing and not the other way round.

I brushed these thoughts to one side and glanced down at the Books of Lists beside me. These days it wasn't just a question of one – there had to be three: one for work, one for home, and one for ideas that were strictly confidential. It was difficult to read from them, though, because of their tendency to slide across the leather seat.

Yes, I was pleased, very pleased, with my newfound efficiency and what I liked to call my effectiveness. I stared at the miniature wooden telephone glued to the dashboard and wished I could speak to Loveday on it. I wanted to hear her voice, wanted her beside me, but she was with her parents in the country. The phone had been a present from Harry and Jessica, complete with its own miniature black curled cord. I laughed as I remembered the message that had been attached to it: 'For the man who lives and dies by the phone!'

In an American magazine I had read about how people in the not-so-distant future would really have telephones in their cars. I thought how many calls I could make while sitting in a jam like this one.

Finally, the traffic began to move. I grabbed hold of the gear stick, whacked off the brake, and pushed the accelerator hard down to the floor.

Arriving at the family seat, I revved the engine loudly in the drive, slammed the door, and saw my father's face appear at the window and jokingly scowl as usual. It all seemed to be the same as I remembered; yet it wasn't. I had moved on, but the house and all it represented had moved backwards.

I stood in the porch waiting for the door to open. There was my father, still tall but slightly stooped in his long camel overcoat, moustache, tie and V-neck sweater. He was smiling. A big gentle smile of welcome, but looking all of his seventy-one years.

'How was the journey down? Did you get snarled up at Hangar Lane?'

I mumbled a reply, shook hands and walked straight past him, down the hall into the kitchen, half-expecting someone else to be there.

A greasy mess of unwashed plates and saucepans littered every surface. Newspapers covered in dried mud from the garden, together with what looked like potato peel, stretched in a zigzag pattern across the once shining parquet floor. All the items I could remember being in their usual places were now in different places or had disappeared.

Having had a noisy pee, my father reappeared in the kitchen, all smiles, rubbing his hands together, and started to pull on his Wellington boots. After swallowing the last dregs of some coffee, we got up and walked through the stable doors, through the passageway, out on to the crazy-paving terrace, and slowly across the lawn.

'What are you carrying there?'

'Oh, I'd forgotten. It's a T-shirt for a new record we're releasing. It's a song called "Rhiannon's Café". I thought you'd like it.'

'Rhiannon? Sounds a bit foreign, doesn't it?' he said, stopping to wipe his nose with a large red handkerchief.

'Never mind, Dad,' I said looking at my wet shoes.

He started walking again. 'Is it good, then?' he said in a more positive tone.

'It's going to be a monster.'

'How do you know?'

'I just do.'

'Mmm, I see.' He paused to look up at the oak tree. 'Charles said your company didn't have much money. Don't you need money to have a monster?'

'That's how you get money, Dad. It's difficult to explain.'

'Sounds a bit odd to me.'

'Don't you want to hear it?'

'Well, that's a bit difficult out here, isn't it!' He chuckled to himself and walked down the path a few yards more before turning round to say: 'So, how are things?'

'Great, I think we've turned a corner. I think we're going to have a big hit for Christmas and a fantastic new year.'

'How's Harry these days?'

'Harry? He's heading for New York.'

'Is he? Grand old duke of York! Nice chap, bright, good bowler as well, wasn't he?'

'Yes, Dad, good at everything,' I said impatiently.

We reached the flattened bonfire and I watched my father lift the nearby wheelbarrow and tilt it so that the rainwater collected in it emptied out.

'Dad? Can we talk about something serious, please?'

'I thought we were.'

'Dad, listen, I've found this fantastic house in Chelsea that I want to buy. Without beating about the bush, I just wondered if it was possible to borrow a small amount of money, short term, you know?'

'Why on earth do you want to buy a house when you've already got a perfectly good flat to live in?'

'Dad, I'm twenty-six now. It's time to think about the future. Anyway, there's a lot of money in property.'

'Listen, Timmy, you need to concentrate on the present and not be worrying about houses and suchlike. Why are you thinking like this? Are you getting married or something? Don't you think you should wait?'

'Dad! Whoever got anywhere by waiting?'

'Come on, help me with this wheelbarrow, and let's get some onions and potatoes. Sometimes I think you live in a dream world.'

'I bet you wouldn't be saying this to Charles, would you?'

'Probably not, no, but Charles's world is a bit more, shall we say, secure than yours, and he does happen to understand about money. Pass me that fork.'

He lit the bonfire and started digging in the vegetable garden.

'Aren't you going to put on the T-shirt I brought for you?' I said. 'Go on, it'll suit you, you'll be the envy of everyone in Hedgerly Cross.'

He kept digging.

I tried again: 'Put it over your sweater, that'll stop it from getting dirty and save money on the laundry.'

The obstinate old bugger wouldn't budge but instead started waving an artichoke in my face. 'You put it on, clever clogs. Let's see you put it on.'

So I did.

The cold October wind did not take the edge off my smile or his. In a moment of perverse euphoria something made me take out my matches and cigarettes, exuberantly light two cigarettes and hand one to him. He disdainfully waved it away.

'I don't smoke any more,' he said.

I threw the spare cigarette into the bonfire and walked off, past the oak tree, across the lawn.

I was sitting in the kitchen flicking though a magazine when my father came back into the house. He picked up the pile of magazines covering a kitchen stool and put them on top of the fridge.

'Come over here, Tim, I've got something rather special on the boil.'

I bent over the cooker, lifted the lid off the saucepan and sniffed.

'Smells funny, Dad, what is it?'

'That is the best artichoke soup you are ever going to taste – well, hopefully!'

My father let out an absent-minded laugh and pulled out the second of four kitchen drawers. Like a dog pawing to find a bone, he pushed aside unwanted string, clothes pegs and various bits of paper until he found a handwritten recipe.

'Here you are, you see. She only made it for me once.'

He let out another laugh and stepped over to where I was sitting, but without taking his eyes off the recipe. He pulled up a stool and sat down.

'It was stupid, really, should never have happened.' My father was staring straight ahead, out of the steamed-up kitchen window. 'I never thought she was the hurting type. I told her – well it was a daft thing to say – I told her that her soup tasted awful, too thin, and too salty, at least I think that's what I said. I didn't mean it. It was all because we had had some silly disagreement.'

'About what?' I asked, unable to contain my curiosity.

'Oh, some nonsense, Timmy, you know.'

I didn't know, but said nothing.

'Anyway, it wasn't until I found the recipe last year and made the soup myself and realised it took hours to prepare that I began to understand.'

'Understand what?'

My father smiled briefly, and continued to look out of the window.

'I've understood a lot of things sitting here, peeling artichokes.'

Without taking his eyes from the window, save to turn and glance at the steaming saucepan, he explained how he would make this special soup every Sunday, sometimes twice a week. I put a cigarette between my lips but decided not to light it.

'Each Sunday I get up early, about six or seven, and pick the best artichokes from the bottom of the garden, put them in a wicker basket, and bring them back in here. I then sit fairly uncomfortably, on this wooden stool, still wearing this funny old coat, until I have peeled every one. They take time to peel, so you have to be prepared to spend a while.'

He got up and stirred the soup, his back towards me.

'I've never told anyone this, Timmy. Something between me and your mother, something between man and wife, none of anyone's business.'

'I understand, Dad,' I said lighting my cigarette.

He sat back down and half-grunted, half-laughed, then carried on talking as if we were speaking about some scientific experiment:

'You see, time no longer matters to me, Timmy. It doesn't matter any more whether it's day or night. More often than not this soup is ready for eating at a very odd hour. But it doesn't worry me at all. I always do the same thing these days.'

He chuckled, angling his head towards the hatch of the dining room. 'I always lay the dining-room table, set two places, and just for a bit of devilment always place the salt and pepper on the table as well, just in case.'

There was a pause as he turned and looked up briefly. Then, the man who believed he did not possess a sentimental bone in his body slowly explained how he would sit down with two full soup bowls and proceed to have a conversation with the woman he wished was still alive.

A part of me understood this perfectly. Another part wanted to get rid of my mother's clothes still hanging in the wardrobe upstairs, and not be anything like my father at all. More than anything, I wanted a drink.

Turning off the gas beneath the saucepan, my father mumbled, 'Need to pee all the time these days, bloody nuisance . . .'

While he was peeing, I sprinted into the dining room, took a slug from the bottle of Bells, poured myself a glass and quickly returned to the kitchen. Knowing I had transgressed a family code of never taking before one had asked, when my father returned, I said, 'Can I get you one, Dad?'

'No thanks and I hope you're having water with that. On second thoughts, I'll have a Double Diamond. I'll pour it myself.'

I wanted to ask him again about the possibility of a loan but could tell by the way he was sitting the likelihood was nil. He cleared his throat several times, and turned towards me.

'Talking about Mummy has made me think of your Uncle Michael,' my father said, holding up his glass of beer to the light. 'You never met him, I know. But he was someone who wouldn't wait for things, had no patience whatsoever. He once rode his horse through a shop window thinking it was a pub.'

I tried to lighten the tone.

'Dad, at least I always try to walk through pub doors first.'

'It's not that funny, Timmy,' said my father, raising his voice. He took a sip from his glass of beer.

'Mum told me stories about him years ago. A brilliant maniac! But Uncle Michael was Mum's sad elder brother, Dad, not me.'

My father stood up and wiped his mouth with the back of his hand.

'We'll talk about this another time. In the meantime, you just be careful with your drinking, please.'

On the way back to London, I took a last look at Hedgerly Cross in my rear-view mirror and felt glad that I was leaving its smallness behind. I lit a cigarette and switched on the radio hoping, really hoping, that by some divine stroke of luck 'Rhiannon's Café' would be playing. It wasn't. It was a record I had heard about, but never heard before; like a rousing hymn in a major key. Like a nursery rhyme but with grown-up words. It was fascinating. I wanted to hear it again immediately. It was called 'Stop the Cavalry'.

24

Loveday had issued an ultimatum.

'If you don't stop or cut down, I'm not hanging around any more and I mean it,' she said after a dinner at the Venezia for Harry and Jessica two nights before they left for New York.

'That's a bit rude isn't it? I mean after buying you such a lovely, a lovely . . .' I said knowing I was already pretty pissed.

'No, Tim, I'm not joking this time. You don't realise you go far too far sometimes. You just blow what everybody likes about you.'

'Oh, bollocks!'

'It's not bollocks. Jessica was very embarrassed with you putting your hands on her breasts like that, and I'm sure Harry was going to say something . . .'

'Bollocks again! Loveday, stop being so bloody conventional. Of course she didn't mind. I do know her pretty well, you know.'

I laughed, sat back, and gulped down the rest of my grappa. Loveday stared at me and sighed. She drew breath and was about to say something but changed her mind. I waved my hand at one of the waiters for the bill and turned to Loveday and smiled. 'Come on, stop getting on your high horse. Let's go home.'

'I'm not coming home with you tonight.'

I laughed and took her hand.

'Oh. Well, what about if I come home with you tonight?'

She pulled her hand away and stood up.

'Tim, I mean it. I want you to go and see someone – a doctor or someone who knows about these things. You've got to make an effort to get your health sorted out. You know what I mean.'

Frank the owner brought over Loveday's coat and held it for her as she put it on. It seemed to me that she was making a point of doing everything slowly; almost teasing me about what would happen next, about what could become a permanent gesture. I left the rest of the wine in my glass, just to show her I could, and flicked the Ronson to light a cigarette. But she went for me again.

'And cigarettes too. Don't forget the agreement?' she said tartly.

'You've got to be kidding, haven't you?'

And so I found myself standing in the grim fluorescent reality of Dr Wang's examination room.

'Ah yes, Mr Lomax, come in, please, and shut the door. Now, if you would just take your clothes off – put this towel around your waist – and lie down on the couch. Could you remind me which particular treatment you are interested in receiving? Have you undergone any major surgery recently, please?'

I stood there transfixed, momentarily caught within an enormous arclight of embarrassment.

Take all my clothes off? What, now?

I fumbled around the bottom of my sweater.

'Actually, I'm only here to give up smoking! It's just a matter of having something put into each earlobe, isn't it?'

Dr Wang stepped closer and with a utterly dispassionate look, said, 'Oh, no, Mr Lomax, the practice of Chinese medicine goes somewhat deeper than merely putting a metal stud or two in someone's ear.'

'It does?' It was as much as my chattering teeth could muster.

Judging by his young age and the inordinate number of certificates lining the walls, Dr Wang must have been a child prodigy of acupuncture and Chinese medicine. Less comforting was his chilly face, which seemed to bear an uncanny resemblance to the merciless assassin I had recently seen in a James Bond film. As a consequence, more out of cowardice than anything else, I began pulling off the sweater.

Eventually, the man I had by then christened Dr No stood back and gave his considered verdict: 'Not as bad as I thought, Mr Lomax. Eighteen needles.'

Cheeky fucker! I tried to see if he had an artificial hand.

I lay there, wincing, as Dr No painlessly stuck in his needles, trying to guess what piece of my body he was going to select next. I felt like Gulliver in Lilliput and wondered if this might all be some practical joke perpetrated by Rick and Loveday. It was not difficult to lie 'very still'. I felt quite convinced that if I moved a muscle, one of the needles would wound me fatally. Being calm, however, was going to be a challenge, especially for forty minutes.

My mind soon switched back to Neil and Dave of the Dogs. They were the most enthusiastic pair I had come across in a long time. True, they were obsessed by the Beatles – Dave even wore John Lennon glasses. Star had pointed it out first. Then, annoyingly, Rick also said they sounded too much like the Beatles, but I knew and they knew they would make it.

It had been quite a month already. Meetings. Meetings. Meetings. My days seemed to consist of nothing else. Meetings about sleeves, meetings about adverts, meetings about pluggers, agents, publicity, distribution, why is this and why is that, and in the end meetings about having meetings. I was thinking about changing my middle name to Meeting, I had had so many. Loveday was so pissed off at never getting through to me that even she had said she wanted to have a meeting. Star and Susie didn't bother trying to put any calls through. They just said automatically, 'Sorry, he's in a meeting.'

But I loved every minute of it. We were getting somewhere at last. The Dogs had now been added to every play-list in the country save the national one, and things were really beginning to cook. Yes, there were problems with the distribution, but I was dealing with that.

Or, rather, I would be dealing with that as soon as possible.

Our problems were simple: we were under-capitalised; we needed something big.

All year Rick had been doing a valiant job of keeping the creditors at bay. He was the one who had put up with my gloom, my lack of faith, my outbursts, my unreliability. Now it was my turn to hold the fort, stop the breach, stem the flow, my turn to pick up the ball and run and run and run. But we needed extra ammunition. Up until now we'd been playing with rifles; what we really needed was one, huge fuck-off cannon.

Six forty-five, and still another half hour to go. I looked up at the one-bar electric heater mounted high on the wall above the couch. I lifted my head further and stared down at my stomach and legs and the network of needles resting there. I felt the long paper towel beneath me sticking to my sweating back and concluded that whatever way I looked at it, I was trapped. I lay back and told myself to be still, to try to breathe as deeply as I could. My mind began wandering down a corridor of 007, Spectre and Smersh.

They wouldn't be messing about trying to find the money for this or the money for that. They would have captured a nuclear missile by now. Or taken all the gold out of Fort Knox. They would have had a Big Idea.

The idea came into my head like a thunderbolt – except there was no flash, no fanfare. It was like discovering that the old green vase you had looked at every week in the cupboard underneath the kitchen sink was made of solid gold. It was so simple! Staring at me, right in front of my eyes.

It must have been the conversation with Tom Biffin at the BBC about the Dogs that had caused it. Every week since February 1968 there had been a live concert recorded and transmitted by the BBC featuring the top band of the day. Every group wanted to perform in front of the invited audience, mainly because it meant great exposure but also because the recording facilities were unusually good. The concert was usually transmitted two weeks later, and then the highlights transmitted again at the end of that year. After that the tape was filed away deep within the BBC vaults.

It didn't take long before I had made a mental list of exactly how many fantastic groups had performed on that radio programme: the

Rolling Stones, Led Zeppelin, Jimi Hendrix, Free, the Faces, even the Ox, and Quantum Frog. Now, if you were a fan of any of these groups, it would be extremely important to you to own every single recording the group had ever made. Just think how many fans there are around the world of people like Pink Floyd or Jimi Hendrix – millions! Now, imagine if all those tapes sitting there in the vaults were released on a label called, say, Dead Octopus or Fish Farm, and the groups were paid their royalty, their record company their cut, and the BBC too – well, everybody would be better off! Plus, there would still be an enormous amount of money left over to go straight into the pockets of Rick and myself, not to mention saving Delta from its watery grave. No recording costs but a guarantee of sales from bands with a proven track record. You could build a series and keep releasing records, virtually for as long as you wanted to.

This was my huge fuck-off cannon; this was the thing that would make everything possible.

I was halfway through designing the first six record sleeves and wondering who would write the sleeve notes, when the door opened and Dr No glided in. He looked a trifle anxious. I lifted my head up and leaned on my elbow to greet him.

'Don't look so worried Dr Wang. I feel ten times better already.'

25

I was a big-game fisherman, strapped into a chair, with the rod screwed into my harness and bending so much I thought it might snap. And other than some sage advice from an experienced angler such as Simon Caplow, I wanted to land this fish all on my own. Then I would share it.

I said nothing to Rick.

Prior to meeting the big-wigs at the BBC, I telephoned Tom Biffin, the producer of the Concert radio show, for his advice. He warned me that releasing the Concert series was not something I should undertake lightly. He went on to talk about how the only people who had attempted it before had failed, because in his view there was a curse like Tutankhamun's, preventing the concerts from ever leaving the BBC vaults. I laughed this off, thinking Biffin was winding me up. I thanked him profusely for his help, offered him the incognito job of writing sleeve notes for the series when it happened, and ended the call by making an impassioned plea for more exposure on the Dogs.

The meeting at the BBC went well. It was very businesslike, with the two men from management unemotionally declaring that they still reserved the right to release the Concert series on the BBC's own record label. However, they were interested in listening to my proposals. I had expected a meeting where I could enthuse and waffle for a while, rather than having to say anything concrete. I needed to open and shut my briefcase several times before I plucked the lowest figures from my head, held my breath and proposed an outline of a deal. Much to my surprise, the two men barely hesitated before saying they thought it was a very reasonable offer. Then, as one made notes, the other repeated what I had said.

'So, you want to license thirty-six concerts over a three-year period, and you are offering two thousand pounds per concert and a three per cent royalty as an override to us.'

A quick qualification then followed. 'All of this, Mr Lomax, is subject to you satisfying us about your ability to secure the clearances from the relevant parties and, of course, our finance people must be satisfied about Delta's and its directors' credit-worthiness.'

I gave them a knowing nod and concentrated hard on preventing the butter in my mouth from melting. After some innocent enquiries about dates of concerts and a rough timetable of my plans, I succeeded in persuading them to issue a letter outlining the agreement.

Simon Caplow initially sat well back in his chair behind his desk, creating a fog between us with his pipe.

Instead of explaining why I had never followed up his offer of running the studio, I handed over the BBC letter and the list of artists, and then rattled on about the enormous potential of the Concert series.

Caplow read the list, smoke circling above his head.

I stopped talking.

Nothing.

Did he understand or, worse, was he thinking that the idea was more suited to *his* company?

The reply, when it finally came, was to the point, carefully considered and calmly delivered.

'The first thing is to keep absolutely quiet about the idea and not tell anyone else in case they steal it,' Caplow said, pausing to strike a match. I moved to the edge of my seat, nodding in agreement.

Caplow leant forwards, holding the pipe in his mouth with his right hand and pulling at the folds of skin in his neck with his left.

'As much as I don't wish to make that head of yours any bigger –' He paused, tapping down the ash in his pipe with his finger. 'This is one of the best ideas I've heard in years. It's so commercial I can't understand why it hasn't been done before. It's brilliant; it's the biggest thing you'll ever do. If you play your cards right, this will make a lot of money and I mean a lot.'

My feet were now twelve inches from the floor. 'Thank you very much,' I said, genuinely embarrassed by the praise. I was about to say thank you again when Caplow raised his hand in a businesslike way and asked: 'Who are you going to do this with?'

'Rick.'

'Is that what you really want?'

I shrugged an 'of course shrug' and grinned expectantly.

Another pause and another puff. 'So be it'.

I watched as he turned the cover of what looked like a school exercise book and scribbled down a note. He leant back hard in his high-backed leather chair, chuckled and raised his eyes. 'What a funny thing life is. One minute you're totally down and then the next you're up there on the ceiling. Extraordinary.'

'I guess so,' I said feeling like Mr Humble all of a sudden.

Caplow leant forward again and put his hands together. 'Is there anything I can do to help get you going?'

I felt like a kid being asked exactly what he wanted for Christmas by someone who could buy him anything. I also knew that Caplow meant exactly what he said. So, when I requested whether it would be possible to have a letter confirming that SCG would grant me the rights to concerts recorded by Joe Cocker, T. Rex, Thin Lizzy and Quantum Frog, the answer was immediate and affirmative.

To show further solidarity, Caplow calmly dictated a letter confirming the arrangement and handed me back the list of concerts as if nothing had happened. I sat there, virtually speechless with gratitude, until he suddenly appeared to change his mind.

'On second thoughts,' he said, 'maybe for your sake it's better for me not to write the letter to you at Delta. Maybe you should think this through some more. I'm not saying that you shouldn't do this with Rick, but maybe you should set up a separate company. After all, you don't want to be dragged down by any debts that Delta may have and, also, this is all your idea, isn't it? Think about it over the weekend and let me know how you want the letter addressed. Put yourself in a strong position first, that's always the thing.'

I hailed a shiny black taxi for the ride back to Delta, knowing it was going to take all the cash in my wallet. What the hell, I thought.

I sat back as the cab bounced over the potholes.

It would be a good idea to keep matters under wraps for the moment. It would make sense to stand well back.

In fact, it would only be safe to put the BBC idea into a company free and clear of Delta.

26

Something was wrong with the sales of the Dogs' record: there weren't any. Already 'Rhiannon's Café' had been played twelve times on national radio, not counting being played to death by every regional radio station as well. Something should be happening out there, but it wasn't. Something was wrong. I knew this and didn't need to have it pointed out seven times a day by the likes of Andy Grave.

'How is the band ever going to get into the charts if you can't even get the bloody records into the shops? I knew we shouldn't have signed with you lot,' was the gist of his daily whinge. If I hadn't decided to use him to help me get a mortgage, I would have throttled him long ago. Even Rick had begun to get pissed off.

'You're the expert, Tim: what should we do?'

Maybe other small labels were experiencing similar problems. I studied my list of names, chose the least important one, took a deep breath, and made the call. It was Fred Canter, of Blue Vista, a label specialising in blues recordings that had been afloat for twenty years despite its unfashionable Midlands location, was well respected.

'Thank God you've made this call, Tim! Listen, there are six of us and we do nothing but talk about this very problem on the phone each week.'

'You do?'

'Oh, yes, it's hit an all-time low. What happens when your record is being played to death on the air, but isn't in the shops . . .'

'Exactly,' I said, dragging hard on my cigar.

'I'm not going to name any names, OK?' Fred said in a conspiratorial tone, 'but the situation is out of control. One of the biggest companies, ironically with six brand-new entries in this week's Top Fifty, is sending its reps to all the chart shops not just with a box of free singles of the track they're pushing, but also a box of free albums. Do you get it? They go in and say hello Mr Chart Shop, here is a lovely free box of our new record by the Hopelessly Unknowns; and, oh, by the way, here is a box of free top-selling albums as well.'

'So the chart-shop man feels sexed-up to help the new single on its way.'

'Precisely, Tim! Meanwhile, the likes of us little independents are struggling, and scratching our heads wondering why these shops are not ordering our records.'

'Jesus Christ, that's bloody outrageous!'

'Too right, Tim, but who's going to do anything about it?'

'Well, I bloody will for a start.'

Something about Fred's defeatist tone got my blood boiling. Someone needed to stand up and be counted. Time to summon up Brando, Steiger and Napoleon.

At the end of the working day, I sat back, put my feet on the desk, lit a cigar, and started thinking. What with the news from Simon Caplow and everything else, this was becoming exciting. Moreover, there was another major turn-up for the books: three telephone messages from Shamus Slime at OTE desperate to license the Dogs' record. Huh! I knew exactly what I was going to say to him: *Sorry to piss on your strawberries, Shamus.* Perhaps the moment had come to get lawyers involved with this and the BBC thing too. I knew only two. One was Johnny Darrell and the other was Abe Aberman. I made a note to go and see Johnny Darrell. Abe was in America and America was going to feature strongly in my plans.

I stood up and peered through the hatch. Rick was leaning back in his chair, reading. I sensed that once again he was getting pissed off with me, so I thought I would clear the air. Maybe this would be a good time to tell him about the possibility of the BBC idea.

'What's that you're reading, Rick, anything good?'

Lowering the piece of paper, Rick looked round at me with an ugly smirk on his face.

'It's the bank statement for October, if you really want to know.'

Perhaps not. 'What's our position at the moment?'

'Bad. What do you think?'

I returned Rick's smirk, trying hard to suppress my sarcasm.

'How bad? Quite bad, a bit bad or very bad?'

'Tim, you've never shown any interest in this subject before.'

'Well it's probably a good time to start. What about the annual accounts, got a copy I could see?'

Rick leant forward, took off his glasses, and stared at me replying tersely: 'Look, this is *my* area. You do what you do and I'll do what I do, OK?'

'Rick, cool it! Don't be so defensive, I'm only asking.'

He almost jumped out of his chair. 'Would you please stop smoking those fucking cigars in the office. I thought you'd given up. What's got into you? Why don't you go and get organised for the meeting with Ted Powell at Columbus. In case you'd forgotten, Powell is big and someone who could easily take us out of this shit. Got the picture?'

I leaned further through the hatch, took the cigar out of my mouth and smiled, 'What's got into you lately? For God's sake, Rick, keep your fucking hair on!'

So much for clearing the air. I let out a puff of smoke and closed the hatch behind me. Then I made the appointment with Johnny Darrell.

Ted Powell welcomed us to his twelfth-floor office with what Rick told me was a warmth normally reserved for big shots.

'Hey, it's the guys from Delta! Come on in.'

Powell, physically speaking, looked like a Californian cliché, tall, tanned, blue-eyed and blond-haired, appearing ten years younger than his forty-five years. His office was spacious, its floor and walls covered in white shag-pile carpet. Overlooking the tree tops of Soho Square, it contained the obligatory glass coffee table, armchairs, swanky speakers and stereo, and, most unusually, an Afghan hound lying on the carpet and licking its paws.

'Don't mind Charlie, will you? He spends most of his time asleep,' Powell drawled, patting the dog as he went to sit behind his desk.

Powell had a reputation for supporting new ideas and was someone who liked to be seen as the saviour of maverick talent. Rick kicked off by deliberately talking up his and my track record in finding talent.

'Had we had another company with backing, even in some small way, we would have kept B Square. No reason why it can't happen again.'

'No reason at all, Rick,' Powell said nodding his head.

The meeting continued to go well for another five minutes with a game of conversational ping-pong between Powell and Rick. Throughout this time I had been content to keep lifting my foot on and off the dog's curly tail, if anything a little bored with the conversation. However, once Rick started talking about the Dogs, and the distribution difficulties we were experiencing with 'Rhiannon's Café', I sat up straight, interrupted him by loudly clearing my throat and took charge of the conversation.

'Ted, what does Columbus do about getting records into chart shops?'

Ted maintained an unconvincing toothy smile.

'I'm not quite clear on what you mean. Eh, Tim?'

Putting my elbow down on the desk, I said. 'Oh, come on, Ted, you're all at it, aren't you?'

'At what, exactly?'

'You know, massaging the charts with free gifts and things.'

Ted looked hurt. 'I hope you're not suggesting . . .'

'He's not suggesting anything of the sort, are you, Tim?' Rick interrupted quickly.

I sat back in my chair. 'I am not suggesting it's you doing this, personally.'

Ted's smile had disappeared. 'What did you say?'

'Doesn't matter, Ted. It was a joke.'

'Tim's been working too many late nights in the studio, haven't you, Tim?' Rick said, pushing the heel of his shoe down hard on my foot.

'Ted, I hope I haven't embarrassed you? I can see you're a good bloke even if you do come from LA! Do you know what I mean?'

'I'm not sure that I do. Would you mind if we finish this another time?'

The pair of us walked out of the Columbus building.

'I am cringing at your over-familiarity and lack of respect . . .'

'I just told him the truth. What's so wrong with that?'

Rick sighed a sigh for England, Wales and Scotland and went silent on me.

Well, I wasn't going to bow down and take any blame. I lit a cigar.

Rick sucked his teeth angrily and turned to me, saying, 'You completely fucked that up.'

'Fucked what up?'

'You're drunk, that's what.'

'Whatever are you on about? That arsehole back there?'

'That arsehole back there could have given us a lot of money, could have saved our bacon. *Could* have.'

I wasn't going to put up with this sort of accusation.

'Bollocks! He was only going through the motions. I felt like I was back at school or going for a job interview. Give me a break! Who does he think he is? He was just fishing for information, that's all. All of these guys are just looking to line their own pockets. The only way we're ever going to get a great deal from one of those arseholes is to already have a hit record or hit act. You know it. You said so yourself. If we're that desperate for money, I'll go off and find it myself.'

December 1980 – Part I

27

'So this is what they mean by jet lag,' Loveday whispered out loud to herself, thinking I was fast asleep. She swung her legs out and sat on the edge of the bed. Then, as if she was about to gargle she tilted her head back and inhaled, licking her lips to see whether the air in Harry and Jessica's New York apartment smelled any different to that in her flat in London. She then let out a squeaky yawn and stretched her arms above her head into an A, making her T-shirt rise up over her white embroidered knickers. It was a perfect voyeuristic thrill.

I was feeling rather pleased with myself. I'd managed to get away from the sniping going on in the office in London and had had combined a holiday and a business trip that would keep Loveday happy for years. Rick had seemed gobsmacked when I told him I was off to visit Harry, but perhaps quietly relieved too.

Anyway, I had my own plans for dealing with that situation.

I closed my eyes and smiled ruefully at what Loveday had said before going to sleep: 'Tomorrow, Tim, is going to be a day spent doing something, seeing Manhattan, not drinking, not arguing, but doing what two normal people do. This is supposed to be my holiday, my Christmas present. Remember?'

Now I opened one eye and flipped over, slipping my hand under her T-shirt.

'I s-a-y, Loveday,' I purred, 'you're not wearing a bra.'

Ten gymnastic minutes later the pair of us were lying entwined and still panting on the carpet. For some reason best known to herself, Loveday had insisted on making love on the floor. She had enjoyed it, she said, but was not prepared to let the day go to waste. I wasn't worried about the day; I was worried about getting my breath back and the carpet-burn.

'Come on, Tim. Come on, Tiger, get up!'

Five minutes later I was standing within a cloud of steam and guiding the powerful jets of water over my body when I heard a voice outside the glass shower door.

'Can you hear me in there?'

Was there no peace? Was nothing sacred? Could a chap not have a shower on his own any more?

'Go away, will you? Go away! This is a totally private experience,' I shouted back.

Loveday opened the door. 'Oh, my God, I don't believe it! You're smoking! How can you have a cigarette when you're in the shower? Is there no time when you don't have a cigarette? For God's sake!'

And she slammed the shower door shut.

But half an hour later, Loveday was all smiles again as we listened to Harry pontificate about the timetable for the next forty-eight hours as if he were fine-tuning the last details of a bank raid. Finally, after jokes about synchronising watches and the need to stay in radio contact at all times, we put on several layers of warm clothing, took the elevator together and then said goodbye on the pavement outside.

Curiously, the one non-negotiable item on Loveday's list was St Patrick's Cathedral. For Loveday, churches were where you went at Christmas, were christened, got married, and finally were dispatched in an attractive wooden box. She had never embraced religion with more than a polite handshake, and while God certainly existed for her, he was mostly relegated to a quiet corner of her mind. Nevertheless, as we walked into St Patrick's, bowing her head in some auto-reverential reflex, she recounted her favourite phrase in a strong Belfast accent: 'You can take the man out of a Catholic, but you cannot take the Catholic out of a man!'

Once inside, she was smitten. 'Oh, my God, Tim, it's absolutely beautiful.'

She was transformed into a little child in some architectural heaven and wandered off, her mouth half-open, her head back, marvelling at the interior. The fact that there was no organ recital in progress playing that Bach Toccata only added to her joy.

The faint but unmistakable smell of incense reminded me of the gas the dentist used to give me when I was a child. Scattered like pieces on a draughtboard, people were kneeling and praying within the rows and rows of seats. I walked into the small Lady Chapel, its polished hardwood floors illuminated by candlelight. A woman was kneeling in a single mahogany prayer stall positioned two or three feet from a padlocked donation box and a set of raised tiers of flickering nightlights.

I wondered for a second if I should push some money in the box and light a candle.

Don't be superstitious.

But I did it all the same.

The woman was in her forties, wearing a veil, black gloves and a black coat, and was looking up at a statue of the Virgin Mary while feeding the beads of a rosary through her fingers. I stood for a few seconds with my hands clasped in front of me. Then, compelled by some strange force, I stepped back two paces so that I was behind her and allowed my eyes to linger on her bare legs. The coat she was wearing was short, and rested at the back of her knees like a curtain. Her legs were not fat but rounded and a light tanned peach-colour, with narrow ankles inside elegant patent leather shoes. I stood closer, far closer than I knew I should, and began bending down as if to pray. I could hear the whisper of her prayers. My breathing was getting faster, my mouth becoming drier. I stared at the coal-coloured hem of her coat, urging it up, urging it to lift itself up so that I could see, so that I could press my face against her flesh, so that I could put my hand between her legs. An argument raged in my head about the difference between aesthetics and uncontrollable lust, when I noticed what I thought was a price tag on the soles of the woman's shoes. I shut down the argument, peered closer, and saw a white peel-off label saying: *Sale $18*. I rocked back on my haunches, scowling. *This sort of woman shouldn't be wearing cheap shoes*, I said to myself.

'Why not?' I queried out loud.

Because that's what your mother did all her life, said another voice in my head.

I stood up too quickly and cleared my throat.

The woman stopped praying, turned round and lifted her veil. She had full lips and a strong Slavic face, no make-up and a look about her that said she was tired of crying and tired of being tired. She opened her mouth as if to issue a reprimand, but initially none came. I said nothing but stepped back two paces with my eyes lowered and the palms of my hands held up in apology.

The woman then spoke, slowly, and with an educated French accent: 'Would you leave me alone? Please?'

I said nothing, but walked away, my cheeks glowing with shame and embarrassment. I carried on walking, glancing twice over my shoulder, until I had left the Lady Chapel, well down the side wall of the church. I began counting the Stations of the Cross mounted on the walls. I was desperate for ways in which I could distract myself from what had happened.

I was sailing too close to the wind.

I found myself staring at the Thirteenth Station: Jesus with a golden halo and red wounds in his side, feet and hands. I stopped and squinted to read what the station said: 'The body of Jesus is taken from the cross and laid into Mary's bosom.'

I was going to be sick. It was as if someone had kicked me hard on my mental coccyx and let in a flood of painful thoughts: Mary Lomax, my mother, at her own funeral, getting out of her coffin and dancing down the Lower Hades Road; unclimbable staircases; an allotment; a snarling Rick; a sobbing Loveday; and, in the background, echoes of standing too near the edge of a platform.

Blinking into the sunlight on the steps outside, Loveday threaded her arm through mine. 'Tim? You look terribly pale. Come on, I'm going to buy you an enormous doughnut. That was a beautiful place, but what a bloody awful smell.'

28

The Badsoul receptionist rested her breasts on her typewriter and said in a low voice: 'Oh, Mr Lomax? I'm sorry, but Mr Glarusso is going to be two or three minutes. I hope you don't mind waiting?'

I was mesmerised by her honey-tongued voice and the sight of the two swollen mounds in her black polo-neck sweater. I managed a choked smile and nodded. Picking up a trade magazine as cover, I ran my finger slowly down the top fifty of the R'n'B charts, and then the soul charts, and then the pop charts and lost count after eighteen Badsoul chart positions. After another gawk at the sweater, I turned the page to see a large photograph of a man in a dinner-jacket accepting an award. Mr Garcia himself, the King of Badsoul. I had met Ben Glarusso only in hotel lobbies and over lunch tables at international conventions and had always understood from him that they were successful, but I hadn't quite understood just *how* successful. Jesus, this is serious! I had always liked Ben, but, in the new world of now is now, I was forced to admit that he was now a Number Two. The hand I needed to shake belonged to Mr Garcia.

Twenty minutes later Ben's smart but balding bulk was sitting politely opposite me in an Italian restaurant full of pink tablecloths and anxious-looking waiters. After the usual comments about London and New York, and gossip about a deal that had nearly happened, we hit a lull. Ben stared briefly at the tablecloth for inspiration and was relieved when the waiter arrived with two plates of food. We sat awkwardly until we'd been served and then, somewhat over-enthusiastically, picked up our cutlery and began eating.

Eventually, the conversation swung back to business and I began a lengthy monologue about the ins and outs of being a small fish in a big pond and vice versa, concluding that, although small was indeed beautiful, a big cash supply was the secret. Ben seemed to follow my train of thought with difficulty, but carried on making a series of polite nods and grunts. My brain was obviously working too quickly for him, that's all there was to it. Eventually I got to the point I had been wanting to make since reading the sales charts in Badsoul's.

'Ben, I want to meet your boss.'

He looked shocked.

'You what? You must be kidding!'

'No, Ben, I'm not. I've got a really serious proposition that could be worth hundreds and hundreds of thousands of dollars, and it could benefit you and your company in a big way.'

'Tim, you don't meet with Garcia, he meets with you.'

I took off my jacket, lit a cigarette and patiently explained, without seeming to take breath, the intricacies of the BBC's Concert series. I summed up by reeling off a list of famous groups from the late sixties right up to the present day. In the end, I leaned forwards and raised my glass to Ben's slightly confused-looking face: 'Brilliant, isn't it?'

Ben was silent for a moment.

'Well, great, if you can pull it off . . . sounds like a lot of work to me.'

Clearly, I was not dealing with a Number One.

'Ben, all I want is five minutes.'

He took a deep breath. 'I'll see what I can do.'

Five minutes later we were in his office.

'Just pretend you're not here,' Ben said. 'I'll put this on the speaker phone. And don't, whatever you do, say anything. OK?'

'Thanks, Ben, you're great. Please don't forget how confidential this is.'

Ben took another deep breath as he got through to the president's office.

'Sorry to interrupt you, sir, but I've got an English guy in town, Tim Lomax. We've done quite a lot of business with him in the past, and he says he needs to see you urgently.'

There was a split-second delay and then I heard a disembodied voice, belonging to someone with a large amount of gravel stuck in his oesophagus.

'If it's any more of that British disco shit, I'm not interested.'

'No, it's something to do with the rights to a radio concert series in England. It's extremely confidential. To be honest, I don't know, but it does sound real interesting.'

'How well do you know this guy?'

'Pretty well, and there are other people interested.'

'It better be good. Two o'clock tomorrow. That's the only time I've got.'

Ben sighed with relief as he put the phone down.

'Tim,' he said, 'this better be good.'

Fuelled by my success in securing a meeting with Mr Big, I spent the next two hours in Tower Rock buying every album I had always wanted to own. Harry and Jessica were leaving for London early the next morning and had suggested a farewell supper at home. It was a big pain: Harry had been ordered back to London to attend an emergency meeting on some oil crisis, so he and Jessica had decided to use it as an opportunity to have last-minute tests done on her and the new baby. I took a cab back to their Mulberry Street apartment and on the way picked up a bunch of tiger lilies for Loveday and a case of champagne for Harry and Jessica. I toyed with the idea of calling Rick, but something held me back.

By half-past eight that evening the apartment was hosting an orgy of eating, dancing, smoking and drinking. Tinfoil trays from the local Chinese takeaway lay messily on the kitchen table. Harry's prized copy of the Stones' *Let It Bleed* was pumping out full blast from the sitting-room. By a quarter to ten, even Jessica was singing and dancing, with an unlit cigarette dangling from her lips.

As the drink kicked in still further, Harry and I began dancing unselfconsciously, soon followed by Jessica and Loveday holding and touching each other and swaying perfectly in time. Later, after a successful series of hand signals, Loveday and myself were dancing alone and holding each other close. In those minutes time stood still. It was odd, but I felt able to dance as I had never done before – no unevenness, no selfconscious wish to draw away. Loveday said to me later it was a moment she had only heard people talk about; a moment when you know, a moment of absolute certainty about someone, a feeling of being complete.

Harry and Jessica sat at the table, exhausted but mesmerised, watching us dance. I think they too sensed that this was a major time of change, of things turning a corner into something profoundly good.

The record on the turntable came to an end, and Loveday and I stood, smiling, foreheads lightly resting against each other. I was about to whisper something into Loveday's ear when the metallic bell of the telephone cut in and made us all jump.

The telephone call was for Harry.

A moment later, after a rapid stumbled conversation, he put down the phone and turned round. His face was ashen.

'Jeesus Christ! John Lennon's just been shot.'

29

I lay very still and focused my eyes on the thin red line of the digital alarm clock beside me: 6.29 a.m.

The sombre nasal drone of the newscaster's voice would not stop reverberating in my head: 'John Lennon was shot dead tonight outside his apartment building in Manhattan, at approximately 9.20 local time.'

I had heard Harry and Jessica leave five minutes earlier and wondered if Harry would make it to the airport without throwing up. The two of us had stayed up drinking until half-past two, standing by the television and solemnly toasting it like some coffin at a wake. I didn't want to get up and say goodbye and had pretended to be asleep. In fact, I was uncertain whether I had actually been to sleep at all but knew it was time to move. I edged my legs out from under the duvet and swung my feet on to the floor.

'Fucking hell!' I shuddered as the cold air swept up my legs. Loveday stirred. I took an immense breath as if I was about to dive underwater, and heaved myself out of bed, in the process kicking over the pint of water Loveday had left out for me. I pulled on my clothes, turned to look back at Loveday, blew her a kiss and headed for the front door.

As I stepped out of the building, the sky seemed badly bruised but was shedding light. My tongue felt double-coated and my heart was beating too fast. The gutters were full and rainwater gushed into overflowing drains. I inhaled the damp air, and convinced myself it smelled of cordite. I turned on to Mott Street and hesitated. It was cold, bloody cold.

It wasn't cold back up there with Loveday. *You're still pissed, just turn round and go back.*

I pondered my options and decided to carry on.

In the eerie silence, a blue-and-white police car sped past, its roof lights flashing but its siren strangely mute. I decided to follow it. Both sides of the street were deserted. I pressed on, walking faster to beat the cold, block after block.

A cab appeared, travelling so slowly I thought it was either kerb-crawling or about to run out of petrol. I stood in the middle of the road flapping my arms about until it stopped.

'The Dakota, please.'

'West Highway or Sixth?'

'Don't care – whichever is quickest.'

The cab-driver grunted belligerently, turned his wheel towards Sixth, and accelerated.

A small army of policemen in thick leather coats was standing in pairs beside makeshift blue-and-white barriers. The early-morning mist and shuttered light only enhanced the funereal atmosphere. Several solitary young men stood by the police barriers looking towards the main gates of the building. Nearer the gates, groups of teenage girls were standing, shivering and looking pale. Altogether, I thought, there must be around two to three hundred people here, some singing, some silent. Several camera crews were simultaneously filming their reports and politely ignoring each other. Everyone but the camera crews and police seemed to have, or be sharing, a candle. Two Japanese girls were sitting on the edge of the sidewalk, crying quietly on to each other's shoulders. As my eyes circled the crowd I saw a man in a Spiderman T-shirt vomit into the gutter. A red-haired girl of about sixteen was hoisted up into the air by two friends to take flash photographs, lighting up the dawn with a blinking neon glow. A smart-looking woman in her sixties stood disdainfully to one side, her arms folded across her chest. I stared at her expressionless face, and the cat she was clutching reminded me of Ned back home.

Just as I was passing behind the throng, two people in the middle of the crowd started singing, passionately but out of tune, 'John is gone, John is gone, but John is not forgotten'. A group of serious young men at the front of the crowd then turned around and shouted at them hysterically: 'Shut up! Stop! Stop that!'

Instantly, the rest of the crowd joined in. A tired-looking policeman picked up a megaphone; another stepped forward pressing his baton against the front of his shoulder. It was like being at a party that was about to get out of control. Sensing danger, I walked away, then broke into a trot.

At the entrance to Central Park I stopped and drew breath. I looked back at the Dakota building to see if a fight was breaking out.

I needed to know exactly what was going on. Was there blood on the pavement? Was there a chalk outline of the body? Had it really been John Lennon?

I walked a hundred yards into the park and stopped under a large dripping chestnut tree. I put my hands on the rough wet bark of a low branch, hoisted myself up, and began my ascent. It was slippery but climbable. About seven feet above the ground, I stopped, convinced I had heard a voice.

'Hey man, what ya doin'? I said, what ya doing in my tree, man?'

I froze. A park attendant? A policeman? A nutter?

I cleared my throat loudly and pulled myself up another foot. I felt my hands slipping. The voice came from below again.

'Are ya deaf? I said, whadya doin' in ma tree?'

I saw a grubby, bearded face with a woollen hat staring up at me. I couldn't be precise about his age, but I knew a nutter when I saw one. I opted to be ultra-polite:

'I'm sorry, I didn't realise this was your tree. No offence.'

'Don't jive with me, man. Whadya doin' in my fuckin' tree?' The tone and volume were getting worse.

'I was just trying to get a better view of the Dakota. You know John Lennon's been shot, don't you?'

'You pissing me off, man. I don't like people like you. John Lennon's a friend of mine. A real friend. He woulda told me first if he'd been shot.'

The man was dribbling as he spoke.

I began to slip back down until I was perilously close to grabbing distance.

'OK. OK. Hang on, I'll come down. You can get back in your tree.'

I let go of the wet branch, and with a thud dropped to my feet. Immediately, the man stepped in front of me and put his face two inches away from mine. The upper left half of his forehead appeared to be missing.

'Hi!' I said, shaking like a leaf.

'Who the fuck are you? John never mentioned anyone coming to ma tree. Fuck it, man, I'm outta ma tree for one night and some mugger shit like you just blows in, yes sir, no sir, three bags full, sir!'

The man sounded like a machine gun.

'Hey, hey, keep it cool, man! I'm John's friend as well.'

'John's friend? Oh, yeah, well, fuck you, man, fuck you and yo mother because I'm really, really pissed about this.'

'Look, I didn't realise, I'm sorry but, you know . . .'

'I know? I know what? I know you been in ma tree that's what, and I ain't shitting it! D'you know who ya dealing with, huh? I done 'Nam, man – if you was there for the time I was, you learn to respect other people's shit, man. If you don't, then you get fucking hurt, dig?'

'Absolutely. I completely understand.'

'Ever seen a body bag? Ever been inside one? Eh?'

'Look, I've got the message, I'm going.'

'Plenty of body bags around, man, and I'm telling you, if I ever catch you in ma tree again, you goin' be in one faster than you can say Jack Shit! Now, hand over some fuckin' money, ya hear?'

My wallet contained only a $20 note. He wasn't having that. I grabbed a handful of quarters from my trouser pocket. I had to get away. The man took an unsteady couple of paces backwards and I seized the moment. Throwing the change against the tree trunk, I ran off wildly along the slippery grass towards the path, retching as I ran. I turned to look back, hoping to see the man picking up the coins. Instead, he was right behind me.

He chased me across the park, mostly in diagonal criss-crosses, for the best part of fifteen minutes. Those fifteen minutes felt like fifteen hours, and even after I saw the crazy man eventually give up and dance his way back to his tree, I remained crouched behind the park bench where I was hiding, paralysed with fear.

After an eternity, I walked briskly back towards the main concrete path leading away from the Dakota to the other side of the park. My heels clicked loudly on the concrete. I kept speeding up and slowing down, desperately reassuring myself that the person I could hear behind me was just the sound of my own shoes. Eventually I slowed down for good and commenced an out-of-breath tirade against myself for having left the bed, the warmth, Loveday, the apartment and, finally, for ever having left London in the first place.

Cold sweat dripping down my back, I parted the branches of the tall privet hedge in front of me and, to my great surprise, saw the head of a chestnut-coloured horse, standing outside the main entrance to the Plaza hotel.

I quickly pushed myself backwards through the hedge, ignoring the branches scraping the sides of my head, and emerged on the sidewalk. I walked over and stroked the white forehead of the impassive horse, promising it faithfully that I would return with some sugar.

30

I had been told that the great man Garcia would not keep me waiting more than two minutes. I sat looking at the multitude of gold and silver disks adorning the walls, beside the numerous black-and-white portraits of Mr Garcia shaking hands with unfortunate children or grinning, singers. The only thing that was missing was a series of souvenir dinner plates with Mr Garcia's cheesy photograph on them. Two purple Chesterfield sofas still covered in protective plastic made an L-shape in the corner of the room and for some reason reminded me of two boxers wearing badly fitting suits. Were Shamus Slime and Joe Garcia related in some way, I wondered?

Feeling bold, I got up to have a closer look at another wall, full of framed certificates testifying to the numerous good works that Mr Garcia had undertaken in various boroughs of New York. Peering like a schoolboy behind his desk, I also spotted two small television monitors and to my amusement realised that they were linked to the reception area I had sat in the previous day. I was hoping the camera would focus on the twin peaks of the receptionist but someone was coming, so I scuttled back to my seat.

The short but squat figure of Mr Garcia came bounding into the office, accompanied by Ben. He waved at my outstretched hand, leaned back into his high-backed leather chair, and planted his short legs halfway across the desk. As he began talking, he opened a large silver cigar box, took out a cigar, pierced it and stuck it in his mouth.

'Great to meet you, Timothy. How long are you in town? What's up? Ben tells me you got a hot property, so shoot.'

I was not sure whether to be impressed or insulted by this bullshit. However, I began to explain my plan of attack, ensuring that my

157

salesmanship was operating at maximum strength. After the initial pitch, Garcia took hold of the list of possible concerts and artists that I had been waving around.

'Jesus, this has got The Who, Led Zep, the Moodies, Hendrix . . . The only thing missing, for chrissakes, is the goddam Beatles! Can you really deliver these?' he said, leaning forwards and offering his cigar box.

I blocked the offer with the palm of my hand and calmly took a Marlboro from my packet. After an expertly-timed pause, I continued, 'Look at this letter, it's from Simon Caplow', and laid it on the desk.

'Yeah, I know Simon,' said the president doubtfully, 'and he's one tough sonovabitch. And he's given you Cocker . . . well!'

I leaned forwards again, resting both forearms on the desk for emphasis.

'Mr Garcia, you're a good businessman, and, as we say in London, you know the price of eggs. I have an agreement with the British Broadcasting Corporation for thirty-six of these concerts. Let me ask you a very direct question. How much do you think these would be worth, if I license them to a major corporation such as yours for the territory of, say, South America?' For the first time since the meeting started, Garcia looked me in the eye. There was a long pause. 'Six million dollars, rolling over three years, against eighteen, rising to twenty per cent,' he replied, without moving a muscle.

There was another long pause. I managed to remain impassive.

Garcia started again. 'Listen, I would be happy to take you down to Sao Paulo, and maybe we could talk about a joint venture with one of the big boys for some other territories. We have many friends at Teller and Polygone, hey, Benny?'

I had forgotten that Ben was still in the room and, judging by his startled expression, so had Ben. I was now having considerable difficulty restraining myself from jumping across the desk and kissing Garcia on both cheeks.

'Mr Garcia, I would be very happy to work with you in South America, and maybe even here. Six million dollars sounds just about right. Perhaps we should meet straight after Christmas and thrash out a plan.'

'It would be my pleasure, Timothy. And, hey, by the way, the name is Joe.'

I walked in a daze across Sixth Avenue towards a blue-and-chrome payphone. Narrowly avoiding being flattened by an impatient cab, I looked up at the sky and noticed it was raining again. I dialled Loveday, but the line was busy. I put down the phone and ran through the Garcia conversation once more. Had I misheard? No, I had not! Where was the catch? Maybe he meant more than South America? Five years instead of three? Fuck it, it doesn't matter, one way or the other! I tried calling Loveday again. Finally, the line was free.

'Guess what?'

'What?' she said.

'Six million dollars, that's what.'

31

I inhaled feebly, and exhaled even more feebly, saying: 'Can you fetch me another flannel, but hot this time? Loveday, seriously, I think I'm going to croak.'

Loveday ignored my request and continued staring into the dressing-table mirror, mechanically pulling her left eyelid up and down. She had told me not to eat the oysters when we returned to the room. Worse, of course, I had insisted on having them with whisky. I moaned again. This time she smiled and shook her head in sympathy.

Like a dying man I raised my head from the pillow, shielding the light from my eyes with my hand, wanting to survey the damage. The long chintz curtains were only slightly open. Three ice buckets with upturned bottles surrounded the bed, which now resembled a battle zone covered with sheets, pillows, and blankets. I tried to reach out and grab the striped boxer shorts that were hanging from the right-hand bedside lampshade but collapsed weakly back on to the bed.

Loveday coolly stood up from the mirror and walked over and retrieved them, then bent down and scooped up a pair of jeans, a shirt and a sock, and placed them carefully over the back of the chair by the writing desk. She looked the opposite of how I felt. She was wearing a pale blue cashmere dress and a thin black belt around her waist that outlined the curve of her bottom perfectly.

I shut my eyes, willing Loveday to come back to bed.

She sat down on the bed, shivered, yawned and I heard her kick off her shoes, felt her legs come under the covers, and her body move snug against my own.

Hello, baby – but then again, maybe not.

I had been asleep for five minutes, or was it five hours, when the telephone rang.

Loveday sighed and picked it up. Without looking, she passed the receiver across her chest and let it rest where she thought my ear might be. I grunted.

An angry voice started shouting down the line.

'Tim, what the fuck do you mean by getting this lawyer to write to me with a set of hidden accusations about my skulduggery and this ridiculous proposal of a separation?'

I sat up immediately.

'Oh, that . . . well, I, eh . . .'

'You what, Tim? Don't waffle. Tell me the truth.'

'Look, I merely went to the lawyer to get things sorted out in my head and to find a way of making things clear between us. I didn't realise he was going to send you this so soon.'

'Bullshit!'

'It's not bullshit,' I said, getting out of bed.

'Yes, it bloody well is, and you know it.'

'Rick, calm down, for God's sake! I'm sorry he sent it, OK?' I said, feeling my voice begin to shake.

Rick was relentless and picking up speed.

'No, not OK. He's making accusations. Normally, Tim, lawyers don't make accusations unless they are instructed to. So don't you bloody well hide behind the fucking lawyers, Tim! If you've got something to say, say it to my face. Right?'

'I'm not hiding. I'm merely trying to protect my position. Right?'

'No, wrong! You're trying to score points. That's what you're trying to do. And I can tell you right now for nothing, I can score a lot more points than you.'

By now Rick was close to screaming. I was unable to formulate a reply, and wished somehow that the conversation would go away. Several crackling transatlantic seconds passed before Rick imparted his closing speech.

'So, Tim, get on the fucking phone to your lawyer and ask him, no, tell him, right now, to withdraw this letter immediately. Then get your fucking arse back here and we'll sit down and have a serious talk. Right? Are you there? I said, right?'

I uttered the most reluctant 'Right' I had ever uttered in my life and slammed down the phone.

My face burned with such anger that the only way to calm myself down was to take a shower. I stayed beneath the powerful water jets for nearly twenty minutes, stomping and cursing. It was being treated like a fucking schoolboy that had done it. How dare he boss me around, telling me what to do! How dare he! I shouted at the soap, leapt out of the shower, and pulled every towel off the radiators. I hesitated only when I realised that Loveday might have heard all this ranting, and managed to shout out an innocent enquiry to check whether she was listening. Luckily, there was no reply. Shutting my eyes, I tried to think of a logical solution. Something had to be done, and quickly.

I lay on the bathroom floor and stared at the television playing inside my head. There was my father in the kitchen, talking and making artichoke soup. I immediately tried to switch to another channel. I banged the side of my head but the channel would not budge. I lay there and listened to my father talk. It was a conversation I had heard before. A chat about being patient, taking one step at a time and not riding a horse through a shop window.

Tim, you've got to accept there are going to be certain things in life that are beyond your control; it's that simple.

I stood up and shouted as loudly as I could: 'Thanks, Dad, for those totally useless pearls of wisdom!'

But then I heard another voice, my late grandfather's advice: *Think big and your deeds will grow.*

Now, that was more like it. Sod Dad.

Loveday had left a virtually illegible note saying she had gone downstairs to buy some magazines. I was pleased. I snatched up the phone and lay back on the bed.

My plan was so simple, so audacious, that I was amazed when it worked. It had suddenly crossed my mind that Simon Caplow's friend and sparring partner, the inimitable Aaron Stein, master of the music universe, might possibly, just possibly, have the time to meet me. Nobody knew more about striking a deal than Aaron Stein. And he might have the rights to some of the most big-time acts to have recorded with the BBC.

'Let's find out,' Caplow said cheerfully

'How are we going to do that?' I asked.

'Simple. I'm going to call him on my other line. Hold on to your hat.'

I heard Caplow humming as he dialled the number. It was easy to picture him sitting there with his pipe in his mouth, waving away a cloud of smoke. I heard him connect straight to Stein's assistant, crack a witty joke, and then be put through to Stein himself.

'Aaron, I won't beat about the bush, there's an important young friend of mine, currently in New York.'

There was a pause.

'Do you remember me telling you about Tim Lomax who used to work here? He has a good idea and I think it could make a lot of money for a very low outlay. He already has some interest in New York but I think he needs guidance. He's young, enthusiastic, and has the brains and chutzpah to go the distance. He's a winner, Aaron, will you give him a few minutes?'

There was another pause.

'You're a mensch.'

I heard Caplow laugh, put down the phone and pick up the other receiver.

'Good enough for you, Tim? Call his assistant Helen, here's the number . . .'

I lay back on the bed and let out a huge breath. For about thirty seconds I kept clicking my fingers in time to the beat in my head. I then lit a cigarette and dialled Aaron Stein's office. Within a minute of that call, Helen Donovan, Stein's personal assistant, called back to confirm a breakfast meeting the following morning.

I can make this thing happen.

Inspiring this outburst of activity was the phone call with Rick. For a brief moment, I had thought about capitulating, throwing in the towel and accepting defeat, but no longer. Surrender was not on the agenda. I knew what my problem was, or rather had been – too much passivity, too much being a Number Two. Abe had always told me about nice guys coming second. Well, I couldn't afford to be second, not any longer. Not with everything I had at stake. Even if Loveday and I had to return to London earlier than planned, I was not going to walk into the arena and do battle with Rick without some serious weaponry of my own. And if that meant recruiting new staff, having an office to work from, and retaining Johnny Darrell long-term to deal with the flak – so be it. Simon Caplow was right – this was my deal and I was going to make it work.

Furthermore, I decided, wiping a bit of shaving cream off my left ear, there was no point in delaying the purchase of the house I wanted. It was now or never, whether people were ready or not. I just needed a few more days in New York. I wanted to keep Loveday in her present happy state, but somehow at a distance from all the new activity. I decided on a new approach. Instead of books of lists, my usual modus operandi, I decided to put everything into separate boxes of action. I was about to make a box of phone calls for the day when I heard the door opening and smelled Loveday's perfume.

'Hi! Guess where I've been.'

'To buy some oysters?'

'Ugh!'

'You've been to feed the horse again?'

'No. I've been talking to my friend Frankie – you know, the driver?'

'You only like him, because he calls you Your Ladyship.'

'You can talk! You're the one who likes being called Your Lordship! Anyway, are you in a better mood? It sounded like a nasty call.'

I cleared my throat and hastily gulped down a glass of fresh orange juice. 'Oh that? That was just Rick in one of his stupid moods, nothing to worry about. Guess what?'

Loveday was now on the bed, leaning back against the headboard and turning the pages of American *Vogue*.

'You've brushed your hair?'

'Loveday, stop being stupid! Have another guess.'

She put down the magazine, looked up at the ceiling, and smiled provocatively.

'You've spoken to Ned and he's moving to Brighton?'

'I'm having breakfast with none other than Aaron Stein tomorrow. What do you think about that, eh?'

Loveday put her hand up to her mouth, and fanned it to fake a big yawn.

'Aaron Stein? Isn't he something to do with carpets you cannot afford?'

'Loveday, for God's sake, that's Cyril Lord! Aaron Stein has worked with not only the Beatles but also the Rolling Stones and owns the rights to some of their catalogue as well. So, ergo and all that, he might be able to get me the rights for these and some other top acts in the BBC Concert series – get it?'

'That sounds great, Tim. Let's celebrate when you've done the deal. Now, I've got a little plan, and it's just a little one but I think it would be great fun and it only costs thirty dollars an hour.'

'What is it: a massage, Loveday?' I asked, sliding my hands up her dress on to her bra.

Loveday smiled but kept to her thread.

'No, that's how much it would cost us to rent Frankie's limousine for an hour. What do you think? I'll go halves if you like. Go on, please?'

Expertly unclipping the catch on the front of her bra, I said softly, 'I'm sure we can discuss that a little later . . .'

32

I strode into the sumptuous entrance of 1400 Park Avenue at 8.28 a.m. and announced myself to the two uniformed porters with as much gravitas as I could muster. I straightened my tie, and took the elevator to the seventh floor. Standing outside Aaron Stein's apartment door, I tried to recall everything I had read in the morning newspapers in case I should be called upon to display my brilliant grasp of current affairs. I then crossed my fingers, shined my shoes on the backs of my trousers, and rang the bell. Just as I heard footsteps coming towards the door I suddenly realised I had forgotten the most obvious thing: John Lennon had been managed by Stein when he was in the Beatles.

I was slightly puzzled by how long it took for the door to open, considering that the female voice within had enquired a good minute earlier who was standing outside. When it finally did open, I found myself face to face with a smartly dressed woman in her thirties, extending her hand to me and confirming, so there would be no confusion, that her name was Helen Donovan, Stein's long-standing assistant. As she ushered me into a sitting room, I noticed that she was surreptitiously trying to ease a foot into one of her tight-fitting shoes, while deftly knotting a silk scarf around her neck. Pleased with my discovery of what I imagined to be some top-secret sexual indiscretion, I walked into a room that seemed grander than Grand Central Station. Doing my best not to be overawed, I looked casually at the paintings on the walls and answered Helen's small-talk. She offered me some coffee, pouring it from a jug that looked as if it was worth more than my apartment back home.

Stein came through the doorway like a bull thundering into a bullring. His wide jaw looked like granite, and his neck and shoulders were so powerful that he could have scrummed for Wales. I was shocked to see that he was not dressed, as I had imagined, in some dominating pinstriped suit but in a short, white, towelling dressing-gown.

I shot up from my chair and shook hands, enunciating the words 'Good morning, Mr Stein' so clearly that it sounded almost ironic.

'Excuse the gown. We, I mean I, had a very late night and I've already been on the phone to England for an hour and haven't had time to shower until now. Do you want more coffee?'

He didn't wait for an answer but thrust my cup and saucer towards a hovering Helen, who knew this was her cue to disappear. It was clear to me that there was going to be no small talk at this meeting. Also, I realised I was dealing with a heavyweight, a boxer who started punching before the bell had sounded. I thought it best to say the most difficult thing up-front. I eased forward in my chair.

'I just wanted to say how sorry I am about John Lennon. It must have been a great shock.'

Stein grunted, almost laughed, and took a sip of his coffee. Looking through the window, he said, 'It was a shock and still is, but we're dealing with it.' He put down his cup and saucer and gave me a look that said the subject was now closed. I was relieved. Pointing his finger, he said, 'So, have you and Simon known each other long?'

That was the last time I was able to answer a question while still being able to anticipate the next. For the next thirty minutes, Stein pummelled me with questions ranging from my views on Margaret Thatcher's government to why exactly I had left Simon Caplow to join forces with Rick. Every time I produced a tortured answer, the bull dived in with another question, swooping in and out to direct the conversation wherever he wanted it to go. Stein was like a ferocious prosecutor who knows the answers to his questions before he asks them. Had it not been for a moment of candid soliloquy, when he spoke about having been raised in an orphanage, I would have felt like I was being stripped of all my secrets, all my treasured information. But the fact that Stein, of all people, had told me such an intimately personal thing – however hard he tried, he could not forget those days and that was how he had come to be so successful – had deflected me from thoughts of self-betrayal. Even so, it still felt like the interview to end all interviews; a bluffer hiding his poor exam results before the board of All Souls College. By the time the towelling gown stood up to indicate the meeting was at an end, I felt as if I had failed to answer any of the questions correctly, and had wrecked my chances of admission to the inner sanctum. It was not until Stein enquired whether I was free for lunch that day that I knew I had succeeded. The big boxer frame then walked me to the door.

'You know, you're much brighter than you think. You deserve to be successful. You're the type who should be. Let's talk again over lunch. Call Helen at the office. She'll tell you where. Oh and by the way, it's Aaron, OK?'

Mr Chew's was the smartest Chinese restaurant I had ever seen. The interior was a cross between an Oriental discotheque and the palace of Versailles. Even the waiters, dressed in perfectly pressed trousers and white jackets with golden epaulettes, looked as if they were members of some royal family serving their staff on their day off. Starched table linen and exquisitely polished glass covered every table. The waiter showed me to a discreet corner table, so discreet that it took me a few seconds to see Stein and Helen chatting behind the leaves of a cheese plant. I sat down and began to prattle on about the cab journey and how I just loved Chinese food.

Stein wanted to order quickly, so I dived into my menu. In the ensuing silence, I felt uneasy that the big man was gaining ground, certain that he was observing me before the next round of questioning. I was wrong. He leaned across the table and stubbed his finger at three places on the menu.

'These are good but whatever you do, don't eat the small black things that look like baby turds – they're chillies that'll rip the roof of your mouth off . . . OK?'

As I tried to deal with the thought of eating anything even vaguely resembling a turd, Stein summoned the two hovering waiters without even clicking his fingers. Within thirty seconds the entire meal was ordered and the waiters dispatched, there being no question of anyone else doing the ordering. I was far too nervous to argue with Stein's assumption that we would all drink what he was drinking (diet cola), although I was desperate for a beer. Stein was way ahead of me, as usual.

'I never drink alcohol, never have and never will, never liked the taste.'

'Really?' I said, abandoning all hope of the beer. Then came the next crushing blow.

'Never smoked a cigarette in my life, either.'

But you're pretty flexible when it comes to bonking your secretary, I thought to myself.

'But you still get excited by music, don't you?' I said instead. 'Or is it just the deals that turn you on?'

There was a pause as Stein and Helen turned to look at each other and they both grinned. I worried for a fraction of a second that I had overstepped the mark.

'Very funny you should say that, Tim, because Helen here has been asking me the same thing all week.'

'It's true,' Helen uttered bravely.

'Well, the answer is, I dunno. I mean, I still listen to music, but a lot of what I hear these days leaves me cold. You see, you've got to remember that I've been lucky enough to be involved with some of the greatest musicians working this century. So, frankly, it gets kinda hard for me to get excited about most of the shit I hear today.'

I said that I understood completely, and took a little longer than was strictly necessary complimenting him on the list of artists he was involved with. I hoped that the back-patting might lead to talk about the Beatles or that he might tell me some funny anecdotes about the Rolling Stones. Instead, he said that he still believed Sam Cooke was the greatest writer he had ever encountered and that, had he not been shot, he would now be at the very top of anyone's list. The conversation then dropped a semitone as Stein remembered an unpaid account in London regarding some Cooke material, and queried Helen for two uncomfortable minutes about dates and contracts. There was a momentary lull as the waiters returned and placed a multitude of sizzling dishes, as well as bowls of soup and rice, on the table.

Stein gestured benevolently to the spread of food with a wide swoop of his arm.

'I like to have everything at the same time. Courses are for wimps!'

I laughed on cue, thinking that Stein was probably just a greedy bastard. There was something strange about him that I could not pin down. The monumental ego was obvious, but his reputation as a man who pillaged artists for every penny they possessed seemed unfair. There was genuine humility, genuine admiration, in the way he had talked about Sam Cooke, which did not square with what I had heard from other people. I reminded myself to stay in the present. This was no ordinary opponent, and one, I felt, who had not got where he was by playing by anyone else's rules.

'So, Aaron, just to backtrack, you still like doing deals, don't you?'

The reply came quicker than a lizard's tongue. 'I live for deals. They're better than sex.'

I glanced at Helen for a reaction and, seeing none, shifted my gaze back to Stein expecting at least a nudge, a wink of bashful humour. Nothing. Stein dabbed his mouth with a napkin before continuing.

'You see, with deals you don't have the same complications of emotional commitment and so forth. You don't have the problem of should I call her again or not. When it's done, you come, it's over. Great sex without any of the aftermath.'

'Yessssss, I see,' I said, unable to formulate a riposte with my mouth full.

Stein changed up a gear.

'So, Tim, let's talk about you. How exactly do you think your BBC idea is going to work? Or, more important, I guess, for you, why do you think someone like me should become involved with the likes of you, eh?'

I was taken aback by the tone of the question and picked up my glass to buy myself some time. I tried to steady myself, rewinding everything I had heard about playing hardball.

I leaned forward and, mustering every shred of authority I could still command, stared hard into Stein's shark-like eyes, and began:

'Aaron, this is one of those rare ideas that no one has picked up and run with before because it simply looks too good to be true. The fact is, it really *is* good and in my view it's a potential goldmine. May I remind you that one of the other people who believes in this idea is Simon Caplow.'

I paused for breath and some nod of approval. Stein turned to Helen with a smirk on his face, saying: 'Simon doesn't have the monopoly on being right, we're all aware of that.'

I took another sip of diet cola, smiled, and carried on.

'Let's put Simon Caplow to one side for a moment and look at the strengths. Firstly, in an age of increasing recording costs and huge mixing costs, here we have quality recordings that are already paid for. Unlike every other project in the record business, everyone involved makes money from the start. No advances or costs to recoup, just straight earnings from record one. Marketing costs can be kept to a minimum, as we'll be preaching to the converted, informing existing fans that there's another live recording of their favourite group.'

I paused to see if Stein was still listening. He merely raised his hand. I ploughed on.

'So, obviously, we want to put out the best sleeve notes we can and make a big point of saying these sound recordings were made by the BBC and are of the highest standard.'

His silence was beginning to unsettle me. I was losing concentration.

'And it's obvious that with ten years or so of concerts to choose from, we can establish a unique and extremely collectable series around the world.'

I laughed nervously and drained the diet cola, desperate for a cigarette.

'Finally,' I said, steeling myself not to mention the Beatles or the Rolling Stones, 'it would be very much appreciated if we could have a helping hand in some way at this early stage.'

I looked across at Helen, who smiled briefly.

There was a silence during which all I could hear was Stein unwrapping a fortune cookie. I finished the last mouthful of food and self consciously held my glass up in the air, hoping to attract a waiter to provide me with another drink. Still silence. I knew what Stein was doing. He was like a job interviewer waiting to see if the applicant had any more to say, perhaps hoping he would blurt out something that would incriminate him. The waiter took away my glass. Then, in between bites of fortune cookie, the great man spoke.

'Quite interesting, what you have to say. Hmm. I need to think about it, see if it stacks up. Have a really close look at that list of yours. But there is one possibility I might be able to help you with, straight off the bat. Sam Cooke. The problem is, I don't know the dates, but I do know he did something for the BBC. Interested?'

Oh my God, what timing! My mouth is paralysed. Water, quick! Oh, my God, I'm losing it. Fuck, my mouth is on fire! Call the fire brigade! Say something, anyone, please? My God, all the spotlights are on me now. You're going to have to say something. Swallow your pride, they'll understand . . . Christ, he's enjoying this I'm sure . . .

Stein turned and smiled the sincerest smile he had smiled all day.

I poured the fifth consecutive glass of water into my gaping mouth.

Stein looked up at the ceiling and shook his head. Without taking his eyes from the ceiling he placed a neatly folded wad of cash on to a plate and handed it to the waiter who was standing respectfully nearby. Stein then made what was to be his final address to me that day.

'There are six golden rules you need to remember when doing a deal. These rules are my rules and they're priceless, but I'm going to tell them to you for free. Now, it doesn't matter whether you are buying a record company, a pizza, or a song, the same rules always apply. Are you ready? The first rule is: is it a good idea? Is it a good idea for me to buy this pizza? Or should I, for example, be eating Chinese instead? The second rule is: do I have enough money? I don't mean just for the pizza, but do I have enough money for the beer and then for the tip and also for the cab ride home? The third rule is: do I have the right people to execute the job? So, if I am buying a song, for example, do I have the right lawyer, the right accountant, the right piano player to test the song, do I have the right people in the office to then exploit the song? The fourth one is: is the timing right? Didn't I eat a pizza only yesterday? Didn't all my friends say that they now liked Chinese? Should I wait until the price of dough goes down? The fifth one is: is the market too well served? In other words, let's take oil tankers as an example, are there ten thousand oil tankers on the market already and do we need another one? Do you follow me so far? OK, then, the sixth one. Well, it's pretty obvious, Mr Lomax, isn't it? The sixth one is never eat a little turd when you're trying to do a deal.'

With that Stein banged the salt cellar hard down on the table twice as if to add his own exclamation marks and let out an enormous laugh, followed by a loud, '*A-men!*'

All I could do was laugh along with the pair of them. Then, as if on cue, they got up, and we all shook hands. Before leaving, Stein leaned towards me.

'You know what? Call me after Christmas and let's see if there isn't something we can do. OK?'

'Absolutely. Thank you for lunch. Bye.'

33

I stared at Loveday, wedged into the window seat of the 747 with her back towards me, and flicking through the pages of a magazine. Despite my flowers and the gifts from Saks, our conversation that morning was tired, chilly and sparse. However, after hearing me ask the air hostess to bring another miniature, Loveday must have decided it was time to say something more substantial. She manoeuvred herself round to face me, took a swig from her bottle of water and said: 'Tim?'

'What?'

'Tim, please don't get pissed. I don't want a fight.'

'I wasn't fighting, was I?'

'Look, I was really angry with the way you just announced we were leaving, that's all.'

I didn't say anything but nodded and offered her a cigarette.

Loveday shook her head and paused to cough and blow her nose on some Kleenex. 'Shit! I've caught a cold!' She sniffed and began again. 'I'm grateful for everything, of course, and I've had a great time, but all I really mean is . . .' she hesitated. 'Something's got into you.'

Loveday looked at me. I stared at my cigarette smoke.

'I don't know if it's the pressure of all this work,' she said, 'or whether it's me or what, but you've become – well, I don't know, different. I mean, even Harry and Jessica thought you were act-ing weirdly. And it was just plain rude, leaving the apartment like that . . .'

'I explained to Harry on the phone and he was fine about it. At least he's interested in hearing how the concert business is going. He believes it's got great potential, unlike some people,' I said, sniffily.

Loveday sighed and tutted loudly. 'Oh, Tim, please! All this cleverness, Tim the tycoon treating everybody like they're your personal slave, for goodness sake . . . the Plaza . . . I mean, money isn't everything, Tim. Don't you get that? What's happened to the Tim who was different to everyone else?'

'I thought you said you didn't want to fight?'

Loveday let out another long sigh, frowned and pulled the British Airways blanket up to her chin: 'Maybe we've just been on top of each other a bit too much. Maybe we should have a break.'

There was no question mark at the end of her last sentence, giving me the chance to agree or disagree, only a silence. I stared straight ahead, pretending to smile. The matter was left without further discussion.

I am standing by the emergency exit with its enormous handle inviting me to push and pull it. I'm surprised it isn't covered in more warning signs. I mean, what if a little kid fancied pushing this handle to one side? What if some madman just leaned against it with his bum and slowly eased it open – what then? Yet I feel myself being drawn to it. I'm only six inches away from the handle now, looking out of the small window above it, down on to the thick carpet of clouds beneath. What if I slipped the handle and eased myself outside? I might do some friendly free-falling, and, with an even friendlier air current, swoop back up and tap on the window next to Loveday and wave and smile and ask her if she really thinks we need a break or was this just something borrowed from some book or magazine. Stupid cow!

Why am I getting so annoyed?

Come on, move away from here! I'm beginning to get the horrors, the same sort of pull I've felt on high buildings that makes me want to run and throw myself off.

I need to calm down and keep walking.

As I pass the gormless faces of people crammed into their seats, I wonder at the point of it all.

I pace up and down, the central aisle. Suddenly, I feel my path blocked by something hard and sharp. It's an air-hostess with the drinks trolley. She stares at me, rather too quizzically for my liking, and asks whether I am trying to get past.

'Get where?' I say.

She smiles and looks a little flummoxed. I stare back and ask her for a whisky on the rocks – that's ice, I say, remembering I am no longer in America. She looks perturbed, as if I have just made an intimate comment about her underwear. I give her a powerful smile. She relents and hands me the drink but with a censorious wiggle of her finger that indicates that I should reverse my steps and head back to my seat. I smile contritely but return to pacing. I think back to Stein's golden rules and settle on Rule Two. Have I enough money? I inhale deeply; bite the mental bullet. I then remember Charles's words; that what I really need is capital. I inhale and exhale. The air in the plane is stale. Fuck, I hate planes. Why can't I travel everywhere by train? I stop pacing and realise that I badly need to connect pen to page. Stein's rules in combination with my boxes! As I make my way along the headrests back to sleeping Loveday, I begin compiling two columns with names of the right people, one marked UK and one marked USA. I get out my yellow legal pad and start writing. Before long the sheet of paper has turned into a family tree of projects, personnel and action.

I am about to write down Loveday's name. I look over at her sleeping foetal shape and my eyes take in every detail of her face. 'To sleep – perchance to dream'. Who said that? Shakespeare? Dylan Thomas? I can't remember but I wish I could press a little button in her head to bring about sleep in times of strife. As I stare at the golden fringe, that perfect skin, and her twitching nose nestled on her cashmere-clad arm, I wonder if I have ever told her just how beautiful she is.

34

I marched from the Trafalgar Square branch of the Hong Kong & Shanghai Bank with the B52's 'Rock Lobster' playing full blast in my head. I looked up at Nelson standing on his column and stuck my thumb in the air in celebration, knowing he would understand.

'Bullseye! Got it! Capitalised! Thank you, Charles, eternally grateful for the tip!' Yes, I could have an immediate overdraft of ten thousand pounds. Mr Wilkinson, the bank manager for Charles's company, had agreed to it in less than five minutes. 'We'll need your flat as security, just a formality, you understand?'

A part of me wanted to throw a party at once, to invite everybody to the nearest pub. Another part was saying, shut up, stay calm, and assume some leadership – think Aaron Stein, think Napoleon, think Nelson at Cadiz.

With as much restraint as I could muster I slid along the back seat of the Gaulle without saying a word and looked at my new driver, George, sitting respectfully behind the wheel. George understood immediately and with a conspiratorial grin switched on the engine and handed me a newspaper. Originally from Kingston, Jamaica, he was wearing a khaki army jacket with a Kermit and Miss Piggy badge on each lapel.

'Glebe Lane, George.'

Thoughts were crowding into my head faster than I could write them down. I clicked open my briefcase and took out my books of lists. More than anything I wanted to tell Loveday the news, but she was on a train to Scotland – a training course she had forgotten about. Not only that, she had visited her parents' over the weekend and had only come to see me last night for an hour on her way back. With a great effort, I tried not to think too much about the darker implications of this, and went back to updating my boxes. There were the usual problems to deal with now that I was back, but these, I told myself, were simple necessities, the growing pains of change.

Now was the time to take the offensive.

As the Byzantine tower of Westminster Cathedral loomed up on the horizon, I began laying down concrete objectives for the day. I knew it would not be possible to procrastinate any longer about calling Rick, and briefly chided myself for the amount of time I had let pass already. There would have to be a phone call and a face-to-face meeting. Perhaps we could have a civilised conversation, one in which we each apologised to the other. I then made an agreement with myself: for every unpleasant item on my list I would reward myself with something positive, something new.

A convertible Mercedes 280SE 3.5: the sweetener for this bitter swig of medicine was to sort out the purchase of the Merc. I could secure the car with some cash and a cheque post-dated for January.

I would then call Andy Grave. Call him every sodding name under the sun if necessary, but demand to know exactly where the mortgage was. My reward for enduring this bit of unpleasantness would be a Christmas shopping trip to Harrods. For good measure, purely as a treat but maybe also as a safeguard, I would open a bank account with Harrods Bank as well.

By the time I emerged from my thoughts we had sped past Vauxhall Bridge and Dolphin Square, and the car was alongside Battersea power station. I leaned forward and shouted over the noise of the Dogs on the tape player. 'Carry on straight down the Embankment until you get to a pub called the Crooked Billet, then hang a right and I'll show you from there, OK?'

George swung the car past the Billet into Laurence Street and drove slowly past its smart terraced houses, then curved around a medieval-looking wall until he saw a weather-beaten wooden sign saying Glebe Lane.

'Go through there, George,' I said pointing into what looked like a driveway.

'Are you sure? Looks like it's someone's private entrance?'

'It's OK, just carry on.'

The entrance to the lane was a tunnel or rather a small road passing beneath the first floors of two adjoining houses. George eased the Gaulle slowly down the tunnel and, to help his concentration, switched off the Dogs. Once clear of the houses, the small road became a gravel lane bordered on both sides by high grassy banks and wild hawthorn. After a hundred yards of careful driving along the loose gravel chips, another sign appeared, suspended by a chain from a lamppost.

'Here we are. This is it George, look over there.'

Glebe Lane was a short, tree-lined road with six semi-detached houses on each side, painted pink, blue, or ochre. Sitting by itself at the end of the lane was a tall, detached, double-fronted house painted green. It had a white flagpole just inside its short brown-timbered fence and a wooden garage to one side. It looked as if it had not been occupied for some time.

'Come on, I've got a key – let's have a quick look,' I said, getting out of the car.

We walked through the wooden gate and along a crazy-paving path.

'Never seen anything like it in all my life. It's like them houses you see in Venice!' George exclaimed, as he craned his head backwards to look up at the three-storey building.

'Actually,' I said, somewhat pompously, 'it's an old Victorian pumping station. Fred in the Billet tipped me off about it. By the time I'm finished, there's going to be a big office as well as a separate four-bedroom house. Sexy or what?'

George stared at me. Feeling the need to explain myself, I told him that when the pumping station had been decommissioned, the occupants had continued to live in it. Recently it had passed to their son, an elderly semi-retired estate agent keen to make a quick sale.

'Have you bought it yet?' George asked as I unlocked the front door and waved him through it.

'A minor formality, dear boy,' I said grandly. 'Just a few dots to dot and a few crosses to cross, you know.'

George seemed to be impressed. 'You are pumping, Tim. You're really pumping!'

A driver. A Mercedes. A house.

Hello, baby.

Except, I wasn't telling anyone else. Not yet. They could wait. They could all just wait.

35

I looked at my diary and nearly had a heart attack.

'Jesus fucking Christ!' I shouted to the cat. Ned shook his head at my blaspheming, and trotted out through the cat-flap.

Quarter to eight in the morning. I made myself two pieces of toast, an Irish coffee on account of the cold, and put some food in the cat bowl. The radio was playing 'Stop the Cavalry' a little too loudly, so I turned it down.

I was impressed by how quickly George had taken note of my instructions regarding the Mercedes. It wasn't absolutely essential, I knew, to have it before Christmas, but I wanted it there and then. The Gaulle just wasn't me any more. I had outgrown it and it was beginning to get on my nerves. I decided to relegate it to occasional use at weekends. The payment for the Mercedes was a pain. I arranged to give George some post-dated cheques for January and my Access-America card as an alternative. I hoped they would go for the post-dated routine. I needed to conserve as much cash as possible.

Today was going to be the day to stop fucking about. Today was going to be record company day, clearances for the BBC, the day to get my lawyers sorted out. This I resented. Why did I have to sort lawyers out? Why were they not sorting everything out for me?

As I bit into the toast and the warm glow of the whisky hit my stomach, I felt strengthened and invigorated. I needed pumping up. I needed to take myself in hand and give my brain a hard-on. I knew that a very small part of me smelled of fear, not badly so, but all the same it was there. This was an old situation with a different slant. But, *I could deal with it*. Front, that's what I needed. That's how everyone else did it.

The telephone rang.

'Tim! Tim, is that you?' Loveday shouted, bordering on the hysterical.

I had decided to take a different line with her. I had given the matter a lot of thought and decided that, without doubt, I had been far too pliable, too accommodating in trying to make things work. The whole relationship had become one-sided, her side.

'Well, who else is it going to be?'

'Oh, Tim, it's like being in a fucking freezer up here; they don't appear to understand what heating is. The food is the most disgusting muck I've tasted since school and the course is straight out of the Spanish Inquisition. Oh, and to top it all, there's this man who just won't leave me alone.'

'Oh, yes?' I enquired.

'Oh, it's nothing, really, just some guy on the course who thinks he's in love with me.'

'Is he very short sighted?'

'Very funny! He's not bad-looking, shame he's not my type.'

'Yes, Loveday.'

'Oh, Tim, I've missed you! I needed this time away to work out what I felt. Do you know, every night I've been in this disgusting dump, I've kept your picture under my pillow. Just like you did all that time ago, do you remember? I can't wait to see you. Have you missed me?'

It gave me considerable satisfaction to know I was appreciated.

'Possibly. Maybe a little. Yes,' I said.

'Friday at eight?' Loveday asked cheerfully.

'Yes, that's possibly possible, Loveday,' I said, trying to sound disinterested.

As I put the phone down, I realised that I had not told her anything about the previous day's gains and triumphs. But maybe I didn't need to just yet.

A brief check in the mirror and then of my watch told me it was time for some inspiring music and to change out of my blue boxer shorts into something more assertive. A minute later I was standing in a pinstriped suit, my shirt collar gaping open and a tie hanging around my neck for effect. I had seen this look in *Get Carter* with Michael Caine – confident but casual. It suggested power but also I don't really give a fuck and if you think I do, you'd better think again kind of look. I had bought the shirt at Barney's in New York and its well-fitting cotton felt sensational against my skin. I made a mental note to order a dozen more the minute I got back there.

The cat had returned and was now sitting somewhat anxiously on top of the dining table, following me around the room with his eyes. He was probably in need of some attention. I strode purposefully to the record player, knowing exactly what to put on. Ian Dury and the Blockheads slammed in with the cascading beats of 'Hit Me with Your Rhythm Stick'. I grabbed hold of Ned's front paws and began moving them back and forth in a frenzied tango. Just as the chorus repeated itself, my singing and our dancing were in perfect synch, but when the song reached 'ich liebe dich', the cat leapt down and rocketed out of the kitchen door. I suddenly realised that someone was standing behind me. A disembodied South London voice said: 'Sorry! We tried the bell! Saw the door was open and heard the music and came right on in. Nice dancing.'

I swung round and there were the builder, Billy Crawley, and his mate, Wilf, standing with their arms folded.

'Sadly, the cat has got terrible arthritis and needs constant physiotherapy,' I countered hastily.

Much to my amusement Crawley either pretended to, or really did, take this quite seriously. The two men sat down, perching awkwardly on the edge of their chairs. It was strange having two people I had only met hammering away on the stairs at Lower Hades Road in my home. After one or two prickly references to being legally able to proceed with the refurbishment of the house in Glebe Lane, we ran through the order of works and fittings we had already discussed. Just as I was about to lay a timetable of payments and bonuses on the table, Crawley decided to play the ace he had been saving up his sleeve.

'Please don't take this personal like . . .'

Why do people always say that?

Crawley got over his hesitation. 'It's just that we've 'eard certain things about your credit-worthiness, shall we say, from the people in the Lower Hades Road, that 'ave given us, reservations and the like. I'm not saying that we listen to gossip or that we don't all 'ave financial hiccups from time to time, but I would be stupid or not doing my job if I didn't mention it, know what I mean? In a long way of saying things, we're going to need most of the money up front, Tim. Guv'nor.'

I counted to twenty, took a deep breath and stood up.

'Billy if I give you seventy-five per cent of the money up front, will that make you feel better?'

'That'd be just what the doctor ordered, Tim.'

'I'll do it, Billy, but there's a catch.'

'I'd expect one, Tim!' said Crawley as cheerfully as possible. 'What is it?'

'It's very simple. I want you to have all the work done by the 7th of January.'

'You're joking! The 7th of January, bloody hell, did you hear that, Wilf? You'll still be in the Bahamas, Tim, having your Christmas holidays, woncha?' Crawley joked, nervously fumbling for his notebook.

'No time for any holidays now. It's up to you, Billy. I've got a hell of lot of work to do in the next four weeks and I'd like this house to be ready when I'm finished. If you can't do it, don't worry, I'll find someone else.'

Just as Crawley was about to open his mouth, the sound of an expensive horn blasted rhythmically outside.

'Sorry, gents, I have to go,' I said smiling. 'Can you let me know within forty-eight hours?'

Crawley and Wilf nodded and picked up all their brochures and catalogues from the floor. I put on my jacket, picked up my cigarettes and keys, and waited until they were both ready to leave. Crawley walked slowly to the stairs, scratching his arm and shaking his head. 'I think it's very unlikely, Tim, especially considering the low price, but you never know.'

'Let me know Billy . . . OK?'

As I heard the door close, I rushed back to the window to check that Crawley had noticed the new Mercedes waiting outside. Sure enough, I saw him nudging Will and peering through the windscreen. Then the phone rang. I was amazed to hear who it was.

'Gabe, is that you?'

'Who else?' said the tired Liverpudlian voice. 'I'm at Heathrow man, and my wallet and address book have been nicked and . . .'

'You need a ride . . .'

*   *   *

When someone like Gabe Morass calls, you drop everything.

Six months away on tour, and what a time to be away, I thought, as George and I sped down the motorway with the stereo blaring so loud we could barely hear each other. I was not going to go into too much detail about what had happened but hoped the sight of the Mercedes would tell Gabe that things were way beyond all right.

As we drove into Heathrow traffic complex, I could see the aeroplanes taking off and it made me want to be back on the plane to New York there and then. However . . . I told myself that all things come to him who waits, and what I needed right now was discipline.

Returning to London with Gabe felt a little strange. He insisted on putting his bags in the boot of the car himself, politely declining George's offer of help. I could see that he was suffering not only from jet-lag but also from having been on the road too long. I kept quiet and listened to him ramble on.

'I am never going on the road again.'

'What? Spend your life in the studio, Gabe?'

'Yeah, why not?'

I laughed, knowing this was probably what he always said after such a long time away.

'Either that or I'm packing it all in and going to live in Bangkok.'

'Gabe, I think all you need is a fat spliff and some sleep.'

'I can live very cheaply and be quite happy not being in the music business.'

'I'm sure it's a phase, Gabe.'

Adjusting the time on his watch, he looked at George and smiled. 'So, Tim, how's it all going at Delta? Selling any records? Finding any half-decent bands? Difficult when you're an indie, isn't it?'

'I've left Delta now.'

Eventually, George pulled up at Marylebone station just in time for Gabe's train back to his studio home in High Denham.

As George and I waved him away, Gabe jerked his arm in the air, indicating he had forgotten something. 'Tim, let's speak and make a plan for Christmas Eve. You remember?'

I had forgotten about the Quantum Frog Christmas gig.

'Of course, don't worry.'

'Bye, man.' Gabe shuffled off towards an open train door. He gave a weary shrug, then clambered on board. The train strained and heaved its tired way out of the station, leaving George and myself choking on acrid diesel fumes. I was just about to curse Marylebone station as one of the most useless properties on the Monopoly board, when we both noticed a smart brown-and-cream Pullman standing behind the space left by Gabe's departing heap. It had sex written all over it; sex and comfort.

To own your own train. Now we're talking!

As George peered down at the side engines, I looked inside and had no trouble at all picturing myself conducting meetings in the dining car. I could use the train all over England, the Mercedes carefully secured in a rear carriage. The train could transport Loveday whenever she chose. It could collect Harry and Jessica at Grand Central Station and take them across America. The Dogs could easily use it for long-distance interstate touring as well. Eventually it would pay for itself.

George tapped me on the shoulder and pointed to his watch.

As the doors of the Mercedes clicked shut, he smiled quizzically, paused to consider for a second, and then turned the ignition key.

36

'George! Park next to that blue Cadillac.'

I pressed the switch for the electric window and leaned out, clocking everything around me. It felt good, as if I was a Russian spy taking secret photographs with my Ronson and biding my time until my adversary emerged. But the sight of the pavement, all sticky with trodden-in dog shit, ketchup and chewing gum, brought me back to reality.

I peered into the wing mirror and saw people trudging up and down, looking tired and without hope, people resigned to having no future, so different from the ones I had seen on Fifth Avenue.

But this was something that had to be done. I took a swig from my hip flask and turned up the Pretenders' 'Brass In Pocket' playing on the quadraphonic system. A moment later, I got out of the car and walked across the road. It was only then that I noticed the two flat tyres on the big blue Cadillac.

How small the building looked now! The familiar stairs seemed so insignificant and irrelevant I took them three at a time, wanting to get to the top as quickly as possible. As I climbed towards Delta, I did some mental press-ups.

I walked into the general office. The place seemed deserted, the *Marie Celeste* of the Lower Hades Road. There was a faint smell of grass.

'Hello?' I shouted. 'Hello? Is anyone here?'

'Hi, there!' squeaked someone, slightly out of breath.

Susie emerged like a genie from underneath the table, wearing a sheepskin coat.

'Hello. Isn't it a bit cold down there?'

'What?' said Susie, switching the radio off.

I tried again. 'How are you, Susie?'

'All right, I guess. You know.'

She took a nervous drag from her roll-up, put her hand on her hip, and scowled as if she was trying to remember something. There was an odd silence, in which all I could hear was the spluttering of the heater about to run out of gas.

'Been busy?' I asked, peering at a large box of singles in the corner of the room.

Susie followed my eyes, walked over, pulled a 7″ single out of the box and handed it to me. I wasn't concentrating at first, still slightly confused by the deadly silence in the place. I held the single up to the light and saw that on its coloured sleeve was a hand-drawn picture of tables and chairs outside a café. I smiled and turned the cover over. There were the words 'The Dogs', 'Rhiannon's Café', and a photograph of Dave and Neil above the Columbus logo.

'Very nice, Susie, I must say, very nice. What a super, lovely, fucking awful sleeve!'

Susie was grinning nervously and bobbing her head like a nodding dog.

They've licensed the record without me!

I stared at the terrible sleeve, imagining it had been drawn by Andy Grave himself, and threw the single back in the box.

'But you knew, didn't you?'

'Of course I knew, Susie.'

'It all happened when you were in America. They turned it around in forty-eight hours. Amazing, you know?'

'Yeah, really amazing! Where's Rick? Is he in his office?' I said, straining to contain myself.

'No.'

'What do you mean, no?'

Susie let out a whooshing sigh. 'God how silly of me. Victoria went into labour this morning. Rick had to rush home and take her to hospital. He's there now, and they've had a little girl. Isn't that amazing?'

'Where's Star?' I said, not really interested but trying to collect my thoughts.

'Oh, she's gone to the florists, you know, to send some flowers.'

'And Rick?'

'Oh, he's in a state of shock!' Susie said, hugging her arms to herself.

I nodded knowingly and pushed open Rick's door, still half-expecting him to be sitting at his desk laughing at the elaborate joke about the baby. Instead, there was only his briefcase standing uncharacteristically open on his desk. I stepped into my office, expecting my desk to have been cleared, but to my surprise, apart from a neat pile of post, saw that it was exactly the same as I had left it. Picking up the post I took one last look out the window and walked out.

I never did ask Susie what she was doing underneath that table.

37

The Mercedes was a mobile headquarters, stopping only outside telephone boxes, petrol stations, Harrods, and the glamorous exteriors of various record companies. The atmosphere inside the car resembled a washing machine – pausing and accelerating again with its own distinct cycles of wash, slow rinse, fast rinse and spin.

The mahogany cocktail table folding out from behind the passenger seat made an ideal desk on which to attend to my boxes. Briefly, I imagined life as a cabinet minister, but one where I was the boss, not Mrs Thatcher. I had made long lists of my contacts and, in an effort to save time, decided to approach them directly. Every record company of any stature had now been visited and assessed. Despite the mayhem of the Christmas traffic, double-parked cars, and streams of vigilant shoppers, George displayed patience worthy of Buddha himself.

'I don't know how you keep so cool, George, considering the amount of parking and reversing up one-way streets you've been doing. You'll be able to set up your own driving school soon.'

George grinned, 'Never been involved in anything like this before.'

'Stick with me, George, keep the faith, and great things will unfold.'

'Rhiannon's Café' suddenly pumped through the airwaves.

I began to cheer but then the DJ spun the record straight into 'Stop the Cavalry' and it was too late.

The back-seat/front-seat meeting with the Dogs at teatime that day took place outside Buckingham Palace. In fact, George steered the Mercedes round the statue outside so many times that a police car pulled us over to check that we were not posing a threat to the monarchy. The interruption did not stop the meeting from being an unqualified success.

'Look, you two, excuse the cliché, but it's sometimes hard to see the wood for the trees, standing in your shoes. But, believe me, the reaction to your tape in New York was exceptional.'

Dave and Neil blinked, open-mouthed. 'Really? Do they really like it?'

'They didn't just like it, they loved it!' I carried on with my speech. 'We all want to be successful in our own country but, sometimes, things being what they are, our own country can be the last to recognise its own talent. It's often a question of being too familiar on your own front doorstep – do you know what I mean? My view is that America is the place where it's all going to happen for you.'

I lit three cigarettes, handed them out and continued. 'My dream is to start a company in London and New York. A record company that will market the past as well as discover the future, and a management company that will manage human beings, as opposed to bits of product. A company that will build bridges for artists to walk over, so they can realise their dreams. You guys are essential to my plan. To come straight to the point, I want to be your manager.'

Dave and Neil were speechless with excitement. I put my finger up in the air to mark a point of order. 'However, there's no need to mention any of this to Andy, or anyone else for that matter – not yet, anyway. But so that you know I'm serious, I've talked to Gabe Morass about producing some new tracks with you. He's really interested and I hope you will be too.'

Dave and Neil closed their eyes, shook their heads madly from side to side, then punched each other, unable to conceal their euphoria.

'Just give me bit of time and then we can celebrate, OK?'

That evening, I paced the flat, my head buzzing with the events of the week. I kept telling myself to take it in my stride, that it was all part of a new normality, but I still wanted to tell Loveday about it. Also, I was still being swamped by a series of images of Loveday cavorting across a tartan bed allowing herself to be pursued by Moira's half-naked nephew, a psychedelic sporran swinging between his legs.

I telephoned her hotel and was told that she was not in her room, the bar, nor the restaurant and no, they would not put a call out to the lavatory. Having asked the telephonist in my most English voice to give her a message, I made a mental note to write a letter of complaint to the Tourist Board. I then walked purposefully to the pile of records lying on the VCR and pulled out the coffee-stained cover of *Carmina Burana*. The needle sitting safely in the groove, I turned the amplifier to maximum, swung myself into a central position on the carpet and, with my arms outstretched and eyes shut, let the music swoop over me.

After recharging my batteries, to both sides of the album, I felt invigorated but restless. I decided to head for Shepherd's Bush to have a drink at Proust's.

38

Eight o'clock Friday morning, and the ache in my head and the thickness of my triple-coated tongue had nearly disappeared. What a difference a Screwdriver and some toothpaste can make! It had been a fantastic night at Proust's. God knows what had happened in the end but, thank God, I didn't have the car to drive and took a taxi home instead. It was strange, but I was getting used to not driving any more.

I sat up in bed and stroked the stubble on my chin. The cat was pacing up and down waiting for me to feed him, but I decided I wasn't going to until I was good and ready. Ned had been annoying me lately, rushing about, moulting and meowing everywhere. No, he'd have to wait. It was time to have a bath.

I turned both taps on full and lit a cigarette. I walked into the bedroom and lay back on the bed. The telephone rang. It was Loveday, calling from a phone box in Scotland. I decided to play it cool.

'Why are you calling from a call box?'

'Because there's snow on the line.'

'Sorry?'

'I'm calling from Aber-fucking-deen station and I'm really pissed off.'

'Sweetheart, that's terrible.'

'I tried ringing you a million times last night but you were always busy, and then when I tried again later, you were out. Where did you go to at that time of night?'

'How's Mr McLover, sweetheart? Is he on the platform too?'

'Don't mention Mr Mc-fucking-Loverboy, please! Otherwise I'll throw myself in front of the next train. What were you doing last night?'

'I went to a wine-tasting.'

'What, at half-past eleven?'

'It's what my old pal Elliot calls a late-night tasting.'

'Late night, my foot!'

'When is the snow going to melt, do you think?'

'God knows.'

'How far is it to the airport?'

'What?'

'Maybe you could fly? A bit of snow never hurt a plane.'

'Tim, what planet are you on?'

'Loveday, do you want to get home today or the middle of next week?'

'I really don't care any more as long as I can be with you . . .'

'Say that again.'

'You heard.'

'You mean, you've had enough of having a break?'

'Yes.'

'Well, I've had enough of having your break too.'

'Oh, Tim . . . oh, shit, there go the pips. I've got no more change.'

'Call me back in a minute and I'll sort everything out, OK?'

'Tim, I just want to say . . .'

She'd run out of money and I was left staring at the telephone. I jumped around the room looking for the telephone directory, which I found underneath the laundry basket. My finger slid along the list of airlines until it got to British Caledonian. I was about to call them when the phone rang again. I picked it up, thinking it must be Loveday.

'Hello, gorgeous.'

A distinctly male voice replied:

'Eh . . . hello, Tim, Billy Crawley here.'

I nearly choked on my cigarette.

'Hello, Billy, look, make it quick, I'm expecting a long-distance call.'

Crawley cleared his throat.

'OK, well, I don't know whether you were really serious or not the other day, but I've called all the men and they've said they can do it. Get your new place sorted out by the 7th of January.'

'You really can do it?'

'Yup. I've worked it all out. It'll mean having to work Christmas Eve and Boxing Day and probably New Year's Day as well and it's going to cost you, even at my rates. I've got to look after the men, see?'

'How much are we talking about?'

'I am going to need seven thousand now and five thousand when we finish. Do you want to think about it?'

'No . . .'

'Ah, there you are, you see. I thought it was a bit too steep for you.'

'Not at all, I'd like to proceed. I'll see you at eight o'clock tomorrow morning with seven thousand pounds in cash.'

'Christ! You *are* serious. You'll be there, won't you? I'm going to have eight men working on this and I can't afford to let any of them down, you know.'

'Don't let me down, Billy. See you tomorrow. Bye.'

I put down the phone triumphantly. To celebrate I decided to give the cat some food and myself an Irish coffee. As I walked down the stairs, a voice in my head, sounding disconcertingly like my father's, kept talking about mathematics. I understood this to be a reference to spending more than I had borrowed, but I chose to ignore it.

Johnny Darrell was my opposite: he was serious, meticulous, shy and extremely intense, and the best thing I had done recently was to use him. He was slight, in his mid-thirties and with a boyish face framed by tight black curls. He was always dressed in the same dark suit and a white shirt with a collar that seemed two sizes too big for him.

From my point of view, the meeting that afternoon was an unqualified success, a matter of three steps forward and no steps back. Johnny explained that he had succeeded in postponing the court case for my latest drink-driving offence, until the 2nd of January. He had formed the two companies I requested, and redrafted the separation agreement between Rick and myself.

'Excellent, Johnny, excellent! Did you speak to any of your clients about the BBC idea?'

'I've spoken to two so far, and both indicated that they would be very interested when matters are a little more advanced. How are you getting on with the record companies, by the way?'

'Great, there's no problem, except that most of them seem to have decided Christmas began two weeks ago. I'm seeing the chairman of Columbus in an hour – you know, the American guy who always has the Afghan hound with him? I think Americans understand deals like this much better than the British. Anyway, straight to the top is my motto.'

'It's not your motto I'm worried about, Tim. It's more the Pump House in Glebe Lane.'

'Why what's wrong?'

'Eddie Chivers and Andy Grave.'

'Why are you dealing with Chivers direct? Where's his solicitor?'

'Tim, calm down! He's just like everyone else, trying to get his sale through. But, because you've said you're a cash buyer, he thinks this sale is going through by Christmas and it isn't!'

'*What do you mean, it isn't?*'

'Tim, we're not going to get anywhere here if you get over-excited. The position is simple. I have the survey report and the contracts all drawn up and ready to exchange. What I don't have is the mortgage offer from Mr Grave. I've called him six times in the last forty-eight hours and he hasn't returned one of my calls. Hardly what you would call professional.'

'Johnny, if you had that mortgage offer, how long would it take to complete?'

'Only a matter of days, but you haven't sold your own place yet, have you?'

'It's as good as sold. I might take out a bridging-loan with the bank to cover the shortfall. I'm not going to lose the Pump House, I can tell you . . .'

I was standing stone-cold sober in front of the Columbus reception desk wondering if Ted Powell would have the grace, the common sense, to offer me a drink during our meeting. He had reluctantly agreed to my suggestion that it would perhaps be in both our interests to meet and resolve one or two points. The reception area was more like an advertising agency than a record company, with its tall green plants and zebra-striped sofas dotted everywhere. There were two black-uniformed commissionaires standing behind either end of the desk interrogating visitors with a little too much zeal for my taste.

The receptionist put down the phone and with a sour pout said, 'Mr Powell will see you now. Would you take the lift, please, to the twelfth floor?'

I could see the older commissionaire trying to write my name on a plastic name-tag with a black felt-tip pen. He was concentrating so hard, with his tongue between his teeth, that for a moment I worried he might bite it in half. I was so immersed in thinking about what it would be like to live with only half a tongue that I nearly missed the brown-suited figure loitering by the lifts. I grabbed the name-tag and walked towards him across the tiled floor. Although he had his back to me, I would recognise that brown suit anywhere.

'Hey!' I shouted across the echoing foyer.

He turned very slowly, like a dog that knows it has done something wrong.

'Christ! Look what the cat's brought in. It's Tim Lomax!' Andy Grave quipped in his flat northern tone.

I forced a laugh. Just as he was opening his mouth to say something else, the lift arrived with a bump. Grave pointed his finger upwards as if to say, 'Sorry, I've got a meeting', and then held out his hand. Instead of shaking it, I pulled both of us inside the lift just as the doors were closing, banging my left elbow. There was no way I was going to miss this opportunity.

Andy Grave stood, his mouth and nose twitching like a neurotic hamster, his fingers hovering over the panel of buttons. 'Ha! Which floor, sir?' he joked nervously.

'Twelve, please, Andy.'

He pressed 12 and 8 for himself.

'Now, Andy, let's talk,' I said, leaning against the control panel.

Grave looked up anxiously at the floor indicator. 'What about? I've got a marketing meeting . . .'

I pressed the red Stop button. The lift juddered to a halt.

'What the bloody hell, are you doing?' he yelled in a high-pitched whine. 'Have you gone soft in the head? I've got to get out on the eighth floor, I've got a meeting.'

'You've said that already. Don't be more boring than you already are. Now, you and I are going to have a little talk about mortgages, right?'

I wanted to hit him there and then. The fact that I had never hit anyone before didn't matter a jot. I shuffled closer so I was nearly leaning against him. He tensed up badly, as if someone had just stuck a small tusk up his arse. He wasn't grinning so much as stretching his lips over his teeth. With the baggy black rings beneath his eyes, he looked like Bugs Bunny having a mid-life crisis.

'Look, I didn't want to switch labels; it was Rick. He was the one who made me agree. There wasn't anything I could do about it.'

'Don't hide behind Rick, Andy. Nobody can license an artist to another label without the manager's permission, so don't come out with that old chestnut. Anyway, I didn't say anything about the Dogs, did I?'

He had betrayal written all over his face. I jabbed him hard in the arm with my finger.

'So, what's happening about my mortgage? That's what this is all about. Not that you and Rick went behind my back when I was in America. Well?'

'Oh, eh, well, of course, that's all totally in hand,' Grave said clumsily. After a few sniffs, he remembered some of his more convincing lines. 'There's no problem with the mortgage, Tim! Apart from the postal strike up north and, then, would you believe it,' he sniffed again, 'my bloody phone went on the blink! I mean, I ask you, how do they expect you to run a business?'

I stepped in front of him, meaning to grab his collar, but grabbed his throat instead. I was nervous now, but enjoying the novelty of being a thug.

'Andy, I cannot afford to have any mistakes with the timing of this mortgage. *Do you understand?*'

His lips began to quiver.

'It's a lot of money, Tim. It's not that easy. I have to be careful. You'll get it; I promise!'

I tried to think what movie gangsters did in these circumstances and on instinct grabbed him by the lapels and threw him hard against the metal wall of the lift.

'*You had better get me that money!* Don't make promises you can't keep, Andy!'

Grave shook his head. 'I promised you the money and I won't let you down. Can we go now, I need the toilet'.

'A toilet? Stop fucking about, Andy, or I'll really lose my temper. I need the money before Christmas. Can you do that?'

'Providing the post is working correctly, yes,' Grave said, staring dejectedly at the control panel.

Suddenly, something inside me clicked.

'Andy, you fucking moron, of course the post is going to be cocked up. It's Christmas, for God's sake!'

I jabbed my finger in his chest. Grave's hand flew to his throat as if he was about to puke, and before I had a chance to stop him, he repeatedly pressed the emergency button with the other hand. Every bell on every floor began to ring. We could hear one of the commissionaires on the ground floor shouting and banging on the door.

I lit a cigarette, took an enormous drag, and stared down at the now crouching figure of Andy Grave: 'Now, what the hell did you do that for?'

39

'Hello, Tiger, long time, no see,' Loveday said, a little breathlessly.

'Long time indeed, Tiger,' I said, kissing her.

I knew I was pleased to see her but had no idea just how pleased she was to see me – that is, until we got back to my place. Christ Almighty! Once we were inside the flat, and I mean just inside the front door, she went completely ballistic, pulling my clothes off and throwing them up in the air.

Having thrown her fur coat on the sofa, Loveday peeled off a pair of gold tartan trousers and pink V-neck cashmere jersey in two seconds flat. She then lay face down on the carpet, putting her arms behind her and unhooking her bra. Flipping herself on to her back, and cupping a breast in each hand, she let out a nervous laugh. I knelt down, put my fingers inside the tops of her silk underwear, and slid them down her legs. Then I reached over to the sofa and pulled off some cushions to put under her back, but she threw them aside, as if she actually wanted the rough cord carpet to ride into her skin.

'Kiss me!' she yelled, wriggling her hips beneath me.

I leant down and kissed the beauty spot on her neck.

I carried on kissing her, gently, noisily, quick kisses, long kisses, all the way down her neck to her breasts. Loveday moaned. I moved my mouth up to hers and we kissed passionately, like we used to when we first met. Sliding her open mouth down over my chin, she arched her back slightly and shifted her shoulders, so that she was level with the side of my neck. She took a deep breath, let out a loud tiger-like snarl and sank her teeth into my neck, the hardest bite she'd ever done.

I liked the bus conductor on the No. 37. He wore a cowboy tie, had V-shaped sideburns, and a kept roll-up behind each ear. As soon as we got on board, I could tell he was able to keep his mouth shut and a crowd under control. Nevertheless, I handed him a twenty as an incentive to encourage passengers to stay downstairs and not interrupt Loveday and I who would be dining on the upper deck.

'I'll do my best,' he said, sniffing loudly and sliding the money into his back pocket. He then stepped closer, lowering his voice as if he was letting me into a state secret: 'We go all the way up to the World's End in Chelsea, turn round, and come all the way back down the Embankment, round to Westminster and then the same again. It's a new route, so you can stay up there as long as you like.'

'Great! And you're not going to mind if I play music?' I said, holding up a portable cassette player.

The conductor scrunched his shoulders into a shrug, and let out a short laugh. 'Well, that rather depends on what music it is, doesn't it?'

I whistled half a verse and chorus from 'Night and Day'. The conductor stuck his thumb in the air and nodded. 'Can't go wrong with a bit of Frank, now, can you?' he said.

I grinned and climbed the stairs to join Loveday.

Clinking together in my wicker basket were two bottles of champagne, along with a tablecloth, fresh smoked salmon, crab, prawns, mayonnaise and warm asparagus. For good measure, and because I knew Loveday loved them, I had also bought grapes, a smidgeon of Stilton and four baby Florentines.

The upper deck of the bus was bathed in a soft yellow light. We sat right at the back where there was more room and where we could get a better view.

'Tim, you know, I love you so much when you do this sort of thing,' Loveday said, moving her face softly against mine, while discreetly pushing a shiny black PVC holdall behind her.

'I had a hunch you would like it. Are you comfortable, madam, or would you like to move to another table?'

She smiled and shook her head, then turned to her left and pressed her face against the steamed-up window.

'We're just passing Battersea power station, so the funfair must be coming up soon!' she whispered enthusiastically, as if she didn't want anyone else to hear.

I leaned across her and marvelled at the towering chimneys silhouetted against the moon. Loveday took a long sip of champagne and, handing me the glass, nudged me to get out of the way. I stood up. As she passed me, she rubbed her breasts against my chest and held her hand between my legs while gently squeezing her lips into an irresistible pout. I lowered my mouth to meet hers and kissed her softly. Then I pulled her towards me and kissed her hard on the mouth, her tongue darting up and down as if it were a hummingbird. Suddenly she tweaked my nose and walked across to the other side of the bus. I stood there, still holding the glass of champagne, wondering what had hit me. Loveday turned round, shot me a coy smile, and said: 'I told you, Tim, it doesn't have to be New York!'

I motioned to her to come back, but teasing, she turned away. Pretending to ignore her, I picked up the cassette player, took out the Sinatra tape and put in Dionne Warwick instead. Catching my eye, Loveday ambled back, sat down sideways on my lap and draped her arms around my neck. I smiled at her, and, as we began a lingering kiss, pressed the button on the machine and 'The Look of Love' began to play.

Eventually, Loveday brought her knees up to her chest, and let out a happy sigh.

'Are you hungry?' she asked, squeezing a lemon on to some crab and putting it into my mouth. I managed to grunt my approval and watched as Loveday produced a black silk scarf from her pocket.

'Trust me,' she said, tying the scarf around my eyes. My thoughts turned to firing squads. 'No peeking! Ready in a minute.'

'Is this the scene where I wake up to find myself naked and handcuffed to a bus seat, while you ride off into the sunset on a motorbike?'

'You should be so lucky. Open wide, please.'

I opened my mouth and felt her finger gently touching my tongue. I licked the fingertip and then the whole finger, soon realising there was a taste of asparagus. I sucked her finger clean and loudly hummed my appreciation. Then, pretending to scratch my nose, I lifted the corner of the blindfold and saw that she had wrapped each of her fingertips with fine strands of smoked salmon and asparagus. One by one, she put them in my mouth.

The bus lurched to a stop just past Chelsea Bridge. I nudged Loveday and pointed across the moonlit surface of the Thames to the hundreds of lights twinkling on the far side, all the way to Albert Bridge. 'Don't you think that's really something?'

She leaned forwards and nodded. 'It's amazing to see things from this height. You get a completely different perspective, don't you? I mean, the lake is over there so the funfair must be over there and your apartment is behind them all.'

'And where's the Crooked Billet?' I asked.

Loveday was too entranced with the view to notice me standing up. 'Somewhere near here, isn't it?'

'It's the next stop.'

'Are we getting off, then?'

The wicker basket creaked loudly as we walked around the bend on Glebe Lane, towards the wooden gate of the Pump House. Loveday seemed concerned.

'Tim, it's really dark here. What's happened to the moon?'

'It'll be back in a minute. Come on, we're nearly there.'

I held Loveday's hand, guiding her along. There was only one streetlight, positioned on the far side of the lane.

When we got to the doorstep, Loveday gripped my arm.

'Tim, it's a bit spooky, isn't it?'

I felt in my pocket for the copy of Chivers's key I'd had made. 'Now, sweetheart, *you* have to cover your eyes and prepare for a big surprise.'

I heard a voice behind me whisper, 'I'm not Goldilocks, Tim.'

'No, and you're certainly not Little Red Riding Hood either.'

I turned the key in the lock.

'Tim, who does this belong to?'

I stepped inside and ran my hand along the wall until I found the light switch.

'Lights! Action! Shazam!' I shouted.

Loveday took my hand and stepped inside the door on to a cream sheet covered in masonry dust. I could tell immediately by the way the house was so well illuminated that Billy Crawley and his men had changed the old lighting for two industrial fluorescent strips suspended from the ceiling.

'God, it's big,' Loveday said, wide-eyed.

'So it is,' I said nonchantly.

'Look up there!' Loveday pointed at the galleried landing and the line of the banisters on the stairs.

'It's great, isn't it?' I said grinning a discreet proprietor's grin.

'You could fit my flat in here at least six times. Tim, who does this belong to? I mean, have you and Rick decided to rent it?'

'*Rick?*' I said incredulously.

'Well, who does it belong to?'

'It belongs to me,' I said in as a deadpan a voice as possible.

'Oh, good,' said Loveday facetiously, obviously not believing a word. 'Is there room for a post office by any chance?'

'That's the whole idea.' I laughed. With a sweep of my arm, I waved her towards the stairs.

On the landing, I was still anxious that she wouldn't like the place, but I could tell by the way standing on tiptoes to look up at the cornices that she was more than interested.

'Who's doing all this building work?' she said, pointing at the wheelbarrows downstairs.

'Ah,' I said.

'Ah what?' Loveday asked.

'Ah, well, it was all supposed to be a surprise.'

'You mean, you *really*, seriously, have bought it?'

'I'm going to divide the place in two. I'm going to make the new office downstairs and then have a separate house upstairs and around the courtyard at the back. I wasn't going to show it to you until after Christmas, when it was all finished, but I couldn't resist it.'

'So that's what you've been doing.'

'Well, as I said, it was supposed to be a surprise. Isn't it great?'

Loveday hugged herself and let out a nervous laugh that echoed loudly round the house. 'Tim, I don't want to start a row . . . but, a new office? Courtyard? Builders? How the fuck can you afford to do all this?'

Now it was my turn to laugh. 'Listen, it's something to celebrate!' I said in my most reassuring tone. 'Don't look so worried! Bridging loan is my new middle name.'

Loveday didn't look up.

'Look, sweetheart, if you are going to do something . . .' I said.

Loveday looked up, but she didn't look at me. Her eyes went to the vaulted ceiling, and then she closed them altogether.

'Do it properly,' she sighed.

'Absolutely right. Now let's go and celebrate!'

40

I woke up the next morning feeling as if I had been head-butted by a lamppost. I lay back in bed, trying to work out whether I was still dreaming or not. I opened my eyes, manoeuvred my head towards the bedside clock, and saw that it was ten past nine.

The telephone rang.

I cleared my throat loudly, and lifted the receiver.

It was Charles. An angry Charles.

'Why haven't you returned my calls?'

'Hello?'

'Tim! Are you there?'

'Who is this?'

'It's Charles, you bloody twit!'

'Oh . . .'

'What on earth's the matter with you? Are you still in bed?'

'Can I ring you back?'

'No you can't! Now, look, I'm bloody annoyed that you haven't had the courtesy to at least call me and let me know how you got on at the bank. And another thing . . .'

Charles proceeded with his lecture as I feebly gripped the telephone, holding it away from my ear.

'. . . so I think the very least you can do is to make sure you come down at the same time as me. We can go for a long walk in the afternoon after lunch and then be in good shape for Christmas dinner. Agreed? Good. See you at Dad's, then, around midday tomorrow. Bye.'

I heard the click of the telephone cutting off but carried on holding the receiver, half-expecting someone to walk in and put it down for me. After a few seconds of suspended animation, I tried to put it back on its cradle but missed. The phone clattered noisily to the floor and my head fell back on to the pillow.

Suddenly I glimpsed something out of the corner of my eye. I pushed the duvet back and turned right round to look at the pillow. It was dotted with blood.

How the hell did that happen?

I went back under the duvet and, as if flicking back and forth through the chapters of a book, tried desperately to remember what had happened last night. I knew that I had come back to the flat in a cab. Loveday wasn't with me. Why not? *Where is she now?* We saw the house and then took a taxi.

I remembered scanning the ground floor of Proust's, its windows steamed up from the heat, a crowd of people bending towards each other, almost eating each other's faces, pecking and gnawing at bits of conversation. I had walked straight up to the bar, and greeted my pal Elliot, the owner.

'Wotcha, cock. How are you?'

'Treating them mean, keeping them keen?' he had said, looking over towards Loveday.

I had ignored the jibe, shaken hands with him, and then proceeded to make comments about the television types filling the place up before returning to Loveday. Save for one long wooden table, the place had been emptied of its furniture and was filling up by the minute. Each time the door opened there was a bloody awful draft – yes I remembered that.

Oh, God, of course. It was all coming back: sitting with Loveday in the only quiet corner in the room – nearly dropping the bottle of wine – squashing together on one chair. And how, like Father Christmas, she had unzipped the mysterious PVC holdall she had been carrying all evening and had handed me an endless stream of presents, each individually wrapped and one with a special message hand-engraved on its back – a Seiko diving watch. How no-problem-at-all she had been about not receiving any presents from me, but how she was 'happy to wait until I came down to her parents' on Boxing Day'. When did I agree to that?

I fast-forwarded to conversations with other people in the room; to drunken banter with people I had never met. Three of the television types tried to impress me with their accomplishments and I put them, quite nicely I thought, in their place. Then that poncy Welsh actor, Robert Tilly, with the deep voice, shaggy black hair and big eyebrows had made a play for Loveday.

'Oh, Tim, darling, one hears such great things about you from young Elliot, such prowess, such muscularity in the fickle world of pop! Don't ask about my world, it's just too boring, having to get up each day at five and spend three hours having your face put on. Oh, hello, dear, you must be Loveday, ah, and with a face that could launch a thousand ships . . .'

Smarmy bastard. Oh, it was all becoming clear now. There was the conversation about what really did happen in the hotel in Scotland. How I had pretended not to take it seriously until the point where she had said she was surprised that I didn't seem to mind. There, of course, I had had to put her right. I was fucking furious.

The evening had gone on and on and on. I wasn't the only one who was drunk, for God's sake! Most of the people there were. How had it all happened? *What* had happened?

I brought my left arm out from beneath the duvet and squinted at the chunky diver's watch weighing down my wrist. Jesus – Loveday's Christmas present! It was Christmas Eve! I threw off the duvet, ran my hand over my face a few times and walked out to the bathroom. I didn't want to look in the mirror, so with my eyes half shut, I lit a cigarette, had a pee and ran a bath. I slouched back into the bedroom, sat down on the bed and picked up the telephone.

'Elliot?'' I asked cautiously, listening carefully for any hint of hostility.

Elliot sounded hungover but relatively cheerful. 'Ha-ha! I was wondering how long it would take you to call.'

'Eh, was there a bit of a problem last night?'

'What! Don't you remember?'

'Not an awful lot.'

Elliot laughed, and then hesitated. 'Have you spoken to anyone else this morning? Loveday, perhaps?'

'Don't be daft, of course not – that's why I'm ringing you!'

'Mmm, I see. How is the nose this morning – a bit sore?'

'It's all sore, Elliot. Don't be a bastard. Just tell me what happened.'

'The short version is that by about one o'clock, Loveday was tired and wanted to go home. Apparently she asked you more than eight times if you could both leave.'

'That's right, she kept pulling at my bloody sleeve, annoying me.'

'Well, unfortunately, I didn't see this, but you weren't interested because you were immersed in an argument with some bloke from the BBC. Just after two o'clock, Loveday asked you again, and, unfortunately, Tim, this time you lost your temper. Tim, you took a swing at her.'

'Christ! I didn't . . . did I?'

'You certainly did. Only the good news is that the barman and I were there to stop you. I grabbed your right arm and he grabbed your left, otherwise you would have hit her. Loveday, however, didn't have anybody holding her back and she whacked you straight on the nose. You weren't at all pleased, because I think it hurt quite a lot. She was quite right, though, you were bang out of order . . .'

Several minutes later, I was staring into the wardrobe mirror. My nose was more swollen than I had thought. I held the bridge between my thumb and forefinger, half-expecting, half-wanting it to be broken, but discovered that it wasn't. I had asked Elliot repeatedly what mood Loveday had been in when she had left the wine bar. All he said was: 'When I got her a cab she seemed upset but OK. No real damage done. Yes, she was still a bit upset, but smiling.'

I held out the palms of my hands, the left one holding upset and the right one OK and attempted to balance them. The left hand was easily tipping the scales.

No, Elliot didn't understand Loveday. For her even to reveal that she *might* be upset meant that she was bloody upset. This was bad, very bad indeed.

I dialled her number. I knew immediately from Monica's tone that I was in big trouble.

'She's gone to her parents. You've missed her. Bye.'

Remorse and recrimination multiplied into a swarm of butterflies in my stomach. I decided to get into the bath. Stretching the telephone cord into the bathroom, I rested the phone on the edge of the tub and eased myself into the water. It was so hot it was nearly unbearable but I took comfort in its purging quality. As soon as I had become used to the heat, I leant back and smoked a cigarette. A battle began in my head between what do to about the butterflies and how to proceed with the rest of the day.

The telephone rang again. I leaned forward on my knees and picked it up, praying it was Loveday.

'Tim? It's Johnny Darrell.'

I let out a big sigh of disappointment.

'Oh . . . hi Johnny. Sorry, I thought you might be someone else.'

'Tim, you're lucky that it isn't anybody else. I want you to listen extremely carefully to what I've got to say. Don't say anything to me unless you're completely sure of the implications. Right?'

'Right,' I said, as I draped a hot flannel over the bridge of my nose. Johnny sounded angry.

'Problem one. Yesterday morning Mr Chivers, the *owner* of the Pump House, returned from his holiday a week earlier than planned. While away, he changed his mind about selling his late father's property. In short, Tim, Mr Chivers paid a visit to Glebe Lane and discovered not only nine builders drinking nine cups of tea but all the interior walls of the ground floor and basement of his house demolished. He was not happy. Mr Chivers telephoned the local police station, where, for some reason, he seems to have personal connections, and within half an hour a Mr Crawley and eight builders were taken to Chelsea police station – where, I might add, they remained until eleven o'clock last night. The legal implications for the person who authorised the builders to enter and do the work . . . provide me with a substantial amount of money on account for defending any of these charges . . . I already have a message to call Messrs Curd and Curd acting for Mr Crawley, and a rather unpleasant letter from Rick Fraser's lawyers in the post as well. So, you had better come and see me within the next three hours. Remember, it's Christmas Eve. As far as we're concerned, we close at three this afternoon. This is serious. OK?'

I let the receiver drop on to the bathmat and let out another long sigh. 'Not good, but not the end of the world,' I muttered to myself. I lit a cigarette, and inhaled deeply; noticing that my hand was shaking, I started to whistle.

Goddamn it, I was whistling 'Stop the Cavalry'. I could at least whistle 'Rhiannon's Café'.

I took another drag of the cigarette, poked it out in the bathwater and lobbed it into the toilet bowl.

41

I am standing in the kitchen dressed in a white shirt, dinner-jacket, black trousers and bowtie, and plates with the debris from last night's Indian takeaway are littered everywhere. I don't mind the mess; I don't mind the echoes of yesterday ringing in my head. What I do mind is Ned and Loveday not talking to me. Ned is sulking in the sitting room with his back towards me as if there's been a row. Maybe Christmas morning doesn't mean anything to him any more; maybe he's grown out of it. Loveday is never in when I telephone her parents' home to speak to her.

I had intended to have a different morning, very different indeed. By rights I should now be having mulled wine, kissing my sister, psyching myself up for the walk from hell, but Thai grass makes you sleep. Not to mention Gabe and the rest of the band going on and on and on, into the early hours of the morning. Even George had been unable to drive the Mercedes home and had to hire a mini-cab. Anyway, I'm sure they can do without me for a little while down there. Guess who answered the telephone when I rang to say I was going to miss lunch?

'You're joking, aren't you?' Charles said.

I was forced to take control because I could see we were going to have a row.

'Charles, get a grip. I'm ringing from the Middlesex hospital. I'm bringing Christmas cheer to patients. Put Diana on and I'll see you in a while.'

He didn't say anything but shouted tersely for Diana. When I spoke to my sister she was annoyed too, but more concerned that I would at least be in good time for the dinner. She told me that lunch was going to be simple: Dad's artichoke soup followed by cold ham, poached salmon, etcetera, so as far as she was concerned, provided I arrived in time for dinner, I would be forgiven. Just.

I had fully intended to go to Mass that morning but was not going to take any chances by driving with the roof down. The steep wide steps leading up to the Brompton Oratory struck me as too dangerous and deserted, just the sort of place I could be picked off by a sniper with a telescopic sight. So instead I drove the car to Westminster Cathedral.

I parked on Ambrosia Avenue overlooking the piazza and the main entrance. I opened the car door wide, stubbed out my cigarette, and stepped out on to the pavement. A smartly dressed crowd was already pouring out of the church and congregating at the bottom of the steps, shaking hands and kissing as if for the very last time. Elderly women, dressed in fur hats and red woollen coats, walked arm-in-arm with husbands with slicked-back hair and well-trimmed moustaches. Younger and more expensive-looking parents tightly clutched their expensive children's hands.

Perhaps I should wait a while and then go in for a discreet word.

But you can never be sure quite how private these places are, can you?

I stood back and began scanning the crowd for a sight of the Cardinal. As in everything else these days, it was so much better to go straight to the top. I briefly imagined him spotting me and apologising to whomever he was with, then coming over and getting into my car.

'Tim, we need to talk, do you fancy Italian?'

'OK, Humey, jump in.'

Soon we would be in the Santa Croce, biting into fresh radishes while parrying in the air with our breadsticks and arguing about the existence of free will.

The sound of the midday church bells flipped me back to reality. I got back into the Mercedes and drove back to Prince of Wales Drive.

Lunch with Ned was an unqualified success in terms of restoring the two of us to speaking terms. In fact, the cat positively purred the loudest purr I had ever heard as he ate the smoked salmon I presented him with. However, to my chagrin, he drew the line at lapping up the champagne I poured out for him in a special saucer. So, instead, over a series of toasts to past and future triumphs, I finished the remainder of the bottle myself.

It was George who saved the day, waking me from the three-hour coma I'd fallen into with his phone-call. My shouts of distress on hearing that it was after six o'clock worried him so much that he said he would come round immediately and drive me to Hedgerly Cross in time for dinner.

By the time George reached the flat, though, I no longer felt sleepy.

'Come in, George. Have a drink. Happy Christmas and all that.'

Pumped up, cracking jokes, pacing the floor, I was like a boxer skipping from foot to foot at the beginning of a fight. I was a matador and a bull tied together in the same ring.

'Please be careful, steady now,' George kept saying as we crossed the road to get to the car.

When the Mercedes pulled into the driveway of my father's house, I took a final swig from my hipflask, wiped my mouth triumphantly and screwed the top firmly back on. Still a boxer, still a matador, still a bull, and not taking any prisoners. George managed to brake just in time as he spotted the illuminated backlights of the cars lining the driveway.

'Christ! There's no bloody room to park. You think they'd leave some space, wouldn't you? Oh, well, here we go. I'll get out here, George.'

'OK, Tim. Thanks again for the Christmas presents, it was very kind of you.'

'Stick with me, George. You know it makes sense.'

We both laughed and shook hands. I turned and walked slowly along the gravel drive towards the porch.

George didn't move.

'Call me if you want anything, Tim,' he said. 'You've got the number, haven't you?'

'Yeah. I've got it somewhere. Wish me luck.'

'Well . . . OK then. Good luck and please be careful.'

Standing in the porch, I watched as George got back into the car and fastened his safety-belt. I took a deep breath, rang the bell, and eyed the broken porch-light impatiently.

The door swung open, letting out a gust of unexpected heat. Diana stood with one hand on her hip and one on the door, wearing a long black chiffon dress. I stepped forward, smiled broadly, and kissed her hello.

'Hello, sweetie. Sorry I'm a bit late. Everything OK?'

Diana silently closed the front door behind me, and then gave a loud sigh.

'Tim, I told you this was important! Look, *I* don't mind about lunch but don't bugger up this dinner or I'll kill you. I've already had to blow the candles out twice.'

'Who *does* mind?' I said, staring at my reflection in the mirror, and pushing my hair back from my forehead.

Diana raised her eyebrows to heaven and nodded her head in the direction of the sitting room.

'You can guess, can't you? Please? They've all been waiting for you. They may not show it, but it's a very important night for everyone, especially Dad.'

'All right, got the message, programmed to respond. Why are you whispering?'

Diana suspended transmission temporarily, as she leant towards the gold-leaf hall mirror to reapply her lipstick, noisily rubbing her lips together.

'Tim, get into that room! Have you not brought any presents?'

'As if I would forget!'

I opened the front door again, dragged in a black plastic sack and smirked at her.

'Hello, everyone, good evening and welcome!' I said as I marched into the sitting room, carrying the sack on my shoulder like Santa Claus.

'You're late,' said Charles.

I ignored him by waving a high-speed greeting to everyone else.

'Hello, Dad, didn't know you were going to be here! Just a joke! Any chance of a drink? No, don't worry, I'll help myself.'

My father, who was having difficulty finding a safe place to put down his glass, stood up and said, 'Now, just hang on a minute, Timmy. Come and say hello properly before you do that.'

But it was too late. I was already halfway to the dining room.

I overheard Charles enunciating rather loudly to my father: 'Don't call him Timmy, Dad. He's not Timmy. He's Tim, as in grim.'

My father didn't reply. I walked back into the room carrying a very full glass of whisky, aware that I might be on the cusp of an argument with Charles. Diana's husband, Stuart, stepped in front of me, gripping two small wrapped gifts. 'Tim, these are for you!' Flat-footed and cheerful, he was not wearing his usual strength glasses.

'Presents, eh? Stuart, this is most unexpected. Thank you!'

'Yes, well, I think we shouldn't open them now,' Charles said, looking across at my father for support. 'I think we should wait until after dinner. After all, it's nearly nine o'clock.'

Stuart smiled compliantly as I transferred the tumbler to my left hand, walked up to my father and shook hands.

'Dad! Hello properly. Get it? Hello *properly*. Funny eh?'

My father grinned briefly but said nothing. Sensing a transgression, I turned to the safer territory of Diana.

'Beautifully laid table in there. Anything to do with you?'

'I'm surprised you even noticed,' she said.

'I thought it was Christmas and we were supposed to be nice to each other.'

'We have been nice to each other,' Diana said. 'Since this morning.'

'My, God, Charles, that must have tested your reserves.'

'Yes, it has.'

'Are we not opening presents?'

'We waited until teatime, Tim, hoping that a certain person was going to join us.'

'Suit yourself. I think it's rather nice of me to provide you with the opportunity of having two present-opening sessions.'

'Are we ready to sit down and eat, Diana?' Charles asked, putting his glass down on the mantelpiece and staring at Maya.

'Yes. Well, we can wait a little longer. It's up to Dad. What would you like to do, Dad? Would you like to eat now or would you rather wait?'

'Whatever you think best. I don't mind when we eat.'

There was a palpable downturn in the atmosphere but no one could find the necessary words to reverse it. Stuart jumped in.

'Tell me, Tim, how was America? I haven't seen you since you got back.'

'Good point: how was America? I often ask myself that. No, to be serious, it was great. We must talk about it soon because there may be some opportunities for you there too. I can't say much about it at the moment until one or two little legal matters have been, shall we say, progressed.'

I was aware of being observed, in particular by Charles. I decided to take cover by speaking individually to everyone else in the room. Maya was standing reading Christmas cards by the mantelpiece in a sexy strapless olive-coloured dress. She was wearing sparkling drop-down earrings and a necklace that made her cleavage seem enormous.

'Hello, Maya, you're looking rather delicious tonight. Are those earrings real or paste?'

'They're diamonds, actually, a Christmas present from your brother.'

'Oh, well then, things must be looking up. I expect you and Charles will soon be posing for photographers on your new estate in Wiltshire?' Before she had a chance to respond, Charles stepped between us.

'Tim, I want to talk to you . . .'

'Sorry, Charles, I've just got to say hello over here.' I quickly took a step backwards, turned round and stood in front of Stuart.

'So, as I was saying, America looks like being the future for me. Are you interested in being there?' I said, pulling a cigarette from the packet with my teeth.

'I wish I could, but your sister is afraid of flying. You never know. Speak of the devil . . .'

Stuart's attention was taken by Diana waving to him from the sitting-room door.

'Sorry, Tim . . .'

He padded away leaving Charles and me alone. Predictably, and with everyone else nearly out of earshot, Charles got straight to the point.

'Right, why are you avoiding me?'

'For God's sake, Charles, sensitive doesn't suit you.'

'Stop playing silly buggers, I want to know what's happening at the bank, and what's going on with this deal in New York.'

'Everything's fine. It's all under control. Why are *you* so worried?'

'I'm not worried. I'm just concerned that you're doing things properly, that's all.'

'Everything is OK. Under control and going according to plan.'

'Are you getting everyone to put things in writing? Are you keeping accurate accounts, receipts for all you've spent?'

I counted to five. 'Look, Charles, do you understand how big this thing is? I wouldn't have asked you for your help with the bank unless I bloody needed it, you know.'

'Tim, I know that. Have you got everything in writing?'

I counted to ten.

'Tim! Are you listening to me? For Christ's sake, tell me what's going on.'

'Look, Charles, I've got lawyers dealing with the paperwork both here and in New York, and I can assure you once again I am not going to blow a deal that is worth six million dollars. OK?'

I drained my glass. Time for a refill. 'Do you want one?' I asked.

Charles looked at me wearily. 'No thanks. We're about to sit down and eat. Don't you think you've had enough?'

I was already halfway down the hall, giving Charles a 'V' sign.

'Naughty, naughty,' said Diana, standing in the doorway of the dining room. 'I'll tell Charles.'

'Sweetie, you can tell who the fuck you like because I don't give a shit, OK? Now what time are Morecambe and Wise on television and where's that bottle?'

'What are you talking about Morecambe and Wise for?' Diana said. 'We're going to be eating any second. Come on.'

I took the bottle into the sitting room and sat down next to my father who had returned from somewhere and immediately asked, 'Is it time?'

'Time for what, Dad?'

'Time to sit down for dinner, I suppose.'

'It's up to you, Dad. You could stay with me and watch Morecambe and Wise if you like. You know how much Mum used to love them.'

'No, I think we had better go in.'

My father stood up and slowly walked towards the dining room. His role of decanting the port had been taken over by Charles; his role of carving the meat had also been taken over by Charles.

He looked back at me and called out.

'I made the soup, Tim, but you didn't appear. You haven't forgotten our conversation, have you?'

'No, Dad, of course not,' I called back.

They were all in there, standing behind high-backed chairs. I could hear them shifting in their shoes, then a host of scraping as everyone acknowledged my father's arrival by sitting down. There was just one empty chair left.

'Could someone please ask Tim to join us?' Diana asked.

I was sitting on the carpet in the sitting room, leaning against the velvet sofa, the black plastic bag of presents to my left, the bottle of whisky to my right, laughing loudly at the television. On the show that night were guest appearances from Woody Allen and Catherine Deneuve, allowing themselves to be sent up as backing singers for a Morecambe and Wise punk rock band, Slash. I roared with laughter.

'Woody Allen! Jesus, this is going to be great.'

'For Christ's sake, what the bloody hell do you think you're doing?' Charles shouted so loudly that I knocked my glass of whisky over the carpet.

'Everybody's sitting down waiting for you, as bloody usual. You've done bugger all to contribute, you turn up late, and now all you want to do is ruin everyone's evening by watching bloody television. Well, I'm not having it.'

I was already riled by the force of Charles's interruption, but when he pulled the television plug from the socket, I exploded.

'*Do you fucking well mind, you fucking prick!* This is not your bloody house in case you hadn't noticed.'

Charles was already halfway out of the sitting-room door when he stopped and, with much control as he could muster said, 'Tim, you're ruining things. Pull yourself together.'

I stared at him for a moment, and then, with my voice somewhat higher than normal, let him have it with both barrels.

'You know what the trouble with you is, Charles? You're a fucking train spotter. You want everything to go like clockwork, everything to proceed according to your own excruciating timetable. Well, I'm different, OK, and so, I suspect, are a lot of other people.'

Charles shook his head and walked off.

For a few moments I could hear an awkward silence around the table in the dining room. I forced open the sliding doors between the rooms and wheeled in the television set. Diana looked at Stuart, Maya looked at Charles, and Charles looked angrily at my father.

'Ah, Timmy.' My father hesitated. 'If you don't mind, I think we won't have the television on in the dining room just now.'

'Jesus Christ, Dad!' exclaimed Charles through gritted teeth.

'Don't listen to Charles, Dad, he doesn't know what he's talking about,' I said plugging in the television.

There was a three-second silence in which we could hear the hum of the set warming up. I sat down, blew a mouthful of cigarette smoke across the table and said, 'That's better. Compromise is everything, don't you think?' Then, as an afterthought, I added: 'I'll tell you something, if Mum was still here she'd be pretty pissed off about all this.'

Instantly my father snapped. He banged his fist on the table, and roared, 'Don't you say that! Don't you ever say that about Mummy! Now switch that bloody . . . bloody television off, *right now!*'

The only sound in the room was an overturned wine glass rolling across the table. Everyone stared straight ahead. The long silence continued.

'Did you hear what Dad said, you stupid bastard?' Charles hissed, his voice beginning to crack.

'Don't you speak to me like that, you arsehole,' I retorted loudly, lurching towards him.

Charles swung himself out of his chair, grabbed me by the arm, and pushed me against the television, which, like myself, toppled backwards against the wall. I sprang back up, pushing Charles hard until he crashed against the door. He grabbed me by the shoulders in what looked like one of our playfights, but as I broke free of his grip, I realised he was deadly serious. While Diana, Maya and Stuart pleaded for the pair of us to stop, I swung my fist at Charles's head. The punch missed, but Charles's reflex backhand caught me hard across my nose. Before I had time to fully register the pain, my father stood up and bellowed: 'Stop it! Stop it you two! Stop it right now!'

While Charles manhandled me to my chair and returned to his own, tears rolled freely down Diana's and Maya's cheeks. I sat there for a few moments, holding my nose between the palms of my hands. My father slumped back in his chair, looking ashen. Maya studiously picked up the wine glass lying by his place mat and belatedly mopped up the spilt wine. Eventually, Charles put down the spoon he had been examining, cleared his throat with two distinct grunts and said, as if he was justifying an unpopular umpiring decision at Wimbledon: 'I'm sorry about that, Tim, but you had gone too far.'

I cleared my throat to make sure my voice was not shaking, blinked to make sure my eyes were not watering, stood up and, with as much sang-froid as I could muster, said: 'I am afraid that you've all become rather too bourgeois for me. Tonight has been like a reminder of a bad play I never wanted to see. You have all allowed yourselves to become trapped into some cesspit of mediocrity that I want no part of. You're all so small, so conditioned by middle-class glue that you're stuck – stuck so far up your own arses that you probably need a torch. Not for me, I'm getting out, whatever you say, I'm off.'

With that, I yanked the silver butter dish towards me and, looking straight into Charles's face, stubbed my cigarette out in the butter. I then strode through the open partition doors, picked up my coat, walked into the hall, wrenched open the front door, and slammed it hard behind me.

December 1980 – Part II

42

'Should be sorted in a minute, Tim!' Gabe called out, leaning his arm on the white counter of the Concorde check-in desk and throwing me a patient smile.

The uniformed hostess reappeared behind the counter.

'Excuse me, love!' Gabe said cheerfully 'Any chance of our tickets? We have been waiting a while.'

The hostess took a deep breath and smiled. 'I'm sorry, there's a slight problem.' Gabe stood up and scratched his head. 'Oh, but we *do* have a reservation . . .'

I stepped up to the counter, sniffed loudly, pulled my coat tight around my shoulders and said to Gabe: 'Leave this to me.'

The hostess laughed a little nervously.

'Oh, Mr Lomax, I was just coming over to explain. I'm sorry for the delay, but your credit card has only just authorised payment for the tickets.'

'I reserved these tickets over the telephone with my Access America card almost twelve hours ago. There shouldn't have been any delay.'

'No, perhaps not, but the trouble is, I'm afraid that the captain has now closed the flight for any further boarding.'

'What did you say?'

The hostess looked down and quickly added: 'There is another Concorde flight in three hours and we do have the Concorde lounge.'

I took a pace forward, gripped the desk with both hands, and let loose: 'Do you know how much money I'll lose as a result of being late for my meeting in New York? Do you? Do you know how much money British Airways are then going to lose? No, you probably don't. Well, if you want to hold on to your job, you sort this out – right bloody now!'

Thirty minutes later, climbing the spiral staircase to the first-class compartment of the Air India flight to New York, I caught sight of Gabe's troubled expression.

'Gabe it was their fucking cock-up not mine.'

'Yeah, but you were a bit hard on that girl and the bloke from British Airways.'

I lowered my voice a little.

'Obviously, that man knew I was completely right but he didn't have the guts to admit it. Which is a shame for him, really, because when I get to New York I'm going to ring my lawyer and instruct him to sue.'

Gabe opened his mouth but thankfully a pretty Indian hostess interrupted, bowing with her clasped hands outstretched.

'Welcome to First Class and the Upper Deck.'

To my immense satisfaction the ten rows of first-class seats were unoccupied on this flight except for an elderly couple at the very front. This meant that Gabe and I had the rest of the seats, and the circular bar complete with bar stools, to ourselves.

While inwardly marvelling at the luxuriously wide leather seats, the opulence and the waiting champagne and canapés, I wished to appear unimpressed and busied myself with setting out my notepads and scattering the contents of my briefcases over a whole row of seats. In the row opposite, Gabe sat smiling happily, allowing the air hostess to buckle his seatbelt.

As I felt the plane tilt backwards, I peered through the window and, seeing the English fields grow smaller beneath us, let out a secret sigh of relief. All morning I had been acting and I knew it. Acting as if nothing was the least untoward, the least bit strange. I told myself, right there, sitting in my first-class seat, that I still didn't care, didn't give a fuck about what anybody thought of me or what anybody was trying to do to me. As the no-smoking signs were switched off, I took out a cigarette and gently rolled it against the bridge of my nose. I smiled at the thought of my next encounter with Eddie Chivers' assistant, promising myself that next time I would be more accurate with my punching.

The incident outside the gates to my flat that morning had unnerved me. It wasn't the fact that I'd had a writ for £5,750-worth of damages stuffed into my hand; it was the way it was done.

Returning from the local corner shop, I had noticed a man with his hands deep inside his overcoat pockets, pacing up and down outside my gates. As I got closer, the man put out his hand and greeted me cheerfully.

'Good morning! It is Tim Lomax, isn't it?'

I chuckled and, mistaking him for an old school friend, replied in the affirmative. 'Hello, nice to see you again, eh, I'm sorry I can't remember . . .'

The man slapped a piece of paper in my hand, stood back and smirked.

The moment I realised that I'd been fooled into accepting a writ, I let him have it.

'You cowardly fucker! Is this your idea of serving legal proceedings? Creeping up on people before breakfast and tricking them? You slimy cunt!'

The man stopped smirking and lurched forward, pushing me hard against the wall.

'You've got fourteen days to respond. You bloody conman!'

The thought that I had managed to punch him on the side of his face and hold his neck in a headlock for a few seconds was some consolation. The fact that the man had then succeeded in breaking free of my grip and banged the bridge of my nose with the flat of his fist before running off to a waiting car, however, was less gratifying.

A gentle pressure on my arm returned me to the present.

'Good afternoon, sir. May I offer you a hot towel and a glass of champagne?'

I turned my head and came face to face with the best smile and most beautiful pair of eyes I had seen all day. I hesitated at a roundabout of lust and alcohol. Taking hold of the towel and pressing it against my face, I answered stoically, 'Just a Perrier please.'

The air hostess smiled another beautiful smile and within seconds placed a cut glass fizzing with ice and lemon on my drinks tray. Just as I was commiserating with myself that it looked like a gin and tonic, she said: 'Is your face sore? Can I get you something? It looks painful.'

'No, thank you, it's just a little scratch.'

Nothing compared to the war I was about to enter. This was the eve of the battle; this was the real crusade, the ultimate one. I had to be focused, to aim straight, and to rise above the slings and arrows of whatever might be thrown at me. I had known it was time to jettison all the bourgeois, difficult, demanding, suburban people who were snapping at my heels. My only gesture to the world I had left behind was a short letter to Loveday, saying I was sorry because I knew she would not understand, but to trust me. And to have faith, until I returned, fully equipped to buy as many sub-post offices as she wished.

The plane was too quiet. I needed an adventure. I got up, winked at Gabe, and casually wandered towards the front seats. I walked down the spiral staircase and through the darkened business class towards the curtain protecting the door to the pilot's cabin. Pulling the curtain aside, I knocked politely on the door and opened it.

The cockpit was surprisingly light and its instrument panel reminded me of fifty travel-clocks set within the dashboard of the Gaulle.

'Good afternoon, my name is Lord Lomax. I'm the chairman of Fish Farm plc. Please call me Tim. How do you do?' I said handing each of them one of my new business cards.

The captain and his two moustachioed co-pilots were surprisingly relaxed as they swivelled round to answer. Wearing short-sleeved white cotton shirts and ties, they looked as if they were members of some colonial club.

'I'm sorry, did you say fish?'

I grinned and pointed to the illustration on the card of three fish holding pitchforks, wearing baggy jeans and playing electric guitars.

The captain cleared some papers from a chair and invited me to sit down and talk. The atmosphere was friendly, like sitting around a bar.

'Is Fish Farm a big company, sir?' the captain asked.

'We're doing quite well and should be pretty big by the end of next year.'

I candidly answered the questions put to me about the vicissitudes of running a small empire, including a detailed explanation regarding Badsoul's offer and the nature of my current trip. The three Indian pilots seemed to be charmed by my descriptions of my people in London and New York and were intrigued as I explained my plans for expansion and my belief in the value of owning property.

'I hope this doesn't sound in any way flash, but I wonder how much it would cost to buy a plane like this?'

The pilots looked at each other. Finally, the captain spoke.

'I must say I don't think the idea is at all flash. Considering the amount of travel you're going to be undertaking in the next year or so, it sounds eminently sensible.'

I was flattered that they were taking me seriously. Just a question of good manners and foresight, I told myself. The captain tapped his cigarette packet loudly.

'But I would suggest not buying, sir, but leasing. That way you can always be sure of a modern plane.'

'What a great idea! Do you think you could radio your head office and get them to give me a quote?'

'Certainly, sir, we'll radio Delhi. Go and relax in your seat, and we'll be sure to let you know before we reach New York.'

43

As the stretch Lincoln Continental thundered towards the neon skyline of Manhattan, a sentimental lump came into my throat. The lights of cars blinking over Queensboro Bridge, the juicy smell of Cadillac upholstery, and Frankie's Brooklyn accent all felt intoxicatingly familiar. It was like returning to a village I'd known all my life; almost like Hedgerly Cross, but with a very different family.

By the time the two bellboys had put away the luggage and I had given them each a twenty, Gabe announced he badly needed to sleep. I paced around every inch, every nook and cranny of the three-bedroom luxury suite.

I needed fresh air.

Once outside the Plaza, the cold air smacked me in the face. I looked across the road for the chestnut-coloured horse, and spotted its forlorn figure standing tethered to an empty carriage. I decided, instead of finding some sugar lumps, that I would buy it some roasted chestnuts. I set off purposefully in the direction of Columbus Circle. My mind was busy debating the merits of riding the horse bareback through Central Park when I suddenly collided with an oncoming pedestrian. On a point of British instinct I shouted, 'I am so sorry!'

I smelt and heard a perfumed voice say: 'Nothing broken, honey.'

I stood back, blinked repeatedly and focused my eyes on the pair of legs I had just crashed into. They looked like two shapely redwood trees standing in suggestively high patent heels, rising up to the dizzy heights of a pink miniskirt. My eyes travelled north and located a spandex sweater that looked as if it had been custom-shrunk on to two pneumatic breasts. Above that, a pretty black face in its late twenties, with a big mouth, big lips, big hair, and huge eyes daubed with enough mascara to repaint the Brooklyn Bridge. The girl stood two paces away chewing gum, with one leg tilted against the other, managing to smile and look bored at the same time, like some sexy ostrich contemplating a snack. She leaned down towards me and asked, 'Hi there, honey, doing anything tonight?'

'Funnily enough, I'm not booked up,' I replied, transfixed by the pouting breasts. 'But aren't you cold? I mean, isn't it a bit chilly without a coat?'

'I get warm when I'm in bed. You got a hotel?'

A shiver of excitement passed through me as I registered her directness. I had never been in this situation before, but remembered what Harry had said about life not being a dress rehearsal.

'Listen, my hotel is just back there. Why don't you come back and have some champagne, and maybe we can find a way of warming you up?'

'OK. Let's go,' said the girl, matter-of-factly.

I smiled as she slid her arm around mine. How very different girls in New York were compared to London.

As we came up to the white marble steps of the Plaza, the girl stopped abruptly.

'No way! There's no way I'm going in there. No way.'

'What on earth are you talking about? This is probably the best hotel in New York.'

'I can't go in. They don't like me here, dig? I'm banned. They won't let me in. Let's getouta here and go some other place,' the girl said nervously.

'Won't let you in? Who says so?' I said, locking my arm tightly around her and pulling her up the steps. 'I don't think you realise who I am, do you? Now take that chewing gum out of your mouth and leave this to me.'

I walked purposefully across the large foyer, bypassing the two reception desks, straight over to the squashed pulpit emblazoned with a gold plaque saying security. Leaning over it, I smiled benevolently at the crop-haired security clerk.

'Good evening, I wonder if you could help me?'

'I'll do my best, sir.'

'I think you know who I am? Lord Lomax? Yes?'

The clerk nodded, anxiously looking down at a list. I didn't wait for a reply, 'Yes, that's right. Now, the point is, could you tell me if there is any reason whatsoever why this young lady should not be welcome in this hotel?'

The clerk stroked the plastic nametag pinned to his jacket, unsure whether this was a joke or something more serious. He looked at the girl's face, then down at my hand laid flat on his desk and the hundred-dollar bill peeking out from beneath. He looked back up at the girl, and said cheerfully: 'No problem, Lord Lomax, no problem at all. I think there must have been a misunderstanding. The lady is most definitely welcome in this hotel.'

As we ascended to the twenty-fifth floor, I felt pleased with myself, and fully entitled to put my tongue in my new companion's ear.

'Hey, not so quick,' hissed the spandexed one, putting another piece of chewing gum into her mouth. I laughed, held out my hand and slapped it twice in self-admonishment.

Once inside the sitting room of the suite and having satisfied myself that I could hear Gabe safely snoring through his bedroom door, I poured out two glasses of champagne.

'Here you are, have a drop of this. My name's Tim by the way. What's yours?'

'Betsy,' she said, lying badly and waving the glass away. 'I can't drink that. I only drink Don Perignon. Which way is the bathroom?'

'You only drink *what?*'

'*I only drink Don Perignon.*'

I was becoming a little irritated.

'You're very grand, aren't you? Well, for a start it's not don it's dom. As in dominus.'

Betsy tilted her head and smiled a sexy but petulant smile. 'The bathroom?'

I realigned my mood to the challenge of seduction, stood up and in a series of unsteady flamenco steps showed her to the bathroom. Rushing back, I downed both glasses of champagne, dialled room service, and ordered two bottles of Dom Perignon. Just as I was rearranging all the velvet cushions so that they were pressed up against one end of the sofa, Betsy reappeared.

'Come in, sit down, relax, Dom Perignon is on his way.'

Feeling the perfumed creature brush down beside me, I felt another wave of excitement. This was like being back in England on a third date.

'So, when were you last in London, Betsy? Or are you the type that never leaves Manhattan?'

'I'm the type that never leaves the city. How many bedrooms are there here?'

'Really? You never leave the city? How interesting! Bedrooms, well now that's a thing. There are three actually, but one of them is occupied so that leaves a choice of two. Do you need to lie down?'

'Who's in the other room?'

'Oh, that's my friend Gabriel. He's fast asleep, don't worry.'

'Gabriel? Isn't that a girl's name?'

'Gabriel's a guy, as in the angel? God didn't make girl angels.'

'I'm a Baptist.'

'How nice.'

'It's OK.'

'You're rather shy, I can see that. But you're completely gorgeous that's for sure. Why don't you have a joint? The champagne will be here any minute.'

Betsy exhaled impatiently and stood up. Folding her arms she turned round and looked down at me.

'Look, I don't do drugs and I don't really drink. This is my living, right? So can we get on with it? I charge $150 for a full strip and screw, and anything else on top is extra, OK?'

There was a pause in which, with a flash of abject disappointment, I realised the third date concept was no longer applicable. I sniffed hard, and forced myself to carry on.

'You don't take Access America, by any chance?'

'Cash only.'

'All right, all right, calm down, for fuck's sake. There's no need to get funny with me. I mean, how often do you get offered both Krug and Dom Perignon and such witty company in one of the best suites at the Plaza?'

Betsy's face turned deadly serious.

'OK. One, I'm not a funny person. Two, this hotel is no big deal to me. Three, I don't like being jived around by anyone, and that includes you.'

It was my turn to stand up. 'All right. What do you think this is? A bank or something? Let's just get back to having fun. Right?'

'Money first.'

A knock at the door interrupted my reply. I almost ran across the suite and pulled open the door to a waiter holding a tray of champagne. Quickly folding a tip into his breast pocket, I took hold of the tray and returned to the sitting room.

'Now, that's better, isn't it?' I said, beaming cheerfully at Betsy as the cork shot from the bottle with a bang. Handing her a glass, I enquired in my best hotelier voice: 'Would you like to see the bedroom now?'

Betsy sighed, swung round on her heel and followed me to the bedroom.

She put her bag down on the bedside table, kicked off her shoes, lay down on the bed, and stared at my new watch.

'We've got all night.'

'Have you got the money?'

'How can you worry about money when you've got something as beautiful as me lying beside you?' I said, unzipping my flies and flipping myself astride her.

Betsy let out a long controlled sigh, as I ferreted my way underneath the spandex and placed my hands on each of her silicone breasts.

'Put the fucking money on the fucking table. I don't do this without the money.'

Almost as a remedy, but more because the tune came into my head, I enquired, 'Do you like Abba, Betsy? I think they're great.'

Then moving each breast in a circular motion, and rhythmically grinding my crutch against her midriff, I sang out in full baritone, 'Money, money, money, it's a rich man's world!'

Suddenly, Betsy leapt up and twisted herself off the bed. Her movements were so sudden that I was convinced she was going to be sick. A second later she was back on the bed holding something behind my head. As I felt it touching my hair, I grinned at the thought of some new-fangled sexual accoutrement. Throwing caution to the wind, I impishly turned round and saw her pointing an eight-inch carving knife under my chin.

Feeling the tip of the blade almost piercing my Adam's apple, I nervously forced myself to look away from the knife back up at Betsy's face. Her eyes were voodoo white and staring as if she was possessed.

For a millisecond I thought it might be a joke, but my mouth was dry and my hands had begun to shake.

A vision of not being able to put up a fight and bleeding to death was racing through my mind.

This is ridiculous.

This is so fucking unfair.

A stupid screw?

This was not worth dying for!

Oh come on, God, tell her to fuck off!

I swallowed and felt the tip of the knife hard against my gullet. Betsy spoke, sounding as crazy and hoarse as the tree-man in Central Park.

'Look, motherfucker, give me the money now! Otherwise I'm going to use this. Dig?'

'You can have whatever you want. My wallet's in my jacket on the chair behind you.'

Pressing the knife a fraction further into the skin of my throat, Betsy swivelled her head over her shoulder and motioned me off the bed. The scene became surreal as the pair of us inched slowly towards the chair, me holding my hands in the air and Betsy keeping the knife in place.

Opening my wallet, I saw I had only three twenties.

'I'm sorry, it's not quite the right amount but take whatever I've got, take the lot. Obviously, I don't want anything in return.'

Now she pushed the knife against my cheek. Blood, it felt like there was blood.

Then, the shine of Loveday's watch on my wrist.

'Give it to me.'

'Here,' I said and took it off.

Betsy read aloud the inscription on the back – 'To Tim, with all my love' – and grunted. Taking two strides back she picked up her bag, held the watch up to the light, smiled and, pulling back the spandex dropped it into her bra. Then she calmly tilted her head back and spat a huge gob at me before running out, slamming the door of the suite behind her.

Suddenly, I was overcome by a desperate need to vomit.

44

By 8.20 the next morning, I was sitting calmly at a table in the newly fragrant sitting room, mopping up the last bit of fried egg from my breakfast plate. I was dressed in a double-breasted charcoal suit, white shirt, blue tie, and sported a red carnation in my left lapel. Simultaneously reading the *Wall Street Journal* and the *Daily News*, with two cigarettes burning in separate ashtrays, I felt like Citizen Kane.

To achieve this state of equilibrium, I had stood for ten minutes under the purging jets of the shower, shouted my own lyrics to drown out the Billy Joel medley on the bathroom radio, instructed housekeeping to have the suite cleaned, and ordered the concièrge to fill our rooms with freesias. The sound of snoring continued from behind Gabe's door. I'd never known anyone sleep for so long.

Just as my thoughts about the perils of the stock market began drifting towards Loveday again, there was an ominous knock at the door.

Mindful of the hooker, I bit my lip, and asked who it was. An educated voice replied: 'Lord Lomax? My name is Raymond Lopez. I am the manager of this hotel. With me is Major Serrano, our head of security. We need to talk to you. May we come in?'

I sensed trouble. What did they want? I decided to borrow some of Charles's clipped and haughty tone: 'This had better be important.'

I motioned the two men to the armchairs in front of the sofa, and sat down. 'Now, what can I do for you?'

'Let me come straight to the point. Is it true, Lord Lomax, that you were entertaining a young black woman in your suite last night?'

'Absolutely. What business is that of yours?'

Major Serrano gruffly cleared his throat. 'Sir, the young lady in question was arrested in the lobby of this hotel after she left your room.'

'Had she stolen anything? A watch, perhaps?'

Lopez leaned forward in his chair. 'No, sir, much more serious than that, I'm afraid. She was identified by one of our detectives as the person who stabbed somebody in this hotel last week. On searching her, she was found to be in possession of a knife similar to the one used in the previous attack.'

'Jesus Christ!' I exclaimed, feeling my heart beating twice its normal speed.

'Having questioned her further, she admitted to another incident with you in this suite. The police are currently holding her on a charge of attempted murder.'

I was disturbed – no, not disturbed, edgy would be a better word; edgy about last night and very edgy about this morning. Edgy, edgy, edgy. I knew it might be seen as weakness but right then I needed an affirmation that my instincts and my judgment were correct.

I took the elevator to the lobby, stepped outside the hotel and scanned the semicircle of limousines. Ah, there he was, standing alone, pumping his leather gloves together in an attempt to keep warm.

For a second I looked at Frankie, and wondered in amazement at this brave man. He must be nearly sixty, and like his grey moustache, his tattered coat and cap seemed close to wearing out. But this was why I liked him. He was like an old soldier, an old sergeant who knew all the tricks and would never let you down.

I walked over to him.

'Frankie, I need your advice.'

'Go ahead, sir.'

'Have you ever felt worried about answering a knock on your front door?'

'Only when my ex-wife's in town.'

'Have you ever felt unsafe walking down the street?'

'People say you can never be safe in New York, but that's bullshit.' Frankie hunched his shoulders and stared at me intently. 'Something's wrong, isn't it?'

'Maybe,' I said, and then I let him have it. I backtracked to Battersea, to London three days before. I exaggerated a little about the man punching me as he served the writ and cut quickly to last night, telling him about the hooker sticking the knife in my throat. He grunted and exclaimed, continually touching his mouth with his hand. I told him about this morning and about the attempted murder charge.

'Frankie, to be honest, I'm worried that things are getting out of hand. John Lennon being shot and all – am I being weird?'

Frankie pushed back his chauffeur's cap and stood up straight.

'Listen, you're not being weird. This is fucking dangerous! I didn't spend thirty years with the cops not to know danger when I see it.'

Frankie was in his element; he paused dramatically and wiped the back of his hand slowly across his mouth. 'You know what you need? You need protection.'

'Protection?'

'Go back to your suite, don't speak to anyone and just wait. Trust me, I know what I'm doing. You'll hear from me or from somebody who knows me within the next half hour. Go!'

At precisely 9.48 there was a loud knock at the door.

'Yes? Who is it?'

'Friends of Frankie.'

The voice was deep, calm, and certain. I unlocked the door.

'May we come in?'

'Of course,' I said.

Two goliaths stepped into the room and stood politely to one side as I double-locked the door. Dressed in dark suits and blue and beige raincoats, they were well groomed, had highly polished shoes and were in their late thirties.

'Lord Lomax, I think you were expecting us?'

'Yes, do sit down.' I motioned the two men into the sitting room, trying hard to suppress an instinct to laugh. The situation seemed so make-believe, like being on stage in a black comedy.

'Lord Lomax? Allow me to introduce myself. My name is John, and this is my colleague Bill, and we're here for your safety and protection.'

'Is that it? Don't you have any surnames?'

'No, we do not.'

'Did Frankie explain how we work?' John the blue said in his Jersey accent

'No, he didn't. So why don't you?' I replied politely.

John the blue, the slightly larger of the two polar bears, straightened his lapels and continued: 'OK, we charge one hundred and seventy-five dollars per day, per man. Cash.'

'I see. Well, a hundred and seventy-five has a bad ring to it, so why don't we round it up to, say, two hundred dollars per day per man. Obviously, I will need a VAT receipt.'

'Very generous, thank you, but we can't supply any sort of paperwork. As I said – no names, no addresses, just us.'

I looked down at the bodyguard's highly polished shoes.

'Oh,' I said. 'Fair enough.'

Moving back to the window to think of the next appropriate question, I pulled back the net curtain for inspiration. Instantaneous-ly, John the blue yelled out, 'Get away from that window!'

'Why? What's the problem? I mean, eh . . .'

Bill, the beige raincoat, had already shot out of his seat and was steering me back to the sofa.

'Look, hang on! What's going on?' I asked nervously.

The raincoats looked at each other calmly, and then John, the blue one, said, 'Lord Lomax, please, we know our business. Do not, under *any* circumstances, stand by windows or open doorways unless we tell you it's OK. Please?'

The excitement of realising that I now had two real live body-guards protecting me was almost too much. Trying to compose myself, I adjusted my tone to blasé.

'Yeah, you're quite right. I'm sorry about that. It's been a long time since I've been in this situation. By the way, are you both armed?'

'We are, yes,' John the blue, replied as if stating his religion.

I looked back and forth at each man. There was an awkward silence.

'Oh, I apologize, Lord Lomax,' said Bill the beige, misunderstanding. 'You obviously want to know what we're carrying, right?'

I grinned, briefly.

'We both use Smith and Wesson .45 calibre short and long barrels,' said John, lifting the inside of his right trouser leg, then pulling back the left front flap of his jacket.

'Do you have to use them very often?' I enquired innocently, almost choking on my euphoria.

'Nah. Normally, showing a gun is enough deterrent. To be frank, we're trained to take people out without all of this shit anyway.'

'Right, yeah, I completely understand.'

I was desperate to continue the line of questioning but, in the interests of not making a fool of myself, decided against it. It was time to get serious, but before I could start John the blue stepped over to me and asked: 'You've had a problem with a psycho? A hooker?'

I nodded.

'OK,' he said, loosening a piece of bison stuck between his teeth. 'My advice to you is to forget about going to the DA and forget about staying in this hotel. Between you and me, it's not up to your standards. Not quite top-drawer, is, I think, how you British put it.'

'It isn't?' I said, inwardly amazed.

'You don't need crazy hookers pulling knives on you, do you?'

'No, of course I don't, you're absolutely right. My secretary booked this without telling me.' I looked up and, with a certain amount of largesse, asked: 'Anywhere decent you might suggest instead, gentlemen?'

45

I had chided myself during the journey for allowing myself to be taken, bamboozled and conned out of a substantial negligence settlement from the Plaza. Yet once I had caught sight of the stylish and discreet entrance to the Carlyle, I immediately understood where I had gone wrong. It was so simple. Greed and grubby haggling were for the bourgeoisie, walking away and winning wars were for me, and the aristocracy. Putting a framed photograph of Loveday on the bedside table and kissing it discreetly, I told myself it was time for a new sort of list.

I tiptoed back, unnoticed, into the drawing room and sat behind the grand piano to quietly observe what was going on.

Having successfully investigated in, under and over every door-frame, bed, cupboard, window, in fact any that could space possibly conceal a suspicious device or package in the seven-room Winder-mere suite, John and Bill sat down opposite Gabe on one of the three pigskin sofas. While Bill telephoned hotel security to notify them of their presence in the hotel, John spoke out loud as he pencilled in the last line of a job report in his pocket notebook.

Seeing the bodyguards and wanting an opportunity to break the ice with them, Gabe waited until the two men had finished what they were doing, stood up from the sofa, and pointed at the Japanese silk fresco on the wall.

'John, what do you think? Isn't this fantastic? This is the real thing! I mean, these sofas have got to be worth a fortune.'

John was in the process of taking off his blue raincoat.

'In our work I see a lot of nice places, and, yeah, I guess this is one of the best. But you know what? I'm a mean sonovabitch and I work hard for my money, and what I make I like to keep. You know what I mean?'

'Right, yeah, sort of,' Gabe laughed uneasily, fumbling for another question. 'Do you do much work with musicians? Work with any bands?'

'We've worked with Sinatra, Sammy Davis Junior, Liza Minnelli. Don't do bands; don't like 'em.'

'None at all?'

'None.'

I decided to break the awkward silence with a crashing piano chord. Both bodyguards and Gabe swung round on cue and saw me sitting at the grand piano waving a yellow-lined notepad above my head.

'Right men, fall in! I've made a list of things we all need to be doing, so let's get cracking. Come over here and make yourselves comfortable, chop-chop!'

Like three cheesy songwriters from the sixties, Gabe, John and Bill leaned over the piano waiting to hear my cheesy tune.

'First off, I'm making this area and my bedroom into operational command. That doesn't mean it's completely verboten to sit here, more that I have to have one place to base myself from. OK so far? Good. Right then, John, for today's exercise, I'm making you officer in charge of this list. I've made my own recommendations as to who should do what. You'll see, for example, that I've asked you, Gabe – if you don't mind, of course – to organise a little party for tonight, and so on and so forth. I've got some very important calls to make now in the bedroom, so I suggest we liase in an hour-and-a-half's time.'

I saluted everyone, handed John the list and walked off, closing the bedroom door behind me.

While I overheard Gabe and the bodyguards arguing among themselves and then speaking on the telephones, I was busy writing lists, composing letters I wanted to dictate, and sticking charts drawn in felt-tip pen on the walls. Books of Lists and boxes were inadequate. I needed to see a bigger picture. I was redesigning the bedroom as my war room, a place where top-secret ministerial decisions would be made. I'd received no answer from either Aaron Stein's office or from Joe Garcia's at Badsoul. Curiously this had not annoyed me, but instead only reminded me of my new mottos stuck up on the wall:

IS THE TIMING RIGHT?

IS IT A GOOD IDEA? . . . YES!

SET PRIORITIES

THINK BIG AND YOUR DEEDS WILL GROW

DELEGATE

* * *

An hour and a half later, Gabe knocked on my bedroom door.

'Tim? I've got everything under control. I've got nearly twenty people coming tonight, plus the lamb curry in about two minutes. OK? You happy?'

'Well done, Gabe. I knew you wouldn't let me down,' I shouted back.

'Tim, is there any chance we could have a bit of a chat?'

I opened the bedroom door and saw Gabe standing in his woolly socks with an address book in his hands. 'Yeah, any time you like, Gabe.'

'Tim, would you do me a favour? They said they didn't want to embarrass you with petty cash matters, but could you reimburse John and Bill for the things they've bought? It's only a matter of a few dollars or so. John made a point of saying he likes to keep things straight. When you have a moment.'

Gabe smiled nervously.

I stepped out from the bedroom and put my hand on his shoulder. 'Sure. Absolutely. No problem. I've got to sort some cash out anyway. I haven't got a penny on me.'

With that, I followed Gabe back into the drawing room and, spotting John the blue standing nearby, said, 'Hello, John, any progress?'

'Step this way, sir,' said John smugly.

'Fuck me,' I exclaimed, as I noticed the far end of the drawing room re-arranged around the largest stereo system I had ever seen. 'I didn't know Tannoy made anything like this. It's incredible.'

'OK, so there's the stereo, and here's the name and address of the biggest Midtown branch of Chase Manhattan. You'll see the senior vice-president's name is Mr Warren Cooper. I've arranged for Janice, the best stenographer at the hotel, to be with you here between 2 and 2.30 and she can arrange any further appointments you want. And finally, over there are the red carnations, toothpaste and the herbal you asked for.'

'Well done, John! Well done, everyone! This is how I like things to run.'

I was almost passing out with pleasure at my own management skills. Food, maybe food would help.

'Where's the curry? I'm starving.'

* * *

Frankie steered the limousine close to the Carlyle's entrance.

'Hi, Frankie, how are you doing?' I yelled as I got in the back of the car with John the blue following close behind me. Frankie didn't have time to reply.

'OK,' announced Bill the beige, sitting himself down in the front passenger seat. 'Frankie, it's a one-car operation and we want Chase Manhattan, which is on 5th and 57th and we need to arrive at four o'clock on the button. I don't know how bad the traffic is but do whatever you have to do. Go.'

Frankie nodded and accelerated on to 76th Street. As we sped off, he looked up into his rear-view mirror.

'Hey! Lord Lomax! Great to see you! How do you like your new hotel?'

'Brilliant, Frankie, well done!'

The limousine pulled up outside the bank at precisely 3.59.

Warren Cooper was older than I had expected. The senior vice-president of Chase Manhattan Midtown looked to be in his late fifties, and was tanned, with greying hair. Unlike banks in England, this one appeared to be entirely open plan, a fact that seemed to worry John and Bill no end.

'Relax,' I whispered.

Mr Cooper gestured to a leather chair in front of his desk.

'Please sit down, Lord Lomax, and let me know how I can be of service to you.'

'Well, Mr Cooper, I'm not going to waste your time, and I hope you're not going to waste mine.'

Cooper glanced at his watch and smiled benignly.

'I'm about to launch a new business here as an extension of my UK operation. The business is rights, Mr Cooper, musical rights, specifically the development of the licensing of rights from the BBC in England into a joint venture with a third party in the USA. We are looking for a bank that can give us competitive deposit rates – not lending rates, Mr Cooper, but deposit rates.'

'Well, Lord Lomax, we can certainly help you here at Chase,' said Cooper, reaching for a leaflet.

Interrupting him and feeling mildly irritated at his attitude, I said: 'Let me be absolutely clear, Mr Cooper, we are not interested in a normal high-street mom-and-pop rate. I'll come straight to the point.

You see, the amount with which we wish to open the account is six million dollars.'

'Tea or coffee, Lord Lomax?'

I could tell Warren Cooper had stopped thinking about his mistress or whatever he was thinking about, and had now turned his complete attention to securing our account. I accepted the offer of tea and began to reel off a long list of questions. Mr Cooper interrupted me.

'Forgive me, Lord Lomax, but I think I have a solution. Here is a set of papers relating to the opening of a corporate account. I take it that your company has been incorporated in the US, and that the IRS has adjudicated your status. And that the bank could see your projected three-year earnings, together with audited profit and loss accounts. Which firm of auditors do you use here?'

'I'm sorry, Mr Cooper, could you repeat the last sentence?'

While Cooper reiterated his three-year earnings rant, I clicked open my briefcase, ducked behind the lid, and fanned through some papers, trying desperately to remember all the banking terminology I had heard before.

There was a lull while Cooper answered my ahem with his own.

Had he guessed that I was out of my depth?

'Conversely, of course, you may have a finance man on your board here in New York who could come in and take care of all these matters.'

Mindful of my conversation about petty cash with Gabe, I decided to move quickly. It was time to delegate.

'Yes, perhaps you could note this down, Mr Cooper. The name of our financial director is Harry Freshwater and he will be able to explain the company's structure far better than I can. In addition, he can probably talk you through a short-term overdraft facility we require as well. I would like to meet again this Friday, at 11.00 a.m. Does that suit you? I'll bring Mr Freshwater. Is that enough time for you to have researched your best deposit rate? I hope so, because I don't have an awful lot of time on this trip and . . .' I paused. 'Well, we all know that Chase Manhattan is not the only bank in town.'

Mr Cooper stood up beaming and chuckling ho-ho-ho like Father Christmas.

'Looking forward to seeing you at eleven on Friday then. I take it that we can reach you at the Carlyle if we need to? Excuse me for asking, but what function do the two gentlemen over there in the raincoats have in your company?'

'Let's just say that their function is to provide security for my account, Mr Cooper.'

The senior vice-president walked me to the door of the bank, smiling broadly at the two bodyguards.

Almost bundled into the back of the waiting limousine, I had no time to issue a new set of instructions before Frankie had successfully barged his way into the only moving lane of traffic on 5th Avenue.

'I need to stop,' I said.

'What's the problem?' asked John and Bill in unison.

'There's no problem, gentlemen, I merely need to make a call.'

'Yeah, but we can do that at the hotel. We'll be back soon.'

'No, this can't wait, Frankie. Find a pay phone.'

'That's going to be very difficult in this traffic.'

'No it's not, stop outside the Plaza. There's a call box next to the horses.'

Five minutes later, standing in a temperature of minus 2 degrees centigrade with a wind-chill factor of 9, I took two quarters from Bill's hand and dialled Harry and Jessica's number in Mulberry Street. Amused, but none the less aware of the dangers of being squashed to death by the weight of the two bodyguards pressing in on either side of me, I made the call as brief as possible.

Amid the noise of traffic, I rapped and ranted to an astonished Harry that I was back in New York, staying at the Carlyle, and most importantly needed a hundred dollars in cash or more, immediately, adding it was imperative they bring it to the hotel at seven that night.

Hearing a grumpy yes OK, I breathed out and put down the phone. I broke free from the protective cover of the two raincoats and walked over to feed the chestnut-coloured horse some sugar lumps I had surreptitiously pocketed from Mr Cooper's desk.

46

'Harry and Jessica?'

'Who are *you?*'

'Step this way, please,' said Bill the beige, ushering them inside the suite.

'Now, if you'll just step over here and put your hands on the wall, and your legs apart . . . that's it, we just have to check for any concealed weapons . . . nothing to worry about.'

I walked towards the double doors where Harry and Jessica were removing their coats. The size and grandeur of the forty-foot drawing room and perhaps the unexpected experience of being frisked was making it difficult for them not to gape.

'Harry! Jessica! At last! Great to see you!'

'Eh, great to see you too, Tim.'

I didn't want to say it but Harry and Jessica seemed inappropriately dressed, considering where they were. Harry was wearing the same stupid Russian greatcoat, complete with Russian hat, he had had since Oxford. Jessica was looking like Princess Leia wearing a black skiing jacket, matching ski pants and white fur hat. She was obviously pregnant.

We embraced as normal, two kisses for Jessica, a hug and two slaps on the back for Harry.

Jessica glanced round the room, running her eye along the Japanese fresco and stopping when she caught sight of the grand piano.

'Wow! Quite a place, hey?' she said.

'Don't you think it's . . . a bit on the small side, old sport? Didn't you bring the family?' Harry asked facetiously.

'Don't talk to me about them! They're the last people I want to see. Anyway, it's not bad is it? Nice stereo system, Harry, eh?'

'Planning on having a concert, Tim? I presume the nice man with the moustache we just met at the door is something to do with artist security? Are you here on your own?' Harry asked.

'No, of course I'm not. I'm sorry, let me get you both a drink. Harry, you remember Gabe the drummer from Quantum Frog? Well, he's here as well.'

'Why's Gabe Morass here? Jesus!' Harry asked.

'Jesus isn't here, Harry, not unless he's hiding somewhere,' I joked and handed them each a glass of champagne.

'Cheers and Happy New Year,' I said, clinking my glass against Jessica's and walking across the room towards the record deck.

'It's extraordinary, Tim. You seem more at home here than you do in the flat back in Battersea!' Jessica said, raising her voice.

Carefully pulling the Steely Dan record from its sleeve, I smiled and nodded at how well Jessica had described the situation.

'Yes, you're right, Jess, I guess I do feel at home,' I said, turning up the volume. As the opening bars of 'Rikki Don't Lose That Number' came through the speakers, I looked across at Harry for his approval.

Harry nodded an acknowledgement, then said: 'In some ways you seem at home and in some ways you don't.'

'What do you mean exactly?' I said sensing some imminent criticism.

'Nothing, my old china,' said Harry beaming. 'It's just we're a bit more used to seeing you on a sofa with Loveday and the cat.' Pausing to look over his shoulder, he added, 'And not with a bodyguard in each room.'

I laughed and was about to put Harry in the picture and in his place as well, when Gabe ambled into the room. Swinging his arms and grinning like Fozzie Bear on speed, he walked straight up to Harry and Jessica and shook hands.

'Hello there! I'm Gabe Morass. How do you do? Do you live here in New York?'

Having slept and showered, Gabe was dressed in a brown suede suit, clean white shirt. He looked refreshed and ready for the party that night.

Harry stood up, and shook hands with him, momentarily over-awed.

'I was supposed to meet you at the Speak but Sid Vicious interrupted us!'

'Probably not the only thing he interrupted that night.'

Gabe quickly engaged Harry and Jessica in an animated conversation about life in the Big Apple, how long they'd known me, and about their feelings about living away from England. When he began recounting anecdotes about the inside story of Quantum Frog and other bands he had played with, Harry was transfixed. That is until Jessica piped up: 'So, Gabe, is it a coincidence that you're in New York at the same time as Tim?'

Gabe scratched the side of his head and grinned. 'Funny you should say that. Tim asked me to join him right at the last minute. I thought it was more fun than being in England and I don't mind helping out, you know, mucking in a bit.'

I interrupted the conversation by formally introducing Bill and John, and offering everyone another drink. I put my hands on Harry and Jessica's shoulders and said: 'Come on, let me show you around this place.'

Jessica walked into the bedroom first. She seemed to be taken aback by the sumptuousness of it all, until she noticed my hand-scrawled BBC Concert charts stuck all over the walls with sellotape. She pointed to the bed.

'Do you mind?'

'Of course not, help yourself.' I hoped she wouldn't see the photograph frame lying flat face-down on the bedside table. Jessica eased herself up on to the bed and lay back with a happy groan, careful to keep her boots away from the gold silk eiderdown. Harry and I then lay down as well. For a few moments, none of us said anything but stared up at the ceiling. It was just like old times.

Then Harry got up, closed the bedroom door and erupted with a torrent of questions.

'Tim, what the hell is going on? What are those bodyguards doing here? Why is Gabriel Morass with you?'

'So many questions and so little time. Calm down, Harry, everything's under control!'

'Tim? It's us here – not a couple of people you've only just met. Maybe everything *is* under control, but what is going on?'

'OK, OK, relax. Look, things are really great at the moment, I mean fantastic, in fact, but they've also become a little tricky as well.'

I heaved myself off the bed, and first recounted the tale of Chivers' minion threatening me outside my flat with a writ, followed by the one about the hooker with the knife in the Plaza.

'*What* house? Hookers? Knives? You're joking!'

'I'm not joking. All this has happened just recently! And, of course, don't forget about John Lennon.'

'Does Loveday know anything about all of this?'

Just then Jessica found Loveday's photograph and held it up to Harry.

'Well?' asked Harry like a schoolteacher.

He had gone too far. I jabbed my finger towards his face.

'Christ all-fucking-mighty, Harry! No, Loveday does not know about all of this, and I don't want her to know either. OK? The bodyguards are here to bloody well protect me. Isn't it obvious? And as to why I'm here, well, the Plaza turned out to be rubbish and, in case you didn't realise, I'm here to sort out, amongst a lot of other things, the BB-fucking-C deal. *Comprende?*'

I gulped back a glass of champagne and lit a cigarette. Seeing that Harry and Jessica were now staring, unsmiling, at the wall, I inhaled deeply and exploded again.

'I mean, Jesus fucking Christ, whose side are you on?'

Jessica got up from the bed and smiled apologetically.

'We're on your side, Tim; we only want what is best for you. Now that we understand, that's OK. If you don't want Loveday to know, that's fine, and if you need bodyguards, that's fine as well. Why don't we just finish our drinks now and give you the cash? We've got to get to this dinner with Harry's new boss. Why don't we come back tomorrow and hear the rest of your news then?'

'Great idea! Come back tomorrow and we'll do something fun, something great.' I waited a second for the air to clear and carried on in a slightly more cheerful tone. 'There is something else, Harry, I want to talk to you about.'

'Oh, yeah?' said Harry, smiling and squeezing Jessica's hand.

'Did I mention Friday to you already?'

'What about Friday?'

'You're coming with me as the financial director of Fish Farm plc to meet the big cheese from Chase Manhattan Bank.'

Harry started laughing and rolled back on to the bed.

'Very funny, Tim. Since when did I become a financial director of, what is it, Fish Farm? Very funny, indeed.'

'Harry, you may laugh, but I'm deadly serious. I've already put you on the payroll, and I've told them exactly who you are. I need you suited up and looking the part for midday Friday. I'll do the talking, all you need to do is just sit there and nod. End of story, OK?'

There was a silence. I clapped my hands together and whistled as if I was trying to hail a cab.

Jessica stood up. Again, she seemed to be the only one with her head screwed on.

'That sounds great, Tim, and, Harry, that's even better that you're going to do it.' She gave him a meaningful look. 'Don't worry, Tim, he can be a bit slow on the uptake about this sort of thing, but he'll come round,' she said leaning down and pinching Harry's cheek.

'Thank you, Jessica, for your support and common sense,' I said. Then we both looked at Harry. 'Jesus Christ, Harry. Stop looking so worried, I'm not asking you to have your teeth taken out! You are going to make a lot of money.'

Jessica patted her pregnant belly. 'We could do with every penny right now. Right, Harry?'

The three of us walked slowly back into the drawing room. I was pleased that Jessica was able to see the bigger picture. As I looked up, Gabe was perched on the edge of a sofa finishing a telephone call. He put down the phone and flicked his fingers in two loud clicks.

'Great news, Tim! My friend Patti from Vancouver is on her way over to the hotel right now! Are you all right, you look a bit wired?'

'Couldn't be better, Gabe. Canada is a long way to come just for a party, isn't it?'

Putting my arms around their shoulders, I joined Harry and Jessica by the window. I wanted to kiss and make up but didn't know how to say it. 'Do you really have to go? I mean, why don't you stay and have a few drinks?'

Jessica turned round and patted her bulging midriff. 'One drink is all I'm allowed.'

'I'm sorry, I keep forgetting.'

I put my hand gently on her midriff and shouted, 'John? Bill? Can one of you get reception to tell Frankie that he needs to drive two extremely important people to Chelsea straightaway? Then can one of you escort them to the car?'

'Tim, we can take the subway, really.'

'Subway? Lady Windermere, please! It's out of the question.'

While John helped Jessica into her coat, I gave Harry a hug and felt him slip an envelope into my jacket pocket.

'Shit, I nearly forgot about the money. Thanks, man, and, eh, I'm sorry about losing my rag back there.'

Harry ignored my remark but sniffed loudly, as he looked around the sitting room. Stepping closer, he flicked the outside of my jacket pocket with the back of his hand. 'I think you're going to need a bit more than a hundred to pay for all of this, old bean.'

By half-past eight, a small queue of people had formed outside the Windermere suite. John the blue and Bill the beige had re-positioned a desk close to the double doors, ready to tick off the names of incoming guests from a clipboard, while the other conducted a body search.

Oblivious to the spread of lobster, salmon, pots of caviar and waiters uncorking champagne in the drawing room, Gabe sifted through some albums while Patti, his recently arrived girlfriend, and Janice the stenographer sat next to each other on the sofa and shared a joint. I was playing the piano.

The guests had all been admitted to the inner sanctum of the suite by 9.00 p.m. Called from the pages of Gabe's recently recovered little black book, they were largely musicians, backing singers, waitresses who were really actresses and bartenders who were really rock stars. Dressed in variations of leather, PVC, black, green or mauve, they wore sunglasses, had streaked hair and, in most cases, an extra buckle or zip stitched into their pointed shoes. One surprise of the evening was the arrival of the two air hostesses from Air India. Gone were the saris and on were white polo-neck sweaters, black jeans and ankle boots.

Like a gaggle of plundering geese the guests pecked at the buffet tables as if there was a time limit for eating up the food. By the time the last scrap of lobster had gone, the waiters disappeared. After that, guests removed bottles of champagne, vodka and brandy to various nooks and crannies around the room.

Bob Marley and the Wailers were playing loudly and the air was peppered with the smell of brandy and marijuana. Gabe was happy, circulating round the room with his arm round Patti's shoulder and a large joint in his hand.

'Hey, Tim, this is a great party. Do you think I could sit down?' said Janice the stenographer, a petite blonde in her early thirties with tight frizzy hair, high heels and a pretty but mournful face.

'My second joint,' she added. 'And fourth glass of champagne . . .'

To steady herself she grabbed hold of my arm. 'I'm going to have to sit down now. I am feeling . . .'

I just managed to keep her from falling backwards into the piano as she fainted. I gave her a fireman's lift over my right shoulder and walked calmly towards the bedroom, remarking to a couple gawping at me as I left the room: 'These American girls, they just can't take the pace, can they?'

As I laid Janice gently on top of my bed she came to, and started crying.

'It's all right. I know what will make you feel better,' I said sympathetically.

Pressing a cold flannel to her forehead, I looked down at her face and briefly wondered what she would look like without her clothes on. I pulled off her high-heeled shoes. She began to weep again.

'I must go home. I've got to go. Please! I need my bag, where's my bag?'

'I'll get your bag in a minute. Now, you just stay here and get better. Take your things off and get under the blankets. Have a sleep and you'll be right as rain. I'll come back later to see how you are. Trust me.'

Once I had had a pee in the bathroom and reappeared in the drawing room, I decided to abandon my low profile. I was really restless, needing to stir things up. Picking up the yellow notepad from underneath the piano, I went and stood between the three sofas, banging a fork against a glass.

'Ahem. Excuse me, everybody. This is a staff announcement . . .'

The noise in the room dropped to a murmur.

'OK everybody, stop looking so worried, the party isn't over yet. My name is Tim Lomax and, strange though it may seem, even though this is my party, many of us have not had the pleasure of meeting. Now the point is, apart from launching a new record company, I am also about to make a film. Yes, a feature film about the music business, to be filmed in London and New York. I'm going to be looking for actors, soundtrack contributors, you name it. So, armed with my notepad, I intend to come and talk to each and every one of you. Now, is anyone still hungry? Yeah? Well, I am. Who wants a steak sandwich and a beer?'

The room erupted into cheers and applause. With a case of Budweiser and sandwiches ordered from room service, I began talking to an eager throng, who crowded round, firing questions.

'Is that what you do, then, movies?'

'Do you know, I thought I recognised you earlier.'

'Gabe didn't exactly say what you did. People have always said I should do film music.'

'Is this really serious? I mean, are you connected to a studio in England?'

'Do they have studios in England?'

'How long are you in town? It's just there's someone I'd love you to meet.'

I was enjoying myself immensely. To some people I told the partial truth, to others I lied outright. As I let slip slivers of information regarding my other activities, such as the Dogs, and the BBC Concerts, the people surrounding me volunteered helpful tit-bits of information. So much so that by the time room service arrived, my yellow notepad was full of ideas and contacts.

The steak sandwiches and beers disappeared as quickly as pieces of orange at half-time at a school football match. Gabe turned the volume of the music back up, and the party resumed.

By 2 a.m. only six people were left in the suite. Bill, the beige bodyguard, had gone to get some air before retiring to the spare bedroom for the first of his four-hour rests. John, the blue bodyguard, sat drinking coffee and watching me tape recording myself playing the piano.

I was so engrossed in my rendition of 'Rapper's Delight' that I didn't notice Gabe casually strolling off to his bedroom with Patti and another girl, Sasha.

'Will you be staying up much later?' John the blue enquired, stifling a yawn.

'Yeah, maybe. Maybe no. Maybe an early night might be a good idea.'

Oh, shit! Janice the stenographer.

'Won't be a minute, John.'

As I rushed into the bedroom, I tried to remember whether I had seen her leave, or whether I had gone into the bedroom since putting her to bed.

She was still lying face down on the blankets. I walked around the bed, and saw that her mouth was open and that she had been sick down the side of the pillow. She wasn't moving. I touched the side of her face, which felt damp and cold.

'Janice, Janice! Come on, wake up! Please, fucking well wake up!' I whispered to her motionless body.

My heart was pounding faster and faster.

'Fuck! Oh, Jesus! Shit, no! She can't be. You fucking, fucking, idiot. Oh, my God, please! She can't be dead. Gabe, quick, hurry!'

I sprinted through the drawing room, vaulting two glass tables as I ran. I flung open Gabe's bedroom door, and started screaming for him to get out of bed.

'Tim, I'm a bit up to my neck at the moment, if you know what I mean. Is there some sort of a problem?'

A moment later he was running through the suite after me, clutching a small white towel to his waist.

When we got to my bedroom, we both stopped and started walking backwards, as John the blue came slowly towards us, Janice resting limply in his arms, wrapped in a blanket.

47

I lifted my head from the pillow.

8.48.

I sank back. I felt sick. My eyeballs ached. My nose felt raw.

Shit. Janice.

Was she really dead, or had I dreamt the whole thing? My mouth filled with saliva. I was going to puke. Voices and funereal music were coming from beyond the bedroom door. Something was very wrong.

I tiptoed into the bathroom and leant against the basin, swallowing the bile that was rising in my throat. Staring into the mirror, I saw that I was shaking. I jumped with fright as the telephone rang in the bedroom and on the bathroom wall. What if that's the police? What if I really did kill her?

Feeling an irrational need for decency, I grabbed the towelling gown hanging behind the bathroom door and picked up the telephone.

'Tim? It's Harry.'

'Eh, who?'

'It's me, Harry.'

There was a two-second delay as my fear and paranoia dispersed. Like a tightrope-walker recovering his balance, I steadied myself.

'Harry! Great to hear from you! Ring you back in five?'

'Fine, OK.'

The familiar and reassuring sound of Harry's voice was all I needed to get me walking again. Adjusting my robe, I swung open the bedroom door and marched out into the drawing room.

'Lord Lomax! Top of the morning to you!' John the blue boomed in an unconvincing Irish accent. 'Your breakfast awaits!'

'John, am I glad to see you. Who else has been here?'

'Oh, just the cleaners, and a guy to sort out the stains in the carpet. Hope you don't mind the Mahler, I'm educating myself, you know, learning about the classics.'

'Great, but what about the girl?'

'It depends which girl you mean?' John called out, adjusting the volume.

'You know – Janice, the secretary?'

John returned to the breakfast table and took a swig of coffee.

'That girl was a nut, and if it wasn't for me, she'd be in a coma right now.'

'You mean she's all right, then?' I said weakly.

'The lady's schizoid or something. She was taking fifteen milligrams of Valium a day. Do you know how much that is? Well, it's a lot. You should never mix drugs like that with alcohol. It stops the oxygen going to the brain. Bill saw the tablets in her handbag, rang the hotel doctor, and he said to bring her down immediately.'

'Jesus! Thank God for that. What's happened? Is she OK? She's not going to complain to anyone, is she?'

'How could she?' said John loudly. 'It was her own damn fault. We didn't ask her to drink that much.'

'Yeah, but I don't want any trouble.'

'Hey, listen, we know both the doctors here, so it's OK. Don't worry.'

I returned to the bedroom, delighted at the news of Janice's resurrection, and telephoned Harry and Jessica.

'Hi, it's Tim. Sorry about that.'

'Are you OK? You sound out of breath.'

'I'm fine, absolutely fine.'

I heard a hand being placed over the receiver and a muffled voice.

'Tim? We want you to come over to Mulberry Street for a chat.'

Sensing real anxiety behind their request, I automatically adjusted my manner to super-calm.

'Well, I have an appointment at Teller Brothers at eleven, lunch with someone downtown at one and a visit to Black Sea, and two appointments to be confirmed for four and five. I've also promised Gabe I would help him resolve a publishing dispute with a company based around the corner.' That last item was the only lie I told.

'Hey,' I said. 'Come to the party tomorrow evening. All the best people will be here. And you two are the best people I know.'

'Speaking of best people, why haven't you called Loveday, Tim? She's wondering how you are.'

'You mean, you've spoken to her?'

'Last night.'

'Did she go completely spare?'

'She's not at all pleased with you, but that doesn't mean you shouldn't ring her, Tim.'

'No, of course.'

I played the game correctly with John and Bill as we walked towards the studio, even if it was like being a crab walking through a rugby scrum. The trouble with them was that they didn't have enough to do. They needed more excitement. I thought about offering Frankie a full-time job too. More money going out! No point in being flash, though. I had to think about controlling expenditure at all times; must have budgets, colour-coded budgets, that's the thing. I stopped to take some deep breaths, making sure my mental tyres were pumped up. I knew the visit to the studio was going to be a success.

Black Sea Records was huge and its studios were the most sought-after in New York. Well, that wasn't going to faze me – quite the reverse. I beckoned John the blue and Bill the beige to follow me into the studio reception. It was low-lit, moody and smart. Unlike other studios, it was also spic, span and organised. I didn't recognise the receptionist, but it didn't matter.

'Hello, there, yes, you can help me. I'm here to see Mr Whemli. Tim Lomax is my name.'

She looked up dismissively.

'Mr Lomax, does he know you're coming?'

I decided to bluff. 'He's expecting me some time this afternoon, yes.'

'Would you mind waiting, please? I'll have to walk through to the studio.'

I chuckled to myself. Receptionists in studios never walk anywhere. I knew what she was doing; she was going to check and didn't want me to overhear. I decided to play a game with her, with all the other people here, and not mention who I really was or what I had, but to see if I could wing it purely on the strength of my personality. Of course I could! I knew I could, I felt it in my blood.

The receptionist returned: 'Mr Lomax, I'm sorry, but Mr Whemli is tied up recording right now. Perhaps you could telephone another time?'

'Don't worry, I'll wait.'

'Well, but, eh . . .'

'No buts, it's not a problem. Is Saul here by any chance?'

'You mean the studio manager?'

'Yes. What a coincidence!'

'I'll tell him you're here.'

Saul was a former basketball player who had worked at Black Sea since he was nineteen. In some ways he was Gabe's double, only darker-skinned, taller and more administrative. He was around forty now, maybe older, and had a grey-black beard and a wide smile that spread slowly, like a pair of curtains opening at a theatre.

'Hey, Saul, how you doing?'

'Tim Lomax! My man, *que pasa?*'

'Saul, my man, what's going on?'

'Weeelllllll,' he drawled like a TV cowboy, 'you could say we have quite a full house.'

He pointed to the clipboard in his hand showing the groups that were using the three Black Sea studios. Van Morrison, Average White Band, Chaka Khan and the Bee Gees were all recording that week. Fuck my old boots, I said to myself. Just the sort of people I needed to meet.

'Saul, what are you doing tomorrow night?'

'I don't know, messing about as usual.'

'Great, I'm having a party at the Carlyle. It's in my suite, the Windermere. I want you to come and bring some friends. Chinese food, do you like it?'

'My favourite.'

'Right, then, about eight.'

'OK!'

Saul smiled and looked down at his clipboard then looked up at me.

'So, who did you come here to see? I mean, apart from me!'

'Sedat Whemli.'

'And he's busy?'

'Apparently.'

'Listen, he's got a session with Chaka right now, but I'm going to talk to him. Stay right here.'

Two minutes later Whemli and I were shaking hands and talking about London traffic jams. He was the opposite of what I had imagined: dressed in a suit and tie, sparkling eyes, mid-fifties, a monocle, and charming. Within another ten, I'd told him, surreptitiously of course, about Fish Farm and the BBC idea and how Aaron Stein believed it was an extremely sexy concept. A sixth sense told me to hold the bargaining chip of Joe Garcia and Badsoul in reserve. I stopped talking and sat back.

After asking a few easy questions, Whemli stood and pondered for a while, rubbing his chin. 'How long are you in town?'

'Not long at all,' I replied. 'That's why I'm having a little party tomorrow night at my suite in the Carlyle.'

Whemli put his hand up to his forehead and let out a weary laugh: 'Not another party! I thought Christmas was over.'

'I know exactly what you mean. They all turn into a horrible blur, don't they? Worse than that, you keep meeting the same people you did your very best to avoid at the last one.'

'You're right, Timothy. That is exactly what keeps happening.'

'Well, all I'll say is we do have a few interesting people coming, like the Archbishop of New York and Woody Allen, although I bet he doesn't show up. But I need to get some interesting artists to come, you know, some musicians who might benefit from a few of the things I'm involved in. Obviously, it would be a great honour if you would come but I understand if . . .'

'The Archbishop, my God. I like your style. Yes, I think we should all be aware of what you are about to launch. So, providing I'm invited, I would love to come.'

Whemli then ran off a list of names he was going to try and bring to the Carlyle the following night. Providing he was invited! I laughed to myself. Things were really beginning to happen . . .

Half an hour later, I marched into the suite. Spotting Gabe and Patti on a sofa, I stood up on a chair and, in the style of *West Side Story*, sang out: 'Tonight, tonight! I've got to have a bath! T-o-o-night!'

Leaping down, I ignored the sheaf of messages Gabe held out to me, and accelerated into my bedroom.

Two minutes later there was a knock on the door.

'Tim? Do you mind if I come in? There are a few things I need to discuss with you, all right?'

'Come in, Gabe, come in. I'm in the bathroom on the phone.'

Gabe looked a little embarrassed as he came into the bathroom. I was naked, smoking, sitting on the edge of the bath, jigging my legs in and out of the water, with the phone stretched to my ear, and sipping a glass of whisky. Pointing to a chair, I whispered, 'Come and sit down, help yourself to a drink!'

While I carried on with my phone call, Gabe looked around the bathroom with a bemused expression on his face. Not only were there more lists sellotaped to the mirrors, but also, instead of the usual toothbrush paraphernalia, a neatly organised bar.

'. . . So you were able to do the swans but not the tigers? OK, yes, well, thank you, for your cooperation, and, of course, the costs are all right. You only get out what you put in, don't you agree? Good! Thanks a lot.'

I hooked the phone back into its cradle and slid down into the bath.

'I was just checking on some special catering I've arranged for tomorrow night. One or two surprises. You'll see.'

'Oh, good . . .'

'How did it go with Rolls-Royce? Sorry to put you on the spot.'

'The cost, Tim . . .'

'No buts, Gabe, it's easy, it's just managing money. We'll pay by instalments. What do you think?'

'Tim, that's why I'm here, I want to have a talk . . .'

'What about? The car? What?'

Gabe sighed, laughed and poured himself a drink.

'Tim? I've got to have a serious talk with you. Now you and I don't really know each other that well but . . .'

'Gabe, I can see something is wrong. Spit it out and no buts.'

Gabe laughed again and ran his hand through his hair.

'Tim, I don't want to be the one to pour cold water, but we've just had eight boxes of office equipment delivered.'

'Marvellous, where are they?'

'They're in the kitchen waiting for you.'

'Fantastic! I'll take a look in a minute.'

'But, Tim, what the hell are we going to do with them?'

'Gabe, if you don't mind me saying, office equipment is not exactly your area, is it? There are certain things you're going to have to leave to me.'

There was a distinct silence during which I decided to experiment as to how long I could hold my head under the water. By the time I had re-surfaced, Gabe had poured himself another drink and was ready to read through the messages. Most of them were tedious, but not all.

'The Archbishop of New York's not coming? Fuck him! OK, well it was a long shot and a bit weird, but you do need to mix these parties up a bit, you know.'

'Why's that, then?' Gabe asked.

'Gabe, the Catholics are a very good team to have on your side.'

'Oh, yes, right, I see,' Gabe replied a little wearily.

I decided to give him some reassurance. 'Listen, it may be difficult for you to see at the moment, but things really are coming together. A little time is all I need and then it's going to be completely in the bag. You are going to go berserk with excitement when I tell you who's coming tomorrow night.'

Gabe looked up like a dog that has just heard the sound of a tin opener.

'Who?'

'The Average White Band, Chaka Chan, Van the Man, the Bee Gees, Sedat Whemli and the other big fish at Black Sea, not forgetting good old Saul. That's who!'

'Mother of God, that's fantastic. Did they say they're really coming?'

'As good as,' I said, laughing at his amazed expression. 'You see, I told you, stick with me and it'll be all right. OK now, Gabe? Anything else you want to get off your chest?'

Gabe giggled and gave an embarrassed shrug.

'Look, Tim, it's not that I'm doubting your ability or anything. I was getting a bit worried about money, you know, what with the bodyguards and everything. It's embarrassing to have to tell you this but I came out without any real cash or credit card. Stupid, really, but I didn't have time. Normally, I don't have to think about that sort of thing on tour. I mean, I'm not someone who freeloads, know what I mean? And another thing . . .'

'Gabe!' I had to shout to stop him rambling. 'Relax. Take it easy. We're probably going to need to busk it for a few days and then everything will be fine. Front is everything, remember.' Then, pointing to my eyes and smiling a cheesy smile, I said: 'Eyes and teeth, Gabe, always remember eyes and teeth!'

Gabe stood up, wide-eyed and smiling. 'Oh, by the way, your pals rang to say they're coming tomorrow for breakfast and of course for the party. A guy called Charles rang from London, and said could you call him urgently. And there's another message as well, well, three from the same person, and a telegram too. Here you are.'

Gabe appeared to be hesitating.

'My hands are all wet, Gabe, just read the telegram.'

' "Am arriving tomorrow afternoon on Pan Am 720. Meet me at JFK or else." . . . They're from Loveday.'

'*What!*'

'I think I'll go and make sure everything's OK with Patti.'

'How the fuck did she know I was staying here? What did she say? Who spoke to her?'

Gabe quickly pulled the bathroom door shut behind him.

Breakfast with Harry and Jessica, and another chance for them to bend my ear.

'My God, it looks like you've had a serious party in here!' Harry said, pulling open the curtains and stepping over the bottles and clothes strewn across the floor.

'You just wait until tonight.' I smirked, turning away from the light and coughing.'

'Why don't I go and get some Alka Seltzer from the kitchen?'

'Thanks, Jessica, you're an angel.'

Jessica left the room, sniffing the air as she went. Harry sat down on the bed, shook his head and adopted a stern tone.

'You know that Loveday has been calling you, don't you, and Charles as well?'

'Loveday's arriving this afternoon, Harry, as you probably bloody well know! Was it you who gave her this number?'

'She rang us at the apartment; we had to tell the truth. She also said Rick had called her. He wants you to call him as well.'

Harry shot me an unusually serious look.

'OK, Harry. It was too late to ring last night.' I paused to wipe my nose with the back of my hand. 'But I can tell you for nothing, Charles and Rick can fuck right off.'

Harry grunted.

'Cut the bourgeois bit, Harry, will you? We've got a war to win.'

'*We* have a war to win?'

'Yes, *we*. You haven't forgotten about tomorrow, have you?'

'What about tomorrow?'

'Harry! You're coming with me to meet with Chase Manhattan.'

Harry laughed and lifted Loveday's photograph from the bedside table. 'Very funny, Tim.'

Jessica reappeared quietly, holding a glass of water.

'Harry,' I said, trying to take the photograph from him. '*You* may laugh, but *I'm* totally serious.'

Harry dropped the frame face up on to the bed. Like Mona Lisa, Loveday's eyes seemed to be watching me. 'Listen,' he said. 'I like a good joke, but I've just started work in a job most people would give their right testicle for. I'm not about to do anything that would mess that up.'

Jessica interrupted: 'Don't worry, Tim, Harry's still being a bit of an old bore, but it will all be OK.' Then reaching across the bed with the effervescing glass, she said, 'Here's your medicine. Why don't you take it and you'll feel better?'

I raised myself up on one elbow, briefly imagining the droplets of sweat running down my back were turning into baby slugs.

'You know something? Physically, I really don't feel that great.'

Jessica sat down on the bed and touched my forehead with the palm of her hand.

'Maybe you need to see a doctor. We know a really good one. We had Abe Aberman's number and asked his advice. He said to say hello and that he would call you.'

I was tempted but remembered the crusade.

'I'll be fine, and, yes, it'll be good to talk to Abe. But I cannot afford to fuck up this party. A good shower will knock me back into shape. I'll see you in a minute.'

I waited until Harry and Jessica had left before shouting: 'John! Get in here!'

I paced round the bed, my hands clasped firmly behind my back, trying to avoid eye contact with Loveday's photograph.

'Is everything all right?'

John the blue stood smiling with his arms folded. I stopped pacing and smiled ruefully back as if I was Montgomery addressing his aide-de-camp: 'I like you, John, you're a good man.'

'Great. So what's up?'

'It's time to stop the fucking about and time, as you would say, time to kick some ass. I want you, Bill and Gabe to answer any calls and to write down each one, however trivial, and give them to me. I want the filing cabinets, typewriters, telex machine, and photocopier unpacked and assembled. This is not a holiday! We need to shape up. OK? I want the three real estate agents I'm meeting at lunchtime to be invited tonight, and I want Frankie in here, right now!'

'Why Frankie?'

'Listen, Frankie used to be a cop, right?'

'Right.'

'Well, the watch that the psycho hooker stole from me was a Christmas present from someone very close to me. So I want Frankie to use his influence to get it back. You with me?'

John the blue nodded: 'You're in charge.'

I laughed. 'Funny you should say that, because a few people seem to be forgetting that fact.'

'And, sir, I have a question about being paid?'

'Jesus, John! Talk to Gabe about that sort of thing, not me.'

Bill the beige called out from the drawing room: 'Garcia's office from Badsoul, on the line. Do you want to take it?'

I came rushing through. Harry, Jessica, and Gabe looked at me as if I was about to deliver the verdict of a jury.

'Do I want to take it? Of course I want to bloody take it!'

'This is Belinda from Joseph Garcia's office, how are you today?'

'Never been better, Belinda. Is he there?'

'Well, no, I'm afraid Mr Garcia is not. He's very sorry that he won't be able to attend your party, but as I said to you yesterday, he had intended to come back to the city last night but he's decided to stay in Maine for the weekend. I've told him that you need to see him right away, but he seemed to think it could wait till next week. Mr Garcia has asked Ben Glarusso to come in his place. Could I make another appointment, perhaps?'

I allowed a long pause while I tried to control my rage, then said, 'Belinda, can you tell him to phone me next week and then we can arrange for him to come here to the Carlyle for a meeting. Thanks.'

I put the phone down and turned to Harry, who was now putting on his coat and hat.

'Can you believe it? This is a guy who wants to give me six million dollars and he can't be bothered to come back from his holidays to sort it out. Fucking typical! Well, we're just going to have to allow Chase Manhattan to fund us for a little while! Think you can handle that, Harry? Shall I buy you a new suit for tomorrow?'

Harry turned and bowed with a sweep of his Russian hat, saying in a mock Japanese accent 'Thank you, master, but I already have suit. Don't you think,' he said, changing back to a normal voice, 'that we should postpone the meeting with the bank until after we've met with the six-million-dollar man? I mean, surely . . .'

'No, I don't think we should postpone the fucking bank!' I interrupted angrily. 'Just because that arsehole has let me down, doesn't mean we let other people down.'

'All right, Tim. Absolutely. Whatever you say.'

'Right, everybody, pay attention,' I said, jumping on to the piano stool. 'We've got a very important party tonight and I want everyone on parade and firing on all cylinders. This is our future. And Loveday is arriving this afternoon as well. Where's Frankie? I need to put him on red alert. John, Bill, any calls from Sedat Whemli, Woody Allen's office or Helen Donovan?'

'Whemli's assistant rang to say we should expect a party of at least twenty and Helen Donovan said she'll be here in time for dinner but Stein's going to be a little late. Still waiting on Woody Allen.'

'That's more like it. It's always the same, anywhere in the world: if you want to establish yourself in a new town, invite the right people and throw a fantastic party.'

I jumped down from the stool making a Superman sign with my arms and noticed Harry and Jessica knotting their scarves and buttoning their coats.

'We've got to get moving,' Harry said, sounding rather stiff. 'A few things to do in Mulberry Street before getting ready for the party. Don't forget about Loveday, will you?'

'Loveday is not someone you can easily forget, Harry. Don't worry, everything's under control. You two have a nice time and we'll see you later.'

I turned to inspect my remaining troops.

'John, could you call housekeeping and have them spring clean my room? Can you also move the office equipment into the kitchen or your room temporarily? Bill, I'm going to need some extra herbal, tiger lilies in the bedroom for Loveday and can you double-check with downstairs that they have the right stepladders? Please don't forget the caterers, and the zoo people arrive at two-thirty. Gabe, are you cool? Don't look so worried. You're not? Wonderful. OK, everyone, we're cooking on gas!'

48

I am immaculately dressed in a gold silk suit and speaking in a mixture of French, English, and Italian. By my side is Jessica, looking exquisite in a charcoal-coloured suit with a gold and cream turban. She has been supervising Mr Chews' the caterers, and the waiters and waitresses. I am circulating round the room, talking with as many guests as possible. Periodically I watch as two pigtailed Mandarin waitresses greet new guests, and direct them to Harry standing nearby. He is dressed like James Bond, offering guests champagne and the chance to slip into something more comfortable – a pair of soft Aladdin shoes.

The drawing room is lit by twenty or so Chinese lanterns and silver candelabra that send flickering shadows up each wall. The floor-to-ceiling windows are so clean, it seems almost possible to reach out and touch the nearby rooftops. The grand piano is gleaming majestically in the centre of the room, guarded by ice swans at each corner. The life-sized swans have hollowed-out backs, and are filled with water and floating lychees. My *pièce de resistance*, though, is a shimmering glass sarcophagus suspended from a winch and resting on two stepladders just above the piano lid. It is an aquarium from a transatlantic ship with forty different fish swimming in forty gallons of water. Fixed into the grey gravel at the bottom of the tank is a miniature farmyard, complete with riding stables, a tractor, a plough and a wishing-well. Chrome-plated swimming-pool steps stand next to the piano, for guests to climb up and inspect the occupants of the tank.

I walk Ed Melcher, the chief executive of Black Sea, and Sedat Whemli around the room. The conversation could not be a greater success. Pointing up at the multitude of different fish in the aquarium, I make them both laugh when I say that Fish Farm is looking forward to farming happily in their Black Sea. I go on to explain to Melch about the BBC deal, succinctly but with just enough bait to make it sound irresistible. Remembering a tip Saul had given me about their interest in horseracing, I sum up the idea as if I am describing an undiscovered stud. Melcher nods his head at Whemli, and concludes that I should meet the third man, the president of Black Sea, as soon as possible. Resting my arms around their shoulders and lowering my voice into a confidential tone, I say: 'Personally, I would far rather be with Black Sea than anything else currently on the table.'

Sedat and Ed both look at me and smile, then speak for a few moments in Turkish. I smile back at them, nodding politely as if I understand every word they are saying.

Meanwhile, a sexy but unobtrusive compilation tape of Grandmaster Flash, Sly Stone and John Barry is gently pumping music into the room. I wish I had my own private periscope so that I didn't have to keep craning my neck to check the party is going at full speed. Over in the far corner, near the double-doors, I have a special table set up with a check tablecloth. They are all sitting there, like the teddy bears' picnic. Yes, I've had to give the bodyguards and tradesmen their own separate table. They were becoming difficult, behaving like spoilt brats, making unpleasant threats to Gabe, talking behind my back, and wanting to be paid. On top of this I have already had to deal with the hotel accounts director, Mr Fenn, telling me that there was no more credit! I was speechless and simply referred him to my credit card company, Access America. 'But they have referred me to you,' he said impertinently. Well, there was no point beating about the bush. I told him if there was one iota, one millimetre of trouble regarding room service, or indeed any service, I would be in touch with my lawyers.

Rise above it, I said to myself, rise above it.

I judge from the thirty or forty chattering faces standing around me that everyone has now arrived. Everyone that is, except for Loveday. Rerouted to Montreal because of fog, not expected to arrive for two hours. Can you believe it? My guest of honour? I told Frankie to go to JFK and wait.

'Sure. You bet. No problem.'

I look over at Harry talking to Hamish from the Average White Band, no doubt talking about Oxford and the time the band played there. I look beside me and see Jessica politely laughing at one of Van Morrison's jokes. Harry and Jessica are like two bricks, two Faberge bricks from St Petersburg. I muse for ten seconds at how well they have adapted to their new situation. I am proud of them. Yet a sixth sense tells me to be on my guard with everyone.

Loveday will be here soon. One more hurdle in the morning and then all will be well.

I give the signal for the twenty-two Chinese lanterns to be dimmed for dinner around 9.30 and all the guests sit down. After the first few courses have been served, I wander from table to table, like a perfect host ensuring everyone has someone to talk to and enough food and drink.

'Tim, my man, great party!' Saul calls out in between bites of a spare rib.

'Thank you so much for inviting us!' says Rania, the sexy raven-haired real estate agent, sitting next to the Monsignor.

Before returning to my table, I interrupt Sedat and Ed who are in deep conversation with Gabe and Andy Gibb about some new studio technology.

'Everything OK here, Sedat? I'm sorry we couldn't produce the Archbishop or Mr Allen but Gabe is more than enough compensation, isn't he?'

'I didn't even notice they weren't here.'

Towards the end of the main course, and with more than several cases of sake drunk, the atmosphere in the suite is getting rowdier.

Is it time to make my speech?

I stand up and shout: 'Excuse me? Excuse me, everybody?'

Silence.

I raise my arm slowly upwards, pointing to the spot-lit aquarium.

'Did any of you know there are more than forty different sorts of fish you can have in an aquarium?'

Everyone obediently bends their heads back to look up.

'I had an idea, yeah,' says a deadpan Northern Irish voice.

'Is that why your company is called Fish Farm, Tim?' asks Chaka.

'You mean, because we are involved in so many different things?'

'No! Because of the fish, honey!' Chaka says, angling a toothpick into her mouth.

'Absolutely right, that's exactly why I called it that.'

'To happy farming at Fish Farm, then,' someone shouts.

'To Fish Farm and all who sail in her!' I shout, clinking glasses.

I pour myself more sake. I need to sex up the atmosphere, make enough noise to cover the six hundred thundering inside my head. I tap my glass with my fork and raise my arms like a conductor to the five shadowy figures in the far corner of the room.

'Ready, girls?'

Right on cue the lights dim and a beat-box, trumpet, trombone, double bass and accordion begin to play the opening bars of 'Cabaret'. Standing within a red-and-white spotlight are five girls in their early twenties wearing white T-shirts, black lederhosen, fishnet stockings and kinky boots. Fronting the outfit is a Japanese girl with enormous eyes, a bowler hat, zigzag fringe and a spot of rouge on each of her powdered cheeks. Resting her foot on a chair, she brings a microphone to her lips and begins: 'Willkommen, Bienvenue, Welcome . . .'

Within ten minutes the music has done the trick. By 11.15, while waiters are offering grappa, brandy and schnapps, guests are getting up from the tables to dance. Even Ben Glarusso is unashamedly enjoying himself, dancing with Helen Donovan. But the slightly tense figures of Harry and Jessica remain seated at their separate tables, politely refusing to dance.

I have to get away from them, something is wrong.

I slip out into the quietness of my bathroom.

Stop drinking so much sake and take stock for a moment.

I pour myself a whisky and ginger from my washbasin bar, sit down on the edge of the bath and conclude that although the evening is already a wild success, something is very wrong.

There is a Judas in my life, someone acting as a double agent.

Harry?

Gabe?

Jessica?

Loveday?

Where the fuck is Loveday? Has something happened to her? Has there been an accident? Worse, has she been abducted? She should have landed. I don't like the uncertainty. It is time for the Judas to come out of his lair.

Cannons to the left of me, cannons to the right . . .

I am fed up with being formal, fed up with having to be nice.

I make a beeline for the five girls from Hiroshima. Putting my arm round the singer, I ask, 'Enjoying yourself?'

Before she can reply, Ben Glarusso walks up to me. Looking back over his shoulder at Helen Donovan, he says: 'Tim, it's been such a good party. I don't normally get invited to these things.'

'Ben, I told you it would be a good party. I can see you're getting quite friendly with Stein's bit of stuff.'

'She's his assistant, Tim. Are you crazy?'

'I know they're at it, for sure. Shame about Garcia not coming, isn't it?'

'Yeah, I'm sorry, but he's not a big party person, you know.'

'Well, you can tell him from me that he had better pull his finger out, otherwise there's not going to be any deal let alone any more parties.'

Ben raises his hands as if this is a hold-up.

'Tim? Cool it, for God's sake!'

'You want me to cool it, Ben? OK, I'll cool it. Watch me cool it.' I stalk off.

'Speech!' Speech!' Saul and Gabe shout from the other end of the room.

I sit down on the piano stool and pull the singer from Hiroshima on to my knee. 'You did well tonight. Did you all enjoy it?'

The other girls from the group turn towards me.

'Oh, yes, we all did.'

I look at them and laugh and begin playing the theme to *Cabaret*.

The doorbell chimes. I don't look up but carry on playing. It has to be Loveday. At the very worst it could be Aaron Stein, but if there is any justice in the world it has to be Loveday. I can just hear Harry answering the door, but what happens next is a blur.

I lift my hands from the piano keys, and rub my eyes as if I am in some kind of cartoon. Am I really seeing Simon Caplow lifting his pipe in greeting, alongside Aaron Stein? I bow and wink back, then realise they are not standing there at all. I rub my eyes again and squint across at the tall lady standing in the shadows next to Harry. Who is it? Who is it with bright red lipstick and bright white eyes? It isn't Loveday. No, it isn't Loveday. It is a woman wearing plimsolls, a wraparound raincoat, a belt knotted loosely at the front and a large wooden crucifix hanging from her neck. At first, I can't understand who it is, but then the big mouth starts chewing gum.

Harry steps forward, holding his bottom lip nervously: 'Is this, eh, is this OK, Tim?'

I laugh in the loud and reassuring way that you do when greeting an old friend. My mind is trying to unscramble information. Is Frankie the Judas? Where are the bodyguards? Did Frankie walk this woman past Carlyle security?

I get up from the stool and wink at Harry. 'Of course it's OK. This lady is part of tonight's entertainment. Relax.'

Harry grins, tight-lipped, lets out a whistling sigh and walks back towards Jessica.

'Some party, honey,' Betsy calls out hoarsely. She takes two more paces so that she is beside me.

'You do want your watch, don't you?'

'God, Betsy, how the hell did you get in here?' I ask, waving happily to everyone in the room now crowding round us.

Betsy yawns and takes a can of hairspray out of her pocket. She begins spraying short bursts of it into her hair as if it is some expensive scent. 'God wasn't a Baptist, honey. Jesus is another matter. I need money for the watch.'

'Come on, let's not have a disagreement in front of all these people. Come and meet the fish.'

'I need help, otherwise my arse is ending up in prison. See your ice-swan over there with the marshmallows floating in it? That probably costs more than my bail.'

'Well, take the fucking swan, just don't ruin the party.'

Betsy stares at me. 'You really are a crazy motherfucker.'

I look over at the guests, who seem to be waiting for something to happen and nudge Betsy towards the swimming pool steps. 'Come and have a look up here and we'll sort things out.'

I stand by the steps smiling bemusedly for what must be a minute, as Betsy covers my hair with hairspray. It is going to be like Punch and Judy with a fishy twist. I am transfixed by the erotic smell.

'Now give me the money,' she says impatiently.

I put a cigarette in my mouth, hand Betsy my Ronson, put my hands behind my back, and stand erect like a condemned man.

'Follow me up and light my cigarette.'

I walk to the top of the steps with Betsy close behind me. The people in the party now sound like an audience at a boxing match. Betsy shouts in my ear, 'You really want me to light it? You crazy?'

'Yeah, light it.'

'O – K.'

Betsy pushes the flame of the Ronson into the tip of the Marlboro. A spilt second later, *Vrooomph*, my hair is alight in blue-and-yellow flames. I want to do something for the crowd but, seeing Loveday's watch in Betsy's hand, change tack, lunge forward and grab it from her. She screams, flails her arms round like a helicopter rotor blade, but soon loses her balance. As she falls backwards Gabe manages to catch her and then gently wrestles her to the floor.

The tops of my ears are burning badly and there is the pungent smell of sizzling pork. Holding the watch in triumph above my head, I bow to each side of the room. My scalp feels like it is melting. I grip hold of the sides of the aquarium, and dunk my head into the slimy water. My head sizzles and steams, as if it has just been used by a blacksmith to shoe a horse. I lift my head from the tank, shake the water from my hair, and cheer in celebration. A fat wave of water flops out and bounces through the open lid of the piano on to the strings below. I let out a pantomime laugh. The steps start swaying. Harry, Jessica and Gabe take hold of them and shout, 'Tim! Watch out! It isn't safe! Come down!'

But I can't hear anything. I am on a roaring train, still in my personal boxing ring, waving the watch high above my head.

It is the sight of Mr Fenn and his uniformed security guards bursting through the double-doors, switching on the overhead lights, running and yelling into walkie-talkies, that makes me lose my balance. As I feel myself falling, I try to steady myself by gripping hold of the side of the aquarium, but my weight is too great, as it and I are up-ended and tumble through the open piano-lid below. For the next thirty seconds, I wince breathlessly, blinking amidst cartoon stars, spread-eagled across a smashed piano and looking face down at forty different fish.

January to February 1981

49

They had me sharing a room at first. It was with an eighteen-year-old boy called Bobby, a tennis scholar from Princeton. They kept thinking I was asleep when they wheeled in the electric shock machine, but I never was. I watched very single bit of it, every single time. Putting the Vaseline on the sides of his head, the respirator in his mouth to stop him from choking, his convulsions and, once he had woken up, his endless tears. Eventually, seeing this every day made me want to cry, not for very long but long enough for me to want to get myself out of there.

Three weeks and two days ago, I was drugged and brought here. I know because of the twenty-three nicks I have made on the desk with my twenty-five cent coin.

I am in a single room now, with a single bed, a single chest of drawers under a single wooden desk. There is also a single wardrobe in which I keep my suit, my briefcase and my single book of lists. The door which leads out on to the long wooden corridor has a wire-mesh window, the type you can see through but cannot break. On the other side of the room there is a window above the desk with a faded yellow curtain that lets in light in the early morning. That window does not have bars but it is locked and is the type you cannot open.

I like that it is called the Royal Bedlam, and not just any old bedlam. But that is all I like about this place, except for the ping-pong and the fact that the building is in the grounds of a disused stately home. I have inspected Byron's former home, even called several building firms for estimates, and strongly considered buying it, but was put off by the crows nesting high up in a chimneybreast. The hospital is an L-shaped single-storey, pre-fabricated building, constipated with brown doors, mustard-coloured walls and over-heated with fluorescent strip lighting everywhere.

It is like being back in boarding school, but a million times worse.

It is eight miles north of Oxford, and ninety-six miles east of Wales. Most importantly, it is only four miles to the M40 and back to London. The chances of escaping on foot are remote, because the only way out is along a raised asphalt drive, once a local railway line, and that lasts for a mile before you arrive at the electronically controlled gates. The grounds are covered in bumpy green pasture, big oak and chestnut trees, countless grazing sheep and countless bits of sheep-shit. By around five in the afternoon, everything outside becomes wrapped in a feathery mist that remains until late the following morning.

My so-called 'monopolising' of the wooden hospital telephone booth has decreased now to about twenty-three calls a day. To be honest, it's not that I don't need to make more calls, it's just the bloody awful smell in there. I swear there are people here who never wash, just sit inside that wooden box and sweat. This afternoon I arrived at the booth and heard tearful Bobby talking, blubbing unintelligibly down the phone. I am embarrassed for him and embarrassed for me. How the fuck did I ever get to be in here? I stare down the corridor, think of *The Shining*, start walking and retreat into my head.

I wish that bloody woman with the over-scrubbed face and wire-wool hair would stop crying all the time. I mean, I know it's sad, but there are limits, aren't there? I said to her this morning: 'Good morning, Joan, isn't it a lovely day out there?' She looked out of the window as if there was a funeral going by, turned back to me and said: 'A lovely what?' I tried to encourage her a bit by saying: 'Well, look up at the sky and see how blue it is. Not a cloud in sight!' She immediately started crying. Then everyone crowded round and looked at me as if I had stabbed her or something. Christ! Get me out of here.

Then again, last night, the fat one, Belinda. Oh, God! It was about nine o'clock, lights-out time. I'd been to the bathroom like every other goody-good boy in the place and was walking back down the corridor. She was in front of me, going to her room. I kept my distance, of course, because I know what she can be like and I'd been told she always has a knife. Then, I realised that she was pissing as she was walking. She must have known what she was doing. She was like some giant slug leaving a trail of slime. I don't want to be sanctimonious; I don't want to be like some tosser from Tunbridge Wells with no idea of the suffering these people endure. But some of these people have just given up, they've given up apologizing or helping anybody. I would cut off two of my toes to be out of here.

Even Mark, the 'I-was-at-Eton-actually' bloke, the one who just sits in front of the television in the brown vinyl armchair adjusting it every two seconds and chain-smoking, well, he's almost given up bothering. I don't know, because I thought we had established some sort of long-term-prisoner rapport. Then straight after Mrs Wire-Wool this morning I went to see him. There he was, transfixed, sitting in front of the telly as if he was getting some much-needed cathode rays for his poxy face. I said something fun like: 'Hello, you old wanker, how's it going?' He turned right round as if he was from *The Exorcist* and stared at me. Then he started shouting:

'*Why don't you fuck off! You're just a fucking fake and you've no right to be here!*'

I admit, in retrospect, I should have walked away, like the nurses said, and gone and played ping-pong, but I didn't. No, I just let him have it. Something in that tone something in that look of his just reminded me of too many cunts who had said that sort of thing to me all my life – that man in the Carlyle, Fenn was it? and that jumped-up bastard Adderfort back at school. I don't know why, but I just saw red. I walked right up to him, grabbed his burning cigarette, his cigarette packet and ashtray, and held them in the air.

'Listen, you sad fucking cunt! Don't make judgments about me, and my suitability to be here or not. Unlike you I'm not a sad fucker who spends his entire time masturbating his pathetic cigarette in front of the television twenty-four fucking hours a day. If you think you're entitled to be here, then you're right. As for me, no, I don't want to be here one bit and that's the difference between you and me. You sad stuck-up ginger-haired failure of a *Cunt!*'

I tore open the packet of cigarettes, threw them all over the room and walked out. He just kept a sanctimonious smile on his face. I felt and still feel bad about this incident. I did tell a nurse what had happened and was given a few mournful nods and told to share it with the group the next day, especially if Mark was present. But I'm furious with myself. Not particularly because of that wanker Mark, although I do feel bad as he hasn't come out of his room since, not even for *Star Trek*, but because this is going to go against me in my review meeting with the doctors. One stupid blot on the copybook could put me back inside here for another three weeks or more. I've succeeded in coming off the witnessed-medication programme where you have to have a nurse virtually feel the tablets going down your throat. But even so, I still have to queue up like the rest and take my stupid tablets if I'm to have any chance of getting out of here. Yet I know it's those very tablets that are preventing me, are holding me back, are flattening my power.

What I do know is that I *am* in prison. I never knew what that felt like before; I could never have imagined the feeling of being so trapped against your will. I spend so much of my energy pacing up and down. No one realises that I'm running out of time. I feel so fucking impotent. I am like a tiger with rubber teeth. Someone's taken my mental belt and braces away and I have to walk around holding my trousers up, asking permission to have a piss.

50

I was sitting on my perfectly made bed when the announcement came over the hospital speaker: 'Timothy Lomax, you're wanted in reception. Would Timothy Lomax come to reception immediately, please?'

I got up, pulled my cashmere coat out of the wardrobe, and wondered if there was a restaurant we could drive to. I was nervous. I hadn't seen him since Christmas Day. Nevertheless, I walked out into the middle of the corridor with as much confidence as I could muster. Mark, the bloke I had had the dust-up with, had previously told me that patients seen walking in the middle of a corridor are much more likely to be released than those who walk down the sides. *Rock on, Tommy*, I said to myself, *because I'm walking right down the middle, with my arms outstretched. That will show them!*

And there he was, innocently standing two feet from the drug hatch, hands clasped behind his back, stooping slightly to listen to what one of the nurses on reception was saying. He was wearing his old camel coat, V-neck sweater, woollen tie, old check trousers, brown suede shoes, and was holding a plastic shopping bag. I assumed his Wellington boots were waiting for him at home like two faithful dogs.

'Hello, Dad.'

'Hello, Timmy.'

We shook hands, stepped back and nodded at one another, not quite sure what to say. He had his newspaper under his arm, folded outwards at the crossword. To my dismay, the carrier bag he was carrying was from Gerard's, the men's outfitters in Hedgerly Cross. How would I explain that I had my own tailors these days?

'How was the journey, Dad?'

His eyes lit up. 'Well, actually not too bad, a bit of a problem at the turn-off . . .'

Maybe the drugs I had taken after breakfast were taking longer to wear off that morning, but he seemed to go on about the traffic, the road works and the old petrol station not being there any more for at least half an hour. OK, an exaggeration, it was two minutes, but eventually, I said, 'Dad shall we go and find somewhere to eat? A bit of seafood? A bit of Chinese?'

'Are you sure you're allowed to?' he said, furrowing his brow like a walnut shell. I smiled a patient smile and looked across at the duty sister on the reception desk, who smiled back, shaking her head in the negative.

'Apparently not,' I said, wondering why I wasn't shouting at her.

'Anyway, Timmy, I'm sorry, because I parked the car by the gates. I didn't realise how far away it was to walk here.'

'You walked?'

'Yes, and very nice if you have the time.'

'Ever eaten in a loony-bin before?' I whispered, taking my father's arm and steering him towards the canteen.

My father just smiled politely, asking: 'Do you think they might make me a cheese and pickle sandwich?'

We sat at the end of a long Formica table, its surface recently wiped clean, with a round grey clock ticking loudly on the wall behind, and the smell of boiled cabbage wafting in from the kitchen. We both played with the salt and pepper pots and examined the underneath of the blue-and-white sugar bowl. Drumming his fingers on the table, my father started humming 'I Could Have Danced All Night'.

Sue, the pretty but plump canteen assistant with no teeth, set down two cups of coffee, a plate of biscuits and hovered by my father.

'Two white coffees, here we are! Shall I take your coat?'

'No, thanks, I think I'd rather keep it on, if you don't mind.'

'I just thought you'd be more comfortable, love.'

My father gave her a nod of gratitude and Sue's face contorted into a marshmallow smile. All I needed was for Belinda the incontinent to appear and we could have a party.

'Biscuit?' I asked holding up the small plate of chocolate digestives.

'Perhaps in a minute or two, Timmy.'

I don't think I'm going to be able to handle this if he's going to go at this pace.

'Good of you to come, Dad. Thanks.'

Holding the saucer under his chin, my father slowly sipped from his cup of coffee. I hoped he was not going to take a similar approach to eating his food. He put the cup in the saucer, then down on the table, dabbed his moustache with a handkerchief and said: 'Well, yes.'

'Well, yes, what, Dad?' I said, lighting a cigarette and inhaling noisily.

'Well, yes, it is very nice to be here, to see you.'

I half choked on the smoke. I put my hand over my eyes and coughed. 'Dad, you don't have to say that. Say what you really think; it might help, you never know. I bet you never thought you would end up visiting me here.'

He looked away up at the ceiling.

'Well, I think the grounds are very attractive, and they have some marvellous rhododendrons and some very old oaks. It's almost a park back there, isn't it?'

'Dad this is a mental hospital, not Kew Gardens.'

The instant I made the remark I regretted it. I should have known the subject of me being here was never going to be up for discussion. He really just wanted to see me, check that I was still in one piece, have a cheese and pickle sandwich, and then leave. However, he made a brave attempt.

'I do understand where I am. By all accounts, and according to Charles, you're very lucky to be a patient here. It was quite difficult to get you a place. I think I should have explained, been more forceful, about certain aspects to do with Uncle Michael.'

'Go on,' I said, watching him shift his position in his chair.

'It strikes me, Timmy, they must think you need to be here and if that *is* the case, it is imperative that you do whatever the doctors tell you. Most important is that you take the pills they're giving you, otherwise you could really be for the high jump.'

'Dad, I've got to get out of here and get back on the horse. I can't waste any more time.'

'What horse? You haven't got a horse.'

'Oh, Christ, Dad, have you no idea? Have you no idea of the amounts of money that are at stake here? Don't you realise what I was putting together in America? I've got a lot on the line. And what about Uncle Michael?'

It was only after I had made the reference to the horse that I fully remembered the business with Uncle Michael.

My father picked up a chocolate biscuit, held it between his earth-stained thumb and finger, broke it into pieces and started eating. As he slowly chewed on the biscuit, I noticed two small patches of stubble, in the cleft of his chin and below his lower lip, which his razor had missed. There was an air of fake curiosity in his eyes as he looked around the room. He was getting old and more obstinate. He had changed the channel and was not going to change it back.

So, instead, we talked about his garden, about the others, about the frost attacking his vegetables, about the price of beer going up a penny . . . and, oh, yes, once again, how it was so important to take the drugs and do what the doctors said. I think he felt as if he had come to see his son in prison. Not that he looked embarrassed or ashamed, but I do think he felt a kind of terrible hopelessness at not knowing what to say. Still, it was good of him to come.

* * *

He stayed for an hour and a half. When I walked out with him into the grounds, past the ruins of Byron's house and up on to the asphalt drive, I thought he had changed his mind and was going to tell me something of enormous significance. He stood gazing mournfully into the distance, clearly thinking about something. As the wind blew hard around his trouser legs and made his grey hair flick up and down, he turned to me, and after a long silence said: 'I don't know, Timmy, I just don't know. I think I will have to write you a letter.'

Another silence. It was strange, because my father was the worst actor I'd ever known and yet he was so completely comfortable with silences, it was as if he had a PhD in them. Then, hearing the sound of a passing car in the distance, he looked at his watch and said, 'Better be off now, I want to get home before it gets dark.'

With that he waved goodbye and with long determined strides headed off towards the gates. That's that, then, I thought, and turned round ready to trudge back to the hospital. I stood still, however, closed my eyes and rubbed my finger up and down the face of Loveday's watch. I desperately wanted her to be with me, there and then, on that asphalt ridge. I was concentrating so hard on rubbing the watch again I didn't hear my father's shouts. Then I registered a shadow, looked round and saw he had walked nearly all the way back and was yelling something while holding the Gerard's carrier bag up in the air. For a ridiculous wonderful moment I thought he might be yelling something to me about Loveday. My heart sank at the thought that I was about to be presented with a khaki safari-suit or something similar.

'Nearly forgot this and went home with it,' said my father, slightly out of breath.

Faking a grateful smile, I took the bag from him. 'What is it, Dad?'

'I made it for you yesterday,' he said enthusiastically.

Oh, no, this is getting worse.

'Really?'

I reached inside the bag, expecting to feel some unpleasant fabric but instead pulled out a large blue Thermos flask. It was weighty and full.

'What is it, Dad?'

My father looked disappointed. 'Can't you guess? I thought it might help to build up your strength.'

'Brilliant, thanks a lot, it's great,' I mumbled, still not sure what it was.

Scratching his chin, he stepped closer to me and, squinting at the label on the Thermos flask, said with a mischievous smile: 'Made with a lot of loving care, you know.'

I laughed. Now I understood what it was. I was trying to think of the right words to say in return, ones that would be appropriate, when he threw his hand up in a wave, nodded and walked off.

'Don't forget, Timmy, concentrate on getting well, nothing else.'

'Bye, Dad, thanks a lot for coming!' I called out.

He walked into the distance, sheep scattering behind him. He carried on walking, growing smaller and smaller, until he reached the bend towards the gates and disappeared.

51

'Is there really a chance of getting out of here?'

Dr Hughes anxiously glanced at her loafer shoes, as if I had asked her what colour bra she was wearing.

'Tim, that all depends on what Dr Simmer says.'

I leaned forwards in the brown vinyl armchair I was marooned in, and offered the twitchy Dr Hughes a Marlboro .

'Thanks, I shouldn't, but I will,' she said, pulling a cigarette from my packet.

'I spent two hours tidying my room today. I don't know what else I can do to convince you people that I'm OK.'

Dr Hughes coughed and exhaled as if she had never smoked before.

'I think it's a bit more than keeping your room tidy, Tim.'

'Aren't you part of Simmer's team? Doesn't what you think count? After all, you're the one who sees me most, aren't you?'

'Dr Simmer asks my opinion, obviously, yes.'

Oh dear, this is turning into a number two situation.

'So, will you put in a good word?'

'Tell me about the visit with your father. What's all this about television advertising?'

'The soup you mean?'

'I think so, yes.'

'I got the idea as I was walking past Mark, the miserable-looking bastard in the TV room. Thinking about it, he would make a marvellous person to use as a before and after candidate, you know, here's a picture of me before I started eating Lomax soup and now look! Anyway, it took me nearly an hour to figure out a way of building a factory near Hedgerly Cross, setting up a distribution network, and, in return for all the shares, to put a considerable amount of money in trust for my father. I would also need to contact Andy Warhol about the design for the can, and find a way of completing the purchase of the Pump House in Chelsea to make it the London head office, buy Loveday a new car, and put down a deposit on a sub-post office.'

'I see, did you do all this last night?' Dr Hughes enquired softly, while writing a note on her clipboard.

'Some bastard was in the stupid booth most of the night, so I couldn't put it into effect. Then out of the blue, this morning, Loveday rang to say she's coming down tonight.'

Dr Bernie Hughes laid her pen against the clipboard, and bit her bottom lip.

'I see. How do you feel about that?'

'Delighted . . . but a bit strange.'

'Why?'

'Because she didn't seem very enthusiastic when I told her I was coming out next week. We didn't fight or argue, and I don't know why there wasn't more excitement but anyway I bit my tongue – not literally – and just said, OK, can't wait to see you, sort of thing.'

'Apart from the fact that you invented your departure date from this hospital, was there another problem?' Dr Hughes said, carefully stubbing out her half-smoked cigarette.

'You're probably going to say I'm being paranoid, but she just didn't seem as pleased as I'd be if I were in her shoes.'

'I see.'

'Don't just say "I see" all the time, doctor! Am I being weird or what?'

'You are probably still a little paranoid, but don't worry.'

'OK. It's better to know these things. I'm trying to get at the real me, so to speak.'

'Good, because that's the idea of being here.'

'Seriously, do you think I might get out next week? I'll do whatever it takes.'

'What about the diary that Dr Simmer asked you to keep? I know you said it was "an outrageous invasion of your privacy", but as a means to an end – have you done it?'

'Touché!' I said nodding smugly and pulling out a sheaf of papers from my trouser pocket. 'I have it right here.'

I flattened the foolscap pieces of paper on my lap and looked across at her.

She looked at her shoes again and motioned with her hand for me to proceed.

Clearing my throat, I began speaking but not too loudly in case anyone was listening outside the door:

'Star Log – 28th January.

'OK, OK, I understand now about New York . . . I'd bitten off far more than I could chew. But, Christ, don't lots of people do that and not end up in a place like this? What's wrong with a bit of ambition? I mean, it's all so bloody passive. Just be patient and you'll get well. Come on now, Tim, you've got to take it easy, or you know you'll never get better. Of course, what they're really saying is, you won't get out of here. Well, how do you take it fucking easy when you know your life is on the line out there? Do I act the zombie, or do I act how any normal fucking person would . . . please!! I mean this is worse than some concentration camp, minding your mental Ps and Qs all the time. I know my ideas are good, just got to tie them all together. I know I'm nearly there. All I need is to be out of here and given some space and headroom. Ha, that's a good joke: head room! Even if no one else believes me, I know success is just around the corner. I know it! It's impossible to trust anyone, difficult, imposs-ible.

'I've been told the rumours in the business have now reached epic proportions. I'm running a newspaper empire and taking over from Aaron Stein apparently. Well, why not? I probably could, given a little bit of money and some back-up. Anyway I can just imagine what everyone is saying now. Harry and Jessica? They don't understand. Keep writing to me about taking time for wounds to heal, don't see what I see. And Charles? Well, it's strange, but I think he really does believe me. I trust Charles more ... Christ, I didn't know how much ... but then he just doesn't know the business. Ironically, out of all of them, the only one who does of course is Rick ... and where the fuck is Rick? Hates me with a passion, I'm sure ... burned all my bridges there, Jesus ... He's written me a letter, so I'm told, saying he's terribly sorry and all that. I can't believe he has. I wouldn't ... Then there's this guy called Idwal ... Welsh for Edward, except stupidly he's known as Zeus round here. Mind you, he is seventeen foot tall. Should have started saying something about him when I met him, but I wasn't keeping a diary then. Well, anyway, I understand. God, I'm tired. The central heating and the drugs just make it impossible to stay awake.'

Dr Hughes appeared to have written an essay on her clipboard.

'That is very good, Tim. I think you are gaining some real insight, don't you?'

'I'm gaining what?' I yelled excitedly. 'What is insight, doctor? Can it be converted into cash?'

She laughed and, taking another cigarette from my packet, said: 'Insight is something we doctors believe means having a genuine awareness and understanding of your mental condition, being able to see things for what they are.'

'Super.'

'You'll come out of this just fine, don't worry, Tim.'

'I know the idea. Trust you, because you're a doctor?'

'Same time tomorrow or shall we space it until the day after?'

'Let's space it and live dangerously!'

Idwal was someone who really listened to what I was saying without thinking something else and taking notes. He explained he'd been in the army for fourteen years and had become disenchanted with the lack of promotion; he had left to get a better job and ended up here. I didn't say anything, but wondered if he ended up here in a different capacity first. Maybe he'd been in Northern Ireland? Anyway, found out he's married with two kiddies and lives with them and his wife Lou in the small cottage just behind the vegetable garden. I said that must be handy, and he said if I knew just how much he has to eat each day on account of the weight training and how little he is paid, it was very handy. I wondered at this point whether he'd ever been a bodyguard. But then again, probably not; he lacks that killer instinct. He was a good bloke, friendly and always bending down to put his arm on my shoulder and ask if everything's all right. He always seems to know exactly what I'm talking about and I mean, *exactly*. He doesn't sound that interested in the hospital or the staff side of things. He said, if possible, he gets involved in staff meetings only every other week. I asked him how many other patients he was treating at the moment. He replied somewhat mournfully that I was the only one. I like that point very much. He keeps quoting various bits of poetry, some I know and some I have never heard. God, he likes to talk, though! Told me about his five-year-old treasures. Thought he was talking about some army souvenirs till he said they were his twin daughters. Then he told me about his wife and how they fight like cat and dog, but he's never been more certain about anyone in his life. I hoped the feeling was mutual, but didn't say it. I wondered whether she's built like him or if she's the opposite, which I kind of guess she is. How do they actually do it? I mean, isn't there a danger of her being crushed?

Talking about sex, whatever has happened to me? I'm sure they put bromide or something in the tea. Still, chance would be a fine thing. Anyway, the only one I want to do anything with is Loveday and maybe . . . you never know . . . maybe that is possible.

Anyway, back to Idwal, king of the vegetable garden, and his twin treasures. He asked all about me. I told him about the BBC deal and how it was so close to working and how I had slightly overdone it and hence ended up in here. I didn't go into all the other companies and ideas for fear of overloading him. I thought at first he didn't understand or was being polite. I explained it to him twice and then he responded just as I had hoped! He thought it was great! He went on to say that I shouldn't worry about being a little hyper; that some of the most successful people in history were. This made me feel even better and able to discuss my loss of power. Again he was brilliant! He said he'd seen this sort of thing in other cases, and that largely it was to do with the drugs. He said that it wasn't just the effect the drugs were having on me mentally, but physically as well.

He then went further and in a way that I thought he perhaps shouldn't have, considering his position. But he said that if I was prepared to enter into a training programme with him in the gym and on the squash court, then 'that power of yours would be back in no time!'. This was what I needed to hear! He suggested we could start with the gym tomorrow but first have a 'knock up' on the squash court. Somewhat stupidly, and I don't know why I said it, I told him I'd once been a county player.

Well, half an hour later we were on the court. I've never felt as humiliated, frustrated or embarrassed as I did then. I could hardly hit the fucking ball. I was like a blind beached whale. I don't know why, but I seem to have put on about ten stone in weight and become short-sighted into the bargain. He, of course, was professionally polite and understanding. Obviously, the bullshit about being a county player had not helped the situation either.

Afterwards, when we were sitting talking, he began expounding his philosophy of physical fitness, poetry and positive thinking. I listened to him for a while and wondered if he had understood what I had been talking about. I mean, where do you get these things, at the drug hatch? Anyway, he's convinced me to persevere. What happened next was a turn-up for the books! He told me he had written a bloody book! I sort of explained that I wasn't exactly a book publisher but within a few months I'd be in a position to do something. Again I'm not sure why I said this, because I hadn't planned to expand this quickly. He wasn't having any of it, though, and said that I was the man for him and that he would bring the manuscript tomorrow. You never know, do you?

We walked slowly back to the main building and I decided to tell him about Loveday coming down. I didn't go into all the details, but he seemed to pick up on something about her being a bit distant. He was spot on with his advice again. Told me that he had seen it a thousand times before. However calm women (as in wives and girlfriends) appear on the telephone, coming to a mental hospital was an extremely stressful experience as they were never sure what state their loved one was going to be in. He went on to say that one of the most important issues was to look the business. I took that to mean well dressed or smart. He gave me some cock-and-bull about the army, which in effect was saying that if a man looks smart he feels smart. Right then I needed any help I could get and he provided it. He came to my room ten minutes later with an iron, some starch and dab-it-off cleaning stuff, and helped me sort out my suit, shirt and tie. If this gym, squash, reading poetry and ironing are the way to regaining my power – well, I'll do it every day for the rest of my life.

52

Loveday sat down on my single hospital bed and remained very still. Eventually she looked up at me and said: 'I don't know how to say this.'

I laughed and put my arm around her: 'Just say it and don't worry.'

'I want to resign, Tim.'

The words came out as clearly as if she had just announced she had cancer. My head went into a tailspin, my specially pressed suit creased in a hundred different places. I knew exactly what she had meant but I tried to buy some time.

'Resign from what?'

'You know what I'm talking about Tim. I'm sorry, but it's better to do this sooner rather than later.'

'You can't be serious.'

I looked at her as if waiting either for a joke to be revealed, or for some conditions to be attached that would stop her from taking this action. Loveday stared straight ahead, almost like a waxwork. I rallied.

'Well, I'm not accepting it! It's that simple. You cannot resign, so there!'

Loveday put her hand on her forehead as if she was about to cry, and after a deep breath, began again.

'Tim?'

'What?'

'I mean it. I can't go through all of this again. I don't think you know what it's been like.'

Spotting a chink of light, I quickly replied. 'Of course I do. Look of course, I know. The second I get out of here things are going to be all right. I know they are. Trust me. Please.' I was aware that my voice was beginning to shake. 'Sweetheart, you know me better than anyone. If I haven't got you to trust, who have I got?'

Loveday clenched her hand into a fist, and brought it up to her chin.

'Tim? That isn't the point. You need to stay here for a while and get better. I should go . . . look, I've . . . I hope you don't mind, I've spoken to the doctors, you know, to let them know . . .'

'You've spoken to whom?'

'I had to say something, Tim. I was a nurse once. I do know about these things.'

'You've spoken to the doctors?' I yelled, turning her shoulders towards me.

'Don't get angry, please!'

I looked up at the ceiling in exasperation.

'No! You can't just come down here, not after all this time, not after everything we've been through, and just say: I should go now, I've spoken to the doctors. I mean, that's rich, isn't it? Pop down and pop into the fucking doctors and tell them everything that is fucking private about my fucking private life! I mean, doesn't that mean anything to you? Don't I mean anything?'

I realised I was shouting and out of breath. I stood up and walked up and down the room. Tears were now streaming down Loveday's face as she struggled to pull out a tissue and cigarettes from her bag. I continued pacing like a condemned man, but was determined to find a way to plead for a reprieve. This was the most pain I had felt in a long time. It was like being cut open with a surgical knife. It was affecting every single channel in my head and new ones in my heart I didn't know I had. I was desperate to stem the feeling of quicksand pulling me down. I tried to kickstart my brain into some course of action. I stopped pacing, crouched down in front of her and took hold of her hand.

'Look. I don't know whether you're right or whether you're wrong. All I know is that I cannot accept this right now and especially sitting in this fucking awful place. Do you understand? Do you? Anyway, you can't smoke here. Let's go out for a drive somewhere and talk this through.'

I stared at her intently, pretending to be relaxed, following every flicker in her eyes in case they betrayed some further information.

She eventually sighed an even deeper sigh, stood up and put her bag wearily over her shoulder.

'Tim? I think we both . . . no, OK, let's go outside for a minute, but then I'm going to have to go. Look . . . this isn't a game. What I'm saying is that it's for your sake too. We've got to stop.'

Loveday smoothed down her dress, letting out a long sigh. She then fastened her coat, and came and stood in front of me, pushing the hair from my eyes.

'You need a haircut. The burnt bits have nearly all grown out.'

I nodded and straightened my jacket collar. 'You've had a haircut and you've lost a lot of weight. I didn't notice the last time.'

Loveday puffed her cheeks out like a hamster, and shrugged, 'I needed to. I've always been too fat.'

'Not in my book, you haven't.'

'I'm ready, shall we go?'

We walked out of the room and into the corridor as if we were both following a coffin. The sound of people shouting in the reception area and playing ping-pong grew closer. With every step I took and every raucous shriek I heard, I began to squirm inside at the thought of the looks that we would get as we walked by. However, as we passed, Loveday summoned some composure, smiled at the two nurses framed in the dispensing hatch, and waved goodbye to the group of patients surrounding the table-tennis board. For a second I winced at the thought that I might be stopped and asked why I was going outside and at night. But there seemed to be an implicit understanding from the nurses not to ask. It was only afterwards that I felt some sense of revulsion, when for the thousandth time, I reviewed what had happened and suddenly thought of some possible compassionate conspiracy existing between Loveday and the nurses.

As we pushed through the revolving doors of the hospital and stepped out into the cold January night, there was an uncanny feeling of having been here before. For a split second I forgot where we actually were and almost started looking for a yellow checker cab or Frankie's limousine. Loveday twigged, raised her eyes to heaven, and let out a little laugh. We walked on, unsure whether to laugh or cry; unsure which side of the line we belonged. Then it began to rain. This was no ordinary airy-fairy rain; it seemed like two hundred gallons of rain, jungle rain, forest rain, sheet rain, rain that washes away the sins of your fathers. By the time we reached the car park, we were drenched from head to foot.

I persuaded Loveday that the only way to get the car heater working was to drive a while and then stop at the back of the hospital by the vegetable patch. I asked her to park the car so that its headlights shone across the neat rows of cabbages and potatoes. I explained that I didn't see it as a patch: for me it was a garden where I spent a lot of my time thinking. Loveday seemed enchanted at first, but pissed me off big time with her suggestion that maybe that was what I should continue doing for a while, or at least until I was better. *Who does she think she's talking to? Some fucking loony-bin moron?* I recovered, on the surface at least, and asked her for a cigarette. She pulled one out of her packet and handed it to me.

'Thanks,' I said.

Two short rings of a bell rang out inside the hospital. It was time for my wing's group meeting. I felt a massive wave of smug superiority knowing that I would not be attending.

Loveday leaned forwards, and gazed at her watch by the light of the dashboard.

'Look, I'm sorry, but I really have to be getting back now. It's quite a drive and there are terrible road works beyond Oxford on the M40. Plus, I've got to be up really early tomorrow.'

I instantly recognised the tone. It was one she had borrowed from someone else. I suspected it was a voice she had recently been taught to use by people at her magazine, the one reserved for dealing with men who were no longer welcome.

Flicking the ash from my cigarette, I put my hand on her knee.

'Can I ask you a question?'

'Of course,' she sighed a little sadly.

'Was this all your idea, coming down here tonight?'

Loveday slowly shook her head: 'Does it bloody matter whose idea it was? Do you think I want to do this, you fucking, fuck-ing . . .'

She started to cry. I put my arms around her and cradled her face on my shoulder.

'I meant to say you look lovely. You've made a real effort. You've put the dress on that I bought you. I appreciate that more than you probably know.'

There was a brief silence. I held my breath.

Then she yelled: 'I wanted to! You fool, don't you see that?'

I breathed out and let my arm slip down around her waist: 'Of course I can see that. You look completely gorgeous. I'm the envy of the whole loony bin, you fool, don't you see that?'

We both laughed and exchanged familiar silly looks.

Pointing to the milky curtain of condensation covering the windscreen and the windows, I joked: 'Now this is nice, isn't it? I always did take you to the best places.'

Loveday sniffed several times, dabbing her eyes and nose with her tissue.

'You always did Tim. No one can deny that. I just wish this wasn't happening . . . it's such a fucking fucker!'

I took hold of both her hands and said, as calmly as I could: 'None of this needs to happen. What has happened already has. None of it is the end of the world. I'll be out of here soon, and I'll get everything back, and we can go on being together. Why don't you stay the night at the local hotel here? They'll never notice I'm gone, and we can get up in the morning, and you can go off to work and I can come back to my loony bin in time for the drug hatch and a bit of brekker?'

I nudged her arm, waiting for a laugh or some degree of conspiratorial agreement. There was none. Loveday appeared to have lost interest and had drawn a heart in the window condensation and dramatically put a cross through it. She turned to me with a sad look on her face.

'Tim, you and I have to face it. This isn't going to work.' She paused and took a deep breath. 'We've gone too far round the clock now. You see, it isn't exactly what happened in New York that's pushed things over the edge. I would have done anything for you, and I mean anything. I would have married you, even if it meant never being spoken to by my mother again. But in my heart of hearts I just know deep down we are not meant for each other – and if that's the case, well, then it's better to cut it off now and not prolong the agony. It's better for you, Tim, can't you see that?'

'No, I bloody well can't.'

This was the same bullshit as the last scene in *Casablanca*.

She continued: 'Tim, please? Can't you see that our problem is that we bring out the worst in each other?'

'No. I can't see that. That's complete and utter crap. You've just borrowed that from some stupid magazine. Maybe I bring out the worst in myself, but not in you.'

'You're mixing my words. Look, let's be realistic, cruel, hard for a moment.'

'Are they your new solicitors?'

'Tim I'm being serious.'

'What the fuck do you think I'm being? Pinky and Perky?'

Loveday angrily turned the ignition key, and started the engine, looked in her driver's mirror and then switched the engine off. 'Tim, you need someone to look after you, especially after this, but I need someone to look after me as well . . . don't you see?'

'Yes, I do see, but I can look after you, I know I can, and so do you!'

'But, Tim, think about it for a second,' said Loveday, pausing to take hold of the top of her seatbelt. 'What if we if we had children? What sort of situation would it be for them now? Let alone all these debts that even now you don't realise you've got . . . What would it be like for them? Have you really ever thought about that?'

Loveday's words whistled around my ears like a wave of bullets hitting their target. The car door was open and I got out. Loveday had covered her face with her arm and clung on with both hands to the seatbelt as if it was a strap on a tube train. It was only when she turned round and saw the open passenger door that she realised I had gone.

She leaned towards the door and shouted: 'Tim! Tim! Where are you?'

I crouched down in the furrowed mud of the cabbage patch. Even though Loveday was only ten feet in front of me, because she was inside and behind the windscreen it was as if she wasn't there.

I tore off a dozen or so cabbage leaves and tried to sit down on them but it was too uncomfortable. Instead, I made them into a neat thick pile and knelt on them. I watched Loveday as she sat back in her seat, took another cigarette from her packet, and started smoking, constantly looking out of each window and over each shoulder. Suddenly there was a big gust of wind, shortly followed by what I took to be an owl shrieking or two cats fucking. A second later Loveday had pulled the passenger door shut, switched on the engine, and put the windscreen wipers on at high speed, presumably hoping that if I thought she was leaving, I would run back to the car. She began revving the accelerator pedal but, like a well-trained soldier, I remained at my post.

The rain had settled down into a light drizzle and to my annoyance Albinoni's Adagio in G would not stop playing full blast inside my head. Like a certain point in a wedding ceremony when there is no turning back, so it was now with Loveday and myself. There was another gust of wind, this time bitingly cold. I cupped my hands and blew on them, never taking my eyes off Loveday's car. I could see her shiver. She was freezing. It was time to call a truce. I let out what I thought was a loud wolf cry. She immediately switched her lights to full beam and began frantically clearing the condensation from the windscreen. I think she half-expected to see a maniac leaping on to her bonnet, so she looked somewhat relieved to see me crouching in the middle of a row of spaceman-like cabbages in front of her.

Loveday jumped out of the car and ran towards me.

I did not look up or turn around as she reached me. Instead I stood up and balanced on my tiptoes. Out of breath and dazed, she leaned heavily against me, so much so that I lost my balance and fell backwards into a row of cabbages.

The fall looked far worse than it was. However, I made the most of it.

'Oh, Christ! Tim, are you OK?' Loveday shrieked. 'Oh my God, have you hurt yourself?'

'It's not that bad,' I grunted, sitting up and holding a cabbage leaf in my hand.

Recovering her breath, Loveday said: 'Tim, what on earth's the matter? You fucking well frightened me! Just disappearing like that! What are you fucking well doing out here? It's freezing. And it stinks.'

'I rather like it myself. Nice family atmosphere, you know?'

Loveday bent down beside me.

'Come on, Tim, please! I'm sorry. I didn't mean to upset you. I love you. You know that.'

'Why did you have to say that?'

'What? Say what?'

'All that business about kids and what would have happened if? Why did you have to say that?'

Loveday exhaled tearfully. 'Because it's true, that's why! I never wanted to say it, Tim, but it's just true that's all.'

'That made me feel really fantastic. Thank you.'

'Look, I'm not saying you won't ever have kids. You will. Christ, you'll be an amazing father, I just know it and so do lots of others . . .'

I stood up and interrupted her, looking straight into her eyes: 'And next you're going to tell me I'll make someone a marvellous husband one day, right?'

We both stared at one another. I began to smile, shrugged a what-the-fuck-does-it-matter shrug and held a small cabbage up to the moon. After a few seconds I passed it to Loveday who clutched it to her stomach, seeming unsure whether to laugh or cry.

'You see, it suits you. Go on, have my cabbage, please? Let's have a baby cabbage together. If not, we could always make some bubble and squeak.'

I took two steps away and then the same two back. 'I love you. I l-o-v-e you. Can't you see?'

Loveday took a step back, shouting: 'Oh, please don't say that. Not now! That's so unfair.'

'Why? It's true! I love you, Loveday.'

'Jesus! Of all the times to say that, you go and pick now.'

'What d'you mean, for God's sake?'

'Because you've never, ever said those words before.'

'Well, I am now.'

'Don't!'

'Why not? I want you. I want you to stay. I promise I can do whatever it takes.'

I pulled Loveday hard against me and we kissed slowly and deeply, our mouths crushed against one another, more and more intense, more passionate, and within moments we were pulling at each other's clothing. Without letting go of her, I laid my jacket on the muddy ground and lowered Loveday on to it. Soon her dress was pushed right up to her neck and by the time I had pulled off my shirt and trousers and kicked away my shoes and socks, she lay naked on the jacket. It was cold, windy and bits of mud were sticking to our legs and arms. Despite all this, our bodies were so warm and so ready for one another that a slow ritualised lovemaking took place which we both knew was a validation of our love.

Afterwards, I lay inside and on top of her in an effort to keep her warm, and in a greater effort to keep the two of us connected. Loveday started to cry. She then coaxed me to kneel astride her breasts. I didn't need much coaxing. Her crying then intensified. It was almost as if she knew she was dying and wanted me to see her breasts in all their moonlit splendour. *This is my body and this is my flesh; remember me at the hour of my death* . . .

I sat there, gently rocking back and forth, smiling at her breasts and into her eyes until she beckoned me further forward until I was directly over her face. Then, almost without me noticing, she put my cock into her mouth and proceeded to suck it. Once she felt it harden again, she increased the depth and tempo until I reached a screaming crescendo. She and I knew it would be the last time.

The cold wind and drizzle eventually persuaded us to stand up and dress. It was unspoken that we would not let go of each other until the very last moment. I picked up my boxer shorts and wiped them over the wet leaves of the potato plants, then gently wiped the earth and sweat from the back of Loveday's calves, thighs, back and arms. She had become like a rainbow, crying big tears but smiling happily. Finding her knickers hanging on a cabbage stump, Loveday softly spat on them, and wiped my face, chest, cock clean, before carefully folding them into her handbag.

Meaningless words were uttered sporadically as we traipsed back through the vegetable garden. Inside the car again, we both gave up trying to express how we felt. It was as if we had been together for twenty years and would be for another. The sound of the engine being switched on and a look into each other's eyes told us that we knew our thoughts were identical: whatever had happened, whatever would happen, no one could ever take away the times we had shared. I managed to resist the temptation of joking about 'always having Dartmouth'.

As Loveday steered her car carefully alongside the front porch of the hospital, she looked at her bare mud-splattered legs and dress and seemed proud of what she had done. Despite a hollow feeling in my stomach, I leaned across and kissed her as passionately as I could. Knowing that I was now committed to walk towards the firing squad alone, I joked saying I would see her sooner than she thought.

I walked back into the hospital with tears burning my eyes. The two dispensing nurses remained polite and muttered discreetly but affectionately that I might like to place my dirty suit in the laundry that night. I shook my head proudly in the negative, walked back to my room, and hung the suit on a hanger. I carefully covered it in plastic, placed it in the wardrobe, and sat down on the single bed.

I've never liked hospitals.

Greece

Sunday morning I normally spend in bed. The island is silent save for the sound of a church bell, a few crows, and small fishing boats putting out to sea. Even the dog is quiet.

I cross the dusty stone floor to the bathroom, fully aware that I am a walking paradox. I feel absolutely nothing at all, and yet at the same time I feel everything. I can see in the mirror that I am shedding skin, but feel no pain.

On Sundays I never shave. I've also learned always to feed the dog first, and then to make my cup of coffee.

On the wall opposite my desk is a collage of photographs from my chequered past, exquisitely mounted between a piece of board and glass. Next to the Roberts radio, on which I listen to the BBC, are three books of poetry: Dylan Thomas, C. P. Cavafy and T.S. Eliot. To the right of them is the dusty Olivetti, still sitting in its travelling case, looking forlorn as an unclaimed parcel on a station platform. I walk up to these things and say good morning, giving them a friendly stroke. I don't do it because I know what is going to happen, but to offer them reassurance and solidarity. They are my friends, after all.

Then I go to sit on the terrace with the dog lying at my feet. Out of respect and for my own amusement, I have also called him Ned. (Ned the cat is now happily living in London with Harry and Jessica.) I look down at Ned, his head resting on his paws, his eyes showing uncertainty about whether there will ever be a walk again. I bend down and give the top of his head and ears a reassuring rub.

The sun is nearly up but filtered in an autumnal haze. The air is cool and sharp. I look around the garden and breathe in its strength, and the memories I have of it.

For a small house like mine, for an island like this, it is a big garden – long at the back. When I first arrived, I intended, like so many things in my life before, to make it the best garden of all. Perhaps a garden from my past, a garden I had known many years before. I stroke the dog and laugh at my history of intentions. I then laugh at my naivety in thinking that English horticulture could be applied to an island such as this. Yet I love my garden. There is the old almond tree and the hammock. There are two sloping lawns of geraniums instead of grass. There is the narrow path, full of chickweed in the spring, running down to the patch to where the hosepipe spends most of its time. There is the bench on the side of the patch where Astrid and I always sit after we've had an argument.

I look at my watch and think that, normally, Astrid would be here. Yet she isn't, she is in Germany. In a way I am glad. I wonder what she would have said about the screeching ravens that have perched at the end of my bed for the last three nights. She knows about dreams, does Astrid.

In my dreams, I have allowed those ravens to come on to my bed and peck at my skin. I don't care what they jab at, provided it isn't my eyes. Their beaks are black and made of granite, their talons sharp and made of silver. At first, I couldn't understand what was happening. I was almost prepared to let them take over and eat my flesh. When I woke up I realised I knew them. They had hung around street corners in my mind ever since I was a child. I was never able to control them, and had allowed them to say whatever they liked when I walked past. They were skilled in the way they taunted, clever in knowing at which points to apply the pressure. I've tried many ways of dealing with them. I have laughed at them, told them funny jokes, told them I was moving. I've drenched them in alcohol. I've even changed my name, but they always come hopping back.

I have been on this island for a year, but intend to leave it tomorrow. Before coming here, there were years reversing out of cul-de-sacs; a caravan in Cardigan; a bus in Marrakech; a house in Vilnius selling techno to Lithuanians for lithium and caviar; a beach hut in Santa

Monica. More years of being the dummy and the ventriloquist. The death of my father, fifteen months ago, changed all that. He keeled over in his vegetable garden while picking artichokes, with a travel brochure in his pocket.

I stand up and wander down the path with the dog trotting behind me. I always like to walk slowly to the vegetable patch, imagining rows of perfect vegetables ready for picking. I laugh out loud when I crouch down and find that the only thing there is an ugly-looking onion that not even the dog wants to play with. I put it in my pocket, sniffing out of perverse respect for its many layers. I get up cheerfully, and decide that I will have a bonfire later that afternoon. I pick up a twig and throw it towards the house and watch Ned charge after it as though it is the last twig in the world.

Having come in from the garden and drunk another cup of coffee, I am ready to take a walk. At first I think I will visit the monastery, and then I think about the cave of St John. But I realise I don't need to see the monastery again, and that the cave has done its work already. No, I want a different church. The church I saw from the boat when first arriving on Patmos. It is high up, seemingly balanced on top of a rock, the church of Aghia Paraskevi. I clip the lead on the dog's collar and set off.

The church isn't far from my house, five minutes' walk, no more. There is a choice of a steep rock path or a set of steps leading up to it. I choose the steps. The white-walled building is smaller than it looks from a distance. In fact, with its small domed roof, it resembles an igloo. Surrounding it are pots of red and white geraniums. I am struck by its homeliness and the way it appears to be looked after.

I stand inside the empty chapel for fifteen minutes or more. There are no thunderbolts or flashes, but a feeling of being comfortable, at ease. As I leave, I am aware that I am clutching something in my hand. When I open the palm of my hand I see an old rubber ball. I grip it tightly and carry on. There is now another place that I have to go and see.

The dog and I wander carefully down the path until we hit the cobbled streets of Konsolato, where we turn right and walk towards the fishing boats. The dog becomes excited at the sight of the fishermen mending their nets. I nearly let him off the lead so that he can stay there, but we carry on walking along the tarmac road away from the port. Eventually I find the rocky path that leads down to the cove. It is not a popular place, not particularly beautiful and somewhat difficult for swimming. I set the dog free and climb over a series of small rocks to one standing in shallow water at the centre of the cove.

I breathe in the fresh air and smile. The sea is calm, almost asleep. I stare at it for a long while. I hold my arm up in the air while squeezing the ball in my hand. It is as if I've come to pay my respects to a very old adversary. Someone I've known all my life. I want the sea to look at what I hold in my hand. The sea is like a sleeping lion, lifting one eyelid to see what is being offered. I want the sea to have the ball, to have what now looks such a small and insignificant object. I ready myself to throw it, yanking my arm back and forth. Yet I see no sign, no response from the sea at all.

A minute passes and I lower my arm. I put the ball back in my pocket. I think for a moment and then change my mind. I had wanted the sea to have it, to consume it within its depths, to drown it once and for all. I understand now that the ball is my past, along with the ravens, worm and doubts. I realise that I do not want the ball turning up on some beach, to fall into the hands of some unsuspecting boy. No, that is not the solution. That is not the solution at all.

When we get back up on the road, I know what the answer is. The rubber ball is not going anywhere. I have decided it is going to stay with me. Since it always has been around, I might as well keep it warm and where I can keep an eye on it. It will live in my pocket.

I turn to look at the sea and feel a flicker of embarrassment at not having said a goodbye or thank you. But it doesn't matter, I know that now. I feel as if I'd been reunited with a long-lost friend and there's no need to say anything further. We both know there will be another time.

I whistle to Ned and take the ball out of my pocket. I nearly throw it to him, but then, out of a respect that I hope will become mutual, I don't. Instead, I bounce it happily along the road. I bounce it with my left hand and bounce it with my right.

It doesn't take long to get used to bouncing the ball. After only a few minutes, my mind is free to think about the three things I saw on my desk that morning.

I stop walking, aware that tears are streaming down my face. I look up and let the sun dry them. And then I laugh. I know that I will be staying on the island, not leaving, after all.

Walking on, I decide there and then that the bonfire should be a celebration dedicated to the people in the photographs, and that the dusty cover of the Olivetti will be coming off tonight. *Carpe diem!*

Acknowledgements

My profound gratitude to Hans Zimmer for his lasting belief in this novel, and multifarious generosity in helping and getting me to write it.

I am indebted to the following for providing their invaluable editorial guidance, or for their support before, during or after the writing of this book: Paul Cowan, Jeremy and Gillian Gough, Nigel Ryan, Elene Sanikou, Ellen Sutton, Francesca Gough, Carolyn Altman, Gabby Debus, Kirsty Dunseath, Max Hole, Tim Macauley, Dawn Stoffer, Emma Neave, Nick Stevens, Alice Chandler, Janet Law, Matthew Bates at Sayle Screen, Chris Thomas, Trevor Morais, Anthony Osborn, the Paradise Squash Club, Gerard Noel and Andreas Campomar, Sarah Tyrer, Dr Tony Hughes, John Vaughan and my friends at the Masons Arms, and Art Cafe.

Those who should have been included above have either been named within the text or left out due to my terrible memory. Apologies.

J.T.